I0762262

ALASKA'S HIDDEN HEROES - BOOK ONE

TUNDRA COURAGE

SHE CAME TO TEACH LIFESAVING SKILLS,
WHAT SHE LEARNED SAVED HER

BRENDA BOWIE WISE

Publishing Services provided by Paper Raven Books
Printed in the United States of America
First Printing, 2020

Paperback ISBN 978-1-7354970-0-6
Hardcover ISBN 978-1-7354970-1-3

CHAPTER 1

Meara peered out the window of the twenty-four-seat Saab turboprop she had boarded in Anchorage, taking in the ground below. The brown mixed with patches of red reminded her of the fall foliage that she would be missing back in Vermont. However, the pools of water that pocked the tundra made her think of craters.

"I might as well be landing on the moon. What have I done?" she said quietly under her breath, searching the ground to find something that would provide scale to the size of the round pools of water. She wondered if they were big enough for fish.

She was now at the end of the final leg of the long journey to her new home. The past two months of preparations to leave the East Coast were a blur of packing, yard sales, dump runs, and looking for tenants. She had stretched her days to include some parties and dinners in order to say goodbye to the family and friends who had surrounded her most of her life.

Her body seemed to have let its guard down once the preparation stage was over and she was actually on the road. Within hours of starting the drive across country, she had fallen sick. Her little Subaru seemed to be as strained as she felt as it pulled the weight of its full contents, in addition to hauling a fully loaded snowmobile trailer with a snowmobile and all of her belongings packed around it.

She had been so sick with fever that at times she had felt delusional. She couldn't tell if the heat she was feeling was coming from inside or from the August heat shimmering in front of her on the highway as she crossed the plains. She regretted not taking time out to fix the air-conditioning in her Subaru. She could have kicked herself. Sure, you don't need air-conditioning in Alaska. She had not factored in the scorching 110-degree temperatures she would face getting there.

Opening the windows of the car only allowed moving air that felt like it was coming out of her hair dryer. There had been times that she was grateful for the chills that occurred when her fever would rise. Was that struggle an omen of things to come?

Now the medium-sized plane she was on had crossed high mountains with peaks and valleys buried under snow even at the end of the summer. The height and sharpness of these peaks stood in direct contrast to the flat tundra they crossed over.

A river snaked its way across the tundra to empty into the Bering Sea in front of her. Its path twisted and turned back on itself that at times it came close to doing a full circle before twisting back again to continue to the sea. This roundabout path contrasted with the path of the straight Connecticut River that formed the border of her state with neighboring New Hampshire back home.

Prior to boarding in Seattle, she had left her car and trailer behind at the barge terminal. After removing the two suitcases and backpack that contained the essentials she would need for the next six weeks, she had filled the emptied space with groceries, because she had been warned that her favorite staples would be unavailable or extremely expensive in Agushak.

She would be living in the hub city where the hospital, grocery store, and commercial airport for the surrounding villages were located, most of which were accessible only by fishing boat or small plane. The total area she would serve covered about the same expanse as North and South Dakota combined.

She had dropped off the car and trailer completely filled to the rim with the exception of the driver's seat. She actually turned and waved goodbye to her personal caravan at the barge terminal. The barge was the last one scheduled before the Bering Sea froze over, after which no deliveries would arrive by barge until spring breakup. She quietly begged to her belongings, "Please make it to me before freeze! I don't want to live an arctic winter without a car."

Half smiling with relief, she thought about how she had tucked some Trader Joe's comfort food into the suitcase to hold her over until the barge arrived.

Her head rested against the window. The cool glass gave her a bit of relief from her headache. The conversations of others on the plane were muffled, not just from her head congestion, but also from the earplugs the flight attendant had handed her as she boarded. The combination of the two with the noise of the propellers outside the window left her feeling distant and separate from the other passengers.

An occasional head rose high above the seats, but in general she did not feel like she was the only one needing to strain to see above the seat back. The black hair that predominated the seat occupants contrasted with her shock of red hair. This was not new to her. No matter where she was, the red hair made her stand out. She never totally blended in a crowd.

Below, she noticed a few houses had started to lead into the town ahead. Some were out in the open on the two main roads. Most lay on the sandy bluffs where the confluence of the river emptied into the sea. Multicolored metal roofs added a variety of color to the tundra. The typical black-shingled rooftops she was used to were not present. There were no sprawling Victorians of a New England downtown. Squared buildings in varying stages of construction or destruction scattered the town. She had been warned that houses were often unfinished on the outside because of the short building season each year.

Alaska was in need of a good architect. She gave a long sigh.

The plane banked as it prepared to circle the runway ahead of her on the outskirts of town. A large, yellow building sat to the side. Part of her wanted to stay on the plane and retrace her steps back home, where everything was known and comfortable. But the part of her that had been waiting for this moment for years pushed her forward.

Almost twenty years ago, she had set this as a goal for herself. She had been in graduate school working on her master's degree to become a nurse practitioner. Another student in her class was already a nurse practitioner. However, she had returned to school to get her graduate degree. She had been one of the pioneering nurse practitioners who had started their work with a certificate degree that allowed the complex work beyond their nursing degrees to fill in where physician care was limited. Now this amazing woman had to get her master's degree alongside Meara as the career requirements had been updated. Her experience had captured Meara when she heard of this woman's job, where she commuted from Massachusetts to Alaska to teach in the Community Health Aide Program, CHAP for short.

This program was originally developed to combat tuberculosis in the remote native villages in Alaska. It had been so successful with this problem that it grew to help combat infant-maternal mortality and trauma in the isolated villages.

The Community Health Aides were native villagers chosen by their village council to be the health care providers for their village. After training, these aides would act as an extension of the doctors working in the central city, the hub of all the surrounding little villages. The doctors worked in the small, nonsurgical hospital. This was where the villagers would be taken if they needed to be in a hospital. The doctors sometimes visited the villages, but these visits were short and as infrequent as four times a year.

Meara clearly remembered twenty years back when she had first heard of this program. She knew teaching here was what she wanted to do. Twenty years was a long time to wait to follow your dream. Raising her son as a single parent had to happen first.

The plane bounced as the wheels hit the tarmac, then bounced again. The ailerons and flaps had been lowered to brake the wings. The loud roar of the deceleration announced their arrival. She gathered her book and tucked it into her backpack. When she noticed the agents on the tarmac were fully zipped on this August afternoon, she zipped up her jacket. People stood and gathered bags as the flight attendant opened the door and unfolded the steps down to the tarmac. Slowly they all climbed down and were welcomed by a crisp, premature fall breeze as they followed the agents into the terminal building. A sign welcomed her to the Agushak Airport.

She stepped across the threshold, vowing that she was not turning back.

* * *

Meara followed the other passengers across the tarmac and into the back door of the metal-sided terminal. Once inside, they filed into a throng of welcomers. Families lined up, embracing the arrivals with big hugs. Children ran from the parent they had been home with into the arms of the parent that returned. Couples embraced as they reunited.

Other people were welcomed by what seemed to be business associates. Meara looked around, expecting to be met by someone from her new office. There was nobody there for her.

Traffic flowed to the left past the airline attendants to a garage door on the other side. She followed and waited by the baggage claim. She listened to conversations and realized how fast she spoke with her New England rush compared to the slow and sometimes staggered speech that surrounded her now. Why had she always felt rushed, both in speech and the need to get things done? The local pace seemed awkward but at the same time something she knew that she needed.

Her Patagonia windbreaker, with the layers of other Patagonia beneath, was a contrast to the dress of the others there. There were men and women in camouflage windbreakers and hunting gear. The majority of the feet were adorned in XTRATUF boots. Many women wore gingham loose-fitting shirts with a large pocket in front that had an entry on either side for the hands, reminiscent of a hoodie sweatshirt. The hoods, pockets, and sleeves were lined with trim, some plain and some with appliqué. The colors were bright and cheerful. Many men wore a more cut-off masculine version squared off at the hips and made of solid colors.

The garage door separating the terminal from the back rolled open and two agents started tossing suitcases, gun cases, cylindrical fishing pole cases, and totes onto the stainless-steel platform in the terminal. Totes of all colors and sizes filled the platform. They were fastened with zip ties threaded through predrilled holes and some with large strips of duct tape.

Tote after tote was placed on the stand with a scattering of suitcases among them. Some men toward the front started clearing the closest ones to the side as they worked to the ones in the back. People started grabbing at their bags and worked their way to the doors at the back of the terminal.

Meara caught sight of her own suitcase and moved to the side, where she stood to watch until the pathway cleared. Other people had relaxed in conversation and did not rush toward their luggage like in a normal terminal. The waiting period at the airport seemed to be social time, as accounts of happenings in town since the arriving person had departed were all recounted.

Eventually, most of the people had gathered bags and worked their way to the gravel parking lot. Meara had gathered her own in a pile at the side when she noticed an elder dragging her bags toward the door.

Meara had stepped in to help and was just returning from the parking lot after helping the elder when she heard her name called.

"Meara?" A short, fit, gray-haired woman with a big smile approached her, weaving across the puddled, gravel parking lot. Self-conscious, Meara realized that she must have stood out significantly if she was that easily identified.

"Yes."

"Welcome to Agushak." Her greeter laughed. "I am Nancy, the CHAP director. We interviewed on the phone. So, are you going to stay?"

"What?" Meara hesitated. How had Nancy known that she had wondered the same thing of herself before getting off the plane? "Of course, I am."

"You wouldn't be the first to get off the plane, take a look around, and immediately fly back."

"Really? People don't even give it a chance?"

"Some people find it too rural; some get scared when they realize when the plane leaves that there is no way out until it comes again. So, are you staying?"

"Yes." Meara smiled, attempting to hide the trepidation she felt. "This has been too much of a journey to turn around without a try. And, I am not a quitter."

"Good, we are so glad to have you." Nancy smiled at Meara while she lifted a suitcase and the backpack. "Your experience seems to make you a perfect fit. Let's grab your stuff, give you a tour, and bring you to your rental. Do you need any groceries?"

"I do need a few supplies. Do you have time for this?" She grabbed the bag that Nancy hadn't picked up and followed her across the gravel parking lot to a dust-covered Subaru.

Nancy opened the back, exposing a dog barrier, and tossed the bags inside as if they were light as a feather.

"I don't see that you have a car yet." She winked at Meara. "And I don't want you starving and grouchy at work tomorrow."

Starting the car, Nancy rolled out of the parking lot to the gravel road to the airport and off to the paved main road leading into the village. Nancy drove in the crisp, energetic way that she walked and caused Meara to grab the armrest when suddenly they switched to the wrong side of the road to drive.

She looked over at Meara and noticed the white knuckles right away. "Potholes." She laughed. "Potholes are everywhere. It is part of what happens when you build roads on tundra. I wasn't going to kill us, but the potholes could have eaten us alive."

Loosening her grip on the armrest, Meara laughed, reassured that she wasn't now employed by a crazy woman.

Meara was given a perfunctory tour of the small town that would be her home when she wasn't traveling to the villages. There was a library, hardware store, and a small extension of the University of Alaska. Some scattered housing was mixed into the few businesses.

Then they stopped at the AC Grocery Store. "This is AC. Alaska Commercial Grocery Store. ACs have been around

Alaska since the gold rush and early fishing and trapping days. Unfortunately, the money they make doesn't stay local."

Meara had her list in her head as she walked up the grated ramp. But curiosity kept her from sticking to the list. Her face and spirits dropped when she surveyed the wilting vegetables as they walked through. The iceberg lettuce was pale and disappointing.

Nancy must have seen her face. "It is Tuesday. Grocery shipments typically come in Wednesday. At this time of the week, things are looking pretty limp. But it is worse come winter. A lot of times the subzero weather freezes the vegetables on the tarmac before they even make it to the store."

"I just need some eggs, milk, and bread." She picked a few browning bananas and a couple soft-feeling apples. She was so shocked by the lack of greens, she found herself almost choking back tears.

She gasped as she grabbed a half gallon of milk. $8.49? She walked past a clothing section and couldn't help but notice some housedresses that her grandmother might have worn. Had she gone back in time? This was 2008, not 1974. Did people still buy these?

Nancy talked to the grocery clerk who rung up the bill and knew her by name. She stopped to talk and introduce Meara to a few people leaving the store.

On the way out, a clean-cut, athletic guy wearing a black formfitting sports top bounded up the stairs.

"Hey, Rey." Nancy smiled in greeting. "I want to introduce you to Meara. She is coming in to take over the Health Aide Training. I haven't seen you in a while."

He stopped in front of the coffee kiosk, which was just at the edge of the door. He poured a cup of black coffee into one of the Styrofoam cups stacked there. He turned with his coffee in hand and gave the two of them a big smile. His tight-fitting shirt showed off his muscles and strong physique.

"I have been down in the lower forty-eight. High school reunion. Back to work tomorrow."

"Nice to meet you." Meara smiled as she shook his hand. It felt like there was something familiar about him. She couldn't place her finger on it. She followed Nancy back to the car.

They drove out of town, the mountains outlined in the distance. Their contrast to the flat tundra was stunning. Nancy took a turn off the main road. But in spite of the distant view, Nancy's next comment drained Meara of her remaining optimism.

"Your rental is to the side of town. It isn't much, but housing is at a premium here. I will drop you off and you can get settled in. I will pick you up for work again in the morning."

* * *

That funky smell she could not identify had permeated her senses the moment she walked in the door to her rental. After completing the brief inspection that the size of the cabin required, she had left her bags outdoors. Nothing was coming inside yet. She went to work cleaning out the dark space, hauling the few carpets out the door—each leaving behind a silhouette of their shape made from dust, dirt, and grease. When she passed her hand over the counter, it stuck upon buildup of some kind. She quickly looked under the sink for cleaning supplies, filled the sink with hot water, and went to work. Starting with the loft, she performed a detailed scrub from the top down.

Her tears surprised her as she scrubbed away. "I left my beautiful, sunny home with beautiful views behind to live in this? What have I done?"

She was actually grateful that the tears were taking away what sense of smell that she had left. This was just a part of the process. *You have made homes out of worse in the past.* Her spirits fell even further when she thought about the challenges of doing that here. She knew nobody; she had no car.

"Damn. If only I had packed my pictures." She cursed herself for being efficient in her packing.

She wished she had some music, but her radio had not arrived yet. The silence added to the sense of having made a huge mistake. She missed the friends that she had left behind. She had always enjoyed having people filling her porch with local food, a shared bottle of wine, and great conversation. How could she create that in this space?

She cleaned until exhaustion hit her. Then she brought her luggage in from outside. All the food she had just purchased went into the newly cleaned refrigerator. She pulled out her pots and pans and hung them in the kitchen. Then she pulled out her running windbreaker and cap and hung them over her sneakers set neatly on the floor beneath. Setting up a reminder of her normally favorite activity lifted her spirits a little. Then she pulled out her sleeping pad and spread it on the smell of fresh Lysol.

"Well, this is better than that other smell," she said out loud. She put her head down on her pillow, fully expecting sleep to take over quickly. Instead, it avoided her as she thought about the great unknown outside her cabin. She had no idea of the layout outside. She was so focused on getting home that she hadn't taken in the local street. She knew she was tucked into the trees.

Meara turned in her sleeping bag. Then she turned back. The whole night seemed to have been filled with restlessness. Normally, sleeping in her camping gear would not have kept her from resting.

Some dogs barked over the night, and each time they barked, she woke up wondering what they were warning her about.

Finally, after watching each hour pass, the watch read six.

"Alright, Meara, pity party is over. Time to put on your steel bra and panties and make the most of this."

She got up and slipped on her running tights. She pulled the headlamp out of her pack and put it on her head in preparation for her run. She was so glad that she had picked up a can of bear spray as one of her essentials when she stopped at the store. This went in a fanny pack belted around her waist and with the zipper slightly open. It was an easy quick grab if it was needed.

Turning on the porch light, she peered outside. Nothing moving there. She opened the door and stared into the black dark in both directions, wishing she had the power to see through the darkness into what was out there. It was still, and nothing seemed to be moving out there. An article she had read in the *Anchorage Daily News* the day before said a college professor was mauled to death by a moose when he stepped out of one of the university buildings. How much more dangerous was it for her here as opposed to the city? She was now living in the middle of the Togiak Wildlife Refuge. The refuge covered the area along the Bering Sea between the Yukon Kuskokwim and the Nushagak River.

Her stomach tightened as she urged herself to step out. The run would clear her mind and wake her up for the day ahead. Pressing some buttons on her big running watch, she switched it into map view so it would record where she was going, and if she got lost, she could follow the little arrow back. Considering that she had no idea where she was, she chose to run out and back as an extra safety. Pressing the button of the start screen, she gazed at her heartbeat. 92? Was that from being sick or from anxiety?

"Alright, Meara, remember, you have nothing to fear but fear itself." Pressing the button started the timer, and she ran into the dark that still showed no sign of early dawn. Her feet hit a rhythm on the gravel road in front of her. Running in the dark was not new to her; she enjoyed it. There was something about running in the nighttime with the grayed, dark scenery that always made her feel like she was floating. It seemed like magic.

Today, after running a while, the fear started to melt, although she did notice that she continued to move her hand to her hip pack to check on that can of bear spray. She felt the sick feeling fade away as her lungs opened up. Once she had gone for ten minutes, her heart beat steadied, and with that, her outlook and self-talk changed.

The chance to combine her health care career and the interest of exploring different cultures was an opportunity she had waited a long time for. A temporary non-homey home was just a minor setback. She had what it took for this adventure. There would be no giving up a decades-old dream for a little bit of inconvenience.

After three miles, she turned around and picked up her pace. She wasn't alone; she still had the companionship of running. She had everything she needed. Running was her friend.

Lifting her gaze from the ground ahead of her, she noted a bobbing light heading toward her as the sky was lightening but was not quite the light of early dawn. From the rhythm, she could tell it was another runner. Soon her light illuminated the silhouette of a man. She half smiled with the realization that there were other runners living here. As they passed, she gave and received a quick nod and a "good morning."

She had heard that voice before and had seen that smile. Was that familiarity a good thing?

CHAPTER 2

Meara had been working hard to dive into her new world since her arrival three weeks ago. She had studied the Community Health Aide Program curriculum and had prepared herself to teach the health aides the classwork that was expected on their way to and from training in Anchorage and Sitka.

Nancy would pick her up and bring her back home from work each day. And they developed a relaxing but very busy work relationship.

On Meara's first day, Nancy had apologetically brought her down to the training room.

"I am so sorry this is a mess. We have been trying to fill your position for a long time. We are hoping you can set up a simulation clinic with all of these expired supplies. The tables and chairs can be set up as a classroom, and you have a computer here just like in the clinics." She pointed to a desk that was set up like a reception area. "The health aides can use this space to learn to schedule appointments and check patients in."

Meara looked back and forth and up and down the room. It was a mess of boxes, scattered supplies, and papers. She could visualize using the full floor space to create a simulated clinic with a classroom in front.

"And, this will be a big part of your teaching when the health aides come back from training sessions. This is the AFHCAN cart. This allows the health aide to take in data to do a consult with the physician in town and, at times, specialists like dermatology or ear, nose, and throat."

A computer stood on a cart in the back of the room. It was attached to otoscopes, ophthalmoscopes, and electrocardiogram leads. She learned that this was a "store and forward" means of providing telemedicine. A still image was captured and sent off to the doctor on the other side. There was also a camera in the drawer, which allowed medical images to be captured. Part of her job would be to teach how to take good medical images.

In the back of the room on a shelf along the wall was a collection of Community Health Aide Manuals. These thick and heavy manuals were in boxes composed of four books. The CHAM contained what the health aide needed to perform a health care visit in the field.

Meara pulled one of the heavy collections off the shelf.

"I know I have been looking at this for a few weeks, but it still amazes me that people were able to take just about anything that could happen as a medical need in the village and give direction in such a way that a person with a limited background could be successful in caring for patients."

"I know. It is an amazing piece of work. Dedicated people developed this and keep it up to date. Soon, we hope to see it become electronic," said Nancy. "And, you will be traveling to Anchorage to meet with these people."

"This is ingenious the way this book will guide a health aide from the moment a person walks in the door. It has so much forethought. I am really impressed by how it immediately helps the health aide to recognize an emergency and to take care of it."

The past few weeks, she had spent some time on the phone tutoring math with some applicants. To be accepted into the training program and be able to be recommended for hire, each applicant had to have the equivalent of an eighth-grade math and reading level. This was the state accepted level of proficiency deemed to be required to navigate the CHAM and successfully make it through a visit.

Today, she would be welcoming her first group of students to prepare for session one training. It was a small group because it was her first session teaching.

They had just finished their ETT training at the hospital. The Emergency Trauma Technician was the Alaskan equivalent of a first responder certification in the lower forty-eight. They learned the basic skills to respond to an emergency. Later, they would advance their emergency skills to emergency medical technician levels I, II, and III.

"It is interesting that Alaska has to have its own emergency training system. It is too bad that there is no way for an advanced trainee to get the observation that is needed to get the same certifications as the lower forty-eight. They really need that observation when they are out in the remote areas, but there is no way for them to see the number of patients unless they stayed for months in Anchorage." Meara was starting to understand the complexity that the isolated locations added to health care.

After completing their ETT certification, the students were now here to start their pre-training before they started their first of four full sessions of training.

Each of these trainees had been chosen by their village council to become a health aide. They had been working alongside senior health aides before they came here to learn office management skills, cleaning, making appointments, and filing. The class arriving today all came from different villages. All of these villages were only accessible by small plane.

Meara had been working hard to prepare the space for this debut day. The room looked like a well-organized classroom now. Feeling like a schoolteacher on the first day of school, she shuffled papers on her desk, waiting eagerly for them to arrive.

* * *

Chelsey was the first to come into the training center that morning. She had just finished her emergency medical technician training and was eager to get to her session work. She had done well with her earlier training and was both excited and scared to eventually become the main health aide for her village of eighty people that grew during the summer season to a few hundred. The health aide that she had grown up with had recommended her to the village council for the position and was eager to retire.

The bonus reason that made her really excited about this new adventure was the chance to get to know one of her half sisters. She was in the middle of a troop of six girls that her father had had all around the region. All but the oldest two had different mothers. The older girls lived north in a small village above the Yukon Kuskokwim Delta. Dad had met their mother traveling to sports games in high school. The couple had been together three years before he started traveling around on his fishing boat chasing fish runs. These sisters were all older and had started families of their own.

However, the youngest of these girls was the same age as her next older half sister, Jean. Dad must have traveled a bit that summer.

Then she was born. Chelsey was pretty sure that she was the product of a good catch during cod fishing season off the Aleutians in December. Dad had decided to stay and live with her mother after that. However, apparently he was not done spawning. A year later, he went on to father Verna. Verna had been raised in the village that he was from, and she was raised by their shared grandparents.

Dad had returned to Chelsey's mother after that brief encounter, and Verna's mother had left her behind when she moved to Anchorage. Chelsey never had totally understood why her own mother was so willing to forgive him and take him back after that escapade. She certainly wouldn't have if she was in her mother's shoes. But he had stopped drinking at that point and had promised her that he would remain sober as a condition of his return. Dad's decision-making definitely improved with the elimination of alcohol.

Chelsey was grateful that she was able to grow up with both a mother and a father present. And the fact that Dad had gone on to have the fling that created Verna was not a testimony to the love that her parents shared. In recent years, he had been working on reconnecting with all of his girls, and Chelsey had joined him in the adventure. She had always had the secret desire to have siblings to interact with. Now, she finally did. She had made a great connection with her youngest half sister, Verna, on Facebook, and when Chelsey was accepted as the candidate for her village, Verna had also applied for the position in her own village. They were scheduled to go through training together, which would be their chance to bond as sisters.

But today, she wasn't feeling the love. She slammed her pencil and notebook down onto the table as she whipped the chair out and sat down with an audible huff. If this is what having a sister brought, she could do without it.

She sat back folding her arms in front of her. Taking a deep breath, she tried to calm down her thinking process. Her tapping foot in front of her combined with the fists she couldn't keep from balling up showed she wasn't in control.

Yesterday, she had been as happy as she ever remembered. She had a great boyfriend. He was attentive, fun, and funny as well. She had a new job that she was excited about. And she had the new relationship with her sister. They had bonded so well as they nervously learned the skills of CPR, splinted each other's fake broken bones, and applied dressings to control bleeding and treat burns. The two had also shared a room in the bunkhouse.

Well, that was yesterday. Today, she had a job. So much for the sister and the boyfriend.

She was angry at her sister and at the same time felt horrible that she was angry at her sister. Verna had been every bit as shocked as her. It was no surprise that she would fall for him.

That lying cheat. How could he think he could have gotten away with this? She let out a forced huff of breath upward to push some hairs out of her face that had strayed from her ponytail. She set her jaw as she declared her new resolve.

Last night, when sitting on the couch scrolling through pictures and telling stories of their home villages, they both were eager to share pictures of their boyfriends. When they both opened up pictures of the same husky, curly-blond-haired pilot with the big smile, they were both shocked into silence.

Chelsey had been the first to speak up. "We cannot let him know that we know yet."

"What are you thinking?" replied a paled Verna. Her phone was visibly shaking in her hand.

"I don't know yet. But I think we need to have him fess up to us."

"How are we going to do that?" asked Verna.

"I have absolutely no idea. Yet. But he had no problem keeping this information from us. Why shouldn't we keep our knowing about it from him?"

The door opening to the classroom brought Chelsey back to the present, and she looked up to see Verna. They had avoided each other this morning while they were getting ready for class. Each of them seemed to be trying purposefully to be where the other was not.

Verna's shoulders slumped over, and her eyes stayed to the ground when she came down the stairs moving slowly.

Chelsey realized that she had waited a long time to have a real connection with one of her sisters. She was not going to let some stupid guy mess it up.

Although she was clearly still angry, she patted the seat next to her in the classroom.

Verna walked over, hanging her rounded face down in an attempt to hide her red and puffy eyes with her bobbed hair.

Seeing her sister's mutual pain firmed Chelsey's resolve for vengeance. That jerk deserved to feel as bad as they did. Thank God, he was flying her village route this week. That meant they wouldn't have to see him for a while. This gives them the chance to come up with a plan for revenge.

Meara, the new training director, had just come down the stairs and into the room. Her eyes stopped at Verna's face, and she seemed to immediately notice the tear-reddened puffiness. Then her eyes shifted to Chelsey. Chelsey sat up, uncrossed her arms, and tried to relax the anger so it wasn't so visible.

Meara's face changed. She went from complete professionalism to a softening around the eyes and mouth as she studied them for a second then moved to face the front of the room.

I think she actually feels for Verna. At least we know she isn't heartless.

Verna let out a long exhale.

No mention of the puffy eyes was made, and they set into a day of learning. They were taught how to sort out emergency patients from the moment they walked in the door. If the patient was a limp infant with a fever, they were directed to go to the pediatric emergency section of the CHAM. That would direct them in emergency care of the infant as they tried to get on the phone with the physician to get further instructions.

If the patient was not in an emergency, they would then work through all the questions on the front right page, which would gather basic information about the history of the illness the patient arrived with. After gathering that information, they would then assign the visit a problem like abdominal pain. After that, the manual guided them through all the questions that they needed to ask about abdominal pain and also the physical exam that they would need to assess.

After all this was done, they would have their final "assessment." The CHAM would then direct them with the treatment. Sometimes, the plan was to call the doctor. Other times, they were directed to give medication once they were certified to do that. After this first session of training, they would be seeing patients with other health aides, and they would always be contacting the doctor about their visits. As they got to session two or three of training, there would eventually be problems they could take care of without having to call the physician each time.

The day flew by with a lot of information shared and learned. Chelsey welcomed the distraction from their personal lives, and Verna seemed to have relaxed a bit more as well as they practiced assessment skills. And, while assessing their own problem, Chelsey was focused on developing a plan of her own.

* * *

Rey pulled his four-wheel-drive truck into the parking lot of the police station. His thoughts were not on work.

He had developed a curiosity about the new woman that had come into the grocery store with Nancy. New to town, fit, red hair that stood out, and freckles that actually gave her more appeal than less. Having been single for a while and knowing most of the people in Agushak, he didn't have many dating options. He would often joke about what he was looking for when people would inquire about his dating life. "Full set of teeth, height taller than width, and able to remember who they are in the morning." And after the last woman he dated, "not crazy" had been added to the list.

Now, this new woman certainly surpassed all of those standards. His interest was even more piqued when he passed her the next morning on his run. Well, that was nice. They had something in common. He made sure to get out the next morning at the same time to run the same route, and this paid off. There she was again. They each mumbled good mornings as they passed.

Each time he saw her, that feeling he hadn't had in a long time took over his gut. He started skipping breakfast because the excited-but-nauseous feeling after his run was taking away his appetite. Missing breakfast wasn't hurting him any. He had noted that he'd started to add a little padding over his well-earned muscles. He loved the feeling of being fit, and he especially appreciated that he was able to turn heads when he walked into a room of females. Perfection was important to him. He needed to look perfect physically, and he needed to have the perfect image in the community.

He had worked hard to be the epitome of Dudley Do-Right. Have a flat tire? Here I am to save the day! Deliver the hitchhiker to their destination? Hop on in, of course. Help the old lady with her groceries. Nobody would expect anything less from him. If somebody else noticed, well that didn't hurt. Sometimes, it was tiring to be good enough and to keep that perfect image.

But when he thought about his high school reunion, his heart sank. There he still didn't feel good enough. He had thought that when he showed up fit in his forties and a successful Alaskan trooper that all his insecurities would melt away. He had talked with a few of the women there that he remembered from high school. But each seemed to have a look as they were talking to him. They remembered where he had come from and the reputation he carried from the choices of his mother. He didn't feel he could shake his childhood image after all these years.

At least here, in this small town in the middle of nowhere, he was somebody. Here, he was the go-to guy, the one that made things happen. He was driven to keep that perfect image. He was the perfect regional lieutenant. His guys were doing a great job out here, and their station was noted to be well run. He'd won awards for this.

His mind wandered to his nearing retirement. The picture of the retirement home that he imagined would be his was tacked onto the bulletin board above his desk. He had been saving, dreaming, and planning about his retirement. The same picture was under a magnet on his refrigerator at home. Alaska had been good to him. It kept him far away from his past. And now he was close to being able to retire. When he retired and finally left Agushak, Alaska, and no longer had his impressive and powerful trooper image, this beautiful home would tell anyone that knows him that "someone important lives here." In Alaska, he hid from his past by his badge and the bars on his uniform. He was in charge out here in Agushak; he had full control over that station. When he took off that uniform come retirement day, the beautiful house would be what would speak for him about how perfect he was. People would want to know him.

Now, there was Meara. Beautiful Meara. She would look good next to him and complete that image. He could see her standing next to him in front of that house. He couldn't deny that feeling in his stomach when he saw her either. She stirred something for him that he hadn't felt in a long time. He knew he wanted to be with her, but was he good enough for her? He would never be able to get over that feeling of not being good enough.

He had never been good at dating. Especially when he was in high school. He always suffered for his mother's decisions. She had a tendency to hang out at bars instead of staying home with him and his siblings. She was known to be the town tramp. How other students knew this was beyond him. But they certainly used it against him in their taunts. None of the "good girls" would date him. He was known as poor white trash.

When he became a trooper and moved permanently to Alaska, he left all of that behind. Here, he lived behind his badge. Everyone only knew him as the "good guy around town." Yup, his image could inflate those flat tires that he would respond to. Elder needs a driveway shoveled. Consider it done. Rey Torrenson? Oh yeah, really nice guy.

He passed Meara on a run for a few mornings and the quick "good mornings" certainly didn't seem to have any chance of growing. Each time they exchanged greetings, she would instantly look down at her watch or down at her feet. Her hand would sweep past the bear spray that peeked out of the pack on her hip, and then she would pick up her pace. She clearly wasn't comfortable with running into him in the early morning darkness. He wasn't going to break the ice there. He needed to find a different lead in.

Two weeks ago, he had given up on the idea of being able to ask her out as they ran past each other. He had realized he needed a new strategy. So, he had grabbed the phone and punched in the numbers. "Nancy? This is Rey. You know Meara, the girl you introduced me to? Do you think she would mind if you gave me her number?"

It had been that easy. Nancy had not hesitated. That afternoon, he had followed that call with one to Meara.

For that call, the fingers were more hesitant—almost as if he had to coax his finger to push each number, especially as he got to the final digit. It would be so humiliating if she rejected him.

The phone rang twice, and there it was. Her voice. Even her voice had the stirring effect on him. He could feel his heartbeat in his throat as he cleared it.

"Meara, this is Rey. You know, the trooper you met at the store. I'm realizing now, you probably don't even know that I am a trooper. I wasn't in uniform. We have been running past each other in the morning now for a while, and I was thinking that the dark is getting darker every morning. Would you be interested in some company and police protection from the lions and tigers and bears we have around here threatening you on your runs? I could meet up with you at your place in the morning."

The pause in response seemed like an eternity.

"That would be fine. But I would feel more comfortable meeting out on the run. Let's meet at the corner of Elderberry and Main at 6:10."

Now that they had been running together for a few weeks, the feeling in his stomach had not eased. It had only grown. Every time that he saw her, it was worse. He was not sure how she felt about him. She seemed fine with talking with him as long as they kept topics about running, avoiding bears, and superficial conversation. With those topics, she seemed relaxed. If he started to talk about feelings or past relationships, he could sense an immediate change in her step. Stiffer and more guarded, not her normal easy-flowing gait.

It was obvious that she was not relying on his protection alone on the run. She still carried the can of bear spray. It did seem to him as she peeled away from him to head down her road that her body was a little more relaxed. In spite of this, he was encouraged by the fact that this morning she was laughing more at his jokes as they ran.

Why did she come off as so indifferent? Was it an act? Was she playing hard to get? Well, he was up to the challenge. He thought he had a chance. It was time to ask her out on a real date and pile on the woo and romance. He pulled his truck into the station, removed the key from the ignition with purpose, then sauntered inside with an extra kick to his gait.

CHAPTER 3

Meara walked into the cafeteria. The rays of the sun through the big plate-glass windows greeted her simultaneously with the scents from the cafeteria line. She could smell salmon from the midst of the other smells instantly. She smiled when she thought of all the different ways that she had seen it prepared in the last month. Before she came here, she had never been a fan of fish. However, the fresh salmon here had won her over. It tasted so rich, so firm, and full of flavor, completely unlike the salmon served on the East Coast.

She loaded her tray with a salad that she had also learned not to take for granted. It was Thursday, and today there was no sign of wilting and limpness to the greens. On top, she placed a small serving of salmon cooked with thinly sliced lemon and a garlic vinaigrette. She breathed in the meal, fairly confident it would taste as good as it smelled and looked. Salmon, it's not just for dinner. She chuckled as she tried to remind herself of the advertisement it brought to mind, but she couldn't place it. Since she had arrived, it was a rare day that she did not have salmon at some point.

Salmon didn't just show up in the cafeteria at work. The employees of the training center were always bringing in food to share. Her favorite was smoked salmon. One of the office women made the best. It had a bit of a teriyaki, brown sugar, and smoke blend that made the taste. Some called it Eskimo candy. She could see why. She had very little "won't power" when it came to restraining herself from putting her hand in the bag to grab more. Somebody was always sharing a little abundance from their carefully put away stockpiles at home.

She took her salad and salmon and fully enjoyed the wafting scent as she scanned the big room full of tables and diners. Across the cafeteria, she saw who she was looking for. At the base of two of the big windows sat the two girls that she had been teaching this morning. She zigzagged through the room and the other diners until she came to stand at their table.

She knew that the two girls, who were both in their early twenties, were sisters, but they were so different. Chelsey was slightly taller and thinner. She seemed to always have her dark chestnut hair pulled back into a ponytail, which accented her narrower face. They had similar soft, chocolate-colored eyes that betrayed a kind and gentle humor through the lines that would crinkle at the corners of the tear-dropped shape. Chelsey was quick to speak up and was quick to assess what happened around her. She was also quick to wit, but it came in subtle, underhanded statements.

She and her sister consistently wore *qaspaq*, the traditional Yupik and Inuit top. But even these displayed the differences between the two girls. Chelsey wore ones that had more of a modern twist. They had cowl necks and tighter-fitting knit lower sleeves that could be pushed up and stay up and out of the way. They were also made of brighter, more modern batik prints as opposed to gingham and paisley.

Verna was a direct contrast to her sister in so many ways. She wore the traditional qaspaq with a simple neckline leading to the hood and cuffed sleeves that did not allow the wearer to push them up and out of the way as easily. Hers were made of bright and traditional gingham prints. She was shorter and more solid in stature than her sister. She had a rounder face framed by thick dark glasses. Her jet-black hair was cut in a blunt, shoulder-length bob.

She reminded Meara of an owl. She took the world in by listening with astute ears and observing carefully through those glasses before she would speak up. When she did speak up, she used a slow speech pattern, and her words were carefully planned. Her movements seemed to have more purpose as well. It was like she fluffed her feathers and calculated where the present current in the room would bring them next. Her style was different from her sister's, but Meara could clearly feel that Verna should not be underestimated. Her quietness seemed to increase her perceptive powers.

Meara had been so concerned about the look in Verna's eyes this morning, and she could not shake the worry. Was Verna homesick? In any case, Meara felt a driving need to guide her through the trials of homesickness or whatever else was disturbing her. Verna had demonstrated such potential as a health aide. Meara was afraid that she might quit because of the challenges. And, she could not lose her so early in her training. Now, she stood at the end of the table feeling like a mother bear looking over her young she was determined to protect.

"I am so sorry for interrupting your conversation. But, may I join you?"

Both girls politely smiled. "Sure," they said in unison. Chelsey patted the seat next to her, welcoming Meara to sit.

She purposefully took a moment to settle into her seat and arrange her meal, hoping they would return to their conversation. Despite the welcome, a silence had overtaken the table, interrupted only by the sounds of silverware meeting the plates. It blanketed the table like a thick fog.

"How are you enjoying your training so far?" Meara asked, breaking the awkward silence. She took a bite of the salad and leaned back for a response.

Both girls responded simultaneously. "Love it!" But they did not continue the conversation.

Meara finished chewing and swallowed. "What has been your favorite part so far?" She took a bite of salmon and waited.

Verna replied, "Emergency skills. I feel so much better. Like now if an emergency came into the clinic, I have a plan. I am no longer helpless."

Chelsey responded, "I agree, but I like the CHAM. What I really like about the CHAM is it makes me feel like a detective gathering information to solve a mystery. And, it seems like there are so many mysteries to uncover. It is like each patient that walks in the door is a mystery to be solved. It makes the whole process feel a bit like an adventure." She paused. "Except human lives are connected to the mysteries."

All three laughed, and the tension left the table.

"I never thought about it that way," said Meara. "But that is kind of what the developers of the CHAM did. They took diagnostic reasoning, which is a form of deductive reasoning, and made it into a step-by-step process."

"It is fun in a way. But it is also so different than how a doctor's visit goes. Their visits are similar but so different. And, so much faster," said Chelsey.

"That is because the doctors and nurse practitioners have years of education that allow them to keep the whole deductive reasoning process in their heads. They are able to narrow down their questions. The CHAM allows you to gather the information you need to assess the problem and eventually solve and treat the problem. And if you can't solve it, you will have all the information that the doctor needs to help you take care of the patient."

"It is amazing how much that book has in it," said Verna.

"It will be amazing for you to see how much you have learned by the time you are certified," replied Meara. "What has been the hardest part of being here for training?"

Verna instantly choked back the bite of food in her mouth. Her body stiffened, tears welling up in her eyes. She dropped her head and turned her face away from Meara. "Excuse me, I need to go." She placed her cutlery on the tray and made a beeline for the dirty-dish window.

Chelsey looked at Meara with a pained look then back toward her sister. Chelsey pressed her lips together forming a straight line, then her eyes and head followed her sister. "I am sorry. I need to go be with her."

Meara sat back watching the two girls exit the cafeteria. *There I go again trying to connect with people. I failed.* Why was she so successful with people opening up to her in an exam room and an utter failure when she was just being herself?

* * *

Verna was the first one back to the classroom that afternoon. She had excused herself from her sister and had taken a walk along the tundra behind the hospital compound. She had brought along a small berry-gathering bucket she had created out of an old margarine container she had found in the housing. She strung a piece of yarn into two holes she had punched on either side. She had measured it so that it hung at the level of her bent elbows as she bent over the lowbush cranberries that were in front of her now.

Lowbush cranberries or *tumagliq* were especially sweet now that there had been a frost. The morning she had arrived, she had noted a patch growing here. She had heard from some white elders that they drove away heartache. Verna wasn't sure about that, but she did know that going to gather them would definitely lift her spirits. She didn't think that there was anything that would cure the heartbreak she felt right now.

As she bent over, she thought about her mother. Verna had been lucky in some ways to be raised by an elder. She had been taught many of the old ways. If she were home right now and she were going out with her mother for a day of berry gathering, they both would have put on their prettiest qaspaqs. Wearing a beautiful qaspaq was a way of thanking

God for all the beauty he had given and for the beautiful berries that helped them survive. The heartache did fade a bit as she thought of herself as a little girl. She always thought of God watching over them smiling and laughing as the berries made a *plop, plop, plop* as they hit the bottom of their pails.

Her eyes scanned the beauty of the tundra. The reds, greens, and browns gave her hints of the plants that could be found when she got close. The smell of peat was still in the air, but the moist, earthy aroma would soon be gone and covered by a thick blanket of snow. She was hoping that the snows would hold off a while longer. She needed to gather a lot more berries for her family's use when she got home. Now that Mom was becoming frailer, Verna had to pick up her gathering to keep the family supplied. How did she think she could keep up with her subsistence chores and finish her training?

She reassured herself that having him gone would be a good thing now. Knowing how untruthful he was made him seem like he was a distraction keeping her from doing the things that she needed to do.

Bending over the mat-like shrub, she could see the small, thick, glossy, elliptical leaves that were now roughly the same size as their bright-red berries. If she were at home, they would be going to the same spot where her mother had gathered berries with her own mother before. When she gathered in that spot, she often felt her ancestral grandmothers gathering right alongside her. Often, she would feel them lend her some wisdom or strength.

With the first handful of berries she ate, the bright sweet and tart flavors exploded in her mouth. She hoped that it was going to calm her stomach down. She had possessed little appetite since the revealing last night of Jim's awful deception. He was the first man who she had fully given her heart to. The pain was consuming her, and she had been struggling to keep it together. As she gathered, the tears fell and washed away her pain.

It was not long before she had filled her little gathering bucket. Standing tall again, she was surprised to realize that she had felt the grandmothers beside her during her berry picking, even though she was far from her home patch.

Time would sort things out. Family was first. Sisterhood was most important.

* * *

In the afternoon, Chelsey watched as Meara pulled the CHAM out and gave each set of health aide trainees some case studies to work through. Today she was teaching them how to combine the emergency skills they had learned with the guidance in the CHAM.

Chesley would be the aide, and Verna was role-playing the patient. Chelsey had an anxious feeling that she needed to get everything right. Somehow, she needed to pull together the emergency skills. These role-plays really made her feel like she knew absolutely nothing.

"What did you come to the clinic for today?" Chelsey read from the left front cover of her CHAM.

"My three-year-old daughter is sick," said Verna as the mother in the role-play.

"Okay, because she is three, I need to go to the right front cover to assess a child less than eight years old." She undressed the baby and asked Verna what she was seeing.

"Is the baby difficult to wake up, barely moving, or unconscious?" Chelsey asked as she eyed the mannequin briefly.

"No." Verna faked a child's cry.

"Is the baby crying constantly and cannot be comforted? This feels so awkward. We would normally be seeing this and not asking this," commented Chelsey.

"No," said Verna.

"Is the baby breathing really fast or slow? Working really hard to breathe?"

"Yes," said Verna. "She is grunting and breathing very fast."

"Okay, the cover says I need to go to the emergency section." Chelsey's own heart beat faster even in this role-play scene.

Meara walked over.

Chelsey tightened up in anticipation of being critiqued.

"Good job. Now you have a choice. You can stay in the big CHAM and go to page sixty-eight, or you can use the small Emergency Field Handbook CHAM. Remember when you are out working that the small one was made so you have a guide on hand that is easily put in a pocket or a bag if you have to run out to the scene of an emergency. They both say the same thing, but some like the smaller guide better. Okay, keep going."

"What is the level of consciousness of my patient?" continued Chelsey. Now the stress that this simulation was creating was doubled knowing that Meara was leaning right over watching the two of them. She didn't want to mess up.

"She is awake; she is breathing, so the airway is open."

"How fast is she breathing?"

"Fifty breaths a minute."

"That is fast. I will give her oxygen by blow-by. I am listening to her lung sounds. What do I hear? What are her O2 saturations?"

"She is wheezing. Oxygen saturation is 88." Chelsey took a deep breath. Her hands shook as she turned to the page in the CHAM that guided her to the next steps. She was having a hard time keeping the anxiety down with role-play. How would she be able to do this alone in her village when there was nobody else with her?

"Okay, I need to give her an albuterol treatment. I now need to look at page ninety-nine of the CHAM. I am going to mix 0.5 milliliters of albuterol and three milliliters of saline in a nebulizer and give it to her."

"Here is a nebulizer, saline, and albuterol. Show me how to set this up."

Chelsey and Verna worked together to fit the nebulizer machine with the tubing. Then putting the chamber onto the tubing, she mixed the medications inside it and closed the top. Finally, they switched the machine on and put it in front of their doll patient.

"Good job. I know that it feels really awkward now. This is why we practice this. If you didn't know how to do it, where would you look?"

Verna piped up. "We could look up things we don't know how to do in the reference manual." She picked up a ring-bound book and looked up nebulizer in the index. She quickly put that large manual down and picked up a similar-sized one. "It says to look at page forty in the medicine handbook."

"Excellent. What does it show you there?"

"It tells how to give the albuterol, and there are pages to copy to give to the patient."

"Good. So, you have the nebulizer going. What do you do next?"

"Now I need to check the circulation. I feel the carotid pulse."

"Her pulse is strong but hard to count at around 150. That is a bit fast." Verna read from her script.

"Is she bleeding?"

"No."

"I am now checking her skin." Chelsey read from the CHAM.

"It is pale, hot, dry. Capillary refill is more than three seconds."

"That isn't good. Okay. I finish the nebulizer as I talk to the mother. I am asking about symptoms. Did she have a fever at home? Been coughing or having difficulty breathing?" She continued with more questions, then added, "Does she have allergies, take medications, have a past medical history, when was her last meal? Was there an event that started this?"

"She had a fever for a day then started coughing. She takes no normal medications, no allergies, this is a first time for her. She hasn't had an appetite. Last ate this morning. Brother was sick last week." Chelsey busily wrote all this information into the encounter form in front of her. She felt like her own heart rate was fast.

"Okay. Now I am checking the vital signs. "

"Temperature 99.4, pulse 92, respirations are 30, oxygen saturations are 94," read Verna.

Meara laughed and moved closer to the two. "I bet that you are feeling better already with those changes from your albuterol. Now what?"

"Now I continue onward for my exam. I start at the head, check the neck, work my way down the neck, eyes, listen to the lungs again, listen to the heart, feel the abdomen, and listen to it. Check the muscle tone of the legs and arms and then check the skin for rashes."

"Lungs are now slightly wheezing, skin is pale, neck moves well, heart is regular and strong. Capillary refill is now one second."

"I am feeling much better hearing that. Those vital signs are normal according to the CHAM. I now ask the mother the last time the child urinated and if she has been drinking," said Chelsey.

"This morning, and she hasn't been drinking well. Last time she urinated was last night." Verna responded from the script.

"Alright, I have determined that this child has the assessment of Very Sick. So, now I call the doctor, and I go to CHAM 149 for the Plan of Very Sick Child," replied Chelsey.

"Excellent job, you two." Meara looked at the two of them with a smile.

Verna looked up. "This is scary, and I was shaking here watching Chelsey be a pretend caregiver when we were just making believe. How will we be able to do this all by ourselves in the clinic far away from you or a doctor?"

Chelsey was almost glad to hear that her sister was as nervous as she was. They had a week of training here, then they will go to the training center. How could they ever learn enough in that short time to be ready to be off in their own village with real people and real problems?

CHAPTER 4

Meara was not going to give up trying to get closer to Verna to find out what had caused those tear-swollen eyes earlier in the week. Her first instinct that it was homesickness had certainly been her strongest hunch. Although she had completely blown it with her first try to understand the tears, she had not given up. She had spent time rotating her lunches among her different students.

She made a point to let them direct the conversation and gave words of reassurance here and there. She enjoyed listening to the totally different childhoods they had experienced compared to her own. She also shared stories of developing her own skills as a nurse practitioner and acknowledged how much there was to learn and how many mistakes they were expected to make.

"Have you traveled much outside Quyalaqaq?" she asked Verna at lunch the next week.

"I never got to travel much other than for sports," said Verna. "I played volleyball and basketball in high school. Most of our travel was quick flights between local villages. Sometimes when we won championships we would go to Anchorage or Juneau."

"That seems so fun. Flying to your sports. We only took buses a few towns over when I grew up," said Meara.

"The flying isn't that much fun. Sometimes it can be really scary. But it is what we have to do. We don't even have a school bus in our village even if there was a next town. When there is snow, we have an elder that pulls the school sled behind a snow machine up to the school. In the days without snow, he pulls a wagon behind a four-wheeler."

"Do you miss going to school?"

"Not now." Verna laughed. "You have me pretty busy. I like learning new things."

Verna was one of the youngest new trainees, having just graduated from high school two years ago. Meara had been surprised to get to know an old soul in her youngest student. Her application stated that she was looking for a career that would allow her to stay in her village to remain with her aging parents. Meara knew that Verna was not very confident in her looks. This came across clearly in Verna's self-degrading Facebook account. Although she consistently put herself down, Verna possessed a humble beauty. She had kind dark-brown eyes that seemed to hold an understanding of the world much older than her age. Her round face lit up when she smiled, and the smile drew you to her. She had a self-deprecating sense of humor as well.

Verna was a natural but quiet leader and showed this potential leadership in the classroom. She was quick to grasp concepts and would then turn and explain them in her own way to her fellow classmates. She was obviously a good student, having excelled in all her placement exams. She had proved during her ETT training that she had a natural ability to calmly assess a situation and respond methodically.

When Verna had come in in tears, the emotion had caught Meara off guard. It was totally out of character for this quiet but self-possessed girl.

After Meara's social awkwardness the first day, she was determined to find the cause so she could support her protege. She was attempting to get to it in a roundabout way this time.

It was clear they were not going to open up to her that easily, even though she had felt they had started to bond during the ETT training.

Chelsey added, "Actually, I am having a lot of fun. I don't get out of the village much, and I am always up for an adventure."

"You seemed to have a struggle last week," Meara said to both girls. "Are you feeling better now?"

She was surprised when Chelsey sat taller. "Yes, we are doing better."

"Would you mind me asking what the problem was?"

"It is a long story. Last week, we accidentally discovered that we were both dating the same man. We had just found out the night before we started session. I had been seeing him for about three months," said Chelsey.

Verna fixed her eyes on her food in a thinly disguised veil of trying to hide her crumbling face. "I had seen him two-and-a-half. The hardest part of all of this is we both really cared about him. He seemed to be such a great guy. He does such caring things for people. None of this makes sense."

"How did you both end up seeing the same man? You don't even live near each other."

"He is a bush pilot. He sometimes flies the route down the Aleutians to my village, and sometimes he flies the loop to Verna's village. Right now, he is doing some training down in the lower forty-eight. We are planning to have some fun seeing what it takes to get him to confess." Chelsey piped in with a smile so wide it showed all of her teeth.

"How are you going to do that?"

"Well, we talked to our dad about this. He had his own period of running around. It was interesting to get his thoughts."

"And what did he say?"

"He said 'what comes around, goes around' is the teaching of the elders. He says Jim followed his desires instead of his mind, and that isn't good. However, it is important that we do not do the same as him and follow our emotions. We need to give him a chance to come forward, and we also need to be ready to be forgiving. That does not mean he gets away with this. He needs to make things right."

Chelsey sat back in her chair and crossed her arms across her chest. "Although what the elders say is important, that doesn't mean we can't have some fun with this. We are going to put him into some situations to make him a bit more uncomfortable. Hopefully, he is man enough to come clean. We plan on letting him tell his own story, and we aren't going to let him know what we know or don't know. Eventually, if he is a good man he will confess. If not…mmmm." She hesitated. "We haven't made up our mind about how we will deal with him if he doesn't."

Verna squirmed in her chair and slipped down a little, while she looked at her sister. "I think that he will come clean, and I think that we do need to be responsible to the beliefs of the elders."

"So, how are you two planning to do this?"

"Well, it just so happens that he will be on the Quyalaqaq route when we are all there for training. That is when we will let him tell the truth. We are still working on the 'how.'"

"Please, keep our secret. Make sure you don't let him know that we know. There is a good chance that he will probably fly you out and that you will see him in the clinic."

* * *

Rey nervously waited. He almost wondered if she wouldn't show. She had been so avoidant of time alone with him. She would escape so quickly when she came to her turn off on the daily run that he had had a difficult time actually being able to ask her out. He finally had gotten her to agree to go on a date with him. He was determined to win her over and suspected she enjoyed adventure, and at the same time she was a bit anxious about it. The can of bear spray was always on her when she was outside alone. He was eager to make a great impression on her by combining some adventure with romance. He had proposed a little snow machine trip.

He had a delivery to make to a village that could only be accessed by land when there was snow cover. A large recent storm had coated the tundra with a thick layer of fluffy snow. He had heard that some of the villagers had been coming to town. And this morning when he passed the grocery store and hardware store, a few machines in the parking lot were hauling sleds.

He prepared his two snow machines with one of them hauling a sled. The sled was fully loaded with a couple of totes and some duffel bags. One duffel bag held the ingredients for a nice picnic on the tundra. He hoped she would like his cooking. He had a nice chili in a thermos, with another thermos of hot tea. The night before, he had even ventured into his kitchen to make some cornbread. Everything was strapped in and ready to go as soon as she arrived.

Meara had refused to have him pick her up and had insisted on walking from her cabin to the beginning of the trail. She was approaching from a distance, well bundled in thick, down snow pants, a thick parka to match, a pair of Baffin tundra boots with an L.L. Bean beanie covering her hair except for the long red ponytail flowing from behind.

His body stirred when he thought of her well-toned body in her running tights. It was well hidden today in all her outdoor clothes. He was glad, because he knew from her distancing body language that approaching her would need to be slow and cautious. She definitely was keeping a wall between them, but he was convinced she was just playing hard to get.

"Good morning!" She waved. Her smile illuminated not just her face but also his own.

His cheeks stretched; he hadn't smiled that big in a while. "Good morning! Ready for your lesson?"

"I'm really not too sure about this, but I'm not one to turn down an adventure. I have never ridden one of these before. I tend to stay with woman-powered sports. Is it too far to ski?"

"Yes. By snow machine it is about thirty miles. I don't know that either of us is ready to ski that distance at this point. Later in the season the 'highway' will be packed down better and a lot easier to travel. We can make that a future adventure. It would be fun. Hey, let me introduce you to your horse for today!"

"I am not riding with you?"

"No, riding with two machines makes things much safer. If one breaks down, then you have a backup. You aren't stuck out there in the cold waiting hopefully for someone to find you." He spent about ten minutes introducing her to the sled. He pointed out the accelerator, lights, ignition switch.

"Seriously? Electric hand warmers? That will make this a lot more fun." She gave an audible sigh of relief.

Adventurous but likes comfort, he noted.

Opening up the gear box under the seat, he pointed out the emergency gear including a reflective warming blanket, emergency food, a set of tools, and a spare small jug of gas.

"And we have some extra special toys, I mean tools, courtesy of my job. Here are some thermal goggles for search and rescue. We have my gun because I can always be called to duty, and it isn't a bad idea with wolves this time of year. And the most important rescue tool of all." He paused and gave her a grin.

He pulled out a super-sized dark chocolate bar. He took his gloves off and methodically unwrapped it, broke it in two small squares. Teasingly, he invited her to open up by holding it in front of her mouth. She hesitated a moment but then opened up for him to pop a square in.

Good to know, chocolate was a weak spot.

He nodded to the totes in the sled. "We are taking these to Angus. He is the VPSO, Village Public Safety Officer. The VPSOs are hired by their local communities, but they are trained and supervised by the Alaska State Troopers. They even go to a shorter version of trooper academy. I am his regional supervisor. Village Public Safety Officers are our eyes and ears on the ground in villages. They are an extension of the troopers, only they are not allowed to carry a gun."

"Anyhow, I thought it would be fun to turn my delivery into a date. You know what they say: All work and no play makes Rey a very dull boy. So, we are combining a little of both today. Hop on! Follow me. We will take it slow to start." He leaned over, turned on her machine, and watched her climb on. After hopping on his and giving her a quick lesson on leaning, he took off down the snow highway on the tundra, hoping he was making the impression that he desired.

* * *

Meara listened intently to Rey's instructions as they prepared to go. She had been a skier all her life, so this should be like skiing but with an engine. She twisted the accelerator back, and the snow machine lurched forward. Okay, that was a bit more sensitive than she thought. Easy girl.

She fell in behind him. He started to slow down then started making some figure eights in the snow in front of her, signaling with his hand for her to follow behind.

She was successful with those and started to feel the tension in her jaw relax, and the smile came back to her face. This was actually fun and easier than she thought.

The cold arctic air was buffered by the full-face mask. Her arctic gear proved its worth, and she felt no cold wind coming through her coat. The helmet added to the warmth of her hat. With her hands in the hand warmers, she was incredibly comfortable in spite of the ten-degree weather.

He waved her onto the path, and then he went up around a corner that seemed to bank into a ditch twenty feet below. He and the sled smoothly moved around the corner and went just out of view.

I don't know about this. She stopped and looked at the banking of the path. He wouldn't take her somewhere she couldn't handle.

She followed and slowed down as soon as she felt the pull of the banking of the path. She stood up and threw all of her weight uphill trying to imitate the movements that he had made. This was like skiing. Accelerating, she pushed down on her downhill foot and kept her body upright and hands neutral as if she were approaching a giant slalom gate.

Instead of getting an edge to ride the corner with, the machine slipped. The outside ski lifted up, and she grasped desperately onto the handles as she rolled over. And over. And over.

Meara didn't know how she kept the snow machine from rolling on top of her as they went down, but at the bottom she was stuck. Her head was securely held underneath the treads. It was safely encased in her helmet, but she could not move it. Snow had made its way under the face shield, and she could feel the cold against her skin. When she tried to cry out for help, the snow muffled her voice. She moved her arms and legs. Other than being a bit sore, she seemed to be alright. She moved her arms along her helmet trying to figure out how to free herself.

"Meara!! Are you alright?" Rey yelled.

"Yes, I am stuck," she was attempting to say as the machine was lifted off of her head.

Quickly, she jumped up, half out of embarrassment and partly to prove to herself that she wasn't hurt and most definitely was not a wimp. She forced a smile and attempted to hide her shaking body from him.

"I think my ego is wounded much more than my body." She tried to ignore the pain in her left buttock. She was going to have quite the bruise. But she couldn't give up. She needed to be able to do this.

Rey walked around the machine, climbed on, and drove it in a circle.

"Looks okay other than the break in the windshield. We can continue on with it as is. Duct tape will do the job for now. But I should probably just get you home."

"No, let's go. I'm fine."

He placed his hands on either side of her helmet and looked directly into her face. Could he see right through her act of confidence? She wasn't sure if she was angry at him or reassured with his support.

"Are you sure? Alright, let's try this again." He reached over her shoulders and gave her a quick squeeze. She found herself wanting to relax into this offhand hug.

The two took off across the tundra where the path opened into a flat highway marked by flags stuck in the tundra. The remaining trip to the village was uneventful. They drove a couple of hours. He took out his radio, called into town, and had a brief conversation she couldn't hear.

"Angus is at a family event. We will just drop by the station and leave the totes out there for him."

A few miles before the village, they passed a grove of trees to the left before they crossed a small river, and way up ahead, they could just start to see the buildings of the town. As they came off the path and onto the street of the village, they passed a row of old run-down houses built on pilings along the road. Some were small, not much bigger than sheds. Others looked to be big enough to have a couple of bedrooms. The ones on the left were open to tundra and then to the river. On the right, they were backed to the tundra. After a quarter mile, they turned right. About a hundred yards down the road, they pulled the machines up behind the VPSO building with the village store directly across the street.

"Let's grab a quick coffee before we head back for our picnic." In the store, Rey greeted the storekeeper and another man who were both sitting and having a conversation in Yupik.

"*Cama'i*," he said as he poured a coffee for Meara. And after handing it to her, he poured another for himself.

Meara sipped her coffee and wandered the store. She had heard that village grocery prices were high, but this was unbelievable. Nine dollars for a box of cereal. Fourteen dollars for milk. There were no vegetables to be seen except in the freezer section. The soda section was large. There was an entire endcap devoted to stacked blue boxes with a

1940s-looking little navy sailor on it: Sailor Boy Pilot Bread. Another endcap was stacked with Tang.

"I didn't know they still made this. I haven't had Tang since I was little." She caught herself reminiscing of summer days filled with Kool-Aid and Tang.

The warmth of the store joined the coffee in chasing the cold from their chilled bodies.

"Warmed up?" Rey asked.

"Yes, surprisingly so," responded Meara.

"*Quyana,*" Rey said to the cashier. He seemed to make a point to look and nod at both of the men before he and Meara left the store and stepped across the street. Meara noted the directness of the look and wondered if this was a police thing.

They made short work of unloading the two totes behind the door of the arctic entry of the VPSO building.

"Okay, business is done. Let's go have some fun," Rey said as the two climbed back onto their individual sleds and took off back across the tundra. After about an hour of riding, they left the trail, making a turn to the left, and worked their way up a small and gently sloped mountain. At the top, Rey stopped, climbed off, and went back to the sled.

"We are going to enjoy a meal with a view in total comfort." He grinned at her as he sauntered by.

The sun was still sending its rays across the tundra, illuminating the view of the snow-covered tundra below with the Bering Sea beyond. The tundra was a vast expanse of white with the exception of a few scattered groves of trees. The sea was filled with large chunks of ice the size of Volkswagen buses. There was a foggy mist hanging over the chunks on the ocean that went out as far as the eye could see, but it seemed to stop abruptly at about twenty feet above the water level. The sun played with dispersing the fog, but it did not seem as if it wanted to commit the energy to clear the gray blanket away.

Meara stood captivated by the landscape. She was in awe that as far as she could see, there was no sign of another human being. The vastness of the horizon was like nothing she had ever experienced before.

Meanwhile, Rey went back to the sled and pulled one of the duffel bags out of it, and within moments there was a shelter set up with a window overlooking the magical scene. He returned to the sled and grabbed a couple more bags and went inside.

"Wait here." He smiled and winked at Meara and ducked back into the shelter with another bag.

Meara waited outside, walking in place to keep her feet warm, but in spite of the cold she was enjoying the incredible winter landscape in front of her. The fog would separate in areas and move in waves underneath as an area of the magical mist was caught in a breeze. It reminded her of the vapors that danced above a witch's cauldron.

The tent unzipped again as Rey bowed with his left arm folded across his chest and his right arm stretched out holding the door open and directing her inside. "Madame, your table is ready."

She stepped inside and found the little tent set up with a table for two looking out the window. It was covered with a beautiful yellow, green, and blue tablecloth that made her think of France. A single rose lay across the table. Two little chairs sat at either side. There was a bowl and a bread plate set in front of the two chairs with real silverware. Antique teacups sat in their saucers on the table. The final touch was a propane heater that vented in the back, which emanated a glow as it heated the little structure to a comfortable temperature. "Rey, you have set up dinner for two! Who would think we would find a cozy cafe out here?"

"Fishing shelters can be used for more than fishing." He held her chair for her at the roll-up table.

"This is incredible. I feel like I am at a French cafe with an incredibly not-French view. I can't believe you did all of this. It couldn't be more wonderful."

"Not as wonderful as you." He looked into her eyes.

Meara's cheeks grew hot. She really didn't feel ready to deal with any kind of romance.

He moved over to his chair and sat. Leaning over, he pulled out a small container. From this he served cornbread with a pat of butter onto their plates. Reaching down again, he produced a wide-mouthed thermos. He screwed off the lid, and the shelter was suddenly filled with the aroma of homemade chili.

She took a deep inhale to fill her senses with the smell. The colors were even dramatic with fresh tomatoes added to the darker sauce. Chunks of meat floated in between the brown beans.

One more time, he reached down and pulled out another thermos. Two bowls and two spoons appeared on the table in front of them. The freshly baked bread was put in the center. When he poured the hot chili into the bowl, the aroma filled up the tent again making her mouth water. He then pulled out another thermos and poured them each a cup of warm tea.

"Moose chili. I got a bull last year. I shared some, but even with sharing it, having only my mouth to feed I probably have enough meat till next winter."

"I have never had moose before." Meara gave him a timid smile. She had heard that moose could taste really gamey.

He reached across the table for her hands and bowed his head. "Thank you, God, for a beautiful day and a beautiful companion. Bless us with a safe ride home."

The atmosphere in the shelter totally relaxed Meara, and they made small talk and told stories of their youth until the sun approached the sea.

"I would love to end this by watching the sunset, but we need to get back to town before dark."

Before leaving the tent, Rey took her hand and pulled her to him. He wrapped his arms around the small of her back and pulled her close.

Her heart raced, and her body stiffened. As Rey moved in to catch her lips, she stepped back quickly to move away.

"Rey, I'm sorry. I am just not ready for that yet. I need more time," she said awkwardly.

As Meara climbed onto her snow machine again, she was grateful that she had her own space for the trip back to town.

CHAPTER 5

Meara opened the door to her cabin and walked in after her run the following morning. She had sent Rey a quick text to let him know that she would not be out at her normal time. She chose to run later so she could be alone. She needed to avoid being with him this morning. She knew too well from her past that when attraction was involved, her judgement was poor. Even with the quick run, she had failed to process her state of confusion. She needed a warm cup of tea.

She moved to the little section of the cabin and sorted through the selection of teas she had packed. The small cabin was starting to feel more like a haven now but not quite a home. It no longer had the smell that had made her arrival so miserable. The cleaning had given it more of a welcoming feel. And little things like the box of teas and a small lamp on the table made it feel like hers. The small table held the little lamp made of driftwood with a lampshade made of birch bark. That little space became her comfort nook, where she would read and think as she looked out the window into the grove of arctic pine outside.

She turned on the tea kettle and chose a bag of tea. She opened the lid to the travel mug, which had become her steady companion, and popped a neatly packaged tea bag inside. As she poured the hot water over it, she wondered why life could not be so neatly packaged. Steam rose up from the bag.

She moved over to the little table, leaned back in the chair, and inhaled the steam. Her body was pulled back to the moment in the shelter when he wrapped his arms around her. The warmth in her hands wrapped around the mug seemed to fill her entire body. Yes, there was attraction. She had felt the pull. It was strong. But, the steam of attraction hadn't worked for her in the past. Steam in the right container in the right dose is wonderful. Steam let loose can burn.

He certainly checked out as being a good guy. If anything, he was too good, and she could never match his giving and caring nature. She had checked around the community, quietly asking people if they knew him. Every time she asked, she was told what a great guy he was. He helped one person to move. He had helped another resolve some legal problems. He even protected an old drunk who preferred to live under a dock than to live in a home. He kept the old man's bank card, and they would pull out an allowance together. This protected the old man's money so that people wouldn't take it all, and it protected the old man from himself so that he wouldn't drink all his money. It seemed that everybody had a story of Rey helping them out.

It was all her. What was wrong with her? She was a bit too gun-shy. She couldn't trust anyone enough to get close to them. This guy checked out. What was her problem?

Her thoughts wandered to running with him. He went out of his way to protect her. He would never allow her to run toward the middle of the road. He wanted to make sure that he could keep her safe before himself. He really was a good guy.

So, why couldn't she relax and enjoy the kiss?

She chuckled a little to herself. Kissing created a giant force that sucked all of her brains out of her head.

She was sure that she had chased him away by acting like such an indecisive fool. He definitely was all about decisiveness. She sighed. Probably too late to fix this one, but she was going to try.

Picking up the phone, she tried to call to thank him for the wonderful and thoughtful day. She heard his voice over his message. "Rey, thank you for the wonderful day yesterday. I really enjoyed it, and I hope we can have more adventures like that."

As she hit the button to hang up, she noticed the rabbit outside. She had been watching him with his brown coat snacking on the grass along the edges of the trees. Today, suddenly his coat had changed. In the blink of an eye, he looked like a totally new rabbit. All camouflaged to hide his actions in the tundra. How many other things on the tundra could completely change to not be what they appeared to be at other times?

* * *

Meara rode the bike she had borrowed from Nancy toward the main road. She had been invited to help process some fish. Nancy had asked her if she would be interested in helping a family that could use one more hand to process the "pinks" that were coming in. She was so excited to see how the wonderful smoked salmon that she had been enjoying so much lately was caught and processed.

She pulled into the driveway and was greeted by a wiry old man who appeared to be at least seventy. His crew-cut hair framed his big smile. He wore a thick work jacket with a patch on the left shoulder with the letters ATG and the Big Dipper on it in stars. "You must be Meara. Nancy told me you might enjoy a little work." His eyes twinkled. "You do know how to work?"

She laughed in return. "Of course, I do. As a matter of fact, I am not good at not working. I am so excited to get to learn how all of this fish processing happens."

"Here, take these." She found herself catching a heavy bundle of bright orange gear. She slipped the rain pants on over her jeans and pulled the Grundén-labeled suspenders tighter over her shoulders. Then she pulled the big rain jacket over all of her clothes.

"Hop in." He put a bunch of coolers into the back of the truck.

She went around to the passenger side of the truck and climbed in. She felt awkward, but she had no idea what his name was. She had been sent to the house of Anna. But Nancy hadn't told her any of the other names.

She awkwardly spoke up. "Hi, I am Meara Crowley. What is your name?"

He looked up. "Whoops. I don't encounter new people that often. Around here, I know most of the folks. Except those that come in and out working at that hospital. You are one of them, aren't you?"

"Yes, I work for the health aide program."

"Well, we need to go get some fish." The old man turned the ignition on and backed the truck out into the road. "Do you know how to pick fish?"

"No, I never did it before." She still wondered who she was talking to.

"Well, this is how it works. Each family has a site that they pick out at the beginning of the season. But, most of the sites are known to belong to specific families by tradition. That site is where you set your net and stake your permit." The old man suddenly moved the car to the opposite side of the road. A car headed toward them from the opposite direction. Her hands still clenched the door handles, even though Nancy had initiated her to this odd ritual.

The old man suddenly shifted the truck back into his own lane. "Damned potholes."

"How do you know who is where?" Meara tried to catch her breath and recover from the lane change.

"It is pretty much known. If a newcomer *kusuk* like you were to stake a claim, you would need to come down with a local. Or, you can ask someone if you can set a tide on their site when they aren't doing their subsistence fishing."

"I don't mean to be dumb, but what is subsistence fishing?"

"Subsistence is when you are gathering the fish or game that your family needs each year. It is counted differently than commercial fishing. You really are new around here."

They pulled down a side road that led down to the waterfront, then drove the truck left along the bank. All along the high side of the shore were weathered plywood signs with last names and numbers painted on them.

There were ropes tied to stakes high up on the bank that they were driving over. Down along the shoreline the ropes were clipped with a carabiner to long nets made of a green nylon. Each net was laid out flat by the outgoing tide. Entangled within were the bodies of writhing, large silver fish. Their fins glistened and reflected the sun, and the silver seemed to produce rainbows on their bodies. Most of them continued to fight for their lives despite being stuck out of water. Their fight showed their will to live, their need to return to the water and to finish their cycle of life.

The old man pulled up to a sign labeled Johnson. "Now, Meara, let's see if you can figure out how to pick."

He went to the back of the truck and tossed her a tote and grabbed one for himself. Then he walked down to the net. He took a deep breath, inhaling then holding it. A big, relaxed smile spread over his face. "You have to take the time to smell the fish."

Meara imitated and chuckled to herself. *Well, that was a twist on "stop and smell the roses."* The air was filled with the smell of the sea and the fish that lined the shore caught in their nets.

"Not bad." He smiled and regarded his net. "We even have a few kings in there." He bent over, grabbing the giant twenty-pound salmon in front of him by slipping his gnarled fingers under the gills. From the gaping mouth, he removed the net that had captured the fish and rudely interrupted its homeward quest. He tossed the fish into the tote and worked on the next.

Meara watched and timidly followed suit. The first fish she grabbed started to flap its tail hard when she slipped her fingers under the gills and tried to release the dorsal fin that had him trapped. The net had rolled around him in his fight to get free. She worked the net off the fish with him occasionally flapping at her. When it was finally free, she tossed it in her tote. Looking up, she saw that the old man had four more fish in his and was working on the fifth.

She moved to her second and continued on. She was surprised to find by the time they met the end of the line of floats that held the net up in the water that her arms were already tired. The old man, on the other hand, looked like an excited little boy at Christmas. There was no sign of energy loss with him.

She thought that she had been fit. And now, they still had to process the fish.

* * *

The two drove back to the house where Anna was waiting with a couple of her grandsons. The two nine-year-old boys were all excited to get going. Anna assigned them to gut the fish as they had started performing this job last year. Meara's new friend worked alongside them at first.

He would comment to the boys. "Run your blade straight." "Not so deep." His eyes watched every move they made. Soon they were filling a bucket with bright pink salmon eggs that had never made it to the spawning ground.

Once the boys finished gutting the fish, they rinsed it and tossed it up onto the table where Meara and Anna stood waiting. Anna took a fish for herself and handed Meara another.

"Take this ulu," she said and handed Meara a half circle of a knife with a handle across the top made of bone. "It is nice and sharp. I worked on sharpening them last night."

She laid the fish open down on the incision the boys had made in the belly. "Hold the fish like this. Now take your ulu and run the blade close down the spine. You will be going over the rib cage. Push down hard."

Meara was unsure on how to hold her ulu correctly and watched carefully and tried to imitate Anna. The fish was slippery, and the smell of the skin was strong. The skin had a thin coat of slime even after having been rinsed. She struggled to hold it in place. Her cuts were not as clean and straight as the elderly woman's. After a struggle, she finally was able to remove the spine and had two filets joined together by the tail.

"Now, lay them side by side and take your ulu and run a cut all the way across. You want to go as close to the skin as you can without going through. These slices allow the fish to take on the smoke and allow it to dry."

Meara's first attempts were slow and required her entire attention. She bit her tongue as she focused on the task at hand. The little elderly woman, her hair held back with a purple-flowered bandana, worked quickly. She would have three stripped and ready to hang to each of Meara's.

"Good." Anna said as she walked a couple of fish over to the alder pole that hung on the side of the cutting shed. "You see why we left them connected to the tail?"

The fish tail stood up on the top of the alder pole with either side of the body filleted and hanging down to dry.

"Once we load this pole, we will move it to the smokehouse. Then Norman will tend the smoke, and we will have to keep an eye out for bear until they are done. We have some good drying weather predicted in the next few days."

Meara laughed as she put her focus back down on the shiny silver fish with bright red flesh in front of her. "Norman. So that is his name? "

Anna laughed. "Yes, Norman. Norman Nelson. He is my brother. He came over from Quyalaqaq to help make sure I got enough fish put up for the winter."

"He doesn't live here in town?"

"No, we both grew up here. But when he joined the Territorial Guard during the war, he fell in love with a girl from Quyalaqaq. He married and stayed with her family. I stayed here."

"What is the Territorial Guard?" asked Meara.

"They were a unit of native men and women who volunteered for the United States Army to protect our coastline from Japan during World War II. Norman was quite the soldier, a hero back then. He still wears the patch on his jacket."

Norman moved closer to the ladies at that point. "Alright, lady. Not bad for a beginner. Someday you might be practiced enough to hang a fish you would be proud of. But not bad for a beginner."

They worked until the sun went down before the final fish was prepared. Then Norman set the fire in the smokehouse and shut it up.

"Now is the time for patience." He kicked a chair back so that he could keep a close eye on the processing of the fish. "You had better get yourself home before dark." He laughed. "The bears are hungry, and they come out this time of day."

Meara went on laughing knowing that he was being playful with her and because she was new. He was trying to make her nervous about moving about with brown bears around. She rode her bike, feeling the satisfaction of being able to help some elders get their food in for the winter and gratitude for being able to be taught the old customs. She was starting to get the feel of things and had a greater appreciation for the amount of labor involved in surviving out here. Would she always seem so slow and uncoordinated?

CHAPTER 6

Meara couldn't contain her excitement. It had seemed like an eternity since she left all her belongings in Seattle. They were finally here! The barge line had called her last night letting her know that her car and trailer would be unloaded from its Conex today. Last night, she had the chance to look at the piles of shipping containers and wondered which one contained her belongings.

She called Rey, and he agreed to get her down there, although he wouldn't have time to help her unload. She was grateful for the ride. The wind was blowing, and her bike would not have been fun. They sat in line in his car down at the terminal and talked for a while.

They had returned to running after the awkward date. He would call her, and they had gone on a couple of dates where they sat and talked. He was allowing things to go slow and had not made another attempt to kiss her yet. He certainly had had the opportunity.

One date had been sitting here watching the big arm of the crane swing over to the barge and lift the giant Conexes off and place them on the ground or onto a trailer bed to be delivered. Another was sitting by the dump in his car watching brown bears foraging around. A third was sitting in his car by the river watching belugas swim upstream. His patience and not pushing for a kiss in spite of the opportunities was helping the need to run away dissipate.

Today's encounter was brief. He wasn't clear why he couldn't stay with her to do the unpacking, but she accepted it, and her excitement took away any disappointment. They watched the barge workers open the doors to a container, and when it revealed her car and trailer she felt like she had won a game show. Within minutes, she was signing the bill of lading and was given the keys to her car. She waved goodbye to Rey.

Sliding behind the wheel of her car, she felt a completeness she hadn't felt in a while. Although she had learned that she could easily live with what little she had in her suitcase and backpack, there were items she really missed. And the feeling of being able to go where she wanted when she wanted without having to call for a ride or prepare for extreme weather on a bike made her feel so free—free in spite of the fact that there were only twenty miles of road to drive on.

She almost felt awkward driving. It had been so long, but as she pulled onto the road, it became natural pretty quickly. When she got onto the long stretch of road, she declared that she now belonged, at least a little, by pulling her car over to the oncoming lane and driving there as she declared, "Potholes."

She turned into the wooded grove where her cabin was and started to unload. Her mattress was rolled up and compressed as it was when she bought it at IKEA. She moved her sleeping mat aside, pulled out a knife, and released the mattress from its wrappings as it magically blew up to full size. She couldn't help but lie down on it.

"Ahhhhh, a mattress. I am officially a princess. This has been way too long." She savored the feeling of floating on a mattress after weeks of sleeping on a camping mat.

She didn't lay there long because there was so much more she couldn't wait to pull out. She hauled boxes of books, photo albums, winter clothing, and the living room furniture she had picked up from IKEA for easy moving. The rest of the day was spent putting things together with the little hex keys that were provided.

After hours of assembly, she finally got to sit back as she pulled out pictures of her with her son at various ages and arranged them on her bookshelf that now lined one of her blank walls. She had a comfortable reading nook in the corner surrounded by those left behind for this adventure. Pouring a glass of wine, she made a meal from the comfort food in the trailer. She lit a candle from a box and popped a CD of classical music into the stereo. Then she settled down with a book she had been waiting months to read. Sitting back in her new comfortable chair, she toasted the pictures of her family. "To shared adventures and new homes. I can't wait for you to come and visit me."

* * *

"Cama'i. Winds are up today, but it looks like we can fly. It will be a bit bumpy though." The stocky, curly-haired young pilot gave a big warm smile. "I'm Jim, and I'll be flying you today."

In an instant, Meara's brain calculated that this was the infamous Jim. He was trying to blend the Yupik hello and other phrases into his conversation. It gave him a sense of being almost too eager to be a part of the local culture. Although, she had picked this up, too. She could see what attracted the girls to him.

She had been here in Agushak for a couple of months now. Agushak had a varied population consisting of different native Alaskans, people from the lower forty-eight, and surprisingly quite a few mail-order brides from the Philippines. But in spite of the variety, Yupik was the predominant underlying language.

Living here, she had learned a few basic terms. It was a hard language to hear because there were many *k* sounds that were different, but to her ear much of them sounded the same. Now, in the small plane terminal Jim seemed overzealous with his "Cama'i." What was it about him that allowed him to feel it was alright to get involved with the two girls? She found her maternal sense of protecting her students kick in. She watched with the alertness of a cougar waiting to find his flaws.

This was Meara's first village flight. She had never flown in this small of a plane before, and she was apprehensive right now. Her mistrust of the pilot was not making her feel any better.

She could see the little red plane through the window. It was tied down to hooks on the tarmac, and when a gust of wind blew, the plane would lift, shudder, and settle back down. She thought back to her knowledge of accident statistics. Red. Was red more accident prone in a plane like it was in a car? And on that note, what was going to keep the wind from flipping them over once they got going?

"Okay, steel bra and panties time," she muttered under her breath when Jim called them out onto the tarmac. As she walked across, part of her wanted to turn back and go inside. There were much better days to fly than this for a first flight. She took a deep breath to push the doubts out of her tightened chest and climbed up the stairs. The nine-passenger plane had four seats removed to make way for cargo. Her backpack and tote, which was full of food for two weeks, was already strapped in among the mailbags and food delivery for the village store. Her bags sat on top of cases upon cases of soda. A mesh net was clipped into the ceiling and floor, providing a wall to keep all the cargo in back if it were to slip loose of their straps.

She found herself digging through her brain trying to find the information about the safest place to sit in a plane. As she was waiting for the other passengers ahead of her to buckle so she could move past, Jim interrupted her thoughts.

"I need you to sit up in the front," he said to her. "I need a lightweight passenger up there for balance."

She nodded with compliance, and at the same time her thoughts were screaming. *Where is the safest place? It certainly couldn't be in the cockpit.* It was clear that her memory was not going to cooperate. Best she didn't know anyway. But the idea that her weight difference from the other passengers mattered to balance the plane clearly made her a bit more anxious.

She slid into the copilot's seat, being very careful to keep her big clunky boots away from the pedals on the floor. Her knees were touching the second steering column. What if she moved wrong? Could her actions overtake the pilot's and crash the plane? Trying to reassure herself, she thought at least he could tell her what to do if something went wrong.

She looked at the tangle of webbing that was the seat belt system and tried to make sense of it. Two straps came down over her shoulders, then two came up from the base of the seat, then reaching between her legs, she pulled up the strap that had the connector to hold all five together. She locked them into place then twisted the release to unlock them. The course she had taken to do medical evacuations was coming back to her. She adjusted each of the straps to fit her then patted the pocket of her coat to feel for the knife she had learned to carry. If there was a crash and she couldn't release the clips, then she could cut herself free.

Firmly adjusting the straps over her bulky arctic clothing was not easy. She had been taught that she should dress as if she were going to be dropped off in the tundra and have to survive with what she had on her. She was fully dressed in a down parka and snow pants. Her subzero insulated boots made her feel like she was wearing astronaut boots. They certainly added to her height with the thick felt insoles. She also carried her can of bear spray, matches, an emergency blanket, and a few protein bars in her pockets. Just in case. She sat back hoping that she looked like a confident local instead of a nervous outsider.

Jim took a card from above the visor in the pilot's seat. He read the card, pulled or pushed a lever, then his head went back to the card again.

Anger built up inside watching him. How could they let him fly a plane that he didn't even know how to fly? *My God. He has to read the instructions! I need to get out of here. He doesn't know how to fly this plane. And look at this wind. I am going to die!*

"Excuse me?" She summoned the courage to tap his shoulder. "Have you flown this plane before?"

"Yes." His brows furrowed as he looked up at her. "Hundreds of hours."

"Has something changed in the plane?"

"Why?"

"I noticed you had to read the instructions." She responded calmly. She felt kind of good about her observation.

He laughed. Loudly. "That is the preflight checklist. Not instructions. You haven't flown much, have you?"

Warmth flowed to her cheeks. She felt like a total fool. Perfect. *Oh yeah, here you are scared and on top of it looking pretty dumb!*

Shrinking into her seat, she listened to every detail of his safety briefing. She turned her head in the direction of the emergency locator in the back. She knew what to do about the emergency locator because of her course. But did those big guys blocking the way to it know?

He pointed out the first aid kit and fire extinguishers.

Hopefully, they wouldn't need those. She shuddered as he directed her toward the headsets that she put on.

Jim buckled in, called clear, and started the engine. The ground crew untied the straps. After a brief warm-up, he idled the plane down the tarmac to the runway. The taxi across showed them that the wind had not died down. The plane felt a bit like a bronco when the wind lifted it off the tarmac and dropped it back down. They got to the strip and turned around. Without hesitation, he revved the engines and took off smoothly into the sky. The plane turned north along the coast then turned back in for a route that was over land.

Now that she was in the air, she could again feel the shaking with the shuddering of the wind. Who would miss her if the plane went down? Her son would, but she was already so far away from him. She didn't even have a will finalized. If she was going to have to fly in this weather, she needed to do that.

What about Rey? He had been persistent with calling her and pursuing her. How would he feel if she went down?

Twenty minutes into the flight, Jim dipped the altitude a little and pointed his finger down into a grove of trees breaking through her morbid thoughts.

"Moose." He pointed. "About fifteen of them," he said through the headsets they both wore.

She looked through her little window and could make out the big, dark shapes in the trees. Most were lying down. "I see them! They look so small from up here. But, I thought moose were solitary animals."

"In the winter, they gather together in groups. They circle up with the weaker, more vulnerable on the inside. Safety in numbers against wolves."

She looked out the window, noticing that the village was just ahead of them after crossing another one of those winding rivers.

* * *

The runway was just to the north of the village, connected by a long road leading out there from town. There was a 300-yard gravel landing strip cleared. Off to the side, there was a shipping container with a door and a smokeless chimney coming out of it.

A truck was parked to the side with a couple of men standing around it. Toolboxes, bags, and five-gallon pails created towers on the ground. The men picked up and moved their gear toward the plane as it came to a stop near the end of the road.

Jim turned off the ignition, and the engine's roar was replaced with the quiet business of people stirring to get out of the plane and the movement of cargo. Jim squeezed between the two front seats and tenderly unbuckled the elderly lady who was sitting behind Meara. Reaching for the door, he slipped his hand underneath the lever and unlocked it. Then he slid it open to the side and folded down the ladder.

"Will you stay up here to support her while I watch her from below in case she slips?"

Surprised, Meara heard him give the elder some cheering in Yupik. She was amazed at the gyrations that the elderly woman needed to make as she moved her arthritic body toward the front of the plane. How were people able to get back to their village after a major injury? How in the world would an elder maneuver on this plane after a broken hip?

Once both feet were safely down, he bent over to reach around her stooped body and gave her a big hug.

He certainly knew how to cover up that he was a jerk. She could see how he had fooled Verna and Chelsey. He brought the elder over to the truck where a man sat behind the wheel. The man pulled out a stepladder and both men guided her up and into the truck. Then the driver backed the truck over to the plane. They went to work unloading all of the freight from the plane and into the back of the truck.

"I won't be heading into town this time," Jim said to the other man. "You can do the deliveries. If it works for you, I will do the delivering this afternoon. There are a few people I would like to visit."

Meara looked around, trying to figure out what she was supposed to do next. Her tote was on the ground. She lifted her backpack up to sling it over her shoulders then hefted her food tote. She walked toward Jim and the other man to ask them how to get to town.

Just then, a four-wheeler came down the road toward them. Verna was smiling at the wheel. "Hi, Meara! It is so good to have you here. I thought I would spare you the ride with the agent today." She winked at the agent and purposefully ignored Jim.

Jim stood there with a big smile at first, but his smile faded as his mouth opened and eyebrows came together.

"Throw your tote on the rack." Verna instructed Meara.

She followed the instructions and put her backpack on top as she surveyed the stack, trying to figure out how this should be secured. When no solution was offered, she decided to put her backpack on her lap and use a hand behind her back to secure the tote. When she looked back up, Verna was looking at the four-wheeler intently and kept her back turned to Jim.

Jim stood there scratching his chin with his gloved hand. He quickly shrugged his shoulders and turned to the work of unloading.

"Jim, are you coming back in this afternoon? I am going to get some herring for dinner later. If you are staying here, would you like to join me?" Verna's voice surprised them all, especially after the initial cold shoulder.

Jim's shoulders lifted, and the smile returned to his face as he looked at her with big soft eyes. "I can't think of anything I would rather do. Sounds like a date."

"Swing by the clinic at five. We can go out then." She took a box off the front of the four-wheeler and handed it to Jim. The muscles around Verna's eyes had tightened, and her mouth had firmed. "These labs need to get to the hospital today, *quyana*."

Turning back to Meara, she declared, "Give me that backpack. Climb on behind me. Let's get back to the clinic." Verna loaded the backpack onto the front of the four-wheeler.

Meara hopped awkwardly on trying to figure out what to hold on to with her right hand to steady herself as she reached behind with the left to hold the tote.

The ride to town on the bouncy four-wheeler gave a good view of the side of town that Meara had not seen on her other trip. The main road paralleled the coastline on the right. As they got closer to town, the first few houses rose on stilts above the snow. Some were sided well, and others were covered with tar paper that was ripped in many places and flapping in the wind. The front yards had piles of snow on them. Some piles where the snow had swept off exposed fishing nets and their colorful floats. Most had a boat or two in the yard to go with the nets.

Doghouses lined a few yards with all variety of dogs represented on short chains in front of their individual shelters. They varied in breed from huskies and hound dogs to other mutt variations.

"Sled teams." Verna announced. "Don't get tempted to try to pet them. Some of them are pretty mean when they are tied up. They have mauled people when they have accidentally gotten into their yards."

"I thought sled dogs were huskies."

"You and everyone else. That is the movie version. The real sled dogs are the best available in the village. Sometimes, you can be really surprised by what makes a good sled dog."

As they got closer into town, she noticed there were homes that looked like a typical ranch style familiar to Meara from back in New England. These houses were all new, all lined up, and all looking the same as the one next to it other than the color of the siding.

"HUD housing!" yelled Verna.

The four-wheeler turned in to an alley way next to a big modern-looking clinic with big windows in the front that welcomed the remaining afternoon sun. In comparison to some of the housing they had just passed by, the clinic looked large, modern, and full of light. It truly stood out as a gem in comparison to most of the buildings in the village. She had been told of the Rasmuson grants providing money to build clinics in rural areas, but she thought the buildings would be simpler. This would have been a beautiful clinic back home.

Verna pulled the four-wheeler next to the back door and they unloaded her gear to start her first village teaching assignment.

Upon entering the back door of the clinic, the two women kicked off their snow boots and placed them under a bench along the wall of the entry and removed their snow gear, hanging it on the rack above the bench. Meara pulled a pair of shoes out of her pack and slipped them on. The arctic entry space they had just walked through was lined with backboards, Stokes stretchers, and empty tanks for oxygen that were waiting for a plane without passengers to transport them back to the hospital to be refilled.

Meara had noticed that all houses had an arctic entry, a room that served to hold items that would drag dirt and moisture into the house. Most importantly, it created a buffer area to block the wind and weather from entering the building directly. She had also learned that in Alaska, you removed your shoes there and either put on a dry pair of shoes in the case of a business or you proceeded inside in your stocking feet.

Verna turned left and brought Meara back to a room that served as the break room for the Community Health Aides.

"Cama'i, welcome home," said Verna. "This is your housing while you are working here. Sometimes the dental team comes in, too, but they aren't here now. You will have the place to yourself after clinic hours."

To the back of the room sat two sets of bunk beds lining either side of the room with a window separating them. She slid her tote to the end of one bed. Then laying her backpack on top of the tote, she opened it and slid out an envelope. The fully stuffed manila envelope contained inspection forms, observation forms, and her stethoscope. Putting her stethoscope around her neck, she immediately felt more at home.

"You know that our village is supposed to have four health aides. We have three exam rooms." Verna led Meara through a tour of three identically set up exam rooms.

"When we are fully staffed, one person is off at all times. That is why there are just three exam rooms. But, as you already know, this village is never fully staffed. It is busy here! It can be pretty crazy from what I have been told. Health aides either last a long time, or they don't last very long at all."

"Well, I hope you are one of the ones that last a long time." Meara gave a half laugh. She realized the investment that went into developing a health aide to the point that Verna was. Turnover would be really expensive. Not to mention that there didn't seem to be an abundance of applicants to replace those that quit.

Verna led her into a large room that took up the entire center of the clinic. The room had two trauma stretchers and the same familiar red emergency crash cart that Meara knew from all her past emergency experience with a cardiac monitor and defibrillator sat on top. There were oxygen tanks and a concentrator on the back wall. The other half of the room had a small x-ray area.

"This is the trauma room. On busy days we may see a quick patient in here, but other than that, this is reserved for emergencies. We also have a provider drawer for you, so you can do full advanced cardiac life support. It is kept in the pharmacy when we don't have a doctor, nurse practitioner, or physician's assistant here. I will get that in place in a few minutes once you know your way around."

"It looks like you are prepared for everything." Meara noticed casting supplies over near where the x-ray was.

"We have the small oxygen tanks mostly for transporting patients. The generator takes care of most of our patient needs. Getting oxygen in and out of here is hard because it is a hazardous material on a plane. We can only ship the tanks in or out when there is a flight without passengers. We try to use the tanks only if we need to have a higher flow of oxygen."

Walking though the emergency room into a hallway on the other side, they entered the pharmacy. Meara was impressed with how much Verna had picked up about the day-to-day existence in the clinic already.

"How are you doing on keeping inventory and ordering what you need? Did Nora teach you about your village supply levels yet?" Meara asked Verna.

Two walls of the pharmacy were filled with shelves of bottles of pre-filled medication. Each had a label already put on by the pharmacy in Agushak. The contents and the instructions were there. All the health aide had to add was the name of the patient and the date it was given. A shelf with a notebook sat on the back wall. A refrigerator sat next to it with a small freezer underneath the shelf for keeping refrigerated medications and vaccines. Above the shelf was a lockbox.

"We need to do a narcotic count as soon as I arrive. I guess that would be now," said Meara.

They unlocked the box, and Meara felt like a nurse in any hospital in the lower forty-eight taking inventory of all the narcotics and benzodiazepines. The counting and logging were exactly the same as back home.

After leaving the pharmacy, they entered a room lined with tables where Chelsey, Nora, and another health aide sat. There was an additional desk across the hall that looked into the waiting area.

"Cama'i," they all said simultaneously, looking at Meara.

"Cama'i." Meara smiled. "You must be Nora." She extended her hand to a petite middle-aged woman with long black hair pinned neatly back with a beaded barrette. "And you must be Karen." A short, elderly woman sat next to Nora.

"Yes," said the older woman with short, curled hair. "I will be heading out on the next flight now that you are here. You most likely know that I am an itinerant. I fill in where villages are short staffed. I am heading off to Chelsey's village next."

"It is nice to meet you, Karen. I hope to see more of you. Nora, I am looking forward to working with you. I have heard so much about you." Meara peered out past the desk to the other side of the reception windows into the bright waiting room. There were a few people sitting there. She put her sheets down. "Looks like there won't be too much visiting time right now. Who would like to have the first observation?"

"Why don't you follow me? You don't have to do as many to recertify me. Then you can concentrate on Verna and Chelsey. I have a patient all set to go." Nora was a longtime certified Community Health Aide. Every few years they needed to take a recertification test and be observed during some visits. She had passed her test and needed a few observations in order to maintain her certification.

Meara knew from the training center that Nora had been out here serving Quyalaqaq for about ten years. She was married and had three children between the ages of six and ten. Her mother had been a health aide before her as well, and the two of them had worked together as the backbone of this clinic for more than six years. Meara was looking forward to seeing her experience in action.

* * *

"Cama'i, Lorna." Nora smiled at the mother of the young patient in the room. "Wassily, you keep growing every time I see you. This is my friend Meara. She will be watching me do my job today. Are you alright with her being here? She has to check me off in order for me to keep taking care of you when you are sick." As she spoke, she glanced back and forth between the child and mother. Nobody said no.

"Meara, I brought this chair in for you." She pointed to an exam stool at the side of the room. She had been observing Verna in the few weeks since the new trainee had come home from session. She had been pleased by the training she had received both in Agushak and in Anchorage. It looked as though this new training director had done a decent job in preparing her. Chelsey had just flown in from her village off the Aleutian peninsula this morning in order for her to get her observation time with the instructor. She had had the chance to observe Chelsey this morning. It would be interesting to have Meara here observing the three of them during her two-week visit.

She had heard from the two new girls that Meara did seem to know her stuff. She chuckled to herself thinking, how would they know? But they did say that she really seemed to care. She was glad to hear that, because she didn't care how much these instructors that came and went so quickly knew. None of that mattered if they didn't show that they cared. In any case, she was glad to have her here and hoped it would be a good experience. She always learned something new when an instructor or a doctor was here, even though she had been a health aide for over a decade. She was extra curious to see what Meara might pick up on with the next patient. Something wasn't right there, but she didn't know what she had been missing.

Little Wassily and his siblings had been brought to the clinic over and over in the last couple months with a multitude of different symptoms. He was not much of a talker, and it took a bit to get him to say anything during the visits. There always seemed to be something a little different about his symptoms.

She opened her CHAM and started the visit. She verbally told Meara that she had determined that he was eight years old, so she did not need to go to the special section on page sixty-eight that sorted out emergencies in young children. Her eyes brushed over him, starting her observations. He was sitting quietly, which was no change for him, but his eyes were glued to Meara's hair, and he was totally captivated by that and her face. Nora could not hold back her smile. In spite of all the medical travel that he had been on, he obviously hadn't encountered a person with red hair and freckles yet. His innocence charmed her.

Wassily was a sweet little boy. She had worked with him in her native dance group that she taught in the evening. At least, she taught it when her clinic call responsibilities didn't interfere. He was a very respectful little boy who really wanted to please. When he smiled, his whole face lit up, and his many silver teeth almost decorated his mouth.

"Wassily is in my dance group," she said to Meara. "Yupik dancing and the Yupik language had almost been lost from our villages when I was a little girl. *Aaquk*, Mother, used to tell me stories of how the mission school taught that the Yupik language and dance was shameful and dirty. All of the children of her generation were sent to mission schools. The shame that was taught nearly wiped out our language and our storytelling culture. Yupik dance is one of our ways of sharing our culture, lessons, and our history. We lost a lot of the old dances, but there are still a few elders that danced, and they help teach it to us now. Cousins of my mother's mother are still dancing, and they taught dance to some of us so that we could share it in our villages. They will be here tomorrow for a community gathering at the school. You should come." She smiled at Wassily. "You will get to watch Wassily dance if he isn't sick."

The little boy's grin grew even wider.

"There is a big dance festival called Cama'i held in Bethel every spring around breakup. Breakup is when the winter ice in the rivers break up and the water flows again. People from Yupik villages all over come and dance with their village groups. There are also dance groups from other cultures that perform as well. This festival and the amazing people that are committed to making it happen helped to revive the dance and the language. The first time I went to Cama'i Dance Festival, I was inspired to bring dance back here. Wassily will be dancing there this year with our group."

Nora then turned to Lorna, Wassily's mother. Lorna was a study of opposites. She appeared sweet but would quickly sour when things did not go her way. Her bitter disposition was completely opposed to her endearing and eager-to-please son. Her thin, tight lips were countered by her large breasts that overflowed the shelf they sat on created by her abdomen. Her butt seemed impossibly smaller than her upper half and appeared to be tucked under, like a dog with his tail between his legs. However, she never had the repentant attitude of a puppy getting into the garbage. She owned that garbage and everything around it by her demanding attitude.

Lorna's attitude would also shift dramatically, and Nora was trying to find a pattern to this. As a matter of fact, she had been studying the woman carefully for a while now. Some days she would be relaxed, easy going, and easy to talk to. Today, Nora suspected that her pupils were a bit constricted for the room's bright exam lighting. Other times, she would come across with answers as short as she was. She would move and pace in the room like a hungry lioness. Other times, Nora felt that the smell of alcohol entered the room with Lorna, and that her words were slurred. Regardless of the presenting attitude, she always seemed to have the unspoken goal of needing to travel to Agushak.

Alcohol and drugs in their dry village had become an increasing problem as of late. Quyalaqaq was one of the many dry villages found in Alaska. A large part of the population could not drink socially once alcohol was available. Once alcohol was obtained, the bottle was emptied quickly between the few people possessing it.

She had noticed for herself when she was younger that she did not have an off switch for alcohol either. Once the bottle was opened, the switch was on until it was empty. The empty bottle was the only thing that turned the drinking off.

After a few nights of not knowing what she had done and waking in places she did not remember going to, she decided the only way for her to deal with alcohol was to not drink it at all. She was lucky to have been able to do that.

She had many friends and family members that had done horrible things when they were drunk. She knew of one man who had killed his own son while under the influence. Others had raped, been raped, had drunk-driving accidents, or found themselves in jail for fights.

Their village had decided that the best way to handle this was to not allow alcohol in the village at all. This made their village a dry village, and because it was on native land, it was a federal crime to bring in alcohol. Those that took the chance to smuggle it in made a big profit. An eight-dollar bottle in Agushak could be sold in Quyalaqaq for over one hundred dollars. Drugs had a similar increase in value in the villages.

Lately, there had been a big influx of alcohol into the village. She had no idea where it was coming from. In any case, the brunt of the incoming flow fell onto her, the other health aides, and the VPSO. They worked closely with Angus, the VPSO. They would see each other a lot when there was a new shipment into town.

Angus would bring in people who were not safe because they were under the influence. The health aides would have to assess how safe the imbiber would be to be held in a jail cell without medical supervision. That left them assessing vitals, breathalyzer tests, and behavior then discussing this with the doctor. If they were a danger to themselves because of the alcohol, then the health aides would have to stay and monitor them until they were safe. If that was the case, Angus would also have to stay to make sure that the health aides were safe watching the unpredictable patient.

Or at least he did the best he could. They had always thought that the VPSOs were pretty brave to do their job without a gun for protection. As a matter of fact, the aides were pretty brave to deal with these patients, too. Sadly, some of the nicest people she knew were extremely violent when drunk.

"I have finished my first assessment of Wassily. He is breathing easy, his pulse is steady and not going too fast, he does not have a high fever, his skin is not pale, it is warm and dry." She verbalized her assessment to Meara so that she knew that she had done this first glance that brings in so much information but isn't normally said out loud.

"Now that I determined that he is not a pediatric emergency, I will go back to the right side of the cover of the CHAM and ask the history of the present illness."

Meara nodded back at her.

The prior visits she had had with Lorna and her children gave her the sense that Lorna knew the CHAM. She seemed to know the answers that would lead to an assessment "patient is sick." And, if this was the assessment, then Nora would have to call the doctor about the case and most of the time Lorna and her child would have a flight to Agushak arranged and paid for by their insurance.

This time, she was going to try a different approach. Nora stifled a laugh when she turned back to Wassily. His eyes were still glued on Meara's red hair. Instead of asking Lorna like she normally did, she spoke to Wassily.

"What did you come to the clinic for today?"

At first, Wassily didn't move.

Nora put a hand on his shoulder and repeated herself. "Wassily, why did you come to the clinic today?"

His eyes moved away from Meara's hair as he looked up at Nora. Then he quickly glanced over to his mother, and he watched her before responding. She nodded to him. "My stomach hurts."

"When did your stomach start to hurt?" Nora looked at Wassily.

Again, he looked to his mother before answering. Again, she nodded. "I think it was last night."

"Where does your stomach hurt? Can you show me with your hand?"

He again looked to his mother.

She discretely moved her hand to the left lower quadrant of her abdomen.

Wassily moved his hand in mirror image to his mother, putting his hand over the right lower side of his belly. “Here,” he said.

“What does it feel like?”

“He says it is sharp, stabbing pain that is really bad,” Lorna answered, not giving him a chance to respond.

“Wass, what does stabbing pain feel like to you?”

“It feels like having a fishhook poked into my finger. Remember? You took the fishhook out of my finger last summer. You made it stop hurting.” He smiled up to Nora with big, wide eyes.

“Is the pain there all the time, or does it come and go?”

“It is always there. Nothing is making it better and nothing is making it worse, but it is getting worse with time.” Lorna interrupted the questioning by finishing the final three assessment questions for Nora without her asking. She was definitely in a short mood today. Did Meara pick up on all of that?

Nora moved to the index of her CHAM and looked up abdominal pain. She needed to go there for the rest of the interview. Lorna did not allow Wassily to answer any more questions.

Then it was time for the exam. Her CHAM directed her to go to the “Sick Child Screening Exam” because Wassily was under eight years old. Did she catch Wassily looking to his mother when she placed her hands on his abdomen?

She pressed down on the bottom right side of his stomach.

"Ouch," said Wassily.

"His skin is warm and dry; ear, nose, and throat are normal. He has no swollen lymph nodes. His heart sounds are normal, and heart rate is regular and not too fast or slow. His lung sounds are clear with full expansion, his abdomen is soft without rigidity, genitalia are normal. Peripheral pulses are normal with one plus capillary refill."

Meara repeated the exam, nodding her head to Nora. She did some other physical exams that were not in the CHAM. She also found the tender area in the right lower quadrant.

"Now, I need to get a hemoglobin, blood sugar, and a urinalysis," Nora said to Meara. Turning to Wassily, she added, "Wass, I am going to need to poke your finger. It will be quick, not like having a fishhook caught there. Then I need you to go and pee in a cup for me. Can you do that?"

After she went to the lab and did all the testing with Meara watching her, they returned to the room.

"Wassily's labs are all normal. Now I am reviewing the chart for abdominal pain. Because he has the lower quadrant pain, I am choosing the assessment as Abdominal Pain, Possible Acute Abdomen. The chart tells me to turn to the page for that plan." She turned the page.

"Wassily does not have any emergency symptoms and is moving well, so I don't think he will need any pain medications. I now will call the doctor to review."

Nora and Meara left the room, and Nora called her doctor. It was too late to send a lab in and get Wassily into town if it was abnormal. Wassily and his mother would need to be flown in on the evening plane into town to be seen by the doctor there and get blood drawn. If it was an appendix and it worsened overnight, a nighttime medical evacuation from their village would put other people's lives at risk. After waiting on hold with Denali KidCare, the state insurance for children, the travel arrangements were made. There was only one flight out of town left today, and it was arriving in an hour.

They left and went to the other room to discuss.

"Excellent job, Nora."

"Thank you. Did something not seem right to you in there?"

"It seemed to me that he was looking to his mother for his answers. That can happen at his age."

"I have noticed that in her other children's visits, too. Lorna certainly didn't like me asking him instead of her."

"That is quite true. She seemed to be very practiced on the history. I did notice that she answered the final history of present illness questions without you asking."

"I kind of wonder if her trips have anything to do with the increased flow of alcohol in here lately. I can't confirm it, but there certainly seems to be a connection. I hate to sound selfish, but I am exhausted from the alcohol calls. I want to figure it out so it stops."

CHAPTER 7

Verna watched the clock turn five. It had been so hard to hold a welcoming face when she had gone to the airport to get Meara. Before the discovery at the training center, she had always been so excited to see him. Before she had met him, she had always been determined that she was going to remain single and had convinced herself that "men are gross and so is sex," but somehow, he had gotten past her guard. He had certainly gotten under her skin. Everything had seemed so much brighter since he appeared in her life. Now, part of her couldn't believe that this was a false light.

His kindness was still such a draw to her. It seemed that everything he did was a kind act toward others. He was a good pilot. She had never seen him pull the macho pilot thing of flying in poor weather just for the ego of it. He was not ashamed to cancel a flight for safety. "Time will heal the embarrassment of a too-cautious call. But time will not bring lives back that were lost from risky choices." He always took the extra mile to help elders get on board and to make them comfortable.

She not only hadn't wanted a man, she certainly didn't want anyone in her life that would pull her away from her aging parents and her collection of extended family here in Quyalaqaq. She felt an immense gratitude that her grandparents had given her a home full of love since she was born.

Her face tightened up as she pushed back the tears that were starting to well up again. Why did she feel this way? Especially after what he had done. She should be angry, and instead she just missed him. Why had he gotten to her, and why couldn't she get angry at him like Chelsey?

Then she would think about how it felt to be wrapped into one of his hugs. She loved being held by him and looking way up into that big smile of his. She loved the depth of his blue eyes. They reminded her of the sky reflecting off the upper lake. She could swim in those eyes. The shock of the last few weeks was like jumping into a beautiful lake only to feel the glacial coldness go deep like needles into your skin.

The last few weeks had been hard. She had avoided picking up the phone when she knew he was calling. Seeing him this morning was so painful. When she and Chelsey had discovered that he was lying to both of them, Chelsey had talked about the situation with their father. He had come up with the plan to see if they could make him confess without them directly confronting him. He said that this plan would make him wiggle like a salmon trapped in a net.

And, he had followed up with, "I should know, I was the master of this mess up when I was younger."

She felt guilty that she was using information he had shared with her during one of their private talks. Was she any better than him if she was taking advantage of the secrets he confided to her to make him uncomfortable?

She heard the front door of the clinic open to the waiting room. There he was with that big smile on his face and that warm look in his eyes that had made her think she was everything in his world. Well, she sighed. She was everything in that moment. How many other women did he make feel this way? Her heart sank, and she felt like she had been punched in the stomach.

She stepped up to the window and smiled. "Cama'i, Jim. Come back here with me. I want to introduce you to my sister." She stepped out to the waiting room to him. She was fighting hard to keep her face neutral. She then casually brought him back to the break room where the rest of the women were packing up for the day.

As they got closer, the two could hear Chelsey's voice. Verna slowed down and glanced over her shoulder to look at his face as the voices drifted down the hall. She watched his brows come together as he tilted one ear toward the room, and he slowed his steps.

She reached the doorway ahead of him and stopped there then turned back to face Jim. "I want you to meet my sister, Chelsey." As she nodded toward Chelsey, Jim reached the door and looked in to see Chelsey pulling on her snow gear.

Jim's brows came together, and his smile was replaced with a slackening of his mouth. He took a long, slow, deep breath in.

Chelsey looked up quickly, looked him straight in the eyes, and acted like she had never seen him before. She stood as she pulled on her parka and kept her nose in the air as she extended her hand toward him.

"Cama'i, nice to meet you. My sister has told me so much about you." Giving him no time to respond, she dropped her head back down and went back to her task of dressing for their adventure.

"Chelsey will be going out fishing with us." Verna watched his face as she said that.

No change from that furrowed brow, other than he looked a little stiffer. "Sounds great," he replied after a pause where his head turned between the two girls. He looked back in the corner of the room and half lifted his hand in acknowledgment of Meara.

Nora piped in and broke the awkward silence. "Girls, I forgot to tell you my mother invited you over for a *maqii* tonight. Ever since she retired as a health aide, she has loved seeing new trainees and sharing her wisdom. Eight o'clock at my mothers'. Could you two pick up Meara and bring her there? My husband can't let me go."

* * *

The party of three walked toward the riverbed. The girls walked ahead of Jim and talked about fishing with parents and grandparents in the past. Jim was at a loss with the two girls. They plodded ahead through the snow talking to each other and barely acknowledging that he was there. Did they know that he had dated both of them? They must know something. Both of them were acting so oddly. Why were they not angry and confronting him? What was going on? The warmth that he knew was redness in his face had started back in the clinic when he "met" Chelsey. He felt so awkward. He was also so ashamed. He didn't mean to lead two of them along.

He had established a friendship with Chelsey and had enjoyed her spirited ways. He had enjoyed talking with her and then taking adventures around her village. She was so talkative and very positive. It was after they had been talking that he had met Verna. The first time he met her, he had felt there was something really different about her. As he got to know her more, he enjoyed the depth of her character. She had a wisdom that was unusual for someone her age, and at the same time she had such a calm and youthful spirit. It probably had come from being raised by her grandparents.

She lived in an old world, yet she existed in a bit of the modern world without feeling that she had to take on too worldly of an image. Chelsey seemed to be driven by something out of television shows. When he had met Verna, he was sure that she was the one that he had been looking for. He felt safe with her. Safe and excited at the same time. There was a familiarity about her that reminded him of when he was little and being raised by his mother and grandmother. People would think he was nuts. He was falling for her, and she reminded him of his grandmother. How sexy was that?

He had been planning on telling Chelsey that they would be just staying friends on his next trip to her village. He never would have predicted that he would find himself here with both of them without having made things clear. And they certainly weren't making things very clear either.

Verna told stories of fishing out here for whitefish with the woman that she knew as her mother, who was also both of their grandmother. "When *maurluq*, grandmother, and my mother was stronger, she would bring me out here to fish for whitefish." She looked wistfully across the frozen river with distant eyes.

Her eyes came back to the present, and she looked at Chelsey. "But she always had *Uppa* walk the ice first this time of year to make sure it was safe."

"Jim?" She turned in his direction, but her eyes met the tundra grass that poked up through the windswept snow at the edge of her feet. "We don't have Uppa today. Would you do the honors?"

"What? How thick is the ice? Is it safe?"

"That is your job as the man." Did she turn and suppress a smile looking at Chelsey?

"Here is the ice pick." Chelsey stood taller than he was used to seeing her stand. She put a hand on one hip and with the other hand swung the pick over to him. She kept her gaze up but avoided his.

Jim had never felt safe on early ice. When he was ten, he had had a friend go through the ice when they went out to play on the lake near his house in Michigan. The ice had cracked, and his friend slipped through. He screamed as he disappeared under. Jim had thrown himself onto his stomach to reach for his friend. But other than a couple more quick glimpses of his friend's mitten as he fought to reach the surface, the mitten never came within his reach, and Jim never saw his friend again. Since then, he has always been afraid of going out on ice. Especially early ice.

Had he shared this with one of them? Did they know what they were asking him to do? They wouldn't ask him to do this if they knew what he had gone through. They wouldn't send him out to do something unsafe.

"Uppa used to always break the dorsal fin of the blackfish he ate when he prepared it. He said that when you break it, it protects you if you fall through the ice. If you don't break it, you won't be able to get out," said Verna.

"Jim, when was the last time you ate blackfish? Did you break the fin?" chortled Chelsey.

"I have never eaten blackfish." He worked hard not to show his fear. He wasn't sure what they were up to. Were they so angry at him that they would set him up with a dangerous situation? Did they really want to kill him for what he did? What had they shared with each other about him? What did they both know?

He wanted to clear the air among the three of them, but he was so frozen by the fear of the ice and not losing their respect. Why was he considering this anyway? They probably both hated him. And they definitely both would continue to when he told them the truth.

Chelsey brought the conversation back to the breaking of the dorsal fin of the blackfish. "Well, in that case, you will have to rely on us if you go through," said Chelsey. "But the elders say that we wouldn't be able to help."

"What do you think? Do you think we are reliable? Or do you think the elders are right?" Verna's voice was almost teasing.

Jim was confused and at a loss as to how to bring it up. Verna was teasing him and taunting him innocently to do something that terrified him. Both were so out of character for her. Chelsey was acting like they had never met before. They must know what he hadn't found the time to tell them each individually. How could he have managed to be attracted to two sisters? Then, not be able to tell them his feelings before they found out. His focused back on Verna. But, he couldn't tell her right now. If he didn't man up right now, she would think he was totally unworthy as a man. He would never get her back.

Jim worked his way down the bank and onto the surface of the river. He stopped on the side, waiting to hear the start of a crack. He held his breath, stalling as he looked across the forty feet to the other side. He mustered up his courage, and when there was silence, he moved himself forward a couple feet.

"How deep is it?" he asked as nonchalantly as he could.

"We don't know for sure," said Verna with a serious face. "There are some places on this river where we have never found the bottom."

He breathed in and moved his body a couple feet more. Breathing was tight, like there was a belt around his chest, and it kept getting tighter. He felt like he had no air. The dizziness was getting harder to fight through. Then he pictured her face and knew that he needed to move forward, or she would never respect him even if he was able to explain the mess he created. He summoned his will as he listened. When the ice did not return the deadly call of a forming crack, he moved forward a couple feet more.

"There. That is the spot," said Verna.

Jim was shaking and hoping the girls didn't see his tremor as he picked up the ice pick. Terror took over. He was in the middle of the river. They weren't sure that the depth was deep enough to support him, and now they wanted him to put a hole in it? Tightening his grip on the pick, he started chipping away at the ice.

He worked his way around the hole, constantly trying to judge the direction that the ice would be the thickest so he could move to sprawl himself in that direction if he heard a crack. His hole went deeper and deeper until he could see that the ice was already six inches deep. He was safe. He widened the hole, and the girls came down to sit near him. Although he knew it should be safe, he couldn't relax for more than one reason.

They sat around the hole and took turns jigging with the two sticks they had. Fishing line ran off the sticks and attached to a series of little hooks.

Jim was in awe. Each time the line went down, it came back up with two to three herring on it. It was not long before they had filled the bucket with fish.

While they fished, Verna told stories about the old ways that her grandmother had told her. Stories about fish and how they protected people and how the people needed to respect the fish back to have safety, protection, and most importantly, food. Life was all a natural balance.

Jim listened in as Verna and Chelsey maintained an easy banter as they shared the tales. Verna seemed focused on sharing the stories of their shared grandparents with her sister. They simply paid him no attention. The way they were dismissing his presence made him feel like he had earned much less respect than the fish.

He wished he could have been as lighthearted as the two of them. He knew he needed to have the conversation with them to set things clear. He was near tears with the frustration of the situation. He searched for the right moment to break in and have the conversation. The time never appeared. By the time they walked back to their grandparents' home, his head hung low. His heart was sure that he would not be able to work his way out of this shame, and he knew he had lost the woman that had become his reason for being.

* * *

It was about seven thirty when Verna and Chelsey came knocking at the door of the clinic to pick her up. That is interesting, she thought. They smell like cucumber. She missed the vegetable so much; she couldn't resist asking where they got their supply.

"Where did you find cucumber here?"

Chelsey laughed. "We fished for herring tonight. When you cook herring, it smells like cucumber. A very smelly cucumber. But it tastes so good!!" she said as she rubbed her belly in appreciation of her recent meal.

They opened the arctic entry to a blast of cold air outside. Meara felt the first breath threaten to stick her nostrils together. She lifted her neck warmer to buffer the wind. As they walked toward the end of town, the sound of their talk and laughter was augmented by the sound of the snow. It was so cold that it made the sound of squeaky Styrofoam as their feet moved across it. The wind came in brief gusts that would momentarily make them grab their towels closer. The sky was clear, and there was a waning moon above. Meara thought she saw a wisp of green pass over through the night sky. She didn't see it again but wondered if she had seen the northern lights.

They turned to a blue HUD house toward the end of the village road just before it continued on to the airport.

The house was on the ocean side of the street. The front yard had the standard collection of fishing gear in piles and a little shed to the back of the house, where smoke climbed up into the night from its little chimney. A pile of wood formed a wall to the side of the shed.

They went into the arctic entry and took their snow pants and boots off and knocked on the door. Moments later they were greeted by a short, round-faced woman with her salt-and-pepper hair pulled into a loose bun. Her eyes were soft and almost twinkling with a laughter that came from their arrival. The crow's feet that lined those eyes deepened with her smile.

"Cama'i! I am Sophie. I am so glad you could come. Come in and warm up. I hope you brought an appetite."

The smell of chicken soup wafted from the kitchen where a few people sat around the table talking. Jars of jam sat on the table with a box of Pilot Bread open. A pitcher of Tang and a collection of cups rested on the counter.

"Tang?" Sophie eyed them all and poured into the cups assuming that she would not be turned down. She scooped a ladle into the broth simmering on the stove. "I am not asking if you want the soup. I know you worked hard today, and you need some."

Meara's thoughts drifted to her childhood. Memories of Tang and Kool-Aid brought her back to a day at her best friend's house. They had come inside from the rain after playing outside. After hugging her mother, they moved to the fridge, and Kathy had pulled out a pitcher of purple Kool-Aid and poured it into three glasses. Meara and Susan had sat at the table as they continued to chatter. Kathy opened the polka-dotted Wonder Bread bag and pulled three pieces out and started toasting.

Kathy's oldest sister went into the living room, where their mother was folding laundry, and announced that she was bringing the youngest to an appointment. She stopped to kiss her on the cheek and left with a quick "I love you, Mom."

Shortly after, the two brothers came in and announced they were going outside as they stopped to give their mom a hug and a quick "Love you." The smell of toasting Wonder Bread filled the room as Kathy pulled out the tub of margarine.

A car pulled up in the driveway, and their father made his way into the house. He greeted his daughters with a big smile and made his way into the living room, where he pulled his wife into a big embrace. They hugged like they had been apart forever.

Kathy spread the topping across the lightly browned squares, creating pads of melting yellow on top. When Meara put the simple piece of toast in her mouth, she could taste the love that was in the house that had absorbed into that bread.

Here, she was in her forties and she still could taste the love that was in that toast.

"The men are going to steam first tonight, so we have some time to sit and visit." Winking, Sophie added, "I like it when they steam first, then we will have the benefit of them getting it nice and hot for us."

Meara stood near the kitchen table taking in all the pictures of family that lined the walls. She recognized a younger version of Nora in some of them. Then there was artwork on the walls and refrigerator as well, created by a variety of ages of children.

"You must be Meara." Sophie approached her and gave her a hug. Then the outstretched arms turned to Chelsey. "Chelsey, I am so glad that you were finally able to come here. Your father has told us so much about you when he has come through for fishing. It seems like we have watched you grow up through all the pictures. It is so sad that you haven't been able to get here more often. I think the last time you were here you were five and it was for fishing. Your great-grandparents would have been so pleased to know you were actually here."

She placed the steaming bowls of soup in front of all of them in spite of protests of having eaten earlier.

Meara smelled it. "Beef stew? Color me dumb, I thought I had smelled chicken."

"Caribou. The last that I have in my freezer. The herd has died off around here and moved west lately due to hoof rot. I hope I will be able to get more." Without a pause, she changed the topic. "How do you like the health aide program so far? But before you answer, let's have a quick prayer. Thank you, God, for friends old and new and family, and thank you for this food. Amen."

Meara responded, "Amen. I am enjoying it. But I have to admit that I feel a lot like a fish out of water around here. The good news is that I am slowly learning to swim."

"The health aides have the toughest job in the village. Them and the VPSO. People have high expectations and expect them to be on call day and night. They think that our clinic is the equivalent of the television show *ER*. It will be your job to help guard the health aides. Make sure that they know to teach their villages what a nighttime emergency is and what can wait until morning. Otherwise, the health aides burn out fast. Speaking of which, I am sorry Nora couldn't join us. Her husband didn't want her going out because call has kept her from home so much."

"I am sorry, too. I was looking forward to the chance to get to know her better. I am really looking forward to hearing stories of when you were a health aide."

"It was hard but also rewarding. But, when I reached my fifties, I decided I could be of better service to my village by being a grandmother. So, I retired."

Outside, a knocking could be heard as footsteps approached the back door and snow was knocked off shoes. The door opened into the house, and a crew of happy, red-faced men with wet hair poured in. A couple sat down at the table. The third was an older man with close-cut salt-and-pepper hair, leaning more toward the salt. He was short and wiry, and his hands were all gnarled, giving away his age.

When he looked up, Meara instantly recognized her friend from a month ago. "Cama'i, Norman!" She gave a big smile.

He gave her a brief nod and turned to Sophie with kind but authoritative eyes. "Hang on before you all run in there. I want to haul in some more fresh water. I used the last of it in there to fill the two pots on the stove. You are almost all set to go."

The four women worked their way outside, and Norman followed right behind with a five-gallon bucket of water. He stepped ahead of them and moved into the steam with the two full buckets and emerged a few seconds later with his hands empty.

The stack of wood blocked the entry to the shed, and behind it the tundra stretched outward until it met the bank that dropped down a few feet to the sea.

He came back out again as the women were ready to enter the doorway. "I loaded up the stove for you, and there is enough wood in there to last you tonight."

The women stepped in the entry way, and the two sisters immediately stripped down and hung up one towel on the hooks over their clothes. Both held on to another small towel. They pulled the interior door open, and they were all greeted with a release of steam into the cooler changing room.

Meara hesitated as she undressed. She barely knew these women, but Chelsey and Verna had acted like it was no big deal to be naked in front of the other women. She had brought a bathing suit along out of modesty. As she was sitting in her underwear folding her pants, Sophie broke through her internal debate as if she had read her mind.

"Most *kussuks*, white outsiders, wear their bathing suits the first time. But we are just women, and we don't bite. Besides, a bathing suit gets in the way of getting really clean." She finished undressing and grabbed her small towel and a loofah-like sponge. Her naked late-fifty-something body stepped through the door.

Meara quickly undressed and determined not to look like a *kussuk*. Opening the door, the steam came out to invite her into her first magical maqii.

* * *

Meara entered the steamy room and looked for a place to sit down. Sitting would at least cover some of her nakedness and make her feel less exposed. She felt quite self-conscious about her body and the pouch she had from having her son. No matter how much she ran, she could not make this go away.

"Sit right here." Sophie patted a spot next to her on one of the lower benches that lined the walls. Chelsey sat on the top row across and Verna on the bottom.

"I like the hot seat." Chelsey smiled.

Sophie got up and took a big metal bowl and scooped water into it from a five-gallon bucket on the floor. Then she reached the ladle into one of the two big steaming pots on the top. The water from there steamed on the way to the bowl.

"We want your wash water to be warm but not too hot." She slid the bowl along the floor in front of Meara's feet. "Here is a washcloth for you."

She moved back to the stove and put the ladle into one of the buckets on the floor and dumped its contents onto the stones wired around the old oil drum stove. The water contacting the rocks sizzled and steamed up to the ceiling, and the temperature of the room rose a couple of degrees.

"It could use a few more," said Chelsey. "It has been awhile since I have had a good maqii."

Sophie looked at Meara. "I like to sit and really work up a sweat before I start to scrub. Then when you scrub, the dead skin comes off and you get nice and clean. She leaned over and looked at the thermometer on the wall. "Not hot enough yet." It read 160 degrees.

She scooped three more ladlefuls on top of the stones.

"Does Norman live here with you? Is he your husband?" asked Meara.

Sophie laughed. "No, Norman lives across the street. He and his wife were like second parents to me growing up. My mother was good friends with his wife. We are also second cousins." She reached over to her bowl with her washcloth and wet it in the water then put it over her head to wring it out. She wiped the back of her neck with the spent cloth.

"Norman and his wife helped me raise Nora. He always made sure that I had enough of everything. He would give me extra meat, extra fish. He has always taken it as his job to make sure I was supplied, especially when I was a health aide."

"He sounds like a very good man. Not much of a talker though," said Meara.

"No, Norman talks through his actions. Not through a lot of words. He used to tell me that the protectors needed to take care of each other, and because I took care of the village, it was his job to take care of me."

"What did he do in the Territorial Guard?" Meara asked.

"How did you know about the Territorial Guard? Not

many people, not even Alaskans, know about the people that volunteered to protect Alaska during World War II."

"I met Norman in Agushak helping Anna to process her fish."

"There you go, always taking care of people. Norman is also a great sled master. He signed up for the guard when he was only sixteen. He ran the recruitment runs at first with Muktuk Marston, who led the guard. Later, he ran the supply chain of the Lend-Lease air route. He would run supplies up to caches along the way toward Russia in case a plane went down as it was being delivered there. Most people don't remember that the US provided planes to Russia during World War II. Those supply caches helped with delivering the planes."

"He still runs sleds?"

"Oh, yes. That man is the master of service. He runs his dogs for search and rescue when it is needed around the village."

"It is hot enough now." She filled her cloth up with soap and started scrubbing her body from head to toe. After rinsing out the cloth, she rinsed herself off.

She leaned back and closed her eyes with a small smile on her face, clearly enjoying the buildup of heat again. "When Norman is on his sled, he is a sixteen-year-old again. Just like I am after I get my bones heated up in the steam." She stood and looked at the group of girls. "I am going outside to cool down. I will be back in a minute."

The door to the outside of the steam opened and closed. Had Sophie really gone out into the snow? The outside thermometer had read zero when they arrived.

About eight minutes later, she returned. Meara was feeling more relaxed and cleaned inside and out than she had since arriving to Alaska. Would a shower ever feel sufficient again?

CHAPTER 8

The next morning, Nora walked into the clinic with her head hung down and her face tucked under the hood of her parka. When she pulled her jacket off, she tried to keep her face turned away. "Meara, what did you think about the episode yesterday? The boy with the abdominal pain. Let's look into the computer and see what happened with him." Nora quickly signed into the computer and pulled up his chart.

Meara leaned in closer as she bent over the computer screen. Was that a black eye? She did notice that Nora had makeup on today as opposed to yesterday, where she hadn't had any on at all.

"Just as I suspected." Nora gave a long exhale. She leaned back into her chair and crossed her arms over her chest. "He was flown in, had labs done, which were perfectly normal, then released with an overnight in Agushak. Now, he will fly back with his mother today. Let's see what happens in the community today and when it will be that she comes in with another child that is 'sick.' I have a feeling that the alcohol is going to flow and we will be busy."

Just then, there was a demanding knock on the back arctic door into the emergency room.

Meara opened the door. She had her eyes on the doorstep as she opened it and saw a familiar pair of snow boots leading up to dark snow pants and the familiar light-blue stripe on the dark blue trooper jacket. It took her a moment to recognize that the big smile in front of her. She drew a quick breath when she realized who the visitor was. Rey. Next to him was an attractive young native man a bit shorter but with a friendly smile that emanated from his sparkling brown eyes and dominated his chiseled face. His broad shoulders were quite apparent even under the snow gear.

Rey looked at her like he was trying to stifle his smile in the name of professionalism.

"Hi, Rey, I am surprised to see you." Her senses lit up.

"Hello, I came out today to do a supervisory visit with Angus. We're starting the day checking in with all of you. I hear your clinic and Angus have had to work together quite a bit lately. I apologize for that. I know that the drug and alcohol monitoring cases are no fun for you in addition to all your other duties. I promise, we'll get to the bottom of the importing. So, Meara, what do you think of Quyalaqaq so far?"

"I only arrived yesterday afternoon. I haven't had much time to make a decision. I got in, and we went right to work. But I have been impressed with the clinic and the hospitality of the few in the village I have met. This village seems to have a good heart."

"Not many people say that about Quyalaqaq. The troopers have felt it's a bit of a war zone."

Angus had gone over to talk with the remaining health aides.

"Have you heard any concerns about Angus from your staff or people you have met yet?"

"No, should I?" she asked.

"No, not at all. I just need to get a feel of how he's doing from people in the community." He stood a little straighter.

Laughter interrupted them. She turned to the charting room to see what was going on. It seemed that Angus was doing just fine amongst the health aides. As a matter of fact, they all seemed a bit brighter with his presence and their conversation.

"We need to continue our rounds." Rey gave Meara a big smile that trapped her, and for just a moment, work slipped away and they seemed to be all alone.

His voice stopped her from slipping away the moment before she was lost. "Angus, let's move on and go to the city council."

Angus quickly finished his conversation and sauntered back over to the door. The two men left the building, leaving a big empty space behind.

They worked through the rest of the day with Meara alternating who she observed. She was so busy working that she barely noticed when Nora peeked out the side window then snuck outside and returned about ten minutes later.

At the end of the day, Nora was in a rush to get out. She had a community dance performance with her group that evening at the school gym.

Meara was excited that she was going to have the chance to go and watch it. Her chest tightened thinking of Rey's veiled smile when seeing her earlier. Was he still here in Quyalaqaq?

* * *

The school auditorium was packed. Almost everyone in the village had come for the *yuraq* dance celebration. Nora had invited her elderly cousins to come and dance. Looking at the gathered audience, Nora could tell these two little elderly women drew out people that weren't already coming to watch a child or family member dance.

As the last of the crowd straggled in and finished filling the gym, she looked at the clock and noticed she was a few minutes late, but this was Yupik time. The time was right when the time was right. She let the stragglers come in and settle down before she went out to introduce the first group.

Nora wore a purple qaspaq with a lighter violet trim on the hood, pockets, and sleeve bands. She also wore her own dance *nasqurrun* headdress made of fox fur with beads that hung down in loops below the beaded fur rim. She had a pair of handmade mukluks made of sealskin and lined with matching white fox fur on the tops. The fronts were beaded in a pattern that showed blueberries. She always chose and wore her dance outfits with respect. When she was dressing to dance, she was dressing to please her ancestors.

Before she introduced the first group, she welcomed her two special guests. Elders Maryann Sundown and Agnes Aguchak, who were both in their nineties, considered themselves sister-cousins because they were so close. They had become well known in the Yukon Delta region for their dance. People loved to watch them because they told great stories with their dancing, and they enjoyed making people laugh as they performed. It was clear they had great fun dancing together to tell old stories. Nora felt like their dancing was a nearly lost treasure.

After getting the first group started, Nora moved between the groups of children backstage. She and a group of parents were preparing the preschool children to go out and do their performance. Each of the little ones had their best qaspaq on with the little girls wearing beaded fur headbands. The little girls nervously held their small woven-grass dance fans while some would put them to their faces, hiding their nervous smiles in the fur linings.

She introduced the preschoolers and kindergarteners as doing a berry dance. The girls filed out and stood in a line in the back, and the boys came out in front with their bigger dance fans of wooden circles with feathers adorning the edges. They sat on their knees in front of the girls.

Nora had taught them, as she had been taught, that the fans represented the human spirit. Each of the children seemed to handle their dance fans with more respect once she had taught that lesson.

Three boys sat in back with large drums held out in front of them. One started the *cauyaq*, drumming a steady beat with his mallet, and the sound reverberated through the gymnasium. After about ten beats, the other two boys joined in with their drums. Then they started chanting a song in the background.

The girls with their feet planted in place started bending their knees to the rhythm. The boys moved up and down while sitting on their knees. The dance fans moved from one side to the other. Sometimes both arms would move in unison. Other times a hand would be planted on the hip as a single arm moved the dance fan. Their heads sometimes bobbed with the rhythm and together they all made sour faces in unison as if they all ate a sour berry.

When they were done, the children nearly ran into each other off stage in a rush to get safely back to their parents. After they were reassured and settled down, they went out to the audience to watch the rest of the dances.

Nora stayed on stage introducing each of her groups of students. As each dance group started, she went back and tried to organize her next group in lines for their turn. Organizing children might have been more work than her job. Smiling, she felt much joy in being a part of renewing her culture from the teaching she was doing. Each of the children seemed so proud of their heritage. She played a small part in the recovery of their Yupik traditions, but as small as it was, she felt such a warmth from doing it. She was glad her elderly cousins had defied the suppression, and they were able to teach her how to teach their traditions and to end the shame.

Her husband's voice came from behind her as she was working on organizing the chaos. He wrapped his arms around her from behind and kissed her neck. "Hey, I am taking the girls home. They are so tired they can barely stay awake. I will see you back there. I will try to sneak back to pick you up once they are settled down."

She turned to him and gave him a big hug and a quick kiss. She was happy that she would have a little time to enjoy this. He was so good about making sure she took the time to do the things that made her feel alive.

After introducing Agnes and Maryann for their mosquito dance, she handed over the emcee role to someone else. She was tired but was looking forward to the chance to sit in the audience and watch the adults perform. Looking out at the audience, she noticed Meara sitting by the trooper and Angus. There was a spare seat near them. She walked over and joined the lineup in the chairs. As she approached, the trooper pulled out a thermos of tea as Meara patted the empty seat next to her. Each of them was sipping on a cup of tea.

"*Quyana cakneq*, thank you very much," she said to the trooper as he handed her a cup. How thoughtful of him to bring a warm beverage to share with everyone. She normally felt like the troopers were somewhat standoffish. This was a pleasant surprise.

She sat and sipped her tea, feeling deeply content as she watched the older community members dance.

"Where is your family?" Meara asked.

"My husband took the little ones home. They were getting tired."

"Enjoy the peace while you have it then." Meara smiled.

"I will." Nora leaned back into her chair. She could feel herself nodding with the drumbeat as she watched the dancers on the stage.

She heard movement next to her as Angus and Rey gathered their belongings and got up. "We need to head back to the station to finish some paperwork. Would you mind if I dropped by the clinic for a cup of coffee with you in the morning, Meara? I will be leaving on the early flight."

"Sure." The smile Meara returned seemed hesitant.

What was with that? She quickly left the distractions and returned to enjoying the evening. After about three more dances, she felt incredibly sleepy. Her eyes were dropping shut as her head nodded with the drum. "I am sorry," she looked at Meara while stifling a yawn. "I think all the calls lately have caught up with me. I can barely keep my eyes open. I am going to start home. My husband was going to pick me up soon anyway. Do you know the way back to the clinic alright by yourself?"

"Yes, don't worry about me, I will be fine. I am enjoying the dancing and think I would like to stay a bit longer. See you in the morning."

Nora found her way to the door and was pushed back by the extreme cold. Her nose felt stuck together almost instantly, and the air that made it past had the metallic flavor it did when the temperatures were well below zero. She hunched forward, pushing herself out into the snowy night toward home.

* * *

Meara zipped up her jacket and pulled the hood up and over her hat as she stepped out into the dark night. She had enjoyed this chance to see Yupik dancing and was impressed at all the work Nora had put into teaching culture in their village. It had been such a thoroughly enjoyable evening, and she felt so fortunate to witness the traditions.

Her favorite dance was the mosquito dance performed by the two tiny elderly women visiting from Scammon Bay. Meara had no idea exactly how old they were, but their faces bore the etchings of a long life. The depth of their smile lines conveyed their sense of humor. The other dances had many dancers, but these two performed as a pair. This duo became the equivalent of a female Yupik dancing Laurel and Hardy. They were literally dancing clowns. The two ladies wore long and colorful loose-fitting qaspaqs that seemed enormous on their small bodies.

You could easily interpret the story they were telling as their heads would follow a mosquito off. A hand would “stop” dancing and itch a bite while the other would carry on. Her hips would gyrate as they danced and tried to itch the unreachable itches. They told the story with their entire body to the rhythm of the drums. And their heads bobbed and expressed the story in ways that seemed impossible to

Meara. Then there were the facial expressions. These women were so comically expressive. The audience response ranged from chuckles to roars of laughter through most of their dance, and when the drums suddenly beat rapidly, signaling the end of the dance, the audience stood to honor the pair. Meara smiled at the memory.

"Hey, want a lift?" The sudden voice out of nowhere made Meara startle. She had been so deep in her thoughts she hadn't even heard the truck drive up right next to her.

"Hi, Rey, I thought you had paperwork."

"I did, and I finished early enough to think you might still be out here. I thought I might be just in time to give you a lift. And it looks like I was right."

He had climbed out and walked around the truck before she could answer. He opened the door for her, and she slid into the cocoon of warmth inside.

They drove back the short distance to the clinic. "How did you like all that drum stuff? It certainly isn't what I think of as dancing."

"I loved it! I love the way the drums vibrate you deeply and you get carried into the rhythm. I also love the storytelling. You can see with their movements the story being told. I was so glad that I could follow it and I didn't have to speak Yupik. However, it really did help when I had someone translating for me. It was an honor to be able to attend." She stifled a yawn. Why couldn't he see the experience she saw? "I need to turn in. It has been a long couple of days."

Rey jumped out of the truck and ran around to open the door for her and took her hand as he walked her to the back door. She didn't resist. When they arrived at the door, he pulled her tight to him.

Meara hesitated and stiffened. But, part of her wanted to relax and put her guard down. It was so clear that he was a good guy and her prior judgement with men was not the case here. She pushed back the inner voice saying to keep her distance and stepped into his arms. Tilting her head back and looking into his eyes, she met his lips. All her apprehensions melted as she moved into him and for a moment, she allowed herself to feel a passion she hadn't felt for a long time.

Suddenly, this all reversed as her inner voice screamed, "Not yet!" She pulled her face downward suddenly and stepped backward and away from the kiss.

"I really need to get some sleep. Thank you for the ride." She yanked herself from his magnetic pull and disappeared into the clinic.

* * *

Meara entered the clinic trying to settle the conflicting feelings she felt after that kiss. But fatigue was taking over her racing mind. Within minutes, she had herself in a pair of sweats and had climbed into her sleeping bag on the top bunk. She was so tired that she was fast asleep before her head hit the pillow.

In her dreams, she heard voices from outside of the room. Slowly, she came back to alertness and realized that she was listening to the radio go off at the front desk. The CB radio was still a major form of communication around town. Did she hear something about needing a health aide? She thought she was dreaming and rolled over, trying to wish the sound away while she listened in case she heard more. Nora was on call again after the dance; Meara didn't need to worry.

Minutes later, she heard a truck pull up to the back of the clinic and then a loud knock at the arctic entry.

She looked at her watch. 3:16 AM. Groggily, she slipped out of her sleeping bag, slipped on her shoes, and walked to the back door.

There stood Rey. Before she could start to deal with the conflict of emotions again, he said abruptly, "I have a patient in the back of the truck. She was found unconscious outside of town heading toward the airport. I loaded her in the back of the truck and brought her here quickly. Angus has taken off to find the other health aides."

"Other health aides?" she responded in her sleep-induced confusion.

"Come with me," he replied. "I will need your help getting her in."

"Wait, I'm grabbing the longboard." Meara grabbed the long orange board the length of a standard person clipped with webbing to hold still the person being carried on it. As she pulled it toward the door, she tossed him a roll of tape and a couple more straps from the basin by her feet.

She ran out to the back of the truck and looked at the woman lying in the back. Her long hair fell across her face. She wore a purple qaspaq with lavender trim. Meara's own breath stopped as she looked at the woman and realized that she was not breathing.

"Oh my God! What happened to her?" Meara climbed up into the truck bed. As she moved the hair away from her face, she tried to convince herself that it was someone else. There was clear liquid coming from the woman's mouth. She did not have a mask to ventilate and gave a quick rescue breath anyway followed by another one. She swore that she could smell and taste alcohol.

"Hold her head while we logroll her on. You don't have anything else to add to the story?"

Rey put his hands around the sides of the woman's face, holding the neck still. He counted to three, and they rolled her over in unison to protect her neck. Rey put traction on her head while Meara rolled the patient synchronized with Rey's turning of the head to the side.

She pulled the longboard under the back of her patient. Then she opened the airway and taped the head in place and gave Rey the straps to hold the patient down.

Meara kneeled next to the longboard and felt for a pulse. While she was on her knees feeling desperately for a sign of life, she started the prayer that she always said whenever she had a patient in a life-or-death situation. "God, please give me what I need to be here for this patient right now."

She pushed down all emotion and worked hard to deny the identity of her patient. She couldn't handle it, but she had to. Her hands were already numb from the subzero air. "No pulse. We will do two rounds of CPR here then we need to get her inside." She kneeled in the pickup truck over her patient and started compressions.

Rey shook his head when it came time for the breaths. "I will breathe when we get a mask."

Meara found herself both partially irritated by this and partially understanding his refusal at the same time.

"When we get inside, you take over compressions while I get us organized." If anything, his refusal to breathe pushed her to get their patient into the building even faster. She still couldn't allow herself to believe that this was not some anonymous patient like she wanted it to be. But part of her could no longer deny that this was Nora lying here cold, unresponsive, and without a pulse.

* * *

Inside, the light of the clinic confirmed the horrible fact of the patient's identity. The bright fluorescent overhead lights refused to allow her any more denial as a coping mechanism. It was Nora, the beautiful and vibrant woman who had been sitting next to her at the dance just hours before.

She choked back tears and coughed in doing so. Her emotions and her brain wanted to run away. Every cell of her being wanted to deny the situation, to be able to give it to someone else to take care of. But here she was, hours from assistance other than the police and her trainees. *You are alone to take care of her, and any chance she has depends on you.*

Meara had always been part of a response team and had always taken care of strangers in her big community emergency rooms. Now, here she was alone without even a lab technician. There was no ambulance to whisk them up and bring them to help. She was the person responsible for making sure the best care was given. How could she take care of her patient without the images of Nora and her family dancing in her head and clouding her view? Would her heart get in the way of her head?

"I don't know how the health aides do this. Every patient they see is a friend or a family member." She would need all of God's help she could get.

"Okay, Meara. Don't feel. Just follow your ABCs just like you teach." She moved as quickly as she could. She had already attended to the first "A" when she opened the airway and taped Nora's head in position outside.

Now, it was time for the "B." First, she turned on the oxygen and connected it to an Ambu bag and mask, a bag of oxygen that was connected to a mask and was squeezed in order to breathe for the patient.

"Do you know how to bag ventilate?" she asked Rey.

"Yes, we learned in our CPR training." He reached for the bag as she handed it to him. He started squeezing the bag and breathing for Nora while Meara put the cardiac monitor on and received another confirmation of the absent pulse. Flat line. No pulse. No rhythm. Meara shuddered at Nora's ice-cold skin. It was firm to the touch. She resumed compressions and, thankfully, the chest moved with her efforts. It was not completely rigid.

"You're not dead until you're warm and dead," she said out loud to Nora. Secretly, she hoped that repeating the adage well known in emergency medicine would make it true for her today. "So, Miss Nora, you are not dead." Tears welled in her eyes. *No, no tears Meara. Compartmentalize. Think of her as somebody else. Someone you don't know.*

Angus, Chelsey, and Verna walked in together. As she tried to continue with compressions, they all froze for a moment as the wide-eyed look of disbelief covered their faces. Chelsey ran to the bathroom from which they could hear retching. She returned quickly to the room.

Meara waited while they processed their initial shock as each of them realized who the patient was. Once she saw that they might be able to absorb information, she quickly assigned jobs.

"Rey, stay on airway, but pick it up a little. One breath every ten seconds. You are getting good chest rise when you do ventilate."

"Verna, you are on compressions. As we get more help, you will rotate the compressors and give them feedback. Angus, we need more help. This could go on for a while. Go find us whoever might know CPR. Do you have a fire or ambulance crew? Get them fast. Chelsey, get the defibrillator pads on her. Then grab the clipboard and start recording. You will be the recorder tonight. We are in this together, and we can do this, but it is going to be a long night."

Knowing that her two new health aides did not have the practice to get the initial intravenous started, she quickly grabbed the starter kit from the crash cart and got a large bore in quickly. She was grateful that Nora was a strong woman with good veins even while frozen. She needed to draw labs, but that would have to happen later. She opened the drawer and drew up one gram of epinephrine and a flush.

"One-gram epinephrine given for the asystole. We need to increase her volume. Chelsey, can you grab me one liter of lactated ringers to run straight in, please?"

Chelsey ran to the pharmacy and back with the intravenous fluid.

Meara quickly connected this to the catheter and opened the tubing wide open. The second line would have to wait. She worked her way down the body cutting off clothes and feeling and examining from head to toe. She would not be able to see the back completely now; the CPR was more important.

"Chelsey, let me know when five minutes are up, and please get a rectal temperature. Verna, do you know how much of a supply of epinephrine there is? I only see six boxes in the drawer."

"I think that is it. They only send out one crash cart drawer for the providers."

Meara went into the crash cart and pulled out another epinephrine and a flush. While she prepared it, she searched her brain for the best practice with the limited supply. Her heart raced as if she had just received the epinephrine.

Chelsey piped up. "68 degrees Fahrenheit."

"Stop compressions." Meara switched the monitor to manual. This setting required the provider to make the decisions instead of the machine. She held her breath. The flat line continued. Her heart sank. “Resume compressions. The heart will get more irritable as we warm her. Let’s resume compressions. I am holding this dose of epinephrine. I need to get the doctor in Agushak on the line. Chelsey, can you dial the phone and get them on?

While she waited for the phone, she started the second IV and drew blood during the start. She set the vials on the table. Through all this, she was trying to keep an eye on how her crew was doing.

“Chelsey, let me know when five minutes have passed since the last epinephrine. Rey, ventilations are slowing down again. One squeeze every eight to ten seconds. Try counting. Compressions look good, Verna.”

She quickly gathered intubation supplies. A definitive airway would help them through their struggle. She had the endotracheal tube set on the table with a laryngoscope, a light with a blade to help her see the vocal cords and know that she went down the trachea instead of the esophagus. Going down the wrong tube could cause Nora to vomit and choke and would lose valuable time in resuscitation. Time would not be all that could be lost. She could aspirate on her vomit and cause a pneumonia to fight once she was revived.

She surveyed the crew working around the room. “Rey, Verna, switch places for a while. Verna, you will hand me tape when I ask for it. I have it prepared right here.” She nodded to the tape hanging off the side of the mayo stand. "Everyone is doing a great job."

The oxygen saturations were not being measured because of the cold extremities. They had no idea how they were doing in their work to get oxygen levels up.

"Okay, I am going to intubate. Continue compressions as I do this." She held her breath to give her own personal judgement of how long it was safe to make the attempt. If she couldn't hold her breath, it was a sign that Nora needed more breath. If that happened, then she needed to step back and ventilate with the bag mask again for a few minutes before she could try again. Picking up the laryngoscope and opening Nora's mouth, she could clearly visualize the vocal cords. Sliding the endotracheal tube quickly between the cords, she stopped where she had already measured Nora for size. She injected air into the cuff that would help to hold the tube in place. Then she removed the mask from the Ambu bag and attached a carbon dioxide indicator to the end of the tube. Then she added the Ambu bag. She had Verna ventilate as she listened to lung sounds on each side and saw the indicator turn on the detector.

"Thank God. Bilateral lung sounds."

"Five minutes is up. I have the doctor on the line." Chelsey looked at the monitor. The flat line could not be denied.

"Continue compressions." Meara picked up the phone. "Dr. Forester, we have a patient found unresponsive and hypothermic, temperature 20 degrees Celsius. She is in asystole. We have only six vials of epinephrine here. I used one, and I am thinking we should wait until we get her temperature higher before I use more. Do you concur?"

"Yes. You can also take two-minute rests with the CPR if you are getting fatigued while you get the temperature up."

"Doctor, the patient is Nora, our health aide."

There was a prolonged silence on the other end of the line. Nora was well known and respected by the hospital physicians. "Okay, I will start to organize a medical evacuation. You just focus on what you have there."

Just then, Angus walked in with the village council chief and Nora's mother, Sophie.

"Sophie, do you want a chair by her side?"

"No. I will help," she responded.

"You don't have to. This is too hard; she is your daughter."

"It would be harder to not help. I can't just sit by."

"I can understand that," Meara said. "Verna, Angus, Rey, rotate the compressions. Sophie, would you feel comfortable with the respirations?"

A nod and a move to the head of the bed answered the question. Sophie moved robotically.

"We need warmed blankets, on her trunk only for now. Chelsey, when the first bag runs out, go grab another bag of lactated ringers from the warmer. Make sure to replace the bags in the warmer. With the help we have now, we will continue continuous compressions. Let me know five-minute intervals."

A beep started intermittently. The oxygen saturations were starting to be picked up. Nora must be warming up. Not enough to get a reading, but the beep was a sign that they were moving in the right direction. For now, they just needed to keep the CPR going. When the temperature came up, they would try the epinephrine again.

* * *

Verna watched Meara. She appeared to be so calm in the middle of all of this. She was scanning the room to see what each person in the room was doing. The one thing that seemed to give the anxiety away was the tremor that Verna noticed in Meara's hand.

"Chelsey, can you get another temperature?"

"Temperature 73.4 degrees Fahrenheit," called Chelsey after a minute.

Meara's eyes locked on the cardiac monitor where the line remained flat. "Good job on the CPR all of you. Chelsey, alert me when five more minutes goes by. Let's add some more warmed blankets."

Verna looked at Sophie. Sophie also appeared calm as she squeezed the Ambu bag every ten seconds, and her eyes moved between her daughter's face and her chest. How was she holding it together?

It felt to Verna that this had been going on for hours. She struggled seeing the health aide that had convinced her to apply lying there. Her heart felt like it had fallen down into her stomach. Her head wanted to go somewhere else, anywhere but here. The ABCs that she had learned in training worked as an anchor to keep her here and doing what she needed. She started doubting herself and her ability to do the job she was training to do.

Sophie continued the ventilations. Verna watched, and in between each breath she was desperately trying to will Nora to breathe on her own.

"Five minutes," said Chelsey.

"Let's get another temperature," said Meara.

"82.4 degrees. We are starting to get a wave form on the oxygen saturations. 90 percent. Excellent job with the respirations."

Meara looked at the cardiac monitor. "Still asystole. Continue compressions. I am going to try epinephrine. One milligram given. Followed by flush."

Verna was so glad that Meara was there. If Meara hadn't been there, they would be working with a senior health aide, and all they could have done was the CPR. There were only a few health aides that had reached the level that they could give drugs. Most couldn't.

"Chelsey, let me know when five minutes is up. Okay, how are all you compressors feeling?"

The lineup of people all nodded their heads.

"Five minutes," said Chelsey.

"Stop compressions," Meara said authoritatively.

All eyes stared at the cardiac monitor. Verna knew that Meara was looking to find some vibration on that flat line. It had none. It looked like she was struggling to swallow that realization.

"No shockable rhythm. Return to CPR. Chelsey, can you spin the speckle-top tube and put the rest in the fridge?" She handed the labs over.

After an hour, Meara looked at the monitor. "Stop CPR. Let's see if we have any rhythm."

The line on the monitor was as flat as the tundra. "Let's get a temperature."

Chelsey grabbed the thermometer and went to work to get another core temperature. "86 degrees."

They continued another twenty minutes.

"Stop CPR," said Meara.

Verna scanned the room. All the eyes on the monitor looked as though they were begging the flat green line to move. But the pleading did not work. The green line on the monitor stayed flat, but there seemed to be a little static in it.

"Return to CPR. Repeating epinephrine." Meara administered the dose and flush. "We have only two epinephrine left. We could try some vasopressin when that is gone. How much do we have of that?" She walked across the room to the crash cart and looked. "Two vials. We need continuous CPR now. Chelsey, can you get me the doctor on the line? I wish I could process those labs. I can't assess electrolytes. Wait. We can still get a finger-stick hemoglobin and a blood sugar. Please do that, Verna." Her face was red. Verna couldn't tell if it was from the heat of the room or the stress.

At that point, a priest walked in with Norman Nelson and one other man. Meara looked like she was going to move them toward the waiting room when Sophie spoke up.

"I would like them here, if you don't mind."

Meara looked around the room. They had everything in control. There was no reason to send them away. "I think that would be alright."

The O2 sat monitor was now giving a continuous 90 percent. They were oxygenating fine.

"Let's get another temp."

"Just did. 89.6 degrees," said Chelsey.

"Hold CPR." Again, all eyes pleaded for the green line to move.

"Resume CPR. Epinephrine one milligram given again. Do I have doctor on the line? Let me know when it is five minutes. We have only one dose left." The corners of Meara's mouth had fine twitches.

Verna herself was struggling to keep the sinking feeling from taking over.

"Damn it," Meara said, then she stiffened when she looked up and saw the priest.

He had just made a circle around Nora with everyone that wasn't doing CPR.

The door opened in front, and Sophie went to bring in Zach and Nora's girls. They joined in the circle.

The priest prayed. "Heavenly Father, we ask of you to give healing to Nora. She is so needed here. There are so many people that depend on her. Please bring her healing and help her family to deal with this."

Verna wanted to join as his prayer went on, but she was back doing compressions.

Meara stood back looking like she didn't know what to do. She then looked at the timer, shrugged her shoulders, and joined the circle holding hands and bowed her head.

As the priest gave an amen, Meara said, "I have never had a big group prayer like this in an emergency down south."

"Five minutes," said Chelsey.

"Stop compressions." Meara stared at the monitor.

Could it be? The clearly straight line looked as if there was a little bit of a jagged pattern to it. Barely perceptible.

"Continue compressions. I think we may have fine ventricular fibrillation. Preparing to shock." Meara turned around, set the joules to 200. Took the pads to Nora's chest.

"Clear," she called.

Verna and everyone else stepped back from the bed. Could the prayer have brought this?

Meara looked to make sure everyone was away. "I'm clear, everybody clear. All clear. Shocking."

Nora's body jumped in response to the shock, and everyone in the room did the same in response.

"Resume compressions."

They continued the CPR for the next five minutes.

"Stop compressions." Verna noted that the entire room held their breath as they looked to the screen.

Meara whispered under her breath. "Please give us a rhythm."

Their expressions all fell when they looked at the monitor. Asystole. Verna's heart fell all the way to her toes.

"Start compressions." She heard Meara's voice. "We will try the vasopressin."

At that point, the phone rang. It was handed to Meara. Verna could hear the doctor's voice on the line. "We can't get a crew out for four hours. Bad weather is between us. It may clear, and they will update then."

Meara reviewed the progress with him. "We had fine v-fib five minutes ago. No response to shock. Asystole last check. Temp is 95 Fahrenheit. Vasopressin used once. We have one more dose. We are out of epinephrine."

"Okay. Repeat the vasopressin. It won't hurt to give her a little more CPR if you want to continue. If you don't get a rhythm, you will need to call it."

After one more dose of vasopressin and no conversion, Meara's gaze went to Sophie and Zach. The little girls were sitting at Nora's right hand holding it.

"Mama, wake up," their little voices said.

Sophie's gaze was able to summon Zach to look at her. She shook her head. He nodded in return. They both turned and looked to Meara.

Meara responded to the room as professionally as she could at that moment. "We have her to a normal body temperature. Advanced life support has failed. We have had no shockable rhythm, and we are out of medication. The flight will not get here for at least five hours. It is time to call this." Tears welled in the corners of Meara's eyes as she said what they all knew was coming. "Stop CPR. Attempt is futile."

The noise of the compressions stopped and was replaced by the sobbing throughout the room. Zach threw himself over the arms of his wife and sobbed in great heaves.

Sophie drew her granddaughters to her side as the tears flowed down their faces. Verna wondered how somebody went on after a loss like this.

CHAPTER 9

The dawn had not risen yet to mark the beginning of a new day at eight thirty in the morning. Meara still had not adjusted to how late the sun rose. Having spent the majority of the night fighting for Nora, the continued darkness made it feel like the day would not arrive. It seemed fitting that they all wandered in the dark for a while. In any case, the sun would not shine again for Nora.

The priest remained behind to help support the family. Rey reminded them that they could not remove any medical devices from the body because of the potential autopsy. He and Angus left the building right behind the community members.

Verna went into the reception area to deal with the incoming flock of people arriving with food. There were only a couple of patients out there for medical problems. Meara marveled at how many people already knew about the tragic events of the evening and had shown up with generous support for the family. Verna had found a table and set it up in the waiting room for food.

Sophie was the one that spoke up to provide direction. "We need to prepare her body and the room for visitors. They will not be flying her body to Anchorage right away with this weather, and until they do, I can't bring her home. People will be arriving here to pay respects."

"They come here?" Meara was surprised. Only the immediate family would be expected to come into the emergency room back in Vermont.

"Yes, if she is sent to Anchorage, we will not have the chance to wake her. Family and community will be coming here. That is why food is showing up out front."

Meara was lost. Back in the lower forty-eight, the health care providers were removed from this. The immediate family would come for a short goodbye if they could get to the hospital before the mortician took the body to the funeral home. The nurses would prepare the body, and it would be placed in a body bag hidden from all eyes in the hospital and snuck down the hallways to the mortuary of the hospital. There, the coroner would usually slide into a cargo door hidden from the public. The deceased would be tucked quietly and discreetly into the back of the hearse, and the body would be taken to the funeral home. Everything neat, tidy, and tucked away. Death was hidden as though it was a shameful fact of life.

"Her husband and the girls will be back soon. They went to get some clothes on. He rushed them all out the door in their pajamas last night."

"Sophie, why don't you run home and get yourself ready? Chelsey and I will prepare Nora," offered Meara.

Sophie hesitated but then nodded and left for home.

Meara and Chelsey moved quietly back to the trauma room.

"I will get a basin and be right back," said Chelsey.

In the meantime, Meara snipped tubes she had inserted last night and tucked them out of sight. The endotracheal tube needed to stay in until they had word otherwise. The coroner would look at the original cause of death and would look at anything in their treatment that would have caused her not to be saved. Meara's head spun, reviewing the night and trying to handle preparing the body of her new friend.

Chelsey kept her eyes down and averted from looking at the person in front of her that a day before had been a mentor.

"Have you ever had to prepare a body for a wake?" Meara asked Chelsey.

"No, I have just gone to wakes and funerals. Everything has always been done by the time I was there. I was just a kid." The experiences of last night had stolen some of the kid that remained in Chelsey. Some innocence had been lost in the night.

"It is one of the saddest and most honorable jobs of a nurse or a health aide. We need to keep her body undisturbed for the medical examiner in case there is an autopsy, so tubes will need to stay. But we want to make her look as natural as possible. Especially for her children." Meara stifled tears. "I have never had to prepare someone I knew. This is a first for me as well. When I have lost family members, somebody else did this part."

They tucked Nora discreetly under a hospital gown with blankets on top. Meara tenderly worked the hair that was knotted from tangles of the prior evening. Carefully, she brushed the beautiful silky hair back into order. Then she washed her face. Her hands were brought up and out of the blankets and were laid neatly by her side. Last, they gently closed the eyelids, giving their friend the look of a peaceful sleep. The tube in her mouth was the only visible sign of the struggle.

Nora was ready. They went back to see if Sophie had returned yet. Surprisingly in that short amount of time, Sophie had run home and changed into a clean qaspaq, brushed her hair, and put some makeup on, giving some color to her pale face.

"She is all ready for her husband and children to come in." Meara took Sophie's hand. "Are you ready?"

* * *

Meara went out to the desk with Verna, and they strategized their day. One of them would remain in the trauma room with Nora, and Meara would alternate between the two, seeing a limited number of patients. They rescheduled the appointments that could be delayed. They needed to keep the clinic going in some capacity.

Meara knew that Verna and Chelsey needed time to process the experience of the night before. The first time she had to do CPR on someone, she thought about it for days afterwards. What had she done right, what could she have done better? She hadn't changed. Who was she kidding?

Verna put a sign on the door that they were seeing limited patients today, then went to work on making the calls to cancel the ones they felt could wait. With Nora gone, there wasn't someone to oversee each of the trainees, and Verna was the one who knew the village. She seemed to know that this was her role.

Meara called back to behavioral health in Agushak to see if they would be sending someone out for a stress debriefing.

If they could get here. She wanted to make sure that the trainees and community got the support they needed. She lied to herself thinking she was processing this just fine.

The hardest job was bringing Zach and the girls back. She stiffly shook Zach's hand and led him back. The children seemed to have the resolve of their grandmother, except the visible quiver of their lips and the shaking of their hands as they fumbled to take their snow pants off. The six-year-old seemed the steadiest. Meara knew that this was from her innocence. She probably had no idea what to expect with death and what it meant.

The immediate family gathered with Sophie in the hallway and all went into the room together. Meara lead them back in and slid chairs under Sophie and Zach. The children stood to the side.

Meara knelt down next to the girls. "Your mom went to sleep in the cold last night. We tried to wake her up, but God felt that his sleep was where she needed to be. There are still tubes there from us trying to help her wake up. I am sorry that we cannot take them out right now. It is okay to touch her if you want. If you don't want to, that is okay too."

The littlest tucked her head under her father's arm. The middle one lifted Sophie's arm and climbed up on her lap.

Sophie, at last, started to cry gently. "Your mama was a good mama. She loved you very much. I remember so clearly when she was the one to climb on my lap like you do now."

Meara tried to fade into the background as she walked out of the room. "I will be right outside if you need me." As she shut the trauma room door, she heard a loud knock on the back door.

There was Rey. She had been so numb from all that had happened in the last twelve hours that she felt no quivers, no trembling of her stomach when she saw him. She felt drained.

"I spoke to the medical examiner. Her coat was found with a bottle of alcohol a block from her home. She must have become intoxicated then sat down for a while in the snow, becoming hypothermic. With the hypothermia, she must have removed her outer clothing and wandered off toward the airport where we found her. With such a clear cause of death and the bad weather, he states there is no need for an autopsy."

Behind him, she could hear commotion. Angus was struggling to get an argumentative man, who appeared to be in his forties, up the ramp in handcuffs.

Angus called out, "So sorry to add to your load. We need medical clearance to make sure he is safe for me to bring to the jail to sleep it off. That is trooper protocol. Apparently, there seems to be another shipment of alcohol in the village."

* * *

Meara quickly evaluated the drunk man. His eyes pierced her, and he spoke only Yupik. She could clearly hear *kussuk* here and there mixed into his speech. She shuddered. He very clearly was not happy with the fact that she existed right now. As Angus brought him back, he would throw his head back in attempt to headbutt Angus or would violently twist his arms to the side in the handcuffs in attempt to get out of his control.

"Chelsey, I am going to give you a break on this one, but I want you to see where you would go in your CHAM. I am going to have you do a write-up later on your encounter sheet. Angus, have you done a breathalyzer?"

"Not yet. He has not been the most cooperative, as you can see."

"That would be stating it lightly." She carefully moved around him, making sure to keep her body far out of the reach of a leg or his mouth.

She heard him start to clear his throat, and she turned to him and stared directly back into those dark eyes with a directed scowl. He stared back and actually swallowed the sputum he had been clearly planning to spit in her face. She suppressed the sigh of relief. Dealing with drunks was not new to her. The only difference in alcohol use between here and back home was that the drunks were conveniently tucked aside and ignored. Here, they were connected to the rest of the community as family. With the small community, they were not as easily ignored.

She was able to get a blood pressure cuff around his arm and was glad to use a machine. She stood to his side holding his wrist to assess his heart rate and reached the stethoscope behind him to listen to his lungs. She navigated around him with caution. She had been taught by experience to never let down her guard.

"Has he told you when and how much he drank?" she asked Angus.

Angus's voice was tight with frustration. "He still isn't admitting that he drank. He was throwing rocks at somebody's window, and they called me. I found him staggering down the street."

"Does he know what day it is? His name or date of birth?"

"He won't answer any questions right now. But this is Lawrence Aputuk. He is in your system."

Meara sensed him shifting his weight and stepped back just as a foot lashed to the side attempting to knock her over.

"Well, I think his level of consciousness is good enough to be safe from aspirating or alcohol poisoning now. And he even demonstrated a little balance there." She gave a wry smile. Logging into the computer, she checked his medical records. "The safest place for him is where he can't hurt anyone. He has no conditions that put him at risk. Let me know if anything changes."

He made a hacking sound again.

She ducked quickly. She had dealt with enough drug and alcohol evaluations in the past to instinctively duck.

Angus had performed a breath alcohol, and as long as that was going down, he would be fine in jail. Angus led the man back down the hallway and out the back door. The patient did not leave quietly.

Entering the trauma room again, she felt as if she was moving from the clinic into a wake. The children were sitting to the side. Sophie and Zach stood next to Nora's body. People flowed in steadily from the waiting room, which was now filled with food and people.

Community members moved through the room, approaching Zach and Sophie. Some paused and gave the children deep embraces. Their little bodies stiffened and relaxed as they tried to process their emotions. Their wide eyes showed that they weren't present much at all.

Meara approached Sophie and Zach. She straightened and stiffened as she talked to him. How could Sophie be so friendly to him? Nora still had that black eye.

"The trooper was just here. We can get her prepared to go. There will be no autopsy. They have declared the cause of death to be hypothermia secondary to alcohol intoxication. Where do you take a body for the wake before the funeral?"

Sophie responded. "Home. She can go to my house so the children can get rest. If that is alright with you, Zach." She looked up at Zach.

Anger welled up in Meara again when she looked at Zach.

"Can everyone step outside so we can prepare Nora to go to her mother's house?" Meara said to the other visitors in the room. She then went through removing all the signs of the medical fight that had happened last night.

Sophie prepared the longboard so they could transfer her to her house. A group of men came in and carried her out of the clinic for her last time and to the back of the village ambulance. Verna drove the ambulance to Sophie's.

The group of people in front gathered up all of the food and followed the ambulance to Sophie's home.

Meara was left alone at the clinic while Chelsey and Verna took a break for lunch. Starting in the trauma room, she cleaned up so they would be prepared for another emergency. After that was cleaned, she moved to the pharmacy and took stock of emergency medications and submitted an extra order to replace them. Then she went to straighten up the lab. She opened the refrigerator door and saw the labs she had drawn the night before.

Maybe getting the clinical information from the labs would help satisfy her mind that she had done what she should have last night. She entered the orders into the computer, packaged them, and called the airline for a pickup.

* * *

Meara had barely climbed into her bed when her head started spinning with the events of the day. She hated how she did this. It didn't matter how long the day was since an emergency. When she went to bed at night, she would review over and over again what was done for a patient emergency, what she hadn't thought of, and what she could have done better.

This one was different. She was so angry with herself. She had the chance to help Nora before she died. And she had failed. To start with, she had seen so many red flags with Nora. She had seen them, but she never bothered to ask questions and act on those red flags. First, there was the evening of the steam. He kept her in and didn't let her join the rest of the group of health aides when they steamed with her mother. Then, there was the black eye she arrived with the next day.

Meara, you let the elephant stand in the room and never commented on it. Why were you such a coward? What happened between them that night? Had they been drinking, and he got angry? Did she drink to escape his control? Funny that nobody back in Agushak mentioned Nora having a drinking problem. She hid that well, Meara supposed. Damn. If only she had the courage to ask the other day, then maybe she wouldn't have had the chance to fail at rescuing her last night.

Lying back on her bed, her breath quickened and her heart raced. She was suddenly back in that apartment in New Hampshire. The flashback took over her senses.

She could see the apartment as she moved about it as she packed what little she had for her unborn child. She moved the pieces of the crib. She gathered her clothes into backpacks and duffel bags. Lying in her bed in Alaska, her heart pounded in her chest like it had that night. She kept telling herself she was safe.

Long ago when she was young, she'd had to escape in the middle of the night while her husband was at work. She was convinced he would know what was going on and walk right in that door at any second. She had to search for her bank card that he had taken from her. The clock struck 1 AM.

The phone rang as if he had a timer connected to it. "Hi, Meara! I was just calling to check to see how well you are sleeping. You wouldn't believe the night so far."

Feigning grogginess, she responded, "Yes, I was just starting to dream." *Yes, I am. I am starting to dream of a new life where I have control and I can give my baby a safe home.* She barely heard him speak as he rambled on and he finally hung up.

She went back to work quickly. This hour she planned to get all of the bags loaded into her truck and have it packed before the clock struck two and the phone rang again.

Her wallet was empty. He took all her paychecks as soon as she got them from the two jobs she worked. Then he would give her a twenty-dollar allowance. Twenty dollars was not much money for food and gas for a week in 1987.

He would eat on his own while he was home during the day, and usually he bought himself takeout on weekends. He had no problem at all taking the food that she had purchased with her "allotment."

She worked hard to stretch that money, and she would clip coupons in order to spread it as far as she could. Sometimes she was even able to get some food free by combining coupons. She was feeding her unborn child on processed food, hot dogs, instant ramen, and whatever else she could buy at a reduced price.

The faint flutter in her stomach reminded her of her purpose that night. Her anxiety continued to build. She had thirty-seven dollars in her bank account. At least it had been there when she last went to access it. That account had been wiped out by him. The last time she tried to escape, she had reported this to the police when they responded. He called them saying she was stealing. When she told the police how he had taken her money, they told her that it wasn't a crime for him to take her money because they were married. She prayed that what little still remained was still there when she accessed her account at the ATM down the street. If not, she would not have enough gas to get away.

She quietly opened the dead bolt and the lock and snuck out to the truck with her first load. The sharp night air and the penetrating streetlight did not cut her anxiety. She moved the packed items into the back of the truck, feeling like she was under an interrogator's spotlight. Were any neighbors watching and calling him? He had told her that he had them watching her. Why wouldn't she believe that?

As she stood behind the truck, the memory of the week before returned. She had been delayed on coming home because she needed to stop at a store. Unexpected traffic made her fifteen minutes late. When she neared the apartment building, she could see him pacing in the driveway.

She held her breath as she opened her car door and was afraid to lift her eyes up to meet his.

He stood there with his tense body, the muscles in his face twitching. His dark eyes bored into her, clearly looking to seek any hint that she could be lying about where she had been.

"I stopped for groceries."

"Don't you care about my sleep at all? Don't you realize I have to work all night?"

"Yes, of course. I just ran into the store and would not have been late, but a car accident held up traffic."

"You don't care about anyone but yourself!" He picked up the shovel leaning against the building wall. He swung it back like a batter preparing to take the base.

She kept her eyes on the ground as she quickly ducked past him, her groceries in her arms, nearly running into the house. Fortunately, when she looked back at the door, he was following but the shovel was no longer in his hand.

A thought caught her breath. *Oh no! What if he has disabled my car again? I am going to get caught if it doesn't run. I can't get everything put away fast enough.*

She slid herself back to the present and behind the driver's wheel. *What was I thinking? How could I have forgotten to test it already?* Her truck had a funny way of not running whenever she had something important to do. She had been trying to get back to school for her anthropology degree, but every time she tried to go for her interview, the car would not start. She was sure that she wouldn't be able to get into the program now. They probably believed she was an unreliable flake. She should have been back in school, if only she could have gotten there for the interview.

The keychain tinkled from the shaking of her hand. She put the key in the ignition. Holding her breath, she turned the key. She felt the click in her fingers first, then the vibration of the engine turning over. She exhaled as it settled into the reassuring purr of the engine. She quickly turned it back off and hoped she had not woken up the neighbors.

Back in the apartment, she quickly and quietly gathered her items and loaded them in the truck. Each trip, her eyes scanned the neighbors for any sign of alertness. After it was all loaded up, she went back inside.

In the bedroom, she sat next to the phone waiting for the next call. She had planned this escape for days, strategizing the use of the time between the calls. If she left immediately after the call, she could get a good distance between them before he discovered she was gone.

She sat on the bed and waited. It seemed like an eternity for the clock to move to 3 AM. What if he had called early, while she was outside? If she had missed his call, he could be on his way here now, or he could have called a friend to check on her. The clock moved past his punctual hourly time. 3:01 AM. That minute was filled with "what ifs."

Guilt and fear took over. She was holding her breath, and instead of speeding, her heart was slowing down to join the rhythm of the ticking clock. Was it counting toward her doom?

3:02. That was it. He was on his way here. She was now in a frantic panic and was trying to decide if she should hurry and unload the truck or leave everything there. She was dead. How could she get it all put back before he arrived? And, what would he do if she didn't?

The ringing of the phone shot like an electrical shock through every nerve in her body.

"Hi, sweetie, just calling to check in to make sure you are sleeping."

She exhaled with a moan as if she had just been woken. "Yes, tired, so sleepy."

"Sleep tight. I love you."

"Love you, too." She replied as she slowly hung up the phone.

That was the last slow thing she did. Bounding out of bed, she hurried to the door. She quickly tiptoed down the stairs and slipped into the seat of the truck.

She turned the key quickly and, without hesitation, backed herself out of the driveway. Turning the little truck toward the highway, she headed toward her mother's.

What was asking her mother for help going to cost her? She shuddered.

Meara felt her hands on the sheets of the bed instead of a steering wheel. She looked around the darkened room for a color to help ground herself and bring her back to the present. She reached down to her backpack for a piece of gum to smell and taste. She was lying in the dark bunk bed in a clinic in Alaska.

The flashback surprised her. It had been over ten years since she had experienced one. Her son was now all grown up and on his own.

What happened to Nora could have been her. It could have been her in a different time and a different place. She could not have saved Nora prior to last night's event. She had barely had a chance to get to know her. The red flags were there. His need to control her time. The black eye that she wasn't brave enough to ask about. She had been so cowardly like the rest of the clinic. Everyone danced their own eyes around making sure to look anywhere but right at her and asking about it.

Meara failed Nora then, and to top it off, she failed her last night. Meara reviewed everything she did from the moment she saw Rey at the door. What did she do or not do that might have saved Nora's life? Unlike working in the lower forty-eight, all of the decisions fell back to her. She had no team of other providers to share them with.

She marveled at the response of the health aides. Nora was their friend and leader of their team. Verna had known her since she was a little girl. They both looked stunned and in shock, but they fell into place and kept their calm. They did exactly what they needed to do. Although they followed her orders, she could see their new emergency training shine through. They were anticipating what came next as they worked through the ABCs of saving lives. Airway, breathing, circulation. How would they manage to keep working when every emergency was a friend or family member? What was their trick to coping? How had Sophie done it for so long, and how did she stay so strong when it was her own daughter as the patient?

Meara reviewed and critiqued in her head over and over. Sleep would not come. She felt guilt that Nora did not survive. They had continued past normal body temperature; they had followed protocols. Would it have been different if that storm hadn't come in?

The sounds of the snow machines circling the group of buildings that she was staying in drifted to her. It sounded like a roundup, and she half expected them to stop and to pound at the doors as they came to get her for failing Nora. She had seen that before back home. Angry family members, whose grief had been hijacked by anger, coming in screaming at doctors or nurses after bad outcomes. There certainly had to be someone that would come after her to express their rage.

Finally, the clock struck six. Time to get up, sleep or no sleep. She needed her run.

* * *

Meara got up, put on her windproof running pants, jacket, gloves, and sneakers. She exited the clinic, hid her keys, and took off toward the airport. The cold air entered her lungs, and she pulled her neck warmer up over her face to pre-warm the air. She started the run slowly, still lost in thought. As she passed town, she picked up the pace.

She should have done this last night. Maybe she would have slept. She forced herself into a sprint, where she pushed until it felt like her lungs would burst—a habit she had to work out stress. Usually, a few of these sprints would get her centered. It hadn't yet. She tried again. She ran all the way out to the airport, did a few laps around, then turned back. She was calmer but still felt the overwhelming guilt.

As she jogged past Sophie's, a few people stood outside with mugs in their hands.

Was she awake? It would feel good to see her. She turned up the pathway to the door. "Hello, is Sophie awake?" she said to the group.

Norman was one of them. "Yes," he said. "She is inside."

Meara stepped inside. There were people sleeping on almost every available space in the living room. Voices came from the kitchen, and the smell of fresh brewed coffee filled the air. Because of the sleeping people, she decided not to announce herself. She tiptoed in, navigating cautiously around the sleeping people until she found herself in the kitchen.

Entering the kitchen, she found Sophie on the ground in a circle of women with a mound of dead, white fluffy birds piled in the center. Sophie was sitting in the circle peeling the skin with feathers off of the birds. She looked up and noticed Meara and invited her to join by patting the ground next to her. The other women welcomed her by shifting to make room.

"Have a seat, we are cleaning ptarmigan for a stew later. Want to help?"

Meara tried to hide any sense of repulsion that she had. She had never had to "clean a bird before." She instinctively turned up her nose and realized that was not a good idea. Instead, she took a deep breath to steady her face. The smell of the dead birds filled her nostrils. Taking another deep breath, she remembered how much Sophie had been through and decided she would not let her squeamish fears interfere with her support.

She sat. "What do I do?"

"Grab a bird, then work your fingers in between the skin and the muscle and peel it back. Like this." Sophie made quick work of pushing her fingers through the skin into an area on the chest and wiggling her fingers around to started pull the skin away from the muscle fascia complete with the feathers. She worked her fingers around the bird and swiftly removed the feather coat. She tossed the cleaned bird with a plop onto the pile of completed birds.

Meara reached forward and grabbed a bird, then hesitantly pushed her fingers into where she thought was the chest started. Suddenly a pile of grubs, twigs, grass and berries poured out onto her fingers.

"I think I know what it had for its last supper." Meara grimaced as she held back the gagging feeling in her throat.

"You need to avoid the throat." Responded the woman next to her. "Start on the chest."

"I guess I need to study bird anatomy. Where have all these people come from?" She eyed the living room.

"Family. The news got out to family in neighboring villages, and they all came over yesterday."

"There aren't enough seats on the plane for all these people."

"Family gets together when there is a death or a serious illness. Sometimes it takes extra flights, traveling over the tundra, or arriving by boat. When there is a death or serious illness, family gets together for support."

Meara was thankful for the distraction of cleaning the birds. It allowed her to not talk much, but she was able to listen. She was cleaning one bird to every two or three that the other women did. "This is a lot of birds. Where did they all come from."

"A group of men went out last evening and gathered them. We will have a lot of people to feed. It is *elriq*, everyone brings something to eat. We share what we have, no matter how small. It is a way of sharing food with our departed loved ones."

"I can't believe that Nora would drink. She has always been so adamant about it. It doesn't make any sense." A voice spoke in a hushed-but-loud whisper from across the room.

Sophie heard it and responded directly. "She never did and never would. It does not make sense."

Meara surprised herself when she spoke up. "When she left the dance, she was so tired she could barely keep her eyes open. Now that I think of it, I can't imagine why or when she would have. She was so tired she just wanted to go to bed." So why had she smelled of alcohol? Meara had more questions than answers.

CHAPTER 10

Chelsey and Verna arrived at the clinic and found Meara in the break room finishing her breakfast. The rings under Meara's eyes made Verna grateful that she had been able to get some sleep the night before. Meara looked like she had not slept in two days.

"Good morning. I am sorry, cama'i. Ready to go?" Meara pushed her breakfast dishes away.

The girls didn't have time to answer.

"Okay. Let's get the final checkoff on clinic opening this morning." Meara stood, gathering her clipboard and pen.

Verna felt a bit cut off as she followed behind. She walked across the clinic as though she was trudging through thick snow. Her legs felt heavy, and everything took effort.

Meara was holding the clipboard, reminding Verna of a drill captain, making sure they could do their job well. Was this push from being tired, or was it from pushing the feelings away? Verna could certainly relate to the latter. Either way, she didn't like being pushed. She wanted—no, needed—to slowly process her feelings.

Verna walked through the pharmacy and punched the number to the lockbox that hid the key for the narcotic cabinet. She yanked the key out, opened the external door, and handed Chelsey the inventory sheet. She dug into her scrub top pocket and pulled out her keychain and unlocked the interior door. Reaching in, she pulled the entire contents out and onto the counter in one grab.

"Morphine, six vials."

Chelsey counted the bottles of morphine. "Check."

Verna reloaded the morphine back and counted. "Valium, five vials."

"Check."

They completed the inventory and signed their names on the bottom. Then moved to the vaccine refrigerator.

"Temp, 42 degrees Fahrenheit."

"For the vaccines to be effective they need to be kept at a constant storage temperature. Checking is an important part of the 'cold chain' that needs to be maintained from the moment the vaccine is made to the time it is given to the patient. An unknown power outage, and you may be giving a vaccine that doesn't work."

Verna didn't really care about any of that, as Meara checked both of them off on their skills sheet.

They moved to the next room and pulled out the charts for the patients scheduled to be seen that day. Verna opened each chart and prepared for each visit. She clipped an encounter form to the top of each one and looked at who needed immunizations. As she finished each folder, she dropped them onto the pile. The thump each one made as she dropped it somehow kept her moving forward.

Meara stood behind them with the clipboard, checking them off as they did each step of preparing the front of the office. They were ready to open the door.

Approaching the door with her keys in front of her, she was surprised to see Lorna and her youngest daughter sitting there. So much for a slow start.

"I didn't see you on the schedule today." She led them into the waiting room.

Lorna sat, pulling her daughter onto what little lap she had. Her stomach and breasts covered all but a couple inches of her knees. "We don't have an appointment. This is an emergency. She has kept us up all night with a headache."

Forcing a polite smile on her face, Verna left the waiting room and added them to the schedule. As she pulled the little girl's chart out, she marveled as to how a little person could have a chart so big. She opened it and noticed that there were a lot of no-shows documented in between emergency visits.

"I am going out to bring in our first unscheduled visit," said Verna.

"I'll be right behind you. Chelsey can man the desk," replied Meara.

Verna wanted to be anywhere else. Anywhere else but in this clinic taking care of people. She realized how little she knew and how scary the job seemed now, especially when she wouldn't have Nora to look forward to seeing most days. She pushed those thoughts aside.

They all tucked into the small exam room.

"Do you remember Meara, my instructor? What are you here for today?" Verna opened her CHAM to the front cover and wrapped the blood pressure cuff around the little arm.

She was now angry with herself. That was dumb to ask. They already told her that in the waiting room. She really had no right to be trying to do this job. She faked her smile to the little girl as she squatted down next to her. "I am giving you a little arm hug."

"Like I said, she has a headache," replied the mother from behind Verna.

"How long has it been going on?" Verna felt caught in her stupidity. She kept looking at the little girl instead of the mother as she counted respirations and waited for an answer.

She moved her eyes to the right front cover of the CHAM and decided that she was not a "child that may be very sick" and continued down the normal line of questioning.

"Since this morning at one. She woke up with it," replied Lorna just as the little girl started to respond.

Verna pulled out a picture with a progressive line of faces ranging from grimace to a big smile. "How bad is the pain? Can you point to the picture that feels like your pain?"

The little girl started to move her finger toward the smiley end of the card then stopped and looked up at her mother.

Verna followed with her eyes to see Lorna with a pointed gaze toward the grimacing face.

The little girl's finger followed.

"What does it feel like?"

The little girl shrugged her shoulders in response.

"Has it changed in any way since it began?" Verna worked her way down the history.

"She is dropping things. When she first woke up, her face was drooping. She has been waking up crying through the night saying it is the worst headache she's ever had," said the mother.

"I am now looking in the index for headache." As she finished the past medical history, she flipped the heavy, bulky CHAM over to search the index for "headache." She then flipped the massive book back to find the page for "other headache."

Lorna reached over and flipped the lights off. "I told you she has a headache; don't you know you should turn the lights off?"

Verna surprised herself with how angry she was starting to feel. How was she supposed to save somebody's life when she was so slow using this book? She progressed through a detailed neurological exam, looking at the book then testing the patient and back and forth. By the time she was done, the little girl was crying.

"She has the worst headache of her life," said Lorna. "Will you leave her alone?"

"I have to follow the exam. I am sorry it takes me so long." Verna turned to Meara. "The exam is normal. Now, I need to find my assessment."

Meara smiled at her and nodded.

Verna moved to the assessment chart for headache and found herself confused. "Okay, the worst headache ever would fall under 'Headache, possible bleeding in the brain,' but she doesn't fit the exam for this. The worst headache would fit there or 'other headache.' Either way, I need to call the doctor."

They got up and moved over to the charting room. Verna faxed her encounter form before she called doctor.

"Before you call, review her chart and see if she has been here for this before. I know her mother said no, but let's take a few minutes to review," said Meara.

Verna flipped through, scanning the many pages of the chart. "No, she has come in for a lot of different problems. But not a headache."

She got on the phone and reviewed her encounter with the doctor. "He says he felt it was best to bring her in for evaluation. Even though she looks good right now, she may need a CT scan."

"Great job with her. That was a tricky case. She didn't look that bad, but you can't prove she doesn't have a headache. Traveling was the safe thing to do."

"I know that is the case. This one seemed extra hard because it just didn't feel right. But, I know we aren't supposed to just rely on feeling," said Verna.

"That is true to a point. You will develop a gut instinct with time. And, if your gut is telling you to be cautious, listen and listen well. Move in and double-check your findings if you need to. As time goes on and you become stronger in your skills, the doctors will trust your gut more. I can say from my own experience that the only times I have gone wrong have been when I had gut feelings that I didn't listen to," said Meara.

Verna's mind left the clinic for a moment. Well, so much for her gut sense. It certainly failed her with Jim. "I wish I could trust that sense. It would make me feel safer when you aren't here to work with us, especially now that Nora is gone. She was the one that held everything together here. I can't fill her shoes. I could work by her shoes but not in them."

Meara's hand landed on her shoulder. Verna was relieved instead of irritated. It was all the support she needed right then to not break into tears, but it didn't do anything to give her confidence in her judgement.

* * *

After Verna and Chelsey left for lunch, Meara let out a sigh as she sank into the chair in front of the computer. She was exhausted; the last two nights were piling up on her.

They had barely been able to get Lorna off on the noon flight. What would the doctors find when Lorna and her daughter arrived in Agushak? Nora had confessed to Meara she thought that Lorna was the recent supplier of alcohol. And there did happen to be the coincidence that the last time Lorna returned from town was the night of the dance.

"I need a pick-me-up." She moved back to the kitchen, foraged through her tote, and pulled out a bag of coffee.

Trust your gut feeling. She went back to her conversation earlier with Verna. She wished she could trust her gut in her personal life like she could at work. She measured out the coffee and put it in the filter.

Chelsey and Verna were doing so well. They handled their initiation into a true emergency like professionals. She needed to find some time to stop and talk to them about what they were feeling. She'd blown it. By keeping busy in order to cope, she hadn't reached out to find out how they were feeling.

What was it about her? Why did she not trust her gut for so long with Rey? Nice guy. Leader in the community. He was always helping people out. And did she trust him? Nope.

She sat back, smelling the coffee brew. Closing her eyes, she smiled. But she didn't chase him away with being so evasive. That was a good sign.

She sank further into the chair as she relaxed and found it a relief to move her thoughts to something more pleasant than the events of the night before and the grief that they were all processing now. That kiss was amazing. She felt like she was going to melt away.

She slammed the arm of the chair next to her with her fist. And, then she ruined the moment. Why was she such an idiot?

She got up and rinsed out her mug, preparing it for the cup of coffee she was so ready for. "I am not waiting any longer." She poured herself a cup then held the cup under her nose. The smell seemed to jump right to her brain, and she remembered the labs that she had sent out yesterday. She put the lid on her coffee cup and walked back to the office. Punching in her password, she pulled up the screen of labs to be reviewed.

"Mmm, normal CBC. She hadn't bled from trauma." She clicked another button opening up to the electrolytes. Slight elevation in potassium. That could have been from the blood draw or the tissue damage from the hypothermia."

She clicked again. She stiffened back in her chair, and her forehead furrowed. Her eyes scanned down the screen in front of her, and then she had to go back and review it again. She shook her head and looked back a third time, reading out loud the numbers that made absolutely no sense to her.

She clicked back into Nora's chart and reviewed her medication list and flipped through the pages looking to see if there had ever been a prescription there. "No prescriptions, hardly any prescriptions for anything ever for her."

She returned again to the lab screen showing the toxicology report.

Blood alcohol, 0.0. Benzodiazepines, 1000 milligrams.

She reached for the phone. This doesn't add up. She needed to reach Rey.

Nora needed an autopsy.

* * *

In the afternoon, Angus called in on the radio that he was bringing in two patients for medical clearance. Chelsey went to open the back door when she saw him pull up. He had both handcuffed on either side in the back seat of his truck. She could see the truck rocking from the passengers attempting to wrestle away. He walked to the nearest side and pulled out the same man as yesterday.

Meara passed by Chelsey and did a double take when she saw the first occupant. "Cama'i, Lawrence. We get to see you two days in a row."

"Apparently so," replied Angus. "His buddy said he had a couple bottles left when I pulled him in yesterday. They decided to share it today. It was all fun and games until they started fighting. Neighbors heard some gunshots going off, and I drove up to find Norman shooting into the air and making sure Lawrence knew what it was to be a war hero."

Chelsey looked up at Angus and smiled. "Well, let's get him back. What do you know about how much he drank today?"

"There were a couple of bottles of Jim Beam between them. One was just about empty. The other is in my truck. That one is going to disappear when I get these two settled so we don't have to meet here again tomorrow over their leftovers." He smiled down at Chelsey then shook his head. "Unfortunately, it isn't just these two. There are a few others I have noticed around town drinking from bags. The others just haven't started causing trouble yet, and I can't haul them all in."

"Any idea who is bringing it in?" Verna asked Angus.

"No, it is all the same whiskey, but still no idea who is bringing it. There have been a lot of people from outside the village because of the funeral, but this started before their arrival. And, they are all staying at Sophie's. She would never tolerate any alcohol there."

Chelsey could feel Meara watching her as she got the blood pressure. Lawrence was pretty aggressive with her but not nearly as much as he had been with Meara. And he kept his eyes on Meara like they were boring a hole through her.

"Vitals are all stable. He is able to walk," she reported to Meara. She then spoke a bit of Yupik to him.

He indicated that he didn't intend to answer by suddenly kicking his left foot out.

Chelsey had no time to react, but Angus grabbed the foot and swung it across the stretcher, handcuffing it to the end of the stretcher.

Lawrence looked startled to find himself sitting fully on the exam table now.

Chelsey jumped back in a delayed reaction. "Thank you, Angus." She mumbled some words to Lawrence in Yupik. He did not react at all.

Meara moved forward toward the stretcher. "What did you say to him?"

"That I didn't want to be here doing this to him any more than he wanted to be here. And to be kind."

"Let's see if it works. So, work through the CHAM as much as you safely can do."

Walking over to the cabinet, Chelsey grabbed a monitor and a lancet to poke his finger. "I need to get a blood sugar.

You will feel a little poke." She grabbed a finger from the cuffed hands and poked as quickly as she could, then gathered the droplet onto the little unit.

"148. I can't get reflexes with the way that he is behaving."

"He will be right next door in the cell. We can go over and get another set of vitals in an hour. Angus will let us know if he changes."

Chelsey looked at Angus with a wan smile. "I owe you for that one. I could have been hurt. I need to become more aware of where I am standing with drunk people."

"Unfortunately, it is a skill you will definitely learn on the job."

"I hadn't thought of that before." There were so many things that she hadn't considered when she applied for the job. She definitely had not thought of drunks. How could she have been so naive to think that she would be taking care of sick and grateful people? And back home, she didn't even have a VPSO to help keep her safe. Maybe becoming a health aide wasn't such a good idea. And, how could she not realize that not everyone would live?

* * *

Meara held the door open for Angus to direct Lawrence back to the VPSO station. Norman was still sitting in the back seat of the running truck. She could barely make out his figure through the darkened glass.

She took advantage of the moment to grab the phone. She punched the well-known numbers in quickly, waited three rings again, and there was the message. "You have reached the desk of Lieutenant Torrenson. I am unable to answer the phone. Please leave a message."

She hung up. There was no sense in leaving a message when she had already left two and hadn't heard back. Was he alright? This wasn't like him.

She went back, reviewed Chelsey's encounter sheet, and signed it off after listening to her report to the doctor.

At that point, Angus was coming back in the door with Norman. His appearance set her aback. He slurred out in Yupik. His normally slow-paced speech was even slower. He looked up at her and raised his hand to his eyebrows in a salute.

Meara was washed in concern about her elder friend. She never would have expected him to drink. There seemed to be a theme this week of nondrinkers drinking around here right now. "What did he say?"

"He was talking about seeing a Japanese fighter plane off the coast. Then he saluted you, Major Marston." Angus smiled.

"Who is Major Marston?" Meara raised her eyebrows quizzically. She knew she had heard that name before.

"He was the organizer of the Alaska Territorial Guard. Norman was in the Territorial Guard during World War II. He has some good stories to tell about it. You need to get him to tell you some."

Norman gave her a big smile.

"Well, this isn't good. He knows me, and if he thinks that I am Major Marston, he is in bad shape. Do you know any more of what he was doing this afternoon?"

Verna came in the room. "Chelsey told me it was my turn."

Meara gave her a worried look as she quickly reviewed what was known about Norman this afternoon.

Verna opened her CHAM and gathered the vitals quickly. "Vital signs, blood sugar, and hemoglobin are all normal. He is not oriented to place, time, or person obviously." She winked at Meara. "He is an elder with altered state of consciousness. I need to do a head-to-toe examination to rule out a head injury or any other injury."

She put on gloves and spoke in Yupik to Norman. She searched his head for cuts and soft squishy collections of blood under the skin. There were none. She then looked at his pupils, which were reactive, and made him smile, show his teeth, and stick out his tongue.

He put his hands to his ears to make them bigger as he made a face and stuck out his tongue.

Verna laughed. "It is good to see he hasn't lost his sense of humor and he can follow command." She worked her way down his spine, feeling and looking for a response to pain. When she got to his back and lifted his shirt, she found a small wound about a half-inch long. The blood was hidden in his dark shirt. "Meara, look at this." She briefly talked to Norman.

He shook his head and shrugged his shoulders.

"He doesn't seem to know how he got it."

"We need to see how deep it is." Meara put on her gloves. She opened the wound and probed it with the swab. Deep inside, she could see the white glistening fascia that covered the muscles over the ribs. "Look there, we need to move it around to make sure we didn't miss it going through into the rib cage and lungs. Listen to his lung sounds carefully. Tell me what you hear."

Verna put her stethoscope on his chest and worked her way methodically around listening to the lung sounds. She was frustrated that Meara was asking her to make an assessment right now. Why would Meara ask her? She didn't know what she was doing. If she screwed up, Meara would realize that in spite of all her work, Verna really didn't know anything.

She cautiously put her stethoscope down. "I think they are all clear and present."

Norman declared that he was not still present by giving Verna a sharp salute that was somewhat dulled.

To Verna's relief, Meara listened carefully as well. "Full breath sounds. Okay, follow the intoxication through to the end of that. Then follow the course of treatment for the wound."

"Well, he assessed with acute intoxication and puncture wound, and I will need to call the doctor for further advice. Let me look up the wound treatment." She turned to Norman. "Do you know how you got this wound?"

He growled back. "Damn Japs."

Meara shook her head. "I don't think we are going to find out what happened today. I know he was in the Territorial Guard, but I don't know much more. Did the Japanese ever attack here? Would Norman have fought them on the ground?"

"No, not here. The Japanese captured Attu and Kiska," said Verna. "I have heard some of his stories, but not this one. Norman ran dogsleds with supplies during most of his time in the army. He once told me that he and his team were all over Alaska delivering supplies, people, and helping to build caches." She turned and looked at Norman's glazed eyes. "Right, Norman?"

This time, she met his salute with one of her own. When she did this, he settled back into the stretcher and relaxed as if that salute had just put him at ease.

The two women rolled him on his side.

"Go ahead and call your report in," said Meara. "I will stay here with him."

Verna faxed the encounter form into the doctor. She repeated her orders back into the phone. "Okay, we will monitor him for a few hours and call back. Chest x-ray before we sew the wound. Complete blood count and metabolic panel to go in on the next flight. Thank you, we will call you back in a few hours."

"Let's get some pictures of this and practice your medical photography while we are watching him. Show me how you would do this."

Verna took the camera and put a measuring tape next to the wound and documented the length, width, and depth. Then she uploaded it onto the AFHCAN cart for his medical record.

"Hello, ladies, it's me," came Angus's voice from the hallway. "How is my friend?"

"Well, he has more of a problem than his drinking. He has a stab wound on his back. Not deep. He told us the Japs did it," said Meara. "We need to file a report on that wound. And, we will be keeping him for a while to watch him."

Angus rolled his head to the ceiling. "I wouldn't be surprised if it was Lawrence. He has done that before when he has hit the bag." He lifted the shirt, looking at the hole in it, looked at the wound, then walked over and picked up the jacket and poked a gloved finger through the hole in the coat to match. "And this would indicate that it happened while he was outside. This might keep Lawrence out of the bottle for a while after I complete my reports."

Meara looked at him. "Speaking of reports and supervisors, is there anything that is going on that would affect Rey? I have been trying to reach him all afternoon."

"No, but I will let him know you are looking for him."

Verna wondered why Meara was so eager to reach Rey. It appeared from this conversation that she had been trying to reach him prior to Norm's arrival. And, it was clear that it wasn't personal.

CHAPTER 11

Verna was sitting at the desk filing the encounter forms from the day before that had already been sent to the hub village doctor and had been responded to yesterday. She and Chelsey were alternating sitting at the front desk as the other one went back with Meara to see a patient; in the meantime, she was watching over Norman. She heard the door open, and when she looked up, there was Jim.

Her heart felt like it came to a complete stop when he moved to the counter in front of him. The game that they had been playing to get him to admit what he had done instead of directly confronting him was taking a toll on her. She couldn't understand how he could have done this to them. Their ice fishing adventure had not brought them any satisfaction of getting a confession from him. That was so painful. She really did not have any worthwhile gut instinct.

However, she also could find the humor in the discomfort that he was feeling. He moved up to the counter with the box of supplies in his hands to be delivered to the clinic. She sought his eyes as she took it from him. He looked at the clipboard, the box, his watch, anywhere but at her.

Was that pain that she saw in those wandering eyes? His face was stiff. His hand was finely shaking as he handed her the box. Or, was it a need to get far away from her?

"Good morning. How are you?" he mumbled quietly.

"Good morning. I am alright. Tired." She politely and curtly responded.

"It was fun fishing the other night. How's Chelsey?"

Verna's heart sank. She should have figured. He wanted to see Chelsey. He never would have wanted her over Chelsey. Part of her missed his arms around her so much it hurt. She missed laughing at his storytelling when he would come over in the evening. They would tell each other their stories of growing up. His life was so different from hers. In spite of that difference, she had never thought that his values would have been so different from hers with this whole scenario though.

She had thought they were such a good match. She was sure that he would have been loyal and faithful to his partner, especially after the story that he had shared with her about growing up with a single mother. His mother raised him alone after his father disappeared when she was pregnant with him. She had experienced the same with Joe, except she would see Joe when he would return to her village for the brief few weeks when the salmon ran in the summer. They would set up their fish camp with her grandparents, and her father would come back to help. She was grateful for having a grandfather that was always there and raised her like his own daughter. She had Joe, too. He was a father but also like a brother, because his parents had stepped in to become her own. She had consistent men in her life. Maybe that lack was what tripped Jim up?

Maybe he didn't understand the commitment of a long-term relationship because he has never seen it. And, of course he would want Chelsey. She was prettier, more confident, more outgoing compared to Verna's shy nature. She understood why she would not be the preferred girl.

She knew that is what she wanted since she met Jim. She wanted the relationship that her two "parents" had. Here, they were almost seventy, having been together since they were in their teens. Together, they had raised children and grandchildren and now were also watching great-grandchildren come into the world. She watched them enjoying their day-to-day subsistence lifestyle here on the tundra.

She loved the image of them helping each other into their skiff in the late summer and turning up the river among the belugas also swimming in that direction. Mom would pick out her prettiest qaspaq and would tie a matching scarf onto her head to hold back her hair.

Each time they would prepare to go out, she always told Verna, "It is always important to honor God by wearing the prettiest qaspaq for berry picking. You need to thank him for all the beautiful abundance of berries that we will be picking." The two would head upriver and come back at the end of the day with baskets overflowing with salmon berries, and later once the frosts were hitting, they would return with cranberries.

And here she sat, fully and completely in love with a cheater. He was so unlike her grandfather. She doubted she was going to feel any better when he finally owned up to this. Was this whole crazy plan even worth going through the waiting? Well, this was the first time she was doing something with her sister and her father. It wasn't how she was counting on growing their bond, but it did feel good to be getting closer. She needed to play her part.

She made herself look right at him and held his gaze. "Tonight, we will be steaming at my parents. We would like you to come. I have told my father all about you, and he wants to meet you. Any chance you will be staying here after the last afternoon flight?"

"Yes, I am staying, and yes again, I would like that." For the first time, he looked at her.

"Seven at my parents'." She smiled just before he stopped avoiding her eyes. Her heart sank once more when she looked into his blue eyes without him avoiding hers.

Tenderness, love? Her gut sense was horrible. How could he feel that for her when he clearly wanted to be with Chelsey? She watched him as he walked out the clinic door.

* * *

Meara tucked herself into the pharmacy and punched the phone number again. This time after it rang a bit, she heard his calm and professional life on the other line. Her heart raced, and the giddy feeling rushed to her head upon hearing his voice. Now that she had given in, she really looked forward to hearing his voice. Even the business at hand didn't damper that feeling. "Hi, Rey, I am so sorry we didn't get to say goodbye yesterday."

"I am, too. I tried to stop by, but things were too busy at the clinic. I needed to get back here and get all the paperwork completed and to check on the troopers here at the station. How are you?"

"I miss your company." She still hated to admit that he had worked his way into her heart.

"I miss you, too. I forgot when you told me you would be coming back here. And, I heard you were looking for me from Angus."

"Another week. Thank you for all of your help with Nora. You did fantastic. I was so grateful for having people that knew CPR. We wouldn't have done as well without you. Even though we didn't succeed."

"All in a day's work," he responded.

"So, I have been trying to reach you because I am confused. I got some labs back this morning. They make no sense. You said you found her coat and a bottle of whiskey, right?" She pulled the labs up in front of her again as if looking at them over and over would create an explanation.

"Yes, the bottle of whiskey was just a few feet away from where her parka was found."

"That's what I remember you saying. And, I clearly remember the smell of alcohol when she was brought into the clinic." She tapped her pen against the desk in front of her.

"Without a doubt, she was schnockered."

"That is the problem. No, she wasn't schnockered," she replied back.

"What?"

"Her blood alcohol was negative. None present, not even a drop. And when I talk to people that knew her, they all say she didn't drink. So, negative alcohol makes total sense. However, to add to the confusion, she had an extraordinary level of benzodiazepines in her blood."

The phone line remained silent as the clock on the wall counted its way across the pause with the ticking sound. Meara waited, thinking that he needed the time to get his thoughts together about how he was going to defend Nora.

"I am going to have to reopen the case. Will you do me a favor? It is important for the investigation that you do not mention this to anyone in town, including Angus. And please make sure to talk only to me about it, if you hear anything else. I need your help to keep this information from getting around. I am also Angus's supervisor, and I need to make sure he processes the information correctly. Can you do that?"

Meara thought she heard a shift in his voice. The warmth seemed to change to a stiffness. "Okay, I understand. I am going to be heading over to visit Sophie for a while. Can I call you later?"

"Sure, looking forward to it," he responded.

Meara hung up the phone and picked up the radio and the beeper so she could be alerted for a call. She made short time of pulling on her snow gear, feeling eager to get out of the clinic, and stepped out into the blustering evening to do her last piece of work before going to Sophie's.

* * *

She plodded through the powdery snow in order to reach her destination. Stepping off the road toward the right instead of turning left as she normally did to go to Sophie's was enough to arouse a loud barking alarm. So much for a quiet approach. The sled dogs were all straining at their leads to get to her as she walked up the trodden path to the front door. She was stomping off her boots in the tidy and orderly entry and had just sat on the bench preparing to remove them when the door opened.

Norman stood there looking much more like the Norman that she had come to know.

"Cama'i. Come on in." The old man wore a big, worn-out red flannel shirt and a pair of long underwear with a pair of sealskin slippers on his feet. "Give me a minute to get my pants on." He shuffled off, a bit more hunched over than his normal gait.

Meara stepped inside and was immediately impressed with how orderly the room was. The kitchen was simple but clean. The kitchen table with chairs for two was barren except a couple of pieces of mail. The walls before the kitchen had black-and-white pictures of a young native boy with the badge of the Territorial Guard on his shoulder stiffly standing with a rifle in one hand next to a slight, young native girl with big brown eyes. The look on his face as he regarded her in the picture was certainly not stiff.

There was another picture of the young man standing with his dogsled with a man in an army uniform standing next to him. There were army duffel bags and ammo boxes loaded on the sled. The patch was sewn on his jacket exactly where he wore it now.

The last picture was the girl kneeling in the snow with an army rifle, taking aim at something in the distance. Her arm also bore the same blue patch with the Big Dipper on it.

"Those beautiful eyes were pretty sharp," came Norman's voice as he shuffled back to where she was standing. "There were very few that could outshoot her when it came down to accuracy. Man or woman."

"Was she in the army as a soldier?"

"She was in the guard as a volunteer soldier like me. She was fifteen in that picture. And she shot that well with the guns that the army provided us with. They were antiquated then. The only rifles that were given to Muktuk were leftovers from World War I. Those rifles couldn't hit a whale in close distance, but we drilled enough to become sharpshooters even with those old guns."

"Fifteen and a woman? During World War II? And she was allowed to sign up to be something other than a nurse?"

"The army wasn't too damned picky when they were recruiting us. I know recruits that were twelve when they enlisted. And, the best sharpshooter in the guard was a woman. She was up near Kotzebue. Laura Beltz Wright could shoot an impressive ninety-eight percent bullseye. She outshot all of the men. Now, my girl was not far behind. If you were her target, she wasn't going to miss you. Those eyes narrowed right in on you if she wanted you." Norman laughed in an easy way Meara hadn't seen from him before. "She narrowed right in on me for sure, and I don't regret for a moment being her target."

Meara smiled. "She picked you out?"

Norman gave her a sheepish smile. "You think I was always this old and ugly?"

Meara laughed. "Oh no. It is always the pretty boys that grow to be crochety old men. So, who is this?" She said pointing at the man in uniform with the dogsled.

"That was Major Marston. He was our leader. He had to pull things together really quick up here after Japan started invading islands and then bombed Dutch Harbor. The American military thought Alaska had no military value before then, so they never stationed anyone here, even though they had been warned that this was strategic territory. They changed their minds fast and sent him here in 1942. They had no military bases, and he had the idea to recruit Alaska Natives to protect the territory."

"So, where were your bases? Where did they send you to bootcamp?"

"You sure like to think about it all set up and pretty, don't you? We recruited by going from village to village by dogsled. And Muktuk there, came right along. I was a young man, but I had been training and running my dogs for quite a while at that time. I ended up taking him on a long recruiting run along the coast here and all the way to Kotzebue. The army had no provisions for us. We mostly trained where we were staying, and we supplied our own food. We all signed volunteer decrees promising our services."

"You were all unpaid volunteers? Completely?"

"You seem so surprised. What would you do to defend your home? We even provided the food for some of the food caches," countered the growly voice.

Meara chose not to say that the rest of the US military didn't serve unpaid. She changed the subject instead.

"What do you remember about yesterday afternoon? It seemed as if you were still volunteering," she said slyly. "Do I look that much like Major Marston?"

"Hell no. Why do you say that?"

"You were saluting me as him this afternoon ," she smiled. "What was the last thing you remember?"

"Oh no." He turned back towards her. "Do you want to go for a walk?"

"Alright, Sophie doesn't have a specific time to expect me. I have time."

"I think I know what I was doing." He slipped on his snow pants.

* * *

The walk to the embankment went much faster than Meara expected. The shuffle disappeared from the old man's steps as they walked along the coastline behind the lines of homes. There, in the opening where the bluff of the sea came to a clearing before town was a packed-down area with footsteps in all directions.

"Thought so," said Norman. "I really should never drink. And I normally don't, but Nora's death threw me so badly. She was like a daughter to me. Sophie raised her right across the street from us. My wife and I always made sure that we helped where we could."

He stood next to a lineup of logs. "One of the reasons I don't drink is that I go right back to my army time. And then I do crazy things. Do you know what these are?"

"Looks like a bunch of driftwood put together." Driftwood was set apart in groups every ten feet. A short piece lay on the ground parallel to the shore. A longer piece lay across it pointing toward the air.

"That," he bowed as if he was proud of his creation, "is antiaircraft artillery."

"Oh, really," Meara responded with confusion. "I am not quite getting this. Were you and Lawrence out here playing a game of army?"

"Territorial Guard," he corrected. "I have a tendency to come down here and reenact the war when I drink. Or so I have been told. Apparently, I was trying to scare the Japs off."

"Did you have antiaircraft artillery here during the war?"

"Hell no. Remember, they were short on time and supplies up here by the time we got pulled into the game. But they needed us. So, we used a little ingenuity."

"And that was?"

"This. From above, it looked like antiaircraft artillery. We hoped it would scare them off." He inspected his handiwork. "I was a bit sloppy this afternoon. I never would have produced anything this shabby back then." He stooped forward to pick something up.

Meara noticed the shiny object in the snow. "Hey, don't touch that. We need to give that to Angus. Does this spark any memories?" she eyed the hole in his parka.

"No, unfortunately, I cannot say I remember that."

Meara pulled a tissue out of her pocket and picked up the knife. "I think that Angus should have this. I will run it to him before we head back to your place."

"I am heading back to my place now. And, I am planning to steam tonight."

Meara hesitated before turning back toward the VPSO building. But it was clear that he had come back out of his adventure. "Don't steam long and make sure you drink water! You had quite the bender there."

He saluted her in return and marched down the street.

* * *

Was that the ptarmigan? Meara knocked and peeked her head into Sophie's doorway and was greeted by the smell of spruce intermingled with chicken. She followed her nose through the groups of people scattered in the crowded house to the kitchen, where she found the counters stacked with food. She was grateful that Verna had let her know that she should bring some kind of contribution with her as she placed her meager bag of baby carrots on the counter. It was what she had.

There were two steaming pots on the stove filled with ptarmigan, vegetables, and a green flat vegetable she could not identify. One back wall was lined with cases of soda, and there were giant pitchers of orange drink on the counter. The counter was filled to overflowing with a variety of dishes in casserole containers.

She found Sophie sitting at the counter with a granddaughter in her lap. She and little Nena, Nora's six-year-old, were wearing matching bright blue qaspaqs with berries on them. They sat atop a stool that had Sophie positioned to invite people for food, oversee the people flowing in and out of the house, and serve as traffic control to the back bedroom where Nora lay in wake. Her face looked drawn. Her body was moving in a more rigid way than Meara had seen in the past.

Meara was amazed at how long Sophie had stayed so strong. "Cama'i, Sophie. Nena, you look so beautiful with your grandmother in your matching qaspaqs." She rose from squatting to talk to Nena at her level. "Sophie, is there anything that I can do for you?"

"Yes, you can do something for me. You can eat. I am sorry I can't serve you." She glanced down at Nena. "Make sure you try the whitefish with seal oil and some *agutuk*."

Sophie directed her toward the counter overflowing with food. Meara politely moved over to the full counter. She had been advised that if food was offered, it was very bad manners to turn it down. Seal oil? Visions of cute little seals danced in front of her. She stalled on that taste by serving herself a small bowl of the ptarmigan stew. She had to taste the product of her efforts.

Looking around the room, she tried to find a place where she could sit back and observe and not feel quite so awkward. She found an empty chair at the wall toward the back of the kitchen next to an elderly, round-faced woman with deeply etched smile lines surrounding dark eyes that were surprisingly bright and clear. Meara smiled at her as she sat next to her.

The elderly woman looked up and gave her a grin showing her punctuated teeth. "Cama'i."

"Cama'i." Meara fed herself the first spoon of ptarmigan soup. Mmm, this was good. Like chicken with a hint of pine. Was the pine taste there, or was she imagining it after her experience of cleaning the birds? The green pieces in the soup were salty and had a bit of slippery feel to them, but the taste was not bad. She didn't dare ask what it was.

The elderly woman smiled more at Meara as she finished the bowl of soup with gusto. She had no idea how hungry she actually was when she arrived. The elderly woman directed Meara back to the countertop full of food with a nod of her head and a wave.

Meara scooped *agutuk*—Eskimo ice cream—onto her plate. She knew from conversation that this was a blend of berries and fat. Traditionally, it was made of dried berries in the winter mixed with seal lard. The modern way of making it used frozen berries and Crisco with a small amount of sugar added. She added some salmon to her plate. She was craving its wonderful tasty, smoky smell. Then she arrived at the chunks of uncooked whitefish, hoping she could pick up this arctic sushi and move past the seal oil. *I can't eat a seal,* in spite of how open and experimental she wanted to be. She suppressed a sigh of relief as she stepped by it without Sophie noticing that she had not taken any.

Then she felt she was being approached from behind. She turned and looked down as the tiny elderly woman came up next to her, picked up the jar of seal oil, and poured it onto the uncooked fish on Meara's plate. Her heart sank as the oil moved toward the salmon she was looking forward to. The elderly woman put the seal oil down, looked up at Meara, and patted her belly with a big grin.

"*Quyana.*" Meara smiled down at the considerate elder and then returned to sit next to her.

She took a deep breath and chuckled a little at herself as she prepared to sample some of the new foods. The berries were small and salmon colored, juicy and tart with a sharp, crisp taste a bit like a raspberry but a little more tart. Meara could smell the commercial lard of Crisco. She would never eat that at home. Slipping a spoonful in her mouth, she appreciated the berries and the creamy blend of fat and sweetness. She could see why fat was so desired here. She was actually craving it, too, in this cold weather. The *agutuk* gave Meara a warm and content feeling.

The whitefish glistened at her as if it were taunting her. How could she make this disappear?

She turned and saw the elderly woman smiling attentively at her as she watched her eat her food. She nodded and pointed at the fish and looked up again smiling and inviting her to eat it.

The elderly woman had taken on the duty of making sure she ate the seal oil. There was no escaping. She felt a little trapped in her cultural foray. She stabbed the smallest piece she could find and put it in her mouth.

The elderly's big smile grew even bigger as she nodded and showed the pleasure in Meara's mouthful.

"This is good," Meara forced a smile. The oil had an unfamiliar and awkwardly bitter taste to it. The taste seemed to spread slowly and very solidly. She chewed carefully and moved the fish to the back of her mouth and swallowed.

I did it! She congratulated herself for getting it into her mouth. She smiled down at her coach and patted her belly in feigned satisfaction.

The old woman continued her smile, nodding her head to direct her to eat more. She spoke something in Yupik to Sophie.

Sophie called from across the kitchen.

"She only speaks Yupik. But she is so happy that you are trying her seal oil. She takes great pride in the way she renders it the traditional way. And she is so honored that you like it. She took that from her supply to honor Nora."

Meara forced a smile on her face and tried to hide the feeling in her throat. She realized that she was not going to get out of this. Should she eat it quickly and get it over with, or should she take it slow and manage to get it down? Poor cute seal. Her thoughts went to the cute little harbor seals she would see in the bay when she was a little girl on vacation in Maine. She needed to move past the image in her head.

She looked at the elderly woman, smiled a big smile, stabbed another piece, and put it in her mouth. She dutifully chewed while she made sure she kept a big, satisfied smile on her face.

As she chewed, she took in the rest of the room. People were coming in steadily. There were couples, families, and individuals going back to where Nora lay in a steady flow.

Then Zach came out of the room. He walked across the room and went over to a few men toward the back. His already stiff body seemed to become more erect and tense, and his face flashed a scowl after they exchanged words.

Meara observed his anger and found her own rising inside of her. She was so sure that he had something to do with Nora's death. How could it be proved to bring Nora justice?

Meara looked up and realized that the two elder dancers from the other night were now sitting at the table. Just as she finished eating, she noticed that someone had moved away from the table, leaving an open chair next to them. She could not resist the chance to get to know them and to learn more about their history. Standing, she nodded a thank you to Grace, disposed of her plate, and went over to claim the empty seat.

The two elderly women were chatting in Yupik when she sat. "Cama'i, do you speak English?"

The two smiled and responded with synchronized nods.

"I loved watching you dance the other night, and I have so many questions that I would have asked Nora. Would you mind teaching me?"

The two women nodded slowly, making Meara wonder how receptive they would be.

"The dance that you did. It looked like it was about mosquitoes. What were the words?"

Maryann smiled a sheepish grin. "The *egturyaq*, mosquito, dance?" She looked at her friend. "You want the translation?"

Agnes piped up, speaking with emphasis, "These damn mosquitoes always bothering us when we get to do things."

The smile lines in Maryann's wrinkled face deepened, and suddenly a laughter erupted that engulfed her entire small figure. Her laughter instantly caught Agnes.

Meara found herself laughing deeper than she had in years. Their laughter echoed across the house.

"Well, that was to the point!" Meara wiped tears away from laughing so hard. The images of their antics added to her laughter. As she looked around the room, she realized people at the other side had caught the contagion after watching Maryann's antics.

"Most of our dances are songs about nature around us," added Maryann.

"I have been told that the missionaries made the dance stop. How long ago was that?"

The smile on Agnes's face faded with that question. "The missionaries really started to come to our villages in the mid-1800s. They said that the dance was a heathen thing and we should not do it. And, so for many years the people of our villages stopped."

"But, you weren't around then. How did you learn? If it was stopped so long ago."

Maryann spoke up, "When we were babies, the 1918 epidemic came through our villages killing many of our elders. With their death, we lost a lot of who we are. We lost our lessons of our ancestors. It was then that we realized that we needed to learn as much as we could from the elders that were left. Our dance wasn't heathen, it was our stories. Our history. The stories teach us and our children about our past, our values, and how to survive."

Agnes added, "That was when we started learning what we could from the elders that survived the epidemic. And now we also look for videos that were taken in the past so we can remember more. Disney even filmed in 1953 in Hooper Bay ."

"We would hear the dance in the night when we were little children, hidden from the missionaries and the law," added Maryann. "As we got older, we learned, too. There were little groups in each village that refused to give up traditions and dance after the flu. One priest in Hooper Bay wrote a letter back to his superiors in the church that said these villagers were 'too sophisticated' because they told their priest that they would not give up their culture."

Meara chuckled, "Sophisticated? That is a funny word for that. It makes me think you all sat around sipping tea with your little finger held out."

The two elders chuckled back in return.

"The men would keep the culture going in the *qasgiq* , the men's community hall. This big sod house was where the men would teach each other old customs, like how to build a *qayaq* or *umiak*, dance *yuraq*, and how to stay strong in the winter with the sports that are competeted in what is now the Native Youth Olympics."

"How did you two start preserving dance?"

"My brother pushed me to work to bring it back and to share it with our grandchildren in the family," replied Maryann.

"Eventually, priests from other churches came and encouraged us to dance. The Catholic church now even allows the dance in the church. One Jesuit priest, Father Renee Astrue, really encouraged dancing and a revival of our culture," added Agnes.

"Our family made a commitment to preserving our culture. My husband, Teddy, had a gift that helped. He had a memory where he never forgot a song or a dance once he heard it. That was a big help.

"For a long time, many of our young people were taught to be ashamed of our culture in the missionary schools. But, that has changed. Now, the schools teach Yupik language and dance. Our children are being taught to be proud in who we are."

"Wow," Meara absorbed the information. "You are truly rescuers of your culture. I am sure that some of the knowledge of the past, like medicinal plants or behavior of animals, could help us today."

Looking around the table she noticed that there were many others trying to move closer to the elder women. She caught herself yawning. "I want to stay and talk so much more with you, but I have an early morning at work. Thank you for teaching me and for the laughs."

As she pushed away from the table, her mind was spinning thinking of how many pieces of history and even science were lost because of one culture attempting to "save" another. She thought back to her own Celtic origins and realized how little she knew. *Would I have had the courage to stand up for my cultural identity and have the commitment to do the same if I were in their shoes?* She doubted her own courage.

CHAPTER 12

Meara walked down the street and into the clinic through the arctic entry. She kicked the snow off her boots and put them under the bench. She unzipped her jacket, and instantly the smell of the oil filled the room. The seal oil had left a funny taste on her tongue and lips since she ate at Nora's. Was it all in her head just because she knew she had just eaten seal?

Before she left Sophie's, she had looked for another food that might overcome the taste. But the stubborn taste would not go away. Even pie and cake did nothing.

She stumbled to the break room in exhaustion. But when she saw her backpack, she nearly dove to dig out the packet of cinnamon gum. She chewed it as she stripped off her clothes and put on a set of sweats. She sat down and sniffed.

There was a funny smell in the air around her. The seal oil seemed to be leaking out her pores. She must lack some enzyme to allow her to digest it. She went to the bathroom and, removing her sweats quickly before they absorbed the smell, took a hot and soapy shower in an attempt to eliminate the smell from her pores. She redressed, brushed her teeth, and moved back to the little room that was her temporary home.

Sitting down at the table, she slid the chair closer to the phone. The call radio sat on the table in front of her with the beeper sitting next to it. She was tired. Bone tired. She felt as drained as she did after she ran her first marathon, only today she didn't have any physical pain. The stress of the last few days was accumulating. She wasn't getting solid sleep because of the calls, and the program director had not found anyone that she could free up to come help staff this clinic. When she did get into her bed, her head continued to process the night of Nora's death. Catching sleep seemed to be like catching that elusive runner in front of you in a race. She could make progress in closing the gap, and then it would slip away, leaving her frustrated.

The toothpaste was starting to lose its flavor, and the taste of the oil came back. She got back up and pulled out her toothbrush and toothpaste again. She brushed her teeth and tongue thoroughly. Then licking her lips after finishing, she found the taste again. Pulling out a washcloth, she washed her face and lips thoroughly and brushed her teeth a second time. She had finally found a little reprieve from the taste. She crawled back into bed.

Her heart was so torn. She felt so defeated from losing Nora. Maybe she was not cut out for this. She could give up and go back to the lower forty-eight. She never appreciated how nice it was to be disconnected from her patients down there. When something went wrong in an emergency room, it happened to a stranger. You had your moments of human connection, then the body was taken away and the family left. You could disconnect to protect yourself.

It was so hard to be part of the grieving here. She felt like she failed Nora's family, and now it was so hard to watch them struggle with the grief caused by her failure. She turned over in the bed, trying to find a position that would let her get away from thinking.

She had taken teams for granted all of these years. She never realized how protective it was to have a team to share the burden of decision-making and the responsibility of the results.

How did these health aides handle all of this by themselves? They just had the CHAM and the phone, and then they had the possibility of having their child in front of them needing the skills they have never performed before. She didn't think that she was anywhere near as tough as them.

She turned in her bed again and thought of the one thing she looked forward to now. She could use the protection of the sound of his voice. Hearing his voice made all the burdens of the world lift off her shoulders, and he wrapped her safely in a secure blanket—just like the feeling of being held in his arms during their kiss.

That decided it. She looked at her watch. It wasn't too late. She hopped out of bed, went to the table, and picked the receiver off the wall.

After a few rings, she heard that soothing, deep voice. "Hello?"

"Hello, Rey. I can't tell you how good it is to hear your voice."

"Same with you. It has been a long day here. How are you holding up?"

"I am tired. Stressed. Hoping that I will get some sleep tonight." She felt a bubble of gas escape her. The gas was followed by a noxious smell she had never experienced before. "I can't wait to see you again." Thank God, he wasn't here to smell that.

"Me, too. I was thinking I was going to need to come out to do further investigation and pick up the body for an autopsy, but when I turned in my report to Anchorage, the medical examiner said that it wasn't necessary."

"Not necessary? Even after those lab results? That makes no sense."

"I know. Sounds crazy, doesn't it? Bureaucracy, red tape. I think sometimes the state misses the forest for the trees. But don't worry. I am working on this. I have Angus putting together some of the investigation pieces on the ground there. I've been guiding him through the process."

"Do you have him following up on Zach? You know who I mean, Nora's husband? I am so sure that he has something to do with this. The way he controlled her and that black eye she had the other day. Maybe he was smuggling. Maybe she was catching on to that. Then there is our little importing mom."

"Hey, I know you're caught up in this." His words were reassuring but his tone was stiffer. "You really don't need to play the detective here. And you need to realize that I can't tell you about the details of my work, just like you can't tell me the details of yours. As a matter of fact, I can't have you talking to Angus about this either. Our investigations are confidential."

"I am sorry. I don't mean to try to do your job." She felt chastised for her need to find justice for Nora. She didn't mean to step on his toes. The pressure of gas built in her abdomen again. There was no way of containing it. The smell that had barely left the air filled the room again. On top of that, the taste that was as noxious as the smell was returning to her mouth. It seemed like the same smell of the gas was coming out of her pores. How long would this last? She shuddered with disgust at herself.

"Rey, I don't want to get off the phone with you, but I need the ladies' room. It has been so wonderful to hear your voice. I feel so much better. Let's try to catch up in the morning."

"Okay, sleep tight. And be safe," he added.

"I will. Sleep well yourself. I look forward to talking to you tomorrow."

Meara went into the bathroom and picked up her toothbrush for a third time. As she crawled into the sleeping bag, she had another bubble of gas take over her sense of smell again. "I swear, manners or no manners, I am never eating seal again. She fell asleep wondering how she could get to the bottom of who did this to Nora.

* * *

Jim trudged over to Verna and Chelsey's grandparents' house. The wind was blowing hard, and the snow was stinging what little of his face was exposed. The cold snow meeting the soles of his boots created the sound of Styrofoam being rubbed together. The rhythmic squeaking seemed to announce his doom on his arrival. He leaned his shoulder into the wind and tucked behind it as he resolved that whatever he was going to meet was worth it if he could fix things.

He slipped inside the arctic entry of Verna's home, where the boots, pants, and coats were all neatly lined up just waiting to be filled with a human. The fishing gear on the other side of the room was stacked in neat piles or hung on the wall. He felt like part of the lineup as he knocked on the door next to the coats.

Joe came to the door, greeting him with a big smile that was frugal on the teeth. Jim did his best to relax and smile back.

"So, you like to maqii?" Joe asked.

"I don't know. I haven't yet. I have wanted to, but the opportunity never came up. Thank you for inviting me."

Joe nodded his head and his mouth tightened. He turned toward the back of the house. "Come on in. The women are just finishing up. There is food on the table. Would you like a pop?"

"I would love some water. Thank you for the snacks." Jim reached for some Pilot crackers and spread some salmon across them.

The sound of female voices came from outdoors, and they soon heard the stomping of boots in the entryway. There was an explosion of laughter that suddenly stopped the moment they opened the door and saw him seated at the table. The three women—Verna, Chelsey, and their grandmother—all turned to the kitchen. Their hair was wrapped in towels and steam was rising off their pink, glowing skin.

"Cama'i." Chelsey's mouth tightened just as her father's had. Their mannerisms ran in the family. How could he not have picked up on the relation?

"Cama'i." Jim consciously formed his mouth into his normally friendly smile. His natural expression felt so fake. He was scared but didn't want it to show. The anxiety of meeting alone with their father was really knocking him off guard. He still had no idea what the girls knew about each other's relationships. But he figured they must have talked.

Verna stood to the back. She kept her eyes toward the floor at first, then she bent her head back and shifted her gaze toward the ceiling. She rubbed her eyes briefly.

"I am getting a cold, excuse me." She walked past him.

"I am heading back to help my grandmother," said Chelsey.

"Well, let's get out while the temp is hot," said Joe.

They walked across the yard to the steam that was near the ocean bluff. The wind pushed them backward as they worked their way out. The small changing room was warmer than the outside but still had a chill to it.

The two men stripped their clothes off, leaving their bigger towel with their clothes. Joe opened the door to the maqii and was greeted by a bellow of steamy air that enveloped them both as they slipped into it. He went directly to the stove, where a pot of water sat on top. Grabbing a ladle hanging on the wall, he took two big bowls and poured cool water in from the five-gallon buckets on the floor. He then used the ladle to pour warm water into them until a warm temperature was reached. He handed one to Jim and placed one in front of his place.

He then added some logs to the firebox made out of an old oil drum. He added more water to the pot on the top, bringing that to near level. Then he took the ladle and poured hot water over the rocks that had been wired around the drum. A loud sizzle took over the sound of the wind from the outside, and steam rose up into the air.

Joe looked over at the thermometer. "160 degrees. The women left us a bit cold." He looked across the steam at the two layers of benches and pointed to the upper one. "Jim, the best seat in the house is right up there. You are my guest, please use it," he smiled.

Jim moved himself up as he held the cringe he felt inside. Joe was going to try to heat him out. He had been warned about people being tested by old timers jacking up the heat. And, he knew about the upper bench. He obediently climbed up top, took a swig of water, and watched Joe ladle another scoop onto the stove. So far, so good. This wasn't so bad. He could definitely handle it. The warmth started to penetrate him.

Joe sat back on the other side for a moment and looked at Jim as he rubbed a washcloth between his hands.

"So, tell me how you know my daughters."

"I have been flying to both villages. When I can, I make a point of delivering clinic freight myself. Then I know what the urgency is of anything they need sent in. I have seen you around in both places." Jim failed in his resolve and tried to turn the conversation.

"What do you think about my daughters?" Joe stood, holding Jim's gaze the whole time. He added another three ladles of water to the steam. The steam rose with a sizzle. The temperature rose quickly on the thermometer.

His skin warmed to match. Perspiration beaded across his face and chest. "I have enjoyed getting to know both of them. They are both amazing women. I have learned so much about their different village lives. They both make my village trips enjoyable." What could he say in response that said how he felt? He had messed up.

"Really? Enjoyable, I am sure. What have you learned from them?"

"Fishing and struggles in village life. They have told me about the pride in their families."

Joe looked directly at Jim's face again and held his gaze as he moved over to the ladle. His silence spoke louder than words. He poured another few scoops of water over the rocks, and the sizzling rose to fill the room.

Jim worked hard to appear relaxed, but he was starting to sweat more from Joe's behavior than the steam this time.

Then the door to the steam opened, and the sounds of two sets of feet drifted to him along with the slow cadence of Yupik speech from the front room. After a few minutes of shuffling noises, two men walked in. One was in his forties with a well-defined chest and muscular arms, his hair shaved tight to his head, and his face stern and chiseled.

The other was in his seventies at least; he was short and wiry. He wore a buzz cut and had a grim look to his face. The two set themselves up then sat on opposite sides of Joe facing Jim. Neither of them said a word. They nodded to Joe, then they just sat, set up their washbowls, and stared across the room at him.

Jim had the intense feeling that he was in a Yupik scene from *The Godfather,* as if he were a lamb being brought to slaughter.

All three men sat with deadpan looks on their faces. When they weren't wiping themselves down, they just silently stared at him. He was getting anxious as he thought about what they might be planning to do with him. The heat rose in his face, and this time he wasn't sure if it was from the steam, the guilt and shame that he felt, or the fear that was beginning to take over.

Joe stood again and kept his gaze on Jim as he once more, very slowly and deliberately, ladled three more scoops onto the steam. The three men spoke in Yupik a little.

Jim was sure that he was soon to be dead. He reached for his water bottle and took a big swig then poured a bit of water over his head.

Joe finally broke the penetrating silence. "When I was young, I drank. I was strong, just like this guy," he elbowed the forty-year-old. "I had two girls, and I loved their mother. Unfortunately, I loved the drink even more. When I would travel, if there was drink, I would have it. When I would drink, I would do things I was ashamed of. I ruined my first marriage because of it.

"I then met Chelsey's mother. She was wonderful and strong. She didn't tolerate the drinking for one second. She straightened me out. Then I went on a bender and messed up one more time. But, that mess up brought me Verna. However, it almost cost me my marriage to Chelsey's mother. Verna wasn't a mess up; she is a blessing to me and more so now to my parents.

"Now, I paid dearly for my mistakes when I was younger. And, I owe a lot to my girls. I have hurt them enough. I don't want anyone else hurting them."

Joe again held Jim's gaze as he walked over to the pot and ladled more water to the stove. The thermometer creeped over 190, and the three men facing him looked cool and calm.

Jim reached a washcloth into the cooler water in his bowl and placed it on his face, feigning washing himself. The rim of his bowl was now warm, and the cool water had joined it. The bench around where he was sitting was hot to touch. Was he being delivered to hell at that very moment? He was so hot he couldn't think clearly to explain himself. And, he felt more awkward because he felt he should explain himself to the girls before he did so to their father.

"Do you know what happens to a fisherman who catches more fish than his net can handle?" Joe stared into Jim's eyes.

"No." Jim tried to conceal his shaking. He had the distinct feeling he was going to lose his bladder.

"He drowns."

Jim reached for his washbasin quickly and poured it over his head to disguise the wet spot he was creating at the same time. He quickly got up, grabbing his towel, and went out to the entry room. He threw on only his pants and jacket and shoved his bare feet into his boots as he hurried out the door, expecting the men to follow him out to do him in.

CHAPTER 13

Chelsey was still asleep when Verna had left her house. By this time, she was used to how quickly Chelsey could bound out of bed, get her makeup on, arrange her hair perfectly, and look beautiful within seconds. She was envious of the genes that allowed Chelsey to just be simply beautiful. It certainly hadn't come from their father's side of the family.

Verna had woken up early that morning, as always. *Why do I have to be the ugly duckling?* She thought about the story one of her teachers told her in grade school. Her attempts to make herself look attractive felt futile when she looked in the mirror, and she added to that futility when she put on her dark-rimmed glasses.

She had cooked breakfast for herself and her parents.

Then she stoked the stove and made sure that the outside stairs were not slippery. Her elderly dad insisted on walking daily and would never ask for help. To top it off, he rarely would put the cleats on his boots that she had bought him to prevent a slip on the ice. She feared the day that he finally took a fall in spite of all she did to prevent it.

Even though her father was there and he could take care of his parents while she was at work, she felt she needed to do it. She knew exactly what they liked. She knew their routines. She would be devastated if anything happened to them.

When she arrived at the clinic, she had found Meara sitting in the break room, freshly showered. There was a funny odor in the break room. Meara had a candle out and burning on the table.

"Did you know that we can't burn candles in here?" said Verna to her teacher.

Meara flushed a bit. "It is better than the alternative. I tried seal oil last night, and it is declaring loudly that it doesn't like me."

Verna tried to make her feel better by offering, "Maybe it was a little rancid?" They chatted for a few moments, then Verna started the clinic opening routine.

Meara joined her in the pharmacy, and they counted the medications together.

"How was call last night, Meara?"

"One call. A mom with a child with a cough and a temperature. She hadn't given anything to relieve the fever, and she had some Tylenol. Never heard anything back."

"Nora used to complain about the calls at night for simple things. She was trying hard to teach parents about what to do first before calling. She said she didn't mind the emergencies. It was the frustration of calls that really weren't emergencies in the middle of the night that bothered her. That and the drug and alcohol calls wore her out the most."

The stomp of Chelsey's boots announced her arrival. It didn't take long for her to be dressed and ready to join them at the front desk. She almost seemed to bounce into the room. "We had an entertaining night."

"Really?"

"Dad invited Jim to steam with him with two of his friends. He asked him about us. And then they put the pressure on him." She stopped and laughed. "They all came back in laughing because they scared him so much. He left so fast he almost burned a path home through the snow."

Putting her hands on her hips, she drew her shoulders back and puffed out her chest. "He still hasn't confessed by the way. He is so full of himself that I don't even think he believes he did anything wrong. He must have thought we were a couple of naive little villagers. His loss. The good news is this has brought Verna and me even closer together as sisters, and we are sticking together. Dad said he really turned up the heat on him, and he didn't falter, at least about us. He is also wondering if he is so crooked to hide what he did—dating both of us—so well and without any guilt that maybe he is involved with the drug and alcohol smuggler. He does some odd things, like delivering to us at the clinic. All the other pilots use the agents. The guys in the maqii last night were thinking the same thing. Maybe he is more than just a cheat."

"I'd never thought that about him," said Meara. "I've had other people I have thought could be guilty."

Verna smelled that odd smell again as she was checking the lab temperature. She looked at both her sister and Meara. Meara was squirming uncomfortably in her chair. Her cheeks were a bit flushed. Verna felt bad for her.

"Could I go out to the airport with our labs this morning and pick up anything coming in? I want a chance to watch him in action when he comes back in." Chelsey cut the silence.

Verna's heart sank. She still remained sure he was innocent of the smuggling and was absolutely sure that he had nothing to do with it. She had confidence that he had an explanation for what had happened between them, too. It just didn't fit with the man she felt she knew. It resonated so wrong all the way to her core. Yet, there were so many things that lined up that, if she used her brain, she should see that he could be part of the smuggling issue. The voice of her heart seemed to drown out the voice of her brain.

And now Chelsey was getting another chance to see him alone. Was Chelsey feeling the same way she did, only hiding it better? She was sure that if Chelsey still felt for Jim that he would want her and her beauty and bubbly, carefree personality more than he would want Verna.

She exhaled, trying to hide her disappointment. Her feelings of inadequacy were taking over. If this was what they called sibling rivalry, why did she get gifted with such a short stick?

Meara responded to Chelsey with a nod. "As long as we don't have a full waiting room when the plane comes in, that will be fine."

Verna made a decision. She was not going to play the underdog anymore. She didn't need him. She didn't need anyone. She refused to allow that sinking feeling in her stomach to take charge. She was okay. She had her plate filled with her parents and was soon to be one of the few health aides in this busy clinic. She was too good for all of this petty romance.

* * *

Chelsey stayed back on the road until the plane was on its final approach and coming in for landing. Once it was low enough in the sky, she quickly pulled up and hid herself on the clinic four-wheeler behind the already high snowbank. She was able to see around the towering snow pile without being seen.

The airline agent sat with the engine idling in his big truck with the outgoing passengers sitting and talking with him. The windows were steamed up, and she couldn't clearly see who was in there. The back of the truck was filled with outgoing mail, a few boxes, and the suitcases and totes of the travelers.

Funny how much came in compared to how much went out of the villages. Chelsey pondered as she waited.

Some toolboxes sat to the side of the truck. There must be some contractors leaving. Contractors were always coming in and out. Did they have any connection to Nora and the alcohol traffic? The contractors could certainly be a piece of the alcohol issue.

The plane did a turn on the tarmac and taxied over to the awaiting truck. It couldn't be contractors. It had to be Jim. He was such a lying, two-faced jerk.

The agent pulled the truck to the back of the plane as the engine stopped and the propeller idled to a stop.

Jim opened the door to the rear of the plane from the inside. He lifted that door up and folded out the stairs. After he climbed down, he turned to offer a hand to the few passengers coming off.

Lorna was one of the first to emerge with her daughter following. She carried a small bag. They stood to the side of the stairs and waited for the cargo to be unloaded. A few other passengers followed that she did not recognize.

Jim opened the hold under the plane and tossed mailbags to the ground. Then he went to the wings and opened them, tossing out some backpacks and other narrow packages. Now that the plane was empty of passengers, he went to the rear of the plane and pulled out a big duffle. His face grimaced with the load, and he seemed surprised by the weight of it. There was a box outlined inside. With a heft, he pulled it over his shoulder and brought it to the ground.

One more passenger emerged behind Jim after he pulled the duffel out. The familiar shape of Trooper Torrenson descended the ladder carrying his own tote. Chelsey thought that he must have been hidden on the other side of the plane on the approach. Was he monitoring Lorna? But if that was the case, why did he stay on the plane so long? She watched him, but he didn't seem to be paying any attention to Lorna or her daughter. He walked over to the baggage that Jim and the agent were piling up to the side. They talked for a second, then he grabbed his totes and slid them to the side.

Chelsey watched him and Jim talk for a few moments as the luggage was stacked up. Rey moved in to help the unloading process now that there was enough unloaded cargo space to empty the truck of the oncoming passengers' baggage. Once the truck was empty, they started unloading the remaining incoming cargo of soda pop and boxes of food directly into the truck.

Last, they loaded the truck with the luggage of the passengers who needed a ride to town. She leaned forward to watch Rey lift the hefty bag. If he noticed anything unusual about that duffel, he certainly wasn't showing it. Lorna stood a little straighter and kept her eyes on the bag as he held it.

Angus was nowhere to be seen. Shouldn't he be here to pick up his boss? She looked down the road toward the village and didn't see anyone else heading toward the airport.

She had better deliver the labs. She pulled back the throttle and drove the four-wheeler up to the truck, climbed off, and walked over to Jim and Rey.

Jim gave her that big smile that he always had for her and used to make her stomach flutter and her knees weak.

But now, her stomach felt sour, and her hands clenched as she approached. So much for giving him the third degree now with Rey here. She turned and gave the trooper a polite smile. "Here are the labs. There is an urgent one in there. Any packages for us?" she said curtly and professionally.

"No, sorry. Most of this goes to the store today. I'm going to be taking back off." The agent looked to Rey. "Do you need a ride?"

"No, Angus is on his way. I'll wait for him here."

Chelsey swung her leg back up over the four-wheeler. She watched as Jim secured the plane and climbed back in.

He leaned his head out the window yelling, "Clear." He buckled up and taxied down the runway.

She turned back toward the clinic. As she drove by her grandparents', she realized there was a book she wanted to have at the clinic. She pulled the four-wheeler up to the house and went in. Three minutes later, she was looking out the window as she put her boots back on. She stood and backed out of view suddenly to watch unobserved.

Rey was walking down the road by himself. Moments later, she saw a black Polaris snow machine with a man in black snow gear, black full-faced and tinted helmet, with red gloves heading toward town. Strapped to the back were the totes that Rey had pulled aside during the unloading.

Who was that, and why was Rey walking ahead?

* * *

There was a loud knock on the arctic entry door as Meara walked by it. She opened the door looking down and was greeted by a pair of shiny, polished boots. She followed them up to see the familiar long legs and the big smile.

"Rey! I am shocked to see you here. You never told me you were coming out." She ushered him into the short hall with coatracks. Looking down the hall, she did not see any of the health aides.

With nobody in sight, she relaxed her smile and moved in to receive him with a big hug. She could feel the pull of pheromones at her heart, even through his thick winter clothing. Her breath was taken away with excitement. "It is so good to see you! How long are you here for?"

"Just in to bring some supplies for Angus and get an update on his end of the investigation. He didn't have much new to offer."

"When will they be sending her body to Anchorage for the autopsy? I am surprised they haven't asked by now. The funeral is tomorrow."

"I have filed everything so far. I've even called them regarding the lack of response. They don't see the need for an autopsy with the conditions of death," Rey vented his frustrations.

"I really don't understand this. Those labs really don't make the death so cut and dry. Don't they understand how much more pain this will cause the family to bury her then go back and get her for the autopsy? This makes no sense. I heard they were able to get through the frozen ground with a backhoe, and some of the family just finished digging the grave for the service tomorrow." Meara slammed a chart onto the bench. She surprised herself with her next words. "How can you feel alright about this?"

Rey's voice tightened to match his lips. "Excuse me. When you have worked in law enforcement as long as I have, then you can tell me how to do my job and how I should feel about it. Until then, you need to back off and let Angus and me handle it." Rey pivoted on his heel toward the door.

"You just don't understand," Meara pleaded. "I've heard a lot out in the community that her being drunk makes no sense. And, we know that she didn't have alcohol in her blood test. I just don't get it. Why are they not paying attention to you?"

Now Rey's eyes joined his voice in sending daggers to Meara. "There are always errors. Especially with all the chaos of that evening. Maybe the blood work was faulty. Maybe it had been mixed up with someone else's. The blood work doesn't match the story her body told that night. You do realize how chaotic it was here that night."

He paused for a second, and his body softened. He turned back toward Meara and took her hand. "Meara, I am sorry for losing my temper with you. You have to trust that Angus and I are working this as hard as we can. We really are trying to get to the bottom of this. It is important to us, too. Trust me, I have worked hard to rise to this level. I am one of the best, and I take my role of protector of justice seriously."

Meara stiffened. She had screwed up again. She had the tact of a hyena. She wanted to trust that Rey would do his best, but she also felt that Nora wasn't being given her chance for truth to rise.

She felt Rey's eyes on her. Her jaw set, and her mind started to spin. She now felt like she had been scolded by a police officer at a traffic stop and was being questioned about knowing the rules. She was helpless, and he was in charge with all the power to fix things here. She didn't understand what she had done to make him so angry to start with.

She knew about his reputation, and he was one of the best. She had to trust that he knew his job. She certainly didn't know it. She nodded. "Okay, I understand."

But she went back to looking around as soon as he was gone.

* * *

Verna had already checked in the next patient and was getting the vital signs when Meara slid into the exam room. Her shoulders lowered, and her jaw clenched immediately when she opened the door. Across the room standing behind the exam table was Zach with his ten-year-old daughter.

"Hello, Zach." She made an effort to be pleasant. "I am sure Verna told you that I will be observing her during this visit. I will just be sitting back and watching, and I will also do the exam with her when the time comes."

"No problem," he said.

Pipnik was sitting on the exam table and made little kicks at the drawers under her feet.

Verna got right to business. "What is the problem you have come in for today?"

Pipnik looked to the ground and fidgeted with her hands on her lap. She said nothing in response.

Zach spoke up. "She has been complaining about a bellyache, and she isn't sleeping."

"What other symptoms has she had?"

"Crying, as you would expect. No fever. She hasn't had much appetite but hasn't complained of nausea or diarrhea." He clearly showed what he had probably been taught by Nora.

"How long have the symptoms been going on?" asked Verna.

The young girl blinked rapidly. There was an awkward silence as she said nothing.

"Since the day after her mother…." He stopped himself short and swallowed deeply.

"Does anyone else in the house have it?" Verna broke the awkward silence.

"No. We obviously aren't feeling that great. But, she is the only one with a stomachache." Zach moved closer to Pipnik, putting a hand on her shoulder.

Meara let Verna finish questioning Pipnik.

Pipnik wiped tears and held back a sniffle.

Verna approached her from the other side with a urine cup. "Pip, we need to get a urine sample from you. Make sure to pee a little in the toilet then into the cup. Before you do, make sure to wipe like the pictures show. When you are done, please put it on the shelf."

The adults waited while Pipnik slunk down the hallway to the bathroom.

"How are you holding up?" Verna slid her chair closer to Zach's and looked down at the floor as she waited for a response. She held her silence even as he started to squirm a little in his chair. He finally spoke, providing relief from the awkward pause.

"As good as we can be. We are waiting for the funeral. I am trying to get the girls through this, but I am barely holding on myself. Nora and I have been together since high school. I don't even know how to wake up in the morning without her. It is even harder with the accusations of alcohol."

Pipnik slammed the exam room door back fully open. "My mother wasn't drunk. She didn't drink. She was completely against drinking." Her hands were curled up into fists, and she was visibly shaking. She climbed back onto the exam table and started rhythmically kicking her foot harder against the drawer. The intensity rose. "She wasn't drunk!! People need to stop saying that."

Zach walked over and tenderly put an arm around his daughter's shoulders. "It doesn't matter what is said, Pip. We know the truth about your mother in our hearts."

"It does matter. She wanted so bad to make this village an awesome place to be and to teach us to be proud. And, she taught us to stay away from alcohol and drugs. It does matter. I can't believe it doesn't matter to you." Tears were now flowing continually down her face. "My mother would never have been drunk. She didn't drink, and now everyone will think about her as a drunk."

Meara swallowed back all that she wanted to say. She wished that she could have shared the blood work information with the little girl. She wanted so badly to tell her that she was right. Her mouth was secured shut because of the investigation. Her chest tightened, and she fought back tears as she watched the little girl agonize.

She was not going to quit on Nora. There wasn't any reason that her looking to find out what happened would cause a problem. It was a small community; she should be able to help figure this out. Rey would get over her digging in once they got to the bottom of this.

CHAPTER 14

"Meara, phone call on line two for you." Chelsey popped into the charting room where Meara was doing paperwork.

Meara had been taking a break to review the training certification files. She paused as she held the folder that she had made for Nora. She sighed as she quietly buried it at the bottom of the pile.

"Meara? This is Nancy. How are things going out there?"

"It has been tough, as you know. In spite of all that we have been through, Verna and Chelsey are doing wonderfully; although I think they are a bit gun shy. I need to find some quiet time with them to see how they are emotionally handling all of this. We have some specific skills still to see. Overall, they are both going to be very good. They are surviving this trial by fire."

She continued. "They are working the manual well. They ask appropriate questions about what they are finding on physical exams. They have seen a lot of normal visits with normal exams, and because of this they are picking up on the abnormal. They are still working on being able to describe their abnormal findings though. What I am enjoying watching is how each is starting to personalize the questions to the patient in front of them. They don't just read the question; they make it make sense to the patient's situation.

"They both have their own strengths. Verna is more patient, quiet, and motherly with the way she approaches patients. She has mastered the use of silence; that has impressed me. Chelsey is bouncy and efficient. They are very good and very different; although you can tell that they are sisters."

She looked at the goals they would need to achieve over the next few days. "They have seen plenty of upper respiratory infections. Both of them need to practice splinting and suturing. They both did well with drawing labs, but they haven't practiced much on starting IVs."

"Sounds like it is time for you to roll up your sleeves," Nancy laughed on the other side. "Part of the sacrifice of teaching."

"I know. I keep hoping that the opportunity will come up on a patient." She organized another file of papers. "I have done all of the inspections. They are meeting all the standards out here. I used my new fire extinguisher inspection course. Theirs all pass. Immunizations look good, and temperatures are all in range. I think I have all that busy work done."

"Good. By the way, I am still trying to get you a traveling certified health aide to come out and work with Verna when you go. How are you holding up with having to take all the calls?"

"It goes in spurts. I did get some sleep last night. There seems to be a little break from the alcohol issues. I am praying for some quiet tonight; I need sleep."

"Me, too, for your sake." Nancy hesitated for a moment. "Meara, I just took a patient complaint. The person on the phone wouldn't identify himself. He was native by the sound of his speech. The complaint was that you were talking about patients outside the clinic. He wanted you removed from your job. Considering he wouldn't identify himself or give more details, I cannot do a full incident report. I just need to hear what you have to say."

"Honestly, Nancy. I am very conscientious about talking about patients. I have done a lot of listening to people, but I haven't spoken to anyone."

"Well, somebody has taken a dislike to you. Just continue to be the professional you are. It is a small village. It is inevitable that someone may not like you. Don't lose sleep over this. Good night." Nancy hung up quickly.

Meara looked at the phone. Someone had an issue with her. Who?

* * *

Angus stepped into the waiting room of the clinic and was pushed the rest of the way in by a burst of wind that blew straight through the arctic entry. Chelsey was sitting at the desk, and he couldn't help but feel a bit of a smile trying to form on his face in spite of his trying to subdue it. He needed to be professional and to come across that way. But, whenever he saw her, his whole world brightened.

Maybe the attraction came because of the adrenaline they had when they had worked so closely on the night of Nora's death. They were switching positions and having to brush by each other as they moved in the tight quarters. That night, his heart was racing because of the urgency he felt for Nora. As he stood there now, his heart was racing again, and there was no emergency to explain it. His face heated.

He stepped to the desk. "I have a patient in the back of my truck. He is going to need suturing, but he is a mess. Do you want me to bring him in the back door?"

"Yes." Chelsey looked up from the desk and smiled at him.

His heart skipped an extra beat, and he felt light in spite of his heavy day.

"I will meet you back there. We will put him in the trauma room."

Moments later, he was walking up the back ramp moving behind a young native man who was slinging off a line of profanity in English and Yupik. Angus stayed close behind the poet, holding the handcuffs that held the man's hands behind his back.

Chelsey opened the door and let them stumble inside.

The twenty-something had blood all over his jacket and face, and a rough dressing over the top of his head. The wind blew the smell of alcohol further into the room.

"Apparently, we have had another delivery," Angus sighed. "He tripped and hit his head on a stair. I happened to drive by as he was just starting to sit up."

"You can't bring me in. I just bought that bottle. I want my bottle," slurred the patient.

"Where did you get it?" asked Chelsey innocently as she walked up to him. "Do they have any more? I could use some."

This must have permeated the drunken haze a little. He lifted his eyes up to look at Chelsey directly. "Do you think I would tell you? Are you crazy?"

Angus stifled a smile. She came across so innocent but went right for the question like it was the most normal thing for her to do. She had initiated her very own game of good cop, bad cop for him. He was disappointed. If the man had drunk a little bit more before Angus had found him, it might have worked.

Chelsey was busy working around him getting his vitals. She then gathered material to wash the wound and reviewed her CHAM to get herself set up to take care of him when Meara arrived in the room.

"What time did you pick him up? Did you see if he lost consciousness? Has he had any other symptoms, like vomiting?" asked Chelsey.

"I just happened to have passed by and saw him going down, so I was there to pick him up. No vomiting and no loss of consciousness."

"Do you know when you had your last tetanus shot?" Chelsey looked directly at the patient.

"So," slurred the drunk, "you want to see my butt?"

"I can't say that was my thought. But, if you know, you might save your butt from the shot," Chelsey winked at the drunk.

Angus was about to step in and protect her from the harassment until she so coyly put the young man in his place. "Alright, the lady is here to help you. No more wise comments."

She moved toward the blood-soaked dressing covering the wound. "I am going to take a peek at what is underneath."

There was a two-inch gash exposing the scalp underneath. The bleeding had calmed down. She opened her CHAM and reviewed it, then pulled out a bowl and filled it with water and grabbed a twenty-cc syringe. She had practiced this in the learning lab. She then layered absorbent pads under his head and shoulders and wrapped one around his neck to gather any dripping.

Meara nodded her head to encourage Chelsey to continue.

"Stay still, this is going to feel cold. I need to wash out your wound." She drew up saline then flushed it into the wound, irrigating the debris out of it.

"I would love to have you suture this for the experience," Meara said. "It would be good experience for you. But, in his state, staples would be better."

"Okay." Chelsey washed the site off with Betadine.

Meara pushed the wound edges.

"You may feel a bit of a poke," Chelsey said to the patient. She methodically put four nicely spaced staples into his head just like she did in the learning lab.

"Ouch," said the drunk young man with quite a delay.

"I am going to wrap your head up with a dressing now." After she taped down the gauze, she went back to his chart. "Good news for you. You seem to be accident prone. You have had a tetanus shot."

Angus was impressed as to how she handled the patient and how she did with the repair.

Meara watched over the whole process, and she also seemed to be happy with Chelsey's performance.

"I am hoping that this isn't the beginning of another shipment," said Angus. "I am sorry we haven't figured out where it is coming from yet. I report what I am finding to Rey, but I haven't been able to move forward with leads. He keeps talking about bureaucracy. I am moving as fast as I am permitted."

"We would all agree that it would be nice to solve this," said Meara.

"Hope not to see you later." Chelsey winked.

Angus's mood sank a bit. Did she mean that? He would be better off believing that she didn't want to see him. Then he wouldn't have to figure out how to get around to asking her out.

* * *

Flying into the runway was a bit challenging for Jim this afternoon. The wind was coming strong from the north and was mixed with big crosswinds from the sea. The small plane had been bouncing around like a piece of popcorn in an air popper. Only a popcorn popper would have been smoother than what they experienced in the plane. Each time they got caught in a gust of a crosswind, the little plane would suddenly rise. Then they would drop suddenly straight down. It never ceased to amaze him how a few thousand pounds of freight would find enough freedom within the straps to levitate upwards and slam back down onto the floor of the plane.

"We are good. Plane is still underneath us," he said to the passengers, trying to keep a calm, cool attitude and send it back to them.

He kept his gaze forward and focused on the runway, even though he wanted to turn around to check on his passengers. He didn't dare. He did not want them to see the worry on his face. The last thing he needed was for them to feel any more anxious than they probably already were.

This wind had picked up so suddenly and unexpectedly that there had been no warning of it on the radar. If he had seen it, he never would have flown. He could turn around, but that could be worse. He needed to push forward.

This weather was over the edge of what Jim was willing to fly in. He had been so grateful to work for a company that fully supported his judgement. He didn't care if he lost hours of work. He wouldn't risk people's lives for hours and money. When he made the decision to fly this afternoon, the weather patterns on the NOAA forecast did not show any hint of this storm.

The runway was just a little off. Judging by the winds, they would be safer coming in from the north. He passed over the landing strip, made a half of an approach circle, then lined the nose of the plane up for descent. The plane bounced up and down as each gust hit. That part wasn't as bad as the sudden shifting ten to twenty feet to the left. He would just get the plane corrected and lined up for the runway and another gust would hit.

"God, for the sake of my passengers and their families, please guide my hands in this landing."

The agent's truck waited on the tarmac with the outgoing passengers for this flight. He would break the news when he landed that they would not be going anywhere tonight.

The plane's wheels touched the ground. They lifted then touched again, rolling down the runway. The ailerons were lowered, and they braked quickly. When he came to a stop, he turned to taxi the plane to the agent's truck. Even here on the ground, big gusts of wind were lifting the plane and dropping it with a shudder.

Jim turned to the passengers. "Stay buckled until the plane is secured." The plane was bouncing so much he was afraid that if they unbuckled, somebody would get slammed into the ceiling.

He quickly opened his door, climbed out on the wing, and jumped down. He ran to the rear compartment of the plane and pulled out tie-downs.

"Hey, grab these and copy me on your side," he yelled to the agent, tossing a second set to the other side of the plane where the agent stood. He secured the wings down with the nose turned to the wind. He then moved over to the tail and tied that down as well. The plane shuddered with the force of the gusts but was now secure.

"I will not be flying back out in this," he said to the agent. "Why don't you run the folks in your truck back home? I will keep these folks in the plane until you return." He climbed into the airplane and opened the door. "Okay, folks, I am not flying back out in this. The agent is returning home everyone that he has in the truck, then he's coming back for the rest of you and the cargo. I will keep the engine running and keep us warm in the meantime."

He climbed back in the pilot seat and turned to the passengers, making small talk with them while they waited for their ride. If things moved fast enough, he could stop by the clinic before the girls got out. He hoped that the storm was not an omen of how things were going to go with him straightening things out with the girls.

He could hear the agent radioing into town announcing both the arrival and cancellation of the afternoon flight. Verna made a return comment. He would be finding out soon enough how tough the storming women would be.

* * *

Verna heard the radio announcement that the plane had come in but was not going back out. She was sitting at the front desk when the call came over and was speaking to her dad who was visiting her at the desk. The local radio station broadcast from Agushak was playing in the waiting room.

Joe gave her a big smile. "Excuse me, I will see you back at the house in a little bit."

"Open Line" was the show at the moment. At four o'clock each day, people called in to the radio station to wish family members congratulations, send birthday wishes, say prayer requests, or announce the sale of items they wanted to get rid of. The radio show served as a daily regional social club.

"See you later," she responded. She returned to organizing her encounter slips from the day that she was getting ready to fax to Agushak. Right now, as a level one in training, she would have to send them after every encounter. But, because Meara was there, they were faxing them at the end of the day in one fax.

She chuckled as Meara walked by. "These slips are reminding me of radio traffic when I was a little girl. Every day at three, we would stay around the CB radio in the kitchen and listen to the health aides do medical traffic. The health aides would call report on all of their patients to the doctor on the CB radio. Then the doctor would tell them what to do. Sometimes the transmissions were so bad that other people would get on the radio and correct the doctor if he couldn't hear the health aide through the static. I kind of miss it. It was entertainment. But the fax is a big gain for privacy."

Meara walked back to supervise Chelsey, and Verna got back to filing and was listening to the radio as she worked. "Open Line" and radio traffic were very much alike, now that she thought about it. Everyone tuned in for the entertainment.

The door to the clinic entrance opened and Jim walked in. Even though she had expected him, her heart gave pause, and a huge lump developed in her throat. She wanted to run to the bathroom to get sick.

He looked at her, and his head sank as he approached the desk. "Verna, I need some time to sit down and talk to you and your sister. Could you two make that happen?"

Just as he said that, they could hear voices in the back. The door to the reception area opened, and Chelsey and Meara came back out to the front.

A familiar voice came over the radio, and both girls turned their heads.

"Hello, this is Joe. It is so good to be back here in my home village this week. I want to welcome Jim to Quyalaqaq tonight. He has offered such a compliment to my family. He has found both of my daughters so charming that he could not choose between them. He is guilty of stealing the hearts of two of them. What a man! Apparently, my girls are so beautiful they drained his brain away, and he couldn't make an honorable decision as he should have. We are seeking prayer for him to have his brains return so that he can clear the injustice he has done to them."

Heat rose in Verna's face from embarrassment. Her father had the intention of embarrassing Jim. How could he not have thought about how embarrassed she and Chelsey would be from this?

Chelsey moved up next to her and put a hand on her arm. Her eyes narrowed, and her lips tightened as she looked at Jim. She was clearly still more angry than embarrassed.

How could her anger be directed at Jim right now instead of Dad for this embarrassment? Maybe she was used to dealing with Dad's odd sense of humor. Her head flooded with the confusion of all the emotions. She felt almost numbed.

Jim's face was bright red. His head seemed to sink even lower than it was when he walked in. He was visibly shaking.

"Excuse me, I need to get some paperwork done." Meara stepped out of the room, leaving the three of them alone.

Jim cleared his throat, looking between Chelsey and Verna. "As I was just asking before your Dad spoke up for your honor, I need some time alone to talk with the both of you. I think this might be as good a time as any."

Verna glanced at her watch, got up, and walked around the counter and into the waiting room. She locked the entrance then sat in one of the chairs.

Chelsey came around and sat next to her. Her glare at Jim was penetrating.

Jim sat and took a deep breath. "First, I owe both of you an apology. I never wanted to hurt either of you, and I clearly have. I am so sorry. Please hear me out."

* * *

Meara locked up the back of the clinic. She had finished the end-of-day closing duties in order to allow the girls to meet with Jim. "Ladies, I have sent your slips off and closed out the back. I am taking a walk. You can just lock up and leave when you are done."

She pulled on her outdoor gear and boots and started the walk to Sophie's house. She wanted some time with Sophie. But, since the visit with Pipnik this morning, there was someone else that she wanted to visit.

As she stepped out of the clinic, the wind caught her off guard. The unexpected force of the gusts from the sea pushed her to the side. She needed to lean into the wind to keep from being blown off the road.

She walked up and into Sophie's arctic entry and slipped out of her gear. There were so many coats and boots there, she wasn't sure where to put hers. She knocked lightly then let herself in. Working her way through the groups of people in the living room and into the kitchen, she found Sophie sitting in the same place as last time.

She walked up with her arms wide to give a hug to the older woman. "Hello, Sophie. I have been thinking of you all day. How are you holding up?"

Sophie straightened her shoulders and held her head up, giving the impression that she was well rehearsed with the "I am here, and I am grateful for family." The drawn lines in her face revealed the longing for the one person in her family she didn't have.

"I have not gone in to give my respects yet. May I go in?"

"Of course." Sophie got off the stool, took Meara's hand, and led her to the back bedroom. "Stay as long as you need."

Meara took in the room. The temperature was cold. She wished she had left her jacket on for the visit. She wrapped her arms across herself in a failed attempt to stay warm. The open window was hung with a couple layers of curtains. There was a sheer and a dark-out curtain that ran to the floor and over a pile of boxes containing papers and neatly stacked albums. The window dressings flapped with the wind that forced itself in. The side of the room held a closet without doors. It was filled with assorted clothes. A chest of drawers against the other wall held multiple pictures of Sophie's family members, some of whom looked like a younger version of Nora.

There were folding chairs set up on either side of the bed. Meara regarded Nora lying there. She had been cleaned up more since leaving the clinic and had makeup covering the bruise that had not entirely gone away at the time of her death. She wore a beautiful, bright blue qaspaq with a lavender straight trim. Her hands were crossed over her abdomen.

Meara sat in the chair closest to the bed and turned to Nora. "Talk to me. Help me. Something isn't right about your death. I have heard that you didn't drink. I know your labs; they do not match what the police are saying caused your death. Pipnik clearly knows that you did not drink yourself into carelessness. Help me, Nora. I failed on saving you, but there is more I need to do. Your funeral is tomorrow. Your daughter needs to bury you with the full truth known of who her mother was. You need to be buried in the full truth of who you were."

She clasped her hands, bowed her head, and said a prayer similar to the one she would pray before each emergency at work. "Dear God, please guide my thoughts and my actions now. Help me to find the truth of the situation and allow me to return honor to my friend."

* * *

As Verna and Chelsey walked home, the two were quiet.

"At least he finally confessed to us," said Verna.

"Yes, he did, but what took him so long? I still don't understand why he couldn't have just said something when we went fishing." Chelsey held the edge of her parka closer to the side of her face.

Verna was reaching to do the same. The wind felt like needles being driven into the side of their faces as it gusted off the surface of the Bering Sea. "His delay didn't help us to trust him anymore. I don't know that I will ever be able to grant him forgiveness."

"I don't even have to think about that," replied Chelsey. "I don't trust the man. Period. He had no problem continuing the lie by not clearing it up sooner."

"I think I can understand how his friendships with us got carried away. He was lonely and needed friends. Our beginnings were innocent enough."

"I can give him that. It was very innocent. Innocent physically. But, then he talked to both of us about dreams and futures. To make it worse, he had the audacity to say that I kissed him first. He talked about it as if I lured him into something he didn't want. I think he needed to blame one of us. I don't buy it." Was it the wind or Chelsey's anger that forced her words out so sharply? "I think he is used to being able to travel and get away with things. Personally, I am still not convinced that he doesn't have anything to do with the alcohol runs here in the village."

"I just can't see him doing that."

Chelsey returned the comment with an angry look.

"Doesn't matter. We aren't finding out today anyway. I wonder if Dad cooked. Or if we need to get on it." As they walked the rest of the way silently, Verna's thoughts wandered back to the conversation in the clinic. Jim had said that he had fallen in love with her. Her, not Chelsey. That couldn't be true. Why would anyone choose her over Chelsey? She was everything Verna was not. She was beautiful, smart, and had more freedom to offer because she didn't have the elderly parents to take care of.

Here she was. Verna. Plain Verna. She didn't like her body; she had always been a bit chubby. Her glasses kept her hindered, and she could not remember a time that she could look out at the world and actually see it without them. She was not caught up with the life in the outside world. Even now, her friends were all the people in her village, and her world didn't expand beyond that. And, she didn't really want it to. She was smart, like her sister. Apparently, Joe had intelligence to pass on through his genes.

There was no way she could have heard him right. He couldn't have been planning to tell Chelsey that he wanted them to be friends right when they discovered his secret.

He actually wanted her over her sister. That couldn't be right. But this was not fair. Because no matter what she felt about him and what he felt about her, she could never hurt her sister by seeing him again. Their sisterhood meant more to her than that. Sometimes, the world could be so cruel.

CHAPTER 15

Meara groaned when a call came in at eight in the evening alerting her to a two-year-old with a fever and cough that wasn't improving with a bath or Tylenol. She had been hoping to join Sophie for a maqii at nine. Sharing the call with the health aides was good for their learning, but right now, taking the time to work through a health aide visit was not what she wanted to do.

Chelsey was taking calls with her tonight. When the mother and child met them at the clinic, Meara was pleasantly surprised at how quickly and efficiently Chelsey was getting at working through a patient visit. When she first started, it took over an hour per visit. But tonight, Chelsey had flipped through the sections of the CHAM so efficiently that she had seen the child interviewed, examined, and assessed fairly quickly.

Meara was impressed with Chelsey's ability to pick up the abnormal findings in the exam. The little girl had an ear infection and abnormal lung sounds that did clear after a cough. Chelsey followed the plan through and calculated the antibiotics that she needed, taught the mother how to give them, and had scheduled a follow-up by nine fifteen.

Chelsey's normally bouncy demeanor was not with her tonight. Meara wondered what that was all about and was curious about the visit with Jim, but she didn't want to bring it up until Chelsey did.

Meara let Chelsey head home. She grabbed her towels and clean clothing, put the beeper and radio into her parka pockets, and pushed hard to open the door against the wind. Once it was open, it slammed shut behind her. Leaning against the wind, she pushed her way against it to go down the road to Sophie's.

The men were just finishing up their steam as Meara arrived and some were settling in to eat in the kitchen.

Sophie called out to her immediately. "Meara, can you walk my mother out to the maqii? I don't want her to slip on the way over. If I am not right out, please help her get started. She will let you help her. She really likes you because of how much you enjoyed her seal oil. She brought you some to take home tonight, too."

"I would be glad to." Meara thought about what she was going to do with the seal oil once she got it. She couldn't ever eat that again. The gas, the smell, and the taste were nearly the end of her. *Crap, I can still taste it.* She tried to conceal her shudder at the thought of ever eating seal oil again. She knew that she needed to graciously accept the gift. But she also felt guilty because she knew that she would never eat it.

She slipped the sleeves of the elderly woman's coat over her arms and onto her shoulders, then offered her arm to walk out the door. Grace smiled at her with her big grin.

"Her clean clothes are in the bag on the table," called Sophie.

Meara and Grace slowly worked their way across the backyard, with Meara placing herself between the wind and the wizened woman. They slowly stepped up to the entry room. Meara stood in front of Grace to support her frail body as she lowered down to sit on the bench.

Meara then peeked in the steam. She felt like she almost knew what she was doing in a maqii now, as she noted the temperature of 160 and poured a ladle full of water over the rocks to bring the temperature up for the elderly woman's body.

She knelt in front of Grace and gently helped her to get undressed. She slowly removed shoes and socks. Grace's shoulders were stiff and arthritic, and removing the qaspaq over her head was a bit of a challenge. Meara added the extra pull to help remove the clothing as the elder woman tried to be as independent as she could be.

Meara stepped in the steam and set the towel across the bench in a seat near the fire. She went back and offered her arm to the naked elder and assisted her in. After leaving Grace in the hot steam, Meara went back to the outside room and removed her own clothing.

"Please give me some quiet." She placed the radio by the door so she could hear it, but it would not be affected by the moist air.

She slipped naked back into the steam and set up a wash basin for herself and for Grace. She could not suppress the chuckle she had as she realized that she had given many a bed bath in her career, but this was the first time she had done it naked herself.

She held out a wet washcloth to the elderly woman. Grace took it and muttered something in Yupik. Then she commenced scrubbing herself where she could reach.

Meara would wait for Grace to take a break, and she would take the cloth, rinse it and reapply soap, and hand it back to the woman.

When Grace had completed all that she could herself, Meara pointed to her back and simulated washing with the washcloth. The elder nodded in agreement but pointed to a bunch of Labrador tea stalks that had been tied together and were hanging from a nail on the wall.

Meara handed them to the elderly woman, giving her a quizzical look. The old lady took and slapped the bunch of leaves against her legs with a steady beat. Then she signaled to Meara to do this to her back, shoulders, and neck.

Shortly after, Sophie arrived with the three girls, Pipnik, Sara, and Nena. Pipnik came in and set to work preparing a washbowl for herself and her youngest sister. Sara took care of herself. Sophie put Nena on the bench next to her great-grandmother and started washing her hair.

"I see *amouk*, grandmother, has you treating her arthritis." Sophie got herself settled. "Slapping with the Labrador tea chases the pain away."

Meara heard another voice come in. How many people were steaming? She still was not super comfortable with the group exposure, even with it being all women. She had never felt comfortable with her body, and being exposed to women of all ages felt awkward.

Gentle cooing came from the entry room. Shortly after, a young mother came in with a baby that could not have been more than two weeks old. The scab of the umbilical cord looked fresh.

"Meara, this is my *nurr'aq*, my niece, Ana and her new baby," Sophie introduced. "His cord fell off today. This is his first maqii. It is an important time for him. He will steam with the women until he is old enough to join the men.

Sophie filled a wash basin up for Ana and slid it over to her.

"How is your father holding up?" Sophie looked at Pipnik.

"He is trying to be strong for us. But, I have been hearing him crying when he doesn't think I am listening. He is feeling like this is all his fault."

No wonder, Meara thought.

"He keeps saying that he should have made her come home with us. She was tired that night, but she wanted to see the remaining children's group dance and to see our cousins dance. Then once we got home, he didn't want to leave us alone until he knew that Nena was completely asleep. Nena had a temperature that night and was restless. He had finally gotten her to sleep when Angus came by and got him."

Meara was dumbfounded by this revelation. He had never left the kids, and they were awake the whole time? She had seen Nora later than they had. He couldn't have been the one to murder Nora.

"Your father seemed to be pretty controlling of your mom's time." Meara winced at her own words, knowing that she had pushed it with her awkwardness again. Why was she such a bull in a china closet when it came to small talk?

"Oh yes, he was." Pipnik didn't give any indication that she was annoyed by Meara's question.

Meara felt justified in her earlier judgement and a little proud she had noticed the red flags after all.

"He was frustrated at how much her job and her dedication to the village took from her. By the time Mom came home each day, she was pretty tired. He wanted her to quit, because he was doing well with fishing, but she wouldn't. She loved her job and the fact that she served the community. So, when she didn't have to be out and running around, he tried to keep her home with us. He wanted her to relax, and he wanted us to have family time." This pronouncement from Pipnik took away much of Meara's theory that he was abusive toward Nora.

"Your mom never told us how she got the black eye."

Pipnik smiled wistfully and laughed at the question. "Mom and Dad were joking around. He was pretending to be a great hunter after a seal with Nena being the seal. Mom was cooking dinner. When he pounced on Nena, he knocked a pan from the hook, and it fell, hitting her in the face."

Meara couldn't have made that story up if she tried. So, it wasn't Zach. He had an alibi, and there was a reason for all the red flags. She had been so sure it had been him. So, who was it?

"I am going to go out to cool down. I will be back in for another round," she said to the group.

As she was stepping out, she could hear Sophie speaking, "Pip, would you please bring Amauq in the house and get her settled for bed? I would like a bit of time in here in quiet."

The younger women joined Meara out there with Grace. Her heart was moved by the scene as she watched the children assist their great-grandmother with getting her nightclothes on as they themselves got dressed. She hadn't seen children so young taking such good care of someone so old. The pack surrounded the elderly woman as they slowly left the building. All three of them guided her shuffled steps across the windblown yard.

Ana had poked her head out the door to wave goodbye to the departing girls. She then walked out the door, planted both feet firmly on the ground, and turned around to come back in.

Sophie laughed from behind her. "Ana, how does it feel to not have to step all the way out when you poke your head out the door?"

Ana laughed back. "It is so nice not to have to, but I was so used to it, I forgot I didn't have to anymore!" She continued to dress up her baby.

"When a woman is pregnant, she cannot poke her head out a door to look at the weather. If she pokes her head out, she needs to follow her head all the way out and plant her feet firmly on the ground before she goes back in. That way, she teaches the baby how to properly come out."

Meara smiled. It seemed that every culture had their own old wives' tales. This one was new to her.

After the girls had all left, Meara poked her head back into the steam.

"Do you want to be left alone, Sophie?"

"No, I actually wanted to have a little time with you." Sophie spoke through the mist escaping into the changing room.

"I am almost cooled down enough to come back in. Give me a second."

"Step all the way outside. The wood stack will block the wind and anyone from seeing you. It will feel really good, and it will get your circulation going."

"Are you trying to kill me?" Meara started to chuckle nervously, then realized how inappropriate that comment was at that time. "I am sorry. I mean, you have to be kidding. It has to be negative ten degrees out there."

"No, I am not kidding. You will be surprised to find you are so warm from being in here it will feel good out there. It will get your blood pumping." Sophie gave no indication of being offended by Meara's awkward statement.

"Okay, I'm sure I'll be back in half a second." Meara slipped her shoes on and stepped gingerly out into the night. The wind was blowing hard, but it was blocked like Sophie said by the wood stack. The night was surprisingly clear in spite of the gusts. She stood looking up into the starlit night and noticed a shimmer of green dance across the horizon.

Then, a wave of purple moved up to join it. Purple and green alternated their dance in the sky. Meara felt like she was caught in a web of nature's magic as she stood exposed in the cold of the night with steam rising from her skin and drifting up to join the sky. The magical combination of her warmth with her first experience of the northern lights filled her with an anticipation that she did not understand. She stood there until her body started to feel the cold.

Entering back into the changing room, Meara felt the warmth envelop her as if she were being wrapped in a warm towel after a shower. This time when she stepped back into the warmth of the steam, the heat penetrated deep into her core. She needed to do the outside rotation again sometime. It felt amazing.

"Meara, I have been wanting to catch you alone. I have been watching you and your distaste for Zach. I need you to know he is a good man who truly loved my daughter and made her very happy. They were well matched." Sophie wasted no time in breaking the silence. "Here, let me scrub your back. You will be amazed at how much better you will feel if we get all that old skin off you. When you peel that layer off, you see the world a little clearer."

Meara felt guilty to have her back scrubbed by her friend who had been through so much. She should be doing the favor to her.

"Let me tell you a story. When I was young, I had no confidence. I fell in love with a man that quickly showed that he wasn't a good man once we were married and I was pregnant with Nora." She leaned in, increasing the pressure of the scrubbing massage.

"He would come home at night whether he was drunk or sober and be on edge. I would watch everything that I said or did very carefully to not aggravate him. It was never predictable when he would get angry. Sometimes it was worse when he was sober. The man was simply not a good man. He beat me unconscious a couple of times. He broke my jaw once. It was always my fault, according to him. I deserved it because I made him angry.

"I had thought I was too stubborn, too smart to be in an abusive relationship. And there I was struggling to figure out how to get out of it. Finally, one day I locked him out. His behavior had the neighbors calling the VPSO. He pulled a gun and had it aimed through the window of the house toward me as I was hiding as low as I could. It was enough to get the troopers to charge him with assault. I didn't back down in the testimony, and he never returned here after he was let out of jail. I raised Nora by myself with the help of the village. They gave me strength, and I took good care of them in return when I became a health aide."

Meara listened to her older friend speak and was surprised by the personal revelation. She was even more surprised when Sophie continued.

"Meara, I see your past. I have seen it in your response to Zach and in your defensiveness around him. I know you thought that you knew exactly what had happened, because I could feel where you have been."

Meara's heart sank with shame. Her head followed. She found herself trying to explain herself. "I am so ashamed. I saw warning signs. I felt so bad that I didn't do something to confront her about them."

"You can relax about Nora. You saw the signs wrong in this case. She and Zach had something special when they came together. Nora was able to be so much more because of Zach. You have a good inner knowing, more than you realize. Right now, it still sees the world through your past."

Sophie took Meara by the shoulders and turned her to face her. She gave Meara a knowing smile. "You need to recognize your inner knowing from the true you, not the wounded you. Someday, you are going to find someone that allows you to let down the walls you have built around you. Your inner knowing will let you know when it is safe to let down your guard. When you open up the locks for the right person, you will be setting yourself free. The right person with the right relationship will not only allow you to be your best, but the two of you will lift each other to be more than either of you could have been alone.

"Nora knew that with Zach, and she left a legacy that will continue without her physical presence. When you find your partner, the power of the two of you together will be much more than what each of you brings to the table alone. You will not only be standing strong in yourself, but you will also have the strength of finding your true match. And when that match happens, will you be brave enough to work through the fear of unlocking all those locks and bolts that you have chained yourself with?"

CHAPTER 16

Chelsey heard the radio go off at two in the morning. She put on her clothes and headed out the door with Meara to see the incoming patient. Was the alcohol issue that was so severe in this village as bad as in her own? Maybe she just didn't realize there was a problem because she wasn't in this job before. She didn't think she could do the job very long if it was.

What was it about alcohol that caused such a severe reaction in some villagers? There was no social drinking like she had seen in movies or even on small trips to Anchorage. There, she would watch people sip a glass of wine and enjoy their meal, and that would be the end of it. At home when she saw someone drink, they drank hard and fast until it was gone, or until they passed out—whichever happened first.

Meara was up and waiting at the door when she arrived, and Angus was leading a handcuffed man Chelsey recognized to the door. He was discreetly shushing the man in an attempt to keep things quiet.

"Get your hands off of me! Don't you have any respect, you stupid trooper wannabe?" the man slurred. "You can't put me in cuffs. I am your chief. You need me for your paycheck. You can't treat me this way." The man continued berating Angus as he twisted away from him. Angus tried to keep him from falling as he led him into the clinic.

Chelsey and Meara stepped back as they held the door to the trauma room. Meara probably never thought that she would be clearing the Chief for alcohol abuse. The Chief, intoxicated in his own dry village. This didn't surprise Chelsey. She had seen many a person that were upstanding citizens think they could have just one, get drunk, and do terrible things that were completely out of their character when under the influence.

"I just got a call from his wife. She said he had been having a difficult time with Nora's death. When he had the chance to get some booze, he got it. But once he started drinking, his normal quiet, gentle self got out of control. He started to threaten her. Then he smashed a hole in the wall. When he went to the back room, she heard him opening his gun cabinet. That is when she called me. I just need him cleared so that I can bring him to the cell to sleep this off. Hopefully, he will let me get him there without too many people noticing."

Chelsey stepped forward. "Hi, I am Chelsey. I am just going to get your vital signs." She didn't approach him until he said okay.

"You're going to do what you want to do anyway!" spit the Chief. "No respect. I get no respect." He started to work up his face with clear intent to spit at Chelsey. What was it about drunk people spitting?

Angus quickly pulled a spit shield out of his pocket and slipped it over the Chief's face. "You will be treating the ladies here with respect. They are here to help you. I am sure they would much rather be fast asleep."

"How long has it been since he last had a drink?" asked Meara as Chelsey worked through the rest of her CHAM.

"He ran out about thirty minutes before his wife called. That would be an hour now."

"Well, he certainly isn't in any danger right now, except hurting himself with the agitation. He should be getting better from here."

They reviewed the visit. If Chelsey had seen him alone, she would have had to call to the physician in hub village, but Meara was able to make the decisions.

"Vital signs are stable. Blood pressure is high at 160/92. He is alert and oriented to place. Poor judgement," said Chelsey.

"He will need to come by tomorrow to follow up on that blood pressure," Meara told Angus. "But he should be fine to go sleep it off with you."

Chelsey moved up to the other side of the Chief as they worked to move him to the door.

Angus looked at her briefly and apologetically. "I am so sorry to wake you for this, and I am really grateful for your help. Maybe some good will come of this. He got the alcohol somewhere. Maybe, as he sobers up, he might be willing to let us know where. Would you do me a favor and go across and open the station door?" He nodded across the way at the VPSO building then nodded to his pocket.

Chelsey reached in and took the keychain out. Feeling a sense of protection, she realized she would not have that when she went to her own home. There was no VPSO there. Who would protect her in the night there? She stared at the loaded keychain, trying to figure which one.

"The red one," Angus read her mind.

The warmth she had started feeling around Angus was not as noticeable as the doubt that crept into her mind. She shouldn't be working by herself, because she was not good enough. Now on top of that, would she be safe enough?

CHAPTER 17

Fred tucked himself and his snow machine behind a drift to wait. His black Polaris was tucked into the shadows on this cold morning. He was well dressed for the incredible blow that had taken over since yesterday afternoon. He leaned into his backrest as he waited to see if that woman would go for her run again today. He had been watching her and knew she had been consistent with both the running and the route. The weather today was pretty extreme. If he did see her today, she would earn a lot of respect in his books. It was a shame to do what he had to do.

He had been struggling through the hardest year he had ever had. No matter how hard he had worked and how much he tried, he simply could not make ends meet this year.

Damned engine. Things couldn't have been timed any worse. Everything was working great until the first day of the silver run. Those silvers were a huge part of adding silver to his bank account. First day. Seriously, the first day.

The diesel engine on his fishing rig had frozen up as he was working his way out to the first run. He didn't even get to set one net before he had to struggle home with his backup motor.

He was so humiliated. He didn't just have the cost of the engine repair. The delay in getting parts cost him the majority of the three-to-four-week run. The heaviest part of the run happened the second week. By the time he got his boat back on the water, his harvest was meager. He ended the season with a devastating loss. It wouldn't have been as bad if his wife hadn't been sick all winter and he hadn't had the extra expense of flying his daughters out of Quyalaqaq to Anchorage to stay there with him while he watched over her.

He had no other choice other than to do what he had done. He had been in a major bind. He did not have the money in the bank to make the remaining boat payments to get him through to next year. If he lost his boat, he lost his family's source of support.

That trooper saved his family. That trooper supervisor had come to him late summer and asked him about teaming up to distribute the drugs and alcohol that he smuggled in.

His stomach turned when he thought about what he had done so far and what he needed to do now.

He had a family that needed him, and he failed them.

He kicked the platform of his snow machine. If only there had been some other way to climb out of this hole and take care of his family. But they must never know about any of this.

So far, the deal was working well. He was never suspected by Angus, because he never left town. They had the cover of Lorna and all her trips in and out. Angus seemed distracted by her. As a matter of fact, the whole village suspected her as the smuggler. She provided a perfect cover by doing whatever it was she was doing. And he had the protection of those he sold to.

He scowled. They weren't about to bite the hand that fed them. To put it more correctly, they weren't going to turn off the fountain that quenched their thirst. Those that bought from him would never turn him in. They wanted their drink.

It was all working until now. Now, this lady had come to town and was asking too many questions. The trooper had told him that they needed to discourage this lady because she was asking about the alcohol supplies. He had been watching her over the past few days. He was surprised at how early he had to get up to watch her start her days. But she was up at six every day for a run to the airport. The trooper had said she was like clockwork, and he wasn't mistaken.

Yesterday, he tried calling the hospital to get her out of town by making a complaint. But, damn it. They wouldn't file a complaint without him giving his name. That strategy wasn't going to work. He was hoping that the complaint would be enough to get her to back off or go away. It was clear that the easy way to deal with her wasn't going to work.

Looking down the road, he saw a figure well bundled in running clothes coming down the road toward the airport. He waited and watched her approach. His heart was beating in his chest. His hands gripped the handlebars tighter. He tried to relax, but he was feeling so torn.

Man, have I already fallen off my own cliff. He clenched his jaw. *I am in the free fall, and there is no turning back.*

He would let her pass before he started up the engine.

Each step he watched her take toward him seemed to take minutes instead of seconds. He was so torn about having to follow through with what he had to do.

This all started because he needed to take care of his girls. He couldn't let this woman uncover everything he did. It would destroy his family.

She moved steadily by leaning hard into the wind. He let her go a few hundred feet ahead of him.

He put his hand onto the key and hesitated before he turned it.

God, forgive me. I can't be a failure to my family.

Turning the key in the ignition, his stomach clenched. He quickly and determinedly revved up his snow machine and sped it quickly across the snow toward the unsuspecting woman.

She looked back when she heard the sound and quickened her pace.

He looked down the road and estimated how much space and speed he needed to force her to the edge of the bluff. The bluff sat right off the road with only fifteen feet to the side before the drop-off. Just last year, a young man had gone over on his snow machine. He was still alive in Anchorage but couldn't even breathe for himself, and on the day of his accident the ground was a lot softer.

It seemed like seconds before he was at her side. He kept pushing her farther and farther toward the bank. She was trying to duck behind and around him, but he was able to force her closer and closer. Then, taking his left hand off the handlebars, he gave her a quick shove as he quickly pulled his snow machine to the right. He watched her tumble over the edge with a scream.

There is no looking back. If she is alive, she won't stay that way long. The cold will get her like it did Nora. And, nobody will be looking for her for hours.

He stopped his machine for a moment and paused as he realized what he had done.

There is no going back for me either. I have made my path. God, forgive me.

CHAPTER 18

Meara moaned waking up from what she thought was a dream. She felt cold on one cheek and warm and wet on the other. She reached her hand up to her face then looked at her hand with a wet glove liner on it. She moved her head back and forth looking at the gray-and-white shadows of the coastline, and she wasn't sure if the rushing sound was coming from the ocean or inside of her own head.

"Where am I?" She felt like she was waking from a dream. She rolled to the side and felt more warmth run down her face. Simultaneously, she felt a sharp stab of pain from her ankle. She pushed up on her arms and lifted her head and immediately felt dizzy. A wave of nausea took over, demanding that she put her head right back down.

"Where am I?" she muttered again in her confusion. Moving her head from side to side, she could see the top of the bluff above her and the sandy wall to her side. She was lying on her back amidst refrigerator-sized chunks of ice piled up along the ocean shore.

It started to come back to her. The snowmobile.

The black snowmobile on her run. It came out of nowhere and came right at her. Everything had happened so fast that she didn't have time to think about it. He forced her to the edge and drove her over.

Then she felt the throbbing from the side of her head. Realizing what had happened, she went into health care–provider mode. She looked to where she had fallen from and felt lucky to be alive. Then she put her ungloved hand to her neck and methodically worked her way down touching each vertebra until she got below her neck.

"Nothing painful to touch," she said with relief. She rolled her neck gently from side to side again, paying attention this time, now that she knew what had happened. Then up and down. "No pain."

She was bruised and battered, but the rest of her spine felt alright. Her left hip felt like it had been kicked. She gently tested her hands, then her arms, raising them above her head and back down. All was good.

Next, she moved her legs. She could move them, and there was no increase in pain in the hip from that. Her entire body was shaking. She didn't know if it was from the cold or the trauma.

"I need to get out of here. Nobody knows where I am, and nobody would look for me here."

She attempted to raise her head again, this time with better results. Her head did not spin quite as much. Then she pushed herself up to sitting with her arms.

She looked around and took in the landscape. There was no going back up the twenty-foot bluff she had just fallen down from. She pondered how she survived that fall. She rubbed her hand up and down the jagged, rock-hard ice chunk that she had landed on. Any farther in either direction she would have broken her back for sure. Luckily, it was just the back of her head that fell against the corner of the ice stained red by her own blood.

Just the back of her head? What was she thinking?

Down the beach about three-quarters of a mile, she could see where the town met the sea and there was level ground to walk out onto.

She stood. Then put weight onto the right ankle. Pain shot up her leg, and the ankle gave in. She landed back on her butt.

"How am I going to do this?" She felt down her leg. No obvious deformity, just really swollen. Seeing nothing to splint it with, she stood, keeping her weight on the right ankle and held onto an ice chunk with her left to support herself as she moved along. She could work through this. She had to work through this. Each step sent another shot of pain up her leg as she tiptoed, holding onto the ice to keep from putting weight on it.

A couple of small pieces of driftwood were frozen to the shore ahead of her. She moved closer to them and pulled and twisted until they became free of the ground. Taking off her neck warmer, she put it into her mouth and grabbed it between her teeth to rip it. At first, it didn't tear. Then she worked her fingers into it until she was able to create a small hole. She stretched this until she was able to rip the neck warmer into two pieces. Using this, she tied the driftwood around her ankle creating a splint that allowed her to put some weight on it. She then moved farther on, holding onto piles of ice.

Ahead, she found what she needed to finish the trip: a piece of two-by-four lumber on the ground. She grabbed it and placed it under her right armpit like a crutch and was able to move along better. She was dripping in sweat from the jolts of pain. Little by little and at a snail's pace, she moved her way toward the village. Eventually, she was able to turn in toward town and down the road to the clinic. She worked her way to the back door, bent to pull the key from her hiding place, and reached for the lock. Suddenly, her vision became dark and she collapsed in a pile outside the door.

* * *

Chelsey heard a thump and opened the door. "My God!" The blood drained from her face as she looked at Meara. "Verna, come here! I need you!"

Verna came running out. She also paled when she saw their instructor lying on the ground.

Meara lay there not moving. Her red hair was matted with the dark red of clotting blood. Her pants were torn, and she had wood strapped to her ankle.

"Meara! Can you hear me?" asked Chelsey urgently.

Verna turned into the entry and found a backboard and laid it down next to Meara. The two girls fumbled but were able to get a cervical collar onto her and carefully rolled Meara onto the board. When they rolled her back flat, Meara groaned and opened her eyes.

"What happened to you?" Verna asked as they carried Meara back to the trauma room. They put her onto the stretcher.

Meara's eyes shut again. Chelsey's heart sank. They couldn't do this without their instructor. They simply didn't have the experience. Then she remembered Meara's words: "You will never be alone. Your CHAM will guide you through any situation. When it comes to the emergencies, always follow your ABCs. Airway, breathing, circulation.

And, there is always somebody available on the other end of the phone line."

Don't panic, Chelsey. Breathe. Stay calm now for Meara. "A" was for airway. Her airway was open. "B" was for breathing. She was breathing on her own. "C" was for circulation. Chelsey put her hand on Meara's neck and felt for her carotid pulse. Her heart rate was fast at 100. Her heart was beating but fast. She could be in shock.

Verna was working on the other side of the stretcher. She pulled Meara's arm out of her sleeve and put the blood pressure cuff on and the pulse oximeter on her finger.

"Blood pressure 90/60. Oxygen level's 92."

"I am putting oxygen on her." Verna pulled out a nasal cannula and put the two prongs into Meara's nose and looped it behind her ears. The oximetry level went quickly up to 98.

"Okay, I am going to do a primary survey," Chelsey announced. "You see if you can get a doctor on the line." Then she pulled a pair of scissors out of her pocket and went to work cutting off Meara's shirt and pants, covering her with a sheet.

"I really am not ready to be doing this with just the two of us. Meara, would you please wake up?" Her heart felt like it was beating faster than Meara's. She worked her way through the emergency CHAM.

Meara was a mess. There was blood pooled in her hair around the edge of her cap. She had a scrape on her right cheek. The skin behind the scrape was a ghostly white. Her ankle was swollen to the size of a football and was already a dark purple. She felt Meara's head for any injury that she couldn't see. Other than the gash, her skull was intact. She then worked her fingers down Meara's spine, just as they had learned in their emergency training. There was no obvious deformity, and Meara didn't wince.

Did unconscious people wince?

She put her knuckles down on Meara's chest and twisted her fist back and forth.

Meara groaned and moved her head a little. "Responsive to pain with moan."

"Dr. Forester wants us to get two IVs in and to check her hemoglobin." Verna walked back into the room with an IV bag already spiked with tubing.

"Okay, I am continuing to inspect her. You get that going." Chelsey had no desire to try to start the intravenous herself.

"Yes, boss," snarled Verna. But she was already setting up the tape and the intravenous supplies like they learned in the lab. She had not yet had the chance to practice on another person. They had practiced with fake arms in lab. They all conveniently had holes from where other people had practiced. She wished Meara had a label pointing to exactly where the IV needed to go. She was shaking so hard she didn't know how she would be able to start the IV.

Chelsey watched her sister put the tourniquet on and clean the site as she continued to examine Meara. She put her hands on either side of Meara's chest and squeezed, then she pushed down on top. She took her stethoscope out.

"Lung sounds clear and full. Chest wall stable." She moved her stethoscope to Meara's belly.

"Bowel sounds positive in all four quadrants." She put the stethoscope around her neck. She placed her hands upon Meara's belly and watched her face for any reaction. "Her stomach is soft."

"Yes! I have it." Verna connected IV tubing to the catheter she had just threaded into the vein in Meara's arm. "Starting one-liter bolus of lactated ringers now. Thank you, God!"

Chelsey continued down assessing Meara's body as the intravenous fluid poured in.

"Why are you here? It can't be eight o'clock yet," Meara said in a quiet voice as she looked around.

"Oh yes, it is. It is actually eight thirty. We were getting worried about you, and we were about to come looking for you when you passed out on the steps," Chelsey smiled at Meara.

"Wow, either the walking took me longer than I thought, or I was out for a while on the beach."

"The beach? What were you doing on the beach? What happened?" Verna furrowed her brow.

"I was out running toward the airport. Suddenly, a black snow machine came up behind me, and then he came alongside me and forced me over the cliff. I woke up on top of an ice chunk at the base of the bluff. Most of my body landed in some drifted snow, but I obviously hit something hard." She moved her hand toward her head.

Meara realized she had an intravenous in her arm at that point. She looked at it and smiled. "Whose handiwork is this?"

"Verna did that," replied Chelsey.

Meara tried to sit up.

"Meara," scolded Verna, "you may be the teacher, but right now you are the patient, and you aren't thinking straight. Lie down."

Meara gave in to the scolding by lying back onto the stretcher.

Chelsey worked down Meara's body, noticing and feeling the large bruise on Meara's right hip. Then she worked herself down both legs.

"Aiii, that has to hurt." She palpated the left ankle and felt the pulse. "Peripheral pulses are palpable. Can you feel me touching?" She squeezed Meara's toe. "Capillary refill brisk and sensation intact." She watched Meara's head nod.

The back of her head had a big hematoma with a three-inch gash in it. The hat had helped to pool the blood in her red hair. Other than that, her skull felt firm.

"Three-inch laceration of the right lateral head," Verna declared out loud to Meara.

Meara smiled weakly in spite of her discomfort. "Good job."

The automatic blood pressure cuff went off. "Blood pressure 110/78, pulse 72. IV bolus in. I am going to call Dr. Forester back." Chelsey picked up the phone.

After a few rings, she had the doctor back on the line. "Hello, Dr. Forester, I have a forty-three-year-old patient known to you. It is Meara, our instructor. She was pushed off a fifteen-foot cliff and landed in some ice chunks. She hit her head, losing consciousness for an undetermined amount of time. She has a three-inch gash on her head. Bleeding is controlled. Cervical spine seems intact. She has no pain over the vertebrae. Her circulation and sensation are intact. Chest and abdomen without injury. There is a large contusion on the left buttock, and her right ankle is very swollen without any crunchiness, I mean crepitus, felt. She is able to move it slightly on her own with a lot of pain. She had made herself a splint on the beach and walked in using a crutch made from beach debris. She walked to the clinic, about a mile, then passed out again outside our door. Blood pressure was low but is now 110/78. Pulse 72 after one liter of lactated ringer bolus."

"Are you saying she lost consciousness twice? At the scene and again at the clinic?"

"Yes," responded Chelsey.

"Okay, with that fall and the loss of consciousness, she needs to come in for a CT scan. I am going to call to arrange transport. Get vitals every fifteen minutes. While I am calling to arrange transportation, you need to wash out that head wound. Make sure to irrigate it well. Have you placed staples yet on anybody?"

"Yes, yesterday was my first time," said Chelsey.

"Good, you are an expert then," joked the doctor.

Chelsey welcomed a little lightheartedness with this situation. She didn't like being alone with just her sister out here dealing with this. The doctor was calming her down and making her feel safe in what she was doing.

"By the way, when you send in the team, can you send someone in to work with us? We are both only just finishing our preceptorships for session one training. Neither of us feels comfortable here alone. I am scared."

"We will see what we can find. And by the way, you need to know that you did a beautiful job so far. That was a very well-done, professional report."

Chelsey went back to the trauma room. "They are sending a crew out to get you. You need a CT scan because of the distance of your fall and the loss of consciousness."

"I knew that would be the case," said Meara. "I am feeling better though. Less dizzy."

"Good." Chelsey wasn't sure if Meara was saying that just to make her feel better. "Now, I need to get your head taken care of. Hopefully, this won't make you dizzier. I am rinsing you out with a twenty-cc syringe and normal saline solution. Then we are going to staple your wound shut."

"Excellent. You are making me proud. And, it is a good thing that I have no plans to try a super short haircut! Bald won't be beautiful for me with this scar in the future. And, the bad scar would be my fault, not a representation of your handiwork. I sent Verna out to handle patients coming in at the front desk. I think she can handle some simple patients, and you can stay in here with me."

"You like to be in control, don't you?" Chelsey laughed. "You know it is okay to just be a patient?"

"Yes, but that doesn't mean that I can't help you deal with things from right here while I am down. It takes my mind off my head and ankle."

"As you wish. Tell me, do you remember anything more about the person that pushed you over?"

"Black snow machine, black snow gear, and I remember there was red on the gloves."

"I saw someone like that when I went in to meet the plane yesterday. When Rey came into town. Rey came in with a big tote. He turned down the ride to town, saying that he had Angus coming out to get him. Then, I saw the man on the snow machine with Rey's tote strapped to the back. Rey was walking behind like he wasn't with him."

* * *

Meara's head was spinning. The attempt on her life this morning took her completely off guard. Her head throbbed. She was reassured that she could remember all the details up to the time of the fall and from when she came back to. At least until she got to the door of the clinic.

The thought of having a cranial bleed kept going through her head. What if she did? What if there was bleeding in her brain right now? It would be at least a few hours before they could get her out of here. And the idea of flying with the weather that she just got in from didn't appeal to her. If she got in trouble here, there was nothing that could be done.

What was she doing living and working here? She could die from this, and here she was hours away from more help if she needed it. How did people live here without worrying about that? And, why did she not think of that before she took this job? She closed her eyes and listened to the throb of her head, waiting for the throbbing to talk to her and tell her what was going on. If only she could look inside, sense inside to know that she was alright.

All she could do was wonder. And worry.

She looked down at the intravenous catheters in her arms. The bolus that had helped bring her back to consciousness was done completely by her students Chelsey and Verna. They did it all without her help. They came to her rescue when she needed it. She smiled, thinking that she had forced her fledglings out of the nest.

Her smile disappeared fast, because the cervical collar on her neck pressed on her face. Its restraint felt like it was cutting off the blood flow to her brain. She reached to take it off then realized she should leave it on until she could speak with the doctor about clearing her neck. Then Chelsey wouldn't feel bad if something went wrong.

She thought back to the conversation she had heard between the girls before she was fully awake. She could hear their voices in her head.

"Who would have done this to her?" Chelsey had asked Verna.

"I have no idea."

"Do you have people in this village that hate *kussuks* so bad that they would be willing to randomly knock them out? We had one in our village. He is in jail now. His hate brought him plenty of trouble."

Meara could feel her gently touching her hand and feeling for a radial pulse.

"No, that hasn't been a problem. Except in extreme drunks, and they tend to hate everybody. But you know, I didn't realize how naive I was until I took this job. There is a whole different side to this village that I didn't know about."

The neck collar was irritating her back to the present from her conversation. Could someone she didn't know actually hate her enough because of the color of her skin to want her dead?

"I want this thing off." She reached up to her neck, but the thought of someone wanting to kill her made the choking feeling worse. After all the talk about cervical spine immobilization in training, she knew that Chelsey and Verna would worry. She would leave it on.

Her thoughts moved to racism. Here, she was the minority. Maybe it was good for her to experience a little racism. Nobody should ever have to fight for their life because of the color of their skin.

No, this didn't feel right. He was waiting for her, and he was determined in his mission.

Now the spinning she felt in her thoughts was focused on who it was that would have done this to her, why, and how they would be connected with Rey.

She thought about the comment that Chelsey had made when she said that Rey had come walking into town with this guy fitting the same description as her attacker. What was the connection? Or was there a connection?

Rey was a trooper. A lead trooper. He was the eternal helper, Mr. Dudley Do-Right. He played by the book all of the time. So, then what did he have to do with the man on the black snow machine? Who was the man in the black suit? What were they doing together, and how did they know each other? And most of all, why would the man in the black suit try to kill her?

"Can you get Rey on the line? His office number is in my phone in my backpack."

She knew in her heart that when she heard his voice, everything would come together and make sense.

Chelsey came back within moments with Meara's phone and brought the portable office phone to Meara to use.

Meara's hands shook as she picked out the numbers on the phone. She waited for the ring, and his voice quickly followed.

"Hello, Lieutenant Torrenson speaking."

That instant rush of comfort came immediately from hearing his voice. It almost made her forget the questions she was having about him just moments before. It certainly threw her off balance.

"Rey, it is Meara. I had an accident this morning, and it looks like I will be flown into town."

There was a hesitation on the line before Rey responded. In that time, Meara heard Chelsey pick up the other clinic line and could hear her muffled exchange in the background.

"What happened?" said Rey.

"I missed your protection from lions, tigers, and bears this morning." Meara forced a smile. "I went for my morning run. Someone deliberately forced me off the road and over a bluff."

Again, Meara noticed a hesitation to his response. Was that concern in his pause? Was he at a loss for words? He couldn't have anything to do with this.

"Are you hurt? You are so lucky to be alive!" Rey's words broke the awkward silence.

"I think I am alright, but they want to bring me in for imaging because of my loss of consciousness."

"You lost consciousness?"

"Yes, twice. Once with the fall and then after getting back to the clinic. That isn't a good sign with a head injury. But, I feel alright." She hoped her words would reassure him about her. She wasn't totally reassured herself yet.

"Well, I will say that it'll be nice to have you back in town. But, this isn't the way I wanted you coming back though."

Chelsey poked her head in the room. "Sorry to interrupt. I have bad news. There is no getting you out of here for imaging. Unless you take a turn for the worse. No planes are flying. The winds are supposed to last until tomorrow. Because you are stable right now, they don't think we should call in the Coast Guard."

"Tell them that I am okay. And, I don't feel anything that makes me feel that I need to be flown out urgently. We'll be fine here." She turned back to the phone. "Well, Rey, it doesn't look like I will be seeing you today. Weather is too bad."

"Are you going to be alright? I wish I could do something for you."

"Yes, I'll be fine. I wish you were here, too." She paused. She didn't want to ask him, but she needed to ask. His connection with the snow machine yesterday could have been just coincidental. "Rey, do you know anyone here that drives a black Polaris snowmobile and wears black snow gear and has gloves with red on them?"

For the third time, there was hesitation before he replied, and this time his response seemed a bit stiffer. "Not that I know of. But I don't know all that many people over there. And, I definitely don't know people's snow machines and what they wear."

"Rey, I am sorry to be a pest, but has there been any updates on the autopsy? Sophie really needs to put to rest what happened to Nora. The funeral was supposed to be this afternoon. They delayed it last night because the grave filled in with snow with the wind and some family couldn't get in that they wanted here. It is now planned for tomorrow. Have they looked at the labs? Her cause of death doesn't make any sense. Those labs really make you question what happened to her. I can't believe that your administration wouldn't need an autopsy." The delay had her perplexed. Back on the East Coast, there was no doubt in that the autopsy would have happened. But, this was Alaska. And, Alaska could be different in so many ways.

"No, no change," Rey grumbled. "It is a bureaucracy and you, my dear, are not a criminal investigator. They may have a plan that they haven't filled me in on. It would not be the first time. You do realize that she was just a villager. They have a lot more important things on their plate. I will follow up, if it helps you rest."

Meara felt her neck expand inside the restrictive cervical collar. Her pulse throbbed against it. "Okay, I will stop trying to be the private investigator. I do need to rest now. Take care. I'll be fine."

"You be careful out there. I need my running partner back."

Meara hung up the phone without further comment. She looked at the ceiling, which had been her view since she came to. "I can see things so much clearer now." She thought about her walk back. She had lifted, pulled, and walked all that way, and her neck never hurt. She knew that she could still have a broken neck, but it could be days before she could have the scan. Its restraint felt like it was cutting off the blood flow to her brain.

"This thing is coming off. Nobody and nothing is holding me back now. Nora was not 'just a villager' and I am not 'just a *kussuk.'* Neither of us is disposable. We are both people trying to make a difference. Nora deserves justice, and I am not going to let it avoid her without a fight." The restriction of the collar seemed to be trying to hold her anger back into a neat little obedient package.

She reached up and undid the Velcro that secured the rigid plastic holding her head in one position. Instantly, the freedom of being able to freely change her gaze seemed to help her feel clearer and more oriented.

Chelsey came back into the room. "Meara, why did you take the collar off?"

"I needed to be able to move to think, and I made the judgement that I really put my neck on the line when I tried to get back here. It hasn't hurt. I have full range of motion. I am willing to trust myself that my neck is alright. I accept responsibility for my decision. I have to trust my judgement right now."

Oh yes, I trust my judgement. He isn't going to do anything for Nora because she is nothing to him. Not only that, I am done with being silenced. I am not going to be quiet for any man when someone needs my voice.

She felt the freedom from removing the collar from her neck. Moving her head around and taking in the room, she felt like her vision was so much clearer. Her hesitation about getting closer to Rey might not have been cold feet after all but that inner sense that Sophie had lectured her about.

CHAPTER 19

Angus heard a knock on his station door. Its sound was almost buried in the wind. Things were quiet inside of the station. He was just debating putting his head down on the cot that the troopers would stay on when they came out to the village. A little shut-eye would help him think more clearly. However, he felt some urgency to follow up on the information that he learned from the Chief this morning.

The morning had been productive. When the Chief sobered up, he was a different man. His normal humility and responsibility returned with his sobriety. But the poor old guy was really missing a good chunk of time last night.

The Chief had talked about how ashamed he was. He had scared his wife, and that really upset him. He had been abusive to the health aide. He most regretted that his behavior last night was not at all representative of his normal standards for himself. They certainly were not appropriate for his role as Chief.

"I just couldn't handle the grief," he had said. "I was hurting so badly because of the death of my niece. But drinking didn't help it; it only made it worse."

When Angus told him that everyone that had taken care of him in the night did their best to keep things quiet, he broke into sobs from the gratitude.

The sobbing had caught Angus off guard as much as catching him intoxicated the night before.

When Angus questioned the Chief about where he purchased his supply, the Chief told him where to look.

Now, Angus was deep in thought. A search warrant would take a lot of time. Maybe he could do some looking around on that end of town. It was worth a shot. Progress with a search warrant would be delayed between the weather and getting Rey out here to do the search and getting it through the court. He needed to think about it.

The knock on the door got louder and became enough to break through his thoughts. When he answered, Chelsey stood there wearing scrubs and holding the keyring to his snowmobile.

"Found these in your snow machine," she smiled. She had shot across the way to talk to him without putting any coat on. He pulled her in and shut the door behind her to block the wind.

"Thank you. I have a bad habit of forgetting my keys in the ignition. One of these days, I am going to regret that." He took the keys back.

"I came over to report to you that there was an accident this morning. Only, it wasn't really an accident. Meara was run off the bluff by a man on a snow machine. A black Polaris, with black snow gear and gloves with red on them. I saw a similar snow machine yesterday when Rey came to town. He said he was waiting for you to pick him up. But, then I saw him later walking into town and his tote that he brought for you was on the back of this guy's snow machine. Who brought the tote to you?"

Angus froze with his keys in his hands. He processed the information. Rey was here yesterday? *And he delivered a tote of supplies to me?* He was cautious in his response. "I didn't get any supplies yesterday, so I didn't see this snow machine or the rider."

"I also overheard Meara on the phone with Rey. She was asking about when Nora's body was going to be taken for autopsy. She said something about lab results and that you were working on the investigation. What is going on with that?" Chelsey's added information caught Angus even further off guard.

Again, Angus hesitated in his response as his thoughts started running. What investigation was Rey talking about? There had been no further follow-up on Nora's death. Rey had told him that he would do all the filing for him that night. It hadn't been mentioned since. What were these labs that she was talking about?

"I cannot speak about that right now. However," he turned to look her right in her face, "I promise that I am going to be digging in and getting to the bottom of all of this."

"I need to get back to the clinic." Chelsey stopped and seemed to be searching his eyes.

What was she looking for? Was she trying to figure out what he knew and what he didn't know? Or was she seeking something else from him? The charge that he felt when he was near her was definitely building. Did she feel it, too?

Chelsey turned and walked out the door.

"No nap for me. I think I am going to go take a ride and check out Fred's place." He wearily pulled on his snow pants and jacket. There were so many odd things going on and so many questions. Maybe a trip to Fred's place would make one thing a little clearer. The Chief told Angus that Fred was the one that sold him the booze.

He hopped in his truck and drove to the far end of the village. There was an older home set back from the road. It had a fishing boat parked in front of it as well as a collection of pink and purple bikes sticking out of the snow.

Angus drove by. There was nothing that would help him get a warrant into the house. He continued down to the end of the road and turned around to come back. This new perspective changed everything. Coming from this direction, he could see just the edge of the yellow-and-black tote that Rey used. The trooper logo was barely visible. And, tucked behind the entry was a black Polaris snow machine.

The questions running through his mind turned his stomach. How was he going to handle this?

CHAPTER 20

Rey folded over his cell phone and slammed it onto his desk. His whole world was falling down around him. His perfectly created masterpiece was being put to the torch by the very woman he had envisioned standing next to him in front of that beautiful retirement home. How could part of his image be destroying it? How could she be so destructive without being aware of what she was doing?

He was torn. He really enjoyed that woman. She was smart, beautiful, caring. She had a great sense of humor and loved adventure. She fit well, and she would have taken good care of him. He paced the room, tapping a pen against his leg.

"I can't deny that I care about her." Even thinking about her, he felt stirred. That stirring just added to the confusion he was feeling. His future was so perfect until she ran those labs. Now she was worse than a dog with a bone. She just wouldn't let it go. She hadn't stopped pestering him about the autopsy. And, it was only a matter of time until she said something to Angus.

"Why can't I convince her that I have it all under control? Why doesn't she trust me and have faith that I am doing my job right? Doesn't she believe in me?" How many times had she pressed him even after he had "turned the case into the authorities"?

He stopped pacing, put his hands on the edge of the desk, and leaned in.

"Just look what she did." He found justification for what he needed to do. "She drove me to this point. Apparently, she doesn't appreciate me and what I could have done for her."

He could see no other choice. "I need to solve this Meara problem myself. It was a mistake to have believed that Fred could have handled it. That was a huge mistake leaving a loser to do my work. He certainly failed me."

Fred not only failed. Fred was a failure. How could he have not made sure that the job was completed? Rey Torrenson would never be a failure. "I need to stop her, or I could lose everything." He paced his office, moving back and forth under all the certificates of excellent performance.

Up to now, he had convinced her not to talk to Angus. He could only hope that she still hadn't. He had worked hard to convince her that Angus was new, inexperienced, and most of all not to be trusted. He was pretty sure that she hadn't spoken to him.

Yet.

Yet. That was the key word. She had proven to be dogged. It seemed as though it was something personal for her to avenge Nora.

He had definitely underestimated her tenacity. She always seemed so eager to fix things whenever she stood her ground that he never saw this determined part of her. She had seemed so eager to please when he watched her with other people, too. She was a people pleaser that was eager enough to deny herself of things she wanted in order to please others. He saw it when they went out to dinner. She would always have him order first, and she would move in a direction that she seemed to think would make him happy.

All of those things had made her safe. But he had misjudged her. He would pay if he didn't get her out of the way, and he needed to do it now.

"I hope I am not too late."

He looked out at the driving winds and the blowing snow. Now he had Mother Nature trying to interfere. This storm had already delayed the funeral. He couldn't wait for the funeral. Not only would Nora be laid to rest, but his worries about being found out would be buried with her body. Nobody liked to dig up bodies once they were buried. But, they would if there was enough evidence.

Now Meara was holding evidence, too.

"God, please, please keep her from telling anyone else that piece of information. Please help my stories." He prayed that he had been convincing enough with his stories to have her keep that critical piece of information about the blood work to herself. He prayed that he had convinced her that he was the only one that she could share it with. Was she maintaining that confidence? He deserved all of this to go well after all the things that had been done against him in the past. God had to be on his side.

He had her convinced that he was doing everything in his power to solve the death of Nora. He had held her off with talks of bureaucracy. But now, he was pretty sure she was going to spill the beans.

He pulled on his arctic gear and made sure that his GPS was ready. It would be easy to get lost in this storm. He grabbed an extra couple of cans of fuel and strapped them to the back of his snow machine.

If he left now, he would get there in a few hours. As long as everything went alright. He was taking a chance by riding the tundra in a storm like this alone. But, the life he had dreamed of was completely over if he didn't go take care of this inconvenience. If he was careful, he should be able to get into town undetected. He checked his holster and his ammunition. He also made a romantic meal to nourish her back to health with. And, he had his little additive ready to go.

He had his plan, leaning into the blowing snow as he exited the station. Now, for the execution.

* * *

"Damn, I can't lie here like a patient if I can't get anywhere. There is too much to be done." Her head hurt, but she was no longer dizzy. Her vital signs were now nice and stable, and strength was returning. She couldn't take pain meds because of the head injury, and not being able to be transported would change the ability to monitor her level of consciousness. "I need to keep my mind off the pain."

She disconnected her intravenous tubing and wrapped her arm in plastic. The intravenous access to treat her if she were to go into shock needed to stay a little longer. At least until she showered. Chelsey and Verna had hit gold the first time with starting her lines, and she didn't want to chance them needing a second.

"Chelsey, will you stay in the bathroom with me when I shower? In case I start to go down?"

She sat in the shower chair and rinsed her hair. The warmth flowing over her head felt so good and almost decreased the throbbing. The water flowed down her body in a red river pooling around her feet before it swirled down the drain. Her hair was a matted mess, and she could not work the dried blood free.

"Chelsey, can you get me a bottle of hydrogen peroxide? That's the trick to getting blood out of things." With the addition of the peroxide, the shower floor horror movie scene now had brown, fizzing bubbles mixed in the red, and then finally it worked its way to clear.

Standing up, she ran the hot water over her sore limbs. She tried to put her splinted ankle down. The plastic splint made a horseshoe up and over her swollen ankle to give it support. The pain from putting weight on the left ankle made her lean back to put her weight fully on her right. This splint was not doing the job.

"Thank you for your help. I feel like a new woman," she said to Chelsey as she wrapped herself in a towel. "Sometimes a shower is a great source of healing. I don't know if my head could have handled a maqii right now." The shower had worked miracles for her. She felt more awake, and the stiffness in her muscles was not quite as bad. The only thing that needed more attention was that ankle. But first, she would get dressed.

"Your head is seeping a little. We may need to put a dressing back on it for a while." Chelsey wiped away a small drop of blood working down Meara's cheek.

Meara carefully slipped on pants, a bra, and a long-sleeve shirt as well as her favorite polypropylene sock liners and a tightly knit pair of wool socks. The wool socks had been with her a very long time and had accompanied her on many crazy adventures. She then put a scrub top over her top as a declaration that she intended to work again with the girls. They could just as well watch her working with them as they could if she was lying around. Probably even better.

Her stomach still felt sick, and she had no desire for food. She reassured herself that it was just the nerves from her morning and not a sign of severe head injury.

"Chelsey, would you look in the storage room and see if there are any walking boots?" The air cast that she had on clearly was not giving the support she needed. The swelling of her ankle was too much, and she couldn't walk. She was sure if it had the proper support she would be able to walk.

"Is this what you are looking for?" Chelsey returned with a big boot with a rigid sole and stiff, knee-high sides strapped together with Velcro. She opened the Velcro straps and gingerly slipped her foot down and inside. Her ankle felt like it expanded to fit the space. The padded support provided some relief from the pain as well. She snugged up the supporting Velcro straps, and her lower leg felt like one unit.

"Ahh, instant comfort." She stood and realized she could tolerate weight. She moved down the hall and was able to walk. It certainly wasn't graceful, but she was able to hobble around using the rail that lined the hallways to avoid the pain.

She moved herself back where she could peer into the waiting room. Looking at the occupants, she sighed. There was Lorna again, this time with her son. She couldn't be looking for travel with this weather.

Verna called her out of the waiting room and brought her back to an exam room. She worked her way carefully through the CHAM. This time, he was brought in for a suspected seizure. Lorna didn't give him the chance to answer for himself as she told the story of how he was watching television just prior to arrival when he suddenly arched back, fell to the floor, and started shaking.

While Verna obtained vital signs, Meara took the opportunity to strike up a conversation. "That must have been incredibly stressful. And to think that this has now happened in addition to all the other things that your children have gone through recently. I am worried about how you are doing. How are you holding up?"

Lorna turned toward Meara, tilting her head up to meet her eyes, her shoulders slumped. "I can't tell you how much stress we have been through lately. My mother is sick. She is being treated for cancer. I want to be there with her, but I can't afford to get to town to see her. I just got a call this morning that she was just sent to the hospital. My family in town are saying that she may not make the night."

Meara held Lorna's eye contact as she slid her chair over in front of her. She maintained the eye contact as she slid her hands into Lorna's. She let her gaze drop to their hands then returned them to meet Lorna's. "Is it alright for me to hold your hand?" she queried as she sat knee to knee.

Lorna's own body started to convulse as she held back her tears.

"Tell me more. It seems like you have a lot you are holding onto," said Meara.

Lorna's forehead wrinkled as she tried to stop the tears. "I need to get in to see her tonight. I cannot lose her. I need to be there with her." Lorna let the tears flow. Her sobs echoed in the little exam room.

"Let it out. It is alright to cry; you need to cry," Meara reassured Lorna as she gazed over to look at Wassily.

He was looking at his feet and held his hands on his lap and was fidgeting with his fingers.

"Lorna, may I ask you a question?" Meara asked.

Lorna responded with a nod.

"First, I need to let you know that there won't be any travel tonight. Nobody can get in, including the Coast Guard. That is why you see me here looking like this and taking care of you. It would be too risky for everyone involved. That includes both the patients and the flight crew. Knowing that, I need to ask you if your son really had a seizure."

The little boy turned his head and watched his mother intently.

She looked at Lorna then at the little boy and then back at Lorna's face.

Lorna looked at her son and slumped further into her chair. "No. He didn't have a seizure. I just can't afford to fly in to see my mother. I have taken advantage of the medical travel to get there. It works to get me there but then I arrive with only one child and have to fly back to take care of the rest. I want to stay with her. I have been torn between being here for my children and being there with my mother. If I could only afford to get us all there. But, I don't have money for that. I can barely feed us all. I have been getting extra formula and food when I go in because it is so much cheaper there."

"Lorna, thank you for your honesty. I can't get you to your mother tonight, but I will see what resources we can find to get you and all of your children into town so that you can be with your mother. I can't make promises, but I will try. Can you come by here tomorrow morning? We will see what we can do."

She turned in her chair. "Verna, can you finish this documentation? And make a call into the hospital and ask for the social worker? They should be able to help. And you." She finished by looking at the little boy. "You don't have to have any more arm squeezes or needles today. You don't have to tell stories anymore to help your Momma."

* * *

Verna and Chelsey had just left the clinic for the day and had settled Meara into the break room. The bottom bunk was now set up for her with all her sleeping gear, and she had some food set out to eat. Verna would be on call tonight with Meara.

"I would like to stay here with you tonight. Then if you have problems, I will be right here. I don't like you being alone," said Verna.

"Really, I am alright. You two have set me up with everything that I need. You go home and try to get some rest." Meara leaned into the wall to be more comfortable with her leg up on a pillow.

"I will give you a quick call later." Verna turned then left the room.

Meara reached for the phone. She dialed Rey's number and got no answer. She would try back later. She sipped on a cup of broth that Joe had dropped off for her earlier. She smiled when she thought about what a doting father he was to the girls.

How was Sophie doing? She wished she could have gone down to visit. The delay of the funeral was probably taxing her a bit. But with all the people surrounding her, she seemed to be well supported. Meara was surprised that she had found comfort sitting in the crowded house filled with Sophie's family.

She thought she heard a knock on the door. "Noooo, please don't have a patient for me. I hardly had sleep last night, and after today I am beat." She hesitated to move in her chair, hoping it was just the wind on the door.

The knock returned as a clear, defined bang. There was no denying it. Getting up, she hobbled to the door. She opened it and thought she was hallucinating.

"Rey, what are you doing here? How did you get here? There are no planes flying! Did someone drop you off?" She noticed there was no vehicle around.

Part of her wanted to hug him and feel the protection of his arms. The other part of her was angry and held back remembering the "just a village woman" comment. Was he talking about his own beliefs, or was he referring to the system? It didn't matter, regardless of the answer, her anger at the injustice kept her from drawing him near.

"I felt so terrible about you and your accident I wanted to bring you a little love and attention. I needed to see you with my own eyes to know that you are alright." He took her face in his hands, inspecting her. Then he leaned over and kissed her. Shivers ran through her body as he pulled her tight to him in spite of her hesitations.

She stepped back. "Come in and come back to the break room. I was just sipping some broth." Meara walked back to the break room and put her foot up again.

"Broth? You need more than that to heal." He slipped his backpack off and placed it on the counter.

"I brought you a nice meal of chicken, sweet potatoes, and kale. I'm sorry that it's leftovers from last night, but it's the perfect healing meal, and I didn't have time to plan. Next time, give me a little warning when you are going to run off a cliff. Then I can treat you like you deserve." He set two plates up and prepared them to go to the microwave.

Then, reaching into his backpack he pulled out a large thermos. "Let's start with a cup of tea." He poured out a cup and handed it to her.

The image of the thermos and the sound of his voice triggered the memory of them standing together at the dance. One of the last things Nora did that night was accept his cup of tea.

All of a sudden, her head was turning, and it wasn't from her accident. Images formed in her head. She remembered how Nora had been wide awake and excited about the event. Then they all had the tea that Rey shared at the dance. Shortly after they drank their tea, Rey and Angus had left. Then Nora had suddenly become so sleepy she couldn't stay for the event that she herself had planned.

Sleepy! She stifled the gasp that wanted to come out as all the pieces clicked together into a perfect puzzle. Benzodiazepines, how did he give her the benzos without everyone else getting them at the dance? They explained her sleepiness. But she was found with alcohol, and there was alcohol in her mouth but none in her blood. Where did he find her, and when did he set her up with the alcohol? Was she even alive when the alcohol went into her mouth?

She shook herself back to the present. She smiled at him and tried her best to give him an adoring gaze. Meara picked up the cup with both of her hands and held it to her nose. "Mmmm, smells so good."

Rey lifted his own and took a sip.

Meara tried to put hers back on the table as nonchalantly as she could. She needed to get away from him. But, where would she go? Was Angus part of this? He was there in the gym with Rey that night, and he was there when they brought Nora in. He had seemed like a good enough guy when they had encountered him over this past week.

Sophie's? She couldn't go there and burden Sophie. She couldn't consider leading this man to Sophie's house. Besides, if she tried to walk there, he would catch up to her in no time.

Verna's house? No, she had her elderly parents there. But they would have Chelsey and Joe there as well. But by going there, she would risk something happening to the elders. That wouldn't work.

"I have something to add to this smorgasbord," she smiled at Rey. "I will be right back."

She clunked down the hall past the arctic entry and grabbed her jacket as she passed, hoping that he didn't pick up on the stop. She then cut through the trauma room and slipped to the other side of the clinic. She needed a distraction to give her time.

Her eyes stopped on her dictation recorder on the desk where she had left it after charting earlier. She carefully picked it up and pressed the rewind button. Then she firmly hit play and set it back on the desk. Her voice filled the room. She hoped that the sound of her voice in the room would buy her some time. Then she quietly opened the front clinic door, sneaked through, and she gently shut it and quietly locked the dead bolt behind her.

She found that her gloves had been put back in the sleeve of her coat as she pulled it on, and she welcomed the protection for her hands. She pulled the hood up on her parka, wishing that the hat and scarf had found their way there as well.

Where to go? She looked around trying to make a plan. It had to be quick. Looking in front of the VPSO building, she noticed that Angus's snow machine was outside. She looked again. Was that the keychain hanging there in the ignition? She couldn't believe her luck. She turned the key, and the engine started. Without a clear plan, she took off. If he could get here from Agushak, then maybe she could make it back. She sped off down the back side of the village and toward the direction she remembered coming with Rey on the day of their picnic.

Steering the snow machine across the tundra, she headed toward the "snow highway" back to Agushak. The cold whipped through her hood, and she was feeling the exposure of the cold and wind as it went straight through her pants. How would she make it back without freezing to death?

She would have to worry about that later. Right now, she needed distance in her flight. She could tighten up her clothing once she had put some distance between Rey and herself.

There was the normal group of young teens driving their snow machines in circles in the middle of town. After the nights of interrupted sleep from their noise, she was surprised as to how grateful she felt for their presence right now. Their noise gave her a little camouflage in her flight.

A few miles out of town, she started thinking about who she would go to for help in Agushak. The local police should be able to help her. Rolling her wrist back, she accelerated even more in her quest to get away.

About five miles out, the escape vehicle jolted, sputtered, and then came to a complete stop. She looked at the panel and saw the fuel gauge pointing to E. Out of gas.

Good God. How could she have not looked at that. Wasting no time, she hopped up and went to the back of the sled hoping to find some fuel inside the seat.

Nothing.

She started to panic. He would realize fairly quickly that she had taken off. She needed to get out of here and fast.

She stood and looked around, taking stock of her situation. If he followed her, and he would, she was a sitting duck right here.

The trail in front of her was packed down with occasional drifts of snow left on it. One option was to run down the trail, but she could see miles ahead of her, and that meant that he would also see her ahead of him.

She turned 360 degrees. To the left was the beginning of the mountain range. There would be plenty of places to hide there. One step off of the packed trail, she found her foot sinking knee high into the snow. She couldn't get there without leaving an obvious track in the snow. And, she wouldn't be able to get there fast enough trudging through deep drifts.

On her right, she noticed the grove of trees that she had flown over a few days ago. The packed trail ran close by it.

She looked back down at the snow machine and noticed a first aid kit sitting under the seat. She grabbed that and started running toward the grove. Each step on her ankle reminded her of her extra challenge.

She remembered from Sophie's that the hunters had taken a moose from the grove for the funeral. She was able to find remnants of their footsteps. She carefully matched her steps into the steps of the hunters and moved into the grove as quickly as she could.

She was thankful for the cloudy night sky and the cover it gave her. The wind was cutting through her street clothes, and her feet were cold and wet. Her running sneaker and the walking cast were totally inappropriate out here and not keeping her dry. She was feeling a hard, cold squeeze in her feet. Her injured ankle alternated between sharp pains and a constant gnawing ache. The staples in her head felt like they were conducting the cold directly to her brain.

The moose. She shuddered, but this shudder was not from the cold. She was following these footsteps right toward that pack of moose. They were sure to kill her for invading their safe space, and she was sure they were on guard after the hunt this week.

There was no choice. She needed to follow the hunters' steps in this direction. She could at least find more cover in the trees. She was no hunter, but she did know that she needed to stay downwind of the moose or at least where she had seen them in the grove.

Then she remembered something that scared her even more than the moose. That thermal camera! She might find cover by the trees, but if he had that with him, he would be able to see her clear as day. These trees weren't big enough to hide behind. Hiding her footsteps wasn't going to be enough.

She moved as quietly as she could with her squeaking walking cast, fearing each squeak would be her end. The sound echoed like a doorbell in the wilderness. She stopped and held her breath, not daring to move.

A moose in the pack ahead of her stirred. He was facing in the other direction with his nose to the wind. His head cocked as if he had caught a scent of something.

She needed to get closer to them. Her size would give her away if he had that camera. Her mouth went dry; her heart pounded so hard in her chest she was sure the moose could hear it.

The moose up ahead put his nose toward the ground, bent his front legs, and kneeled. If she wasn't here at this moment in this situation witnessing a moose either praying or giving his fullest moose expression of downward dog, she would be laughing at the scene. He continued to graze. He was clearly not interested in her if he was relaxed enough to be grazing.

She moved forward again. How could they not smell her? She certainly smelled them. The air was filled with earthy smell with an added aroma close to old gym socks. Maybe they couldn't smell her after being around themselves for so long.

She restarted her journey farther back in the grove. Ahead, on the other side of a fallen tundra spruce, was one of the largest moose she had ever seen. He was head down and deeply relaxed in a snooze.

Immediately, she identified him as her personal protector. She lowered herself to the ground to eliminate the sound of the walking boot and crawled parallel to the moose and tucked herself down along the pine. She had barely settled in when she heard the whine of a solitary snow machine approaching on the trail. She curled into a ball and prayed that she was not seen. She hoped that the thermal print of the large moose hid that of her own.

She shuddered, trying to choke back her fear and to control her shaking from the cold and her inappropriate dress. She could maybe be trampled by the moose or definitely be murdered by him. Calculating her risks, she stayed with her plan. She placed her bets on the moose.

* * *

Rey leaned back in his chair and waited for Meara to return to the meal he had prepared while he casually sipped his tea. He waited five minutes as he listened to her talking to herself from across the clinic. He could hear the murmur of her voice but couldn't make out what she was saying. What is taking her so long? He was irritated that she was wasting his time. He had enough to do that night without her dawdling.

He took advantage of her absence to heat the meal. He had not forgotten to add the romance when he threw everything into the bag to go. He had even grabbed a tablecloth and cloth napkins from his house as he rode by. Keeping the romance level up would help him with his final deception. "Not bad for no preparation time." He felt pretty proud of himself.

He could hear her talking still but hadn't heard her moving about for a while. "Meara?"

Just more murmuring was all he had for a response.

"Meara?" he called louder. Again, no change in the rambling of her voice.

He got up and walked through the clinic toward her voice. He entered a side room where he found a long tabletop spreading across the wall. On top of the table, placed squarely in the middle, was a tape recorder with the on button pressed, and from it came Meara's voice talking about patient exams. Meara herself was nowhere to be seen.

He went to the front door. It was dead bolted shut from the outside. There was no key available to open it from the inside.

"Shit."

He went back to the arctic entry and slipped on his pants, boots, and jacket then rushed to the back room. He quickly scanned the room for traces of him. He slipped the thermos into his backpack and dumped the remnants of Meara's tea into the sink. Nobody would ever trace the tablecloth or food to him, so he left them there. He needed to catch her.

He then rushed out the door. No sign of Meara. Looking toward the VPSO building, he noticed that the snow machine that had been there on his arrival was now gone. He could see a funny track in the snow that led over to where it had sat. He took off in a run toward where he had hidden his snow machine just out of town where the snow highway began.

There, along the tracks that his machine had made on his arrival, he noticed another set going off across the tundra. He hopped onto his vehicle and took off in pursuit. She should be easy enough to catch up to. She had already proven herself a lousy rider. She knew only what he had taught her, and she was not an easy student.

He pulled the accelerator back and took off toward hub village. A few miles out, he noticed a dark shape on the trail.

As he grew closer, he realized it was a snow machine. The VPSO snow machine to be exact.

He pulled up alongside it. It was stopped, the engine barely still warm. He turned the ignition, and nothing happened. Then looking at the fuel gauge, he laughed. She may have gotten a jump on him, but luck was on his side tonight. She stood no chance of getting away from him on foot out here. She would be easy to find. The tundra was wide open, and other than the blowing snow disrupting vision, there wasn't much for her to hide in. He smiled. He also had the benefit of having search and rescue equipment.

"I am going to search but there will be no rescue tonight," he declared to the wind. By the footprints around the snow machine, it appeared she went in two different directions then the steps disappeared. The ice pack where the footprints ended would make it a bit difficult for him to track.

He put on the thermal-imaging goggles and scanned the tundra in the direction of Agushak. No thermal print, and there was nowhere to hide in that direction. He scanned the base of the mountains. There was no way she went that way. She would not have been able to hide her tracks.

He hopped on the snow machine and slowly worked his way back toward the grove of trees. She could be hiding in there thinking she could tuck away in the trees. Too bad for her. She should be an easy find with the goggles. He scanned the woods. To his surprise, the grove lit up with large thermal prints. About fifteen of them. Some standing up, most lying down. Moose herding in the grove for protection. Meara would never go anywhere near them; she was petrified of them.

Where could she have gone? If she had taken off away from town, she would be a goner from the weather. Many a person had wandered out onto the tundra in the stormy weather. By the time they were found in the spring, there was nothing left but bones. If bones were found at all. He could search this way later.

If she had not taken off across the tundra and gone in the direction of the village, it would take her an hour or more to find her way back to town.

That is where he would go to search for her. He would give himself an hour or more to search for her, then he still had something to deal with. He needed to deal with the other body and get rid of any evidence. And, get rid of it permanently. Once that was taken care of, he would be able to find her easily enough.

* * *

She had stayed still and could hear the crunch of his boots on the tundra. It sounded like he stayed on the trail.

All was silent for a few minutes. She breathed as quietly as she could and remained still. Finally, the foot tread moved away, and the ignition turned on the snow machine. The sound of the snow machine moved off to the distance until it was a distant hum. She slowly rose to sit in the little hollow she had curled into beneath the fallen alder. She looked around the nearby forest. The moose around had settled down to rest and seemed to have accepted her presence.

She was cold. She could not remember a time that she had been so cold. And wet. Her feet and legs were soaked from the snow that coated her pants, shoe, and sock-covered toes of her injured foot. The snow had stuck there then melted from the warmth of her body. The warmth was now being steadily drawn away from her by the wet clothing. Her feet were now freezing to the point that they no longer hurt.

Her situation was not good. She was quickly on her way to frostbite and hypothermia. She only had a pair of sneakers and that walking cast and no snow pants. She had a long way to walk to get back to the village where she could find safety.

She got up and moved away from her protectors. She did not want to take the chance of disturbing them.

"Thank you, my friends," she whispered back toward the grove as she hobbled out of it into the dark, wide-open tundra. She sat in the snow and opened the emergency kit. The smell of bandages met her when the box opened, and she was glad that she didn't chance opening it closer to the moose. Inside, she found supplies that might help her chances of survival. She smiled when she saw the little packet of handwarmers in the first aid kit looking up and greeting her like they were greeting an old friend. She pulled the pair out of the plastic that kept them from activating and set them down to heat up. Then, she pulled her silver emergency blanket out of her pocket. She opened the sheet and cut it in two with the multi-tool she kept in her pocket. Then removing her sneaker, she slipped a handwarmer on top of her foot under the lacing, a trick she used in her ski boot back east. Then she wrapped her whole left leg with the reflective material and secured it with the medical tape in the bag. Then she slowly and painfully removed the walking cast and wrapped her injured foot and leg the same way and put the walking boot back on.

She was so grateful that she wore wool socks year round. If she had cotton socks on, her feet would already have frozen. The wet wool socks would keep her warm, especially now that there was a means to keep the heat in.

She peeked at her watch. 8:30 PM.

She searched more in the medical kit and found some emergency food bars. She opened one and ate half, chewing and appreciating the food as if it were a long-overdue gourmet meal and also praying that it wasn't her last. She hoped the calories would help her warm up a little and give her the energy she needed to make her way back. She slipped the other in her pocket.

She continued to sort. There was also a small penlight, some matches, and fire-starting sticks. She slipped those in her pockets as well.

Her head throbbed, and the rhythm it made brought her back to the reality of the passing time until Rey tried searching for her again. He wouldn't give up easily. Of that she was sure.

The pain in her ankle felt like an ice pick was being driven into it. She decided to change her perception of it.

"Pain is a sign that I am alive, and I will choose to be grateful for that." She was still alive, although she could not credit her own wits at this point.

"What was I thinking believing that I could run away from the village all the way to Agushak on a stolen snow machine?" She found a roll of gauze and wrapped it around her head and face to give herself more protection from the weather. Then she taped her hood closer to her face.

"Where did I think I was running to? I didn't even check for gas. I wouldn't have had protection in Agushak. He would have come up with some story to have the local troopers stop me." She stood on her newly wrapped legs. Her eyes were adjusted to the pitch-black night. The warmth and the calories seemed to resurrect her rattled brain. And, her determination as well.

"I am done with running away. If I survive this—" She stopped and corrected herself loudly to the wilderness. "No. *When* I survive this, I am going to spend my life running toward what I want. Miss Meara Crowley no longer runs away because of fear. The moose were right. There is safety in numbers and safety in friends."

Between her memory of the flight over and the darkened gray silhouettes made by the landscape, she was able to assess the lay of the land. The river came along here. If she got down and ran back on the frozen ice, she wouldn't leave tracks and wouldn't be seen as easily by Rey's camera as she would be running on top of the tundra. The other benefit would be that she could get out of the driving wind.

But that river was so curved. How long would it take for her to get there? She remembered Jim mentioning on their flight that the headwater was about five miles up in the mountains and they were about five miles from the sea above the grove.

"Pi Day. I remember from last Pi Day that the length of a meandering river can be calculated by multiplying the distance from the headwater to sea by pi." That meant she had about fifteen miles to go if she chose the protected route back.

"No big deal normally. Ice, wind, painful ankle are not going to stop me. If this isn't a steel bra and panties day, I don't know what is."

She started down the river, counting turn after turn. She hoped that the pi calculation ran on the high side.

CHAPTER 21

Angus went back to the station after the quick drive through town.

His snow machine was gone. He knew he had left it sitting outside the station. Looking where it was parked, he could see an odd set of footprints leading up to it. One side looked like a sneaker. The other was squared off like a peg. He went inside and looked for his keys. They were not on their hook where they should have been. "I can't believe I left them in the ignition again." He rummaged across his desk. "I couldn't have. What the heck is it with me? I don't want to be scolded by Lieutenant Torrenson about it being stolen because I was careless."

He didn't want to be scolded by the king, as he thought of the Captain's name. Rey. He acted like he was the king ruling over the area and Angus was just an inconvenient peasant.

There were times when Rey came out that Angus felt like an irritating flea on Rey's pants, like he knew nothing and as Rey would put it, "was just a villager." Angus was pretty sure that Rey had made assumptions and had never bothered to look at Angus's experience before he came out here.

Angus had grown up in Anchorage and graduated from high school in the top ten of his class. Between his scholarships and his wrestling, he had a full scholarship to UAA. He had graduated from there as an honors student in the criminal justice program, and he had a minor in business administration. He would have gone to trooper academy, but his mother had gotten sick when he was supposed to attend, and he needed to stay in Anchorage to take care of his sister. He had accepted placement in the VPSO academy so that he could work in the villages before the next entry to the trooper academy.

It was clear that Rey assumed that he knew nothing. Angus was a bit shy at heart, and he didn't say much. He knew that people underestimated him because of that. However, he had realized a long time ago, when you weren't too busy talking, you could hear a lot more information. At times, he wished that Rey would learn that lesson when he had to listen to him go on one of his lectures about policies and procedures that supported his greatness.

Angus enjoyed being in the village, although he wasn't yet doing the job that he wanted. His grandparents had lived out here in a nearby village, and he remembered fondly the few times that they were able to visit during his youth. It was so nice to get out of the city.

But now, he might have jeopardized his career with his forgetting the keys. The snow machine was missing, but that needed to wait a few minutes. His head was clouded with all that he was thinking now.

First, he wanted to look into what Chelsey had said about the case and about the blood work. That was bothering him more than the snow machine. Why didn't he know anything about an investigation? This made no sense.

He logged onto the computer and waited patiently as the log-in page slowly filled the screen. Then he looked into the database searching for Nora Wassily. There was nothing. No report at all filed about her death and certainly none about an investigation. He picked up the phone.

"Hello, this is VPSO Nanalook in Quyalaqaq. I have searched my database and cannot find the file on a death we had out here. Can you check from your end to see if there have been any files opened on the death of Nora Wassily?"

He could hear the keyboard clicking on the other side of the phone, then a pause of silence. "I don't see any cases under Wassily. Can you spell it for me?"

"W-A-S-S-I-L-Y."

"No, no cases under that spelling. I am trying to adjust the spelling and still nothing," said the dispatcher in Anchorage.

Shaking his head, he searched through the files he had put away in his own drawer. The file was not where he had left it either. "That is odd. Is the Major in?"

"No, he is out on a call right now. Is it an emergency?"

"No, I need to do more digging to find out what is gone. I will call back later. Thank you for your help." He paced for a minute, looking at the file cabinet where he knew he had filed a paper copy on the night of Nora's death. Where could that have gone? He had been the only one in the building with access to the locked file cabinet.

"Except Torrenson." He thought back to what Chelsey had told him. "Meara knew about some labs. Chelsey had seen Rey come to town the other day, but he had never checked in with me. And, he came in with one of my totes. I never got a delivery of any supplies that day. Why would he come here with supplies and never check in with me or deliver supplies?"

He'd walk across to the clinic and question Meara about the labs himself. Outside, he walked up to the clinic, seeing the lights on inside the break room. There was no answer when he knocked loudly on the door. He walked through the snow and peered in the break room window. There was no sign of her in there.

He walked back into his station and grabbed his radio. "VPSO trying to reach clinic. Come in clinic."

He waited for five minutes for a response. "VPSO trying to reach clinic. Come in clinic."

"Hello, Angus, this is Verna. Meara is not picking up?"

"No."

"I am on my way."

* * *

It was nearing eleven when Verna pulled up to the clinic on her four-wheeler. She came to a rapid stop and turned the ignition off at the same moment as she swung her leg off. She wasted no time in moving to the door to open it.

Her heart pounded in her chest. What was she going to find on the other side of the door? And, how would she deal with it? Her mind reeled with the possibilities.

"I should never have left her alone after that fall. But she convinced me she would be fine and that she would call me if she started to not feel well. My God, I hope she is alright." She looked briefly back to Angus as she tried to enter, half expecting him to make things all better.

She jiggled the key in the back entry, trying to get the door to catch. It stuck and wouldn't turn. Realizing that she was holding her breath, she exhaled, took a deep breath and tried again.

"You aren't helping anyone by being panicked. Calm down," she mumbled to herself. Any other time the door lock would have turned with ease. But, the guilt of leaving her patient alone had taken over. Why had she let Meara talk her into leaving her alone? Supervisor or not, she was a patient with a head injury. To top it off, the doctor had said that she needed supervision.

She stomped her foot and tried again. Finally, the key caught, and they got into the clinic. "Angus, why would her coat be gone, but her snow pants and boots still be here? Maybe she came out to get it? Meara?" The echo of her voice seemed to reverberate across the empty halls of the clinic.

No answer.

"I pray she is in a deep sleep." She looked at Angus.

His face was drawn with the same worry she felt.

Neither of them was prepared for what they saw in the back room. There was a meal for two set up at the table. Complete with a tablecloth.

"Who would have had dinner with her?" Verna asked herself as much as she asked Angus.

"And, why didn't they eat it?" Angus regarded the two full plates with clean utensils sitting next to them.

"I can't think of anyone else in the village she knows other than Sophie and her family." She had looked toward Sophie's on her way here, and all the lights were off.

"Where could she have gone? This food is cold. It wasn't recent that she left it here."

"She never would have left without her call radio. She never leaves it far from sight when she is on call." Verna's gaze fell on the radio sitting on the little bunk side table. "Something is not right. Meara is the definition of responsibility."

"What was she wearing for shoes when you last saw her?" asked Angus.

"She had a sneaker on her good foot and a walking cast on the right."

"Do you have a walking cast for me to look at?"

"Sure." Verna walked to the supply room and brought one out and handed it to Angus.

He looked at the base of the walking boot and raised his eyes back to Verna. "Well, I think I know who took my snow machine."

There was a banging on the back door. They rushed to open the door expecting to see Meara. Instead, there stood Fred Chythlook. He stood there in his black snow gear with his visor up on the black helmet. His red gloves stood out in contrast. His eyes were glued to the ground, and his shoulders slumped.

"Angus, I heard you on the radio. I was going to come see you in the morning, but I haven't been able to sleep. When I heard you were here at the clinic, I came to talk to you."

"I would like to talk, Fred. It will need to be another time. We have a missing person here. I think you might know her. She had an accident today." Angus's eyes tracked from Fred's face down to his feet then back to his face. This time, his gaze very purposefully tried to hold Fred's.

"This kind lady was forced off the bluff by someone riding a black Polaris, wearing black gear with a black helmet and red gloves. You wouldn't happen to know anything about that?" The awkward silence hung among the three of them.

Verna anticipated a denial.

"Yes." Fred lifted his head, and he locked eyes with Angus. "As a matter of fact, I do. I am so ashamed. I have let my family down and the village down. I cannot excuse my behavior. I knew it was wrong when I got involved with him. I was wrong, but I was desperate. This summer season was such a horrible loss that I could not see any way to make it through the winter without using my boat. Losing my boat would mean I lose the ability to ever provide for my family as my own boss. When he approached me and asked me to distribute, I saw it as a way out. I knew it was wrong, but I thought that I could do this for a short time—just enough to make my payments.

"Things were going well. I have no idea what that girl did. He definitely had a thing against her. He asked me to get her out of the village. So, I tried calling her work to make a complaint hoping they would fire her. But…they didn't get rid of her. When that failed, he told me to make her disappear, or we would both be in jail.

"I was thinking in fear. Fear of being exposed and being sent to jail. Fear of shaming my family. I wasn't thinking clearly, and the fear drove me to do something I would never do. I was the one that drove her off the cliff. It was wrong. It was all wrong. I tried the bluff because I thought at least she had a chance of surviving the fall. I thought then that the weather would have killed her. Then, I wouldn't feel like I had killed her. It doesn't make sense, I know. And, I betrayed myself. It is not who I am. Take me in, arrest me now. I am guilty. I have no idea what is going to happen to me as a consequence of this, but I accept it. I screwed up and I cannot shame my family anymore. I have my kids to think of."

Verna's jaw dropped, and she and Angus exchanged a quick glance.

"Who is he?" asked Angus.

"Do you know where she is now?" asked Verna.

Fred looked Angus straight in the eye. "She is missing? Are you talking about the woman from this morning? I didn't know what happened to her after she went off the bluff."

"Who is he?" repeated Angus.

"Trooper Torrenson. He promised me if we could keep this on the low that I would have enough to get my payments caught up and some extra."

"Fred, I am not arresting you now. Right now, we need your help. Can you go round up the Chief and the search and rescue crew? She is missing, and my snow machine is as well. She didn't leave dressed to be out, and it appears she has been gone for a while. Meet us back here with a crew as soon as you can."

* * *

Angus left Verna alone to get some emergency gear together for the search and rescue crew. Returning to his office, he dialed the phone to Anchorage again.

"Hello, VPSO Nanalook calling. Can I talk to the Major?" he asked the dispatcher.

"Hold a moment."

"Major Sharp speaking."

"This is VPSO Nanalook. We have some big trouble out here. I have had some alcohol importing lately, and I just had a man come in confessing to the distribution. He also reported that he forced a woman off a bluff this morning to scare her out of town. Apparently, he was asked to do this by his distributor."

"Have you had any identification of the distributor yet?"

"Yes, sir. You will not believe this. He says that Trooper Torrenson has been the distributor."

The phone was silent.

"Sir?"

"Yes?"

"The problem seems to be bigger than that. We had an accidental death in the village three days ago. Nora Wassily. She was our health aide out here for a long time. She was found unconscious with hypothermia. Torrenson was the one to find her. He stated that he found her unresponsive and her jacket was seen near her house with a bottle of alcohol in it. The nurse practitioner here sent out some lab work that came back with some questionable results in regard to her cause of death. I just heard from another health aide that she has been asking Torrenson about autopsy and investigation. He has been telling her that it has been held up by bureaucracy. He had told me that he was filing the report on the night of the death because I was too close to the victim and that he had it taken care of. I just found out tonight that he never filed a report."

"Okay. I am looking into what has been done on this side. I will be back in touch with you."

"Excuse me, sir?"

"Yes?" The major sounded impatient this time.

"There is more, sir. The nurse practitioner that got pushed off the cliff this morning is now missing. We are gathering a search and rescue effort now. We don't know why she would have taken off."

"Okay. You have your hands full. I will look into things on this side, and I will be back with you." The phone clicked on the other side.

Angus hung up, not sure what the major was thinking, but he didn't care at this point. He wanted to make sure that they found out what had happened to Meara and get her back alive.

He went back over to the clinic to join the gathering search and rescue party. When he arrived, he found ten men on snow machines. Among them were Norm Nelson with his sled team and the one man in town who had a search and rescue dog. Fred also joined them with his snow machine. Jim was there as well.

"Hello, everyone. *Quyana cakneq* for coming. We have a missing woman. She was in an accident earlier today. She left earlier on my snow machine under suspicious circumstances. We don't know what time she left. She was injured already and not properly dressed. We believe she went out onto the main trail. She most likely would have turned toward Agushak. Does everyone have a radio? Turn them all to channel twenty-two. If you hear anything, radio in."

He stopped to make sure he turned the radio on the sled he was riding on to channel nine in case he got any other emergency calls from the village. "I will need a small team of four people to head north. The remaining will move with me, and we will start a search and rescue grid just outside of town."

"I have some of her clothes for the search dog." Chelsey handed over the bloodied hat that had been left behind from the morning. "Verna and I will stay here in the clinic to serve as headquarters and to be here in case she comes back."

The snow machines turned on with a loud group roar. Angus climbed on behind Fred on his Polaris. They all took off directly to the trail entrance on the eastside of town. Angus turned his group toward the south.

"Alright, let's spread out far enough from each other that we can still see each other but cover the area from the ocean to the base of the mountain. Radio if you see anything. I repeat, radio if you see anything."

They covered the five-mile distance down the trail quickly to where they found the disabled snow machine. Angus hopped off the snow machine and went over to his. Keys were in the ignition. He tried to turn it over, and it didn't start. His gaze moved to the fuel gauge as he remembered that he had needed to fuel up earlier in the day. "She ran out of gas."

He opened the rear storage compartment and found the emergency kit gone. "She took the emergency kit. Why wouldn't she have stayed with the sled and sheltered?"

Another sharp gust of wind pushed some of the smaller members of the crew enough to make them stagger backwards. This was no night to be out here without snow gear.

"Look around for any evidence of other machines. Could someone have picked her up?"

Everyone stopped to study the tracks on the trail in front of them. The ice pack was fairly well windswept, but about five feet ahead they could see the tracks of a snow machine that had circled back.

"Who would that have been? Did they take her? Let's assume she is on the run. She could be just confused from the head injury and wandering out here." Picking up his radio, he called, "North crew, any sign?"

Static came over the radio initially. "There have been a couple of tracks back and forth this way with big boot prints intermittently when it stopped. But none of the funny tracks you showed us earlier."

"Alright, you guys head into town and search there. The rest of us are going to start a search out here. We found my snow machine." He handed the hat back to the search-dog handler. "Will we get to her in time? This doesn't feel right."

* * *

Meara tucked herself in along the bank out of the wind while she took her glove off long enough to pull out the chocolate bar. She glanced at her watch. 11:05 PM. She was working so hard to keep her thoughts together.

She couldn't walk in spite of the fact that walking felt a lot better on her ankle. It felt better on her ankle, but she didn't generate enough body heat to keep herself warm. She had to keep her movement at a jog.

Each step at a jog was a challenge at first; the jolts of pain made her want to crumple to the ground. But that was not an option. When she ran a marathon, she used visualization to get her through. Each step, she would pour an imaginary bucket of warm water over her leg to wash the pain away. After a while, it worked.

After the first hour, she no longer felt the pain in her leg and she just continued to run. She had no idea the distance she had covered. In good situations, she ran an easy seven-to-eight-minute mile. With the pain, the cast, and the running surface, she doubted she was moving that fast. Two hours in, she calculated that she must have covered at least ten to twelve miles. Her energy was draining, and she needed to refuel. Sitting and resting in the hollow that she had found in the bank felt like a good idea.

She opened the energy bar in her pocket and started chewing. Her mouth was so dry. She hadn't thought about drinking all of this time. Scooping up a little bit of snow, she let it melt in her mouth. It was enough to allow her to swallow, but with her lack of motion, using her heat to turn the snow to water could work against her.

How could Rey have gotten to the point that he would come after her like this? What was worth cheating another person of their life? What had happened to him to make him so callous about the value of another person's life? "Just a villager." She couldn't understand this thought process, and the fact that he felt justified in saying something like that made her angry.

The grief that had been brought on this village by what he had done to Nora was overwhelming. She left a big gaping hole in the community. Nobody would ever miss Meara like Nora was missed.

She started to feel sleepy, and the shivering that had started during her rest was stopping. She had enough awareness to know she needed to get up and start running again.

She stood and resumed the pace. Now she focused on Sophie's kitchen and all the wonderful smells of food cooked with love. That was her target. She would find warmth and safety there, and it was a goal that she would not be denied.

* * *

Rey went back above the village by way of the airport to approach his destination. He had been searching for a few hours now. He had also spent a little bit of time hanging back and watching the clinic in case she returned. It was getting late. He looked at his watch. 11:30 PM. If he could just slip into town and deal with the evidence, then he could go find and take care of her.

He patted his pocket. That part should be easy.

He pulled his snow machine up as close to the village as he dared without being heard, then hid it behind a bank. He left his helmet on. It was providing some protection from this penetrating wind. "She won't last long out here tonight. This is perfect. Nobody knows I was in town, and no one would suspect I was here. What would have triggered her to take off like that? She didn't have anything on me yet. She couldn't have. Now, this was perfect. She took off on the snow machine and got herself into trouble. I didn't even have to drug her. This could not be turning out any better for me."

He audibly sighed in relief. He had felt so vulnerable this morning after she survived the "accident." But now, he didn't have to do anything. She had put herself into harm's way. She was impulsive with running away and by doing so she put herself in danger. The thermometer on the snow machine read negative twenty Fahrenheit. With the way she was dressed when she took off, Mother Nature was going to take care of her for him. If he was really lucky, the blowing snow should make it difficult to find her body.

He leaned into the wind as he walked toward his target. Fortunately, Sophie's house was one of the first as he approached the village. He slipped his coat sleeve up with a gloved finger to peek at his watch. It was approaching 11:45 PM. The prolonged time period before the funeral must have worn out the grieving. There was only one light on in the kitchen. Every other light in the house was out. He worked his way behind the house, stepping carefully into tracks made earlier.

Behind the house, he had no doubt about which room contained Nora's body. The window was wide open. The flapping drapes fluttered in and out of it with gusts of wind. He was pretty confident that there would not be a smoke detector in the room. People didn't seem to value those too much. It wouldn't matter anyway. If the room was like most bedrooms, it wouldn't take long to engulf the room, and the smoke detector would not give much warning against the speed of ignition that curtains, bedding, and paper would give. The room would reach flash point within minutes, and the body would be incinerated.

He moved to the back of the house and pulled the curtain out the window. Then he gathered it in his hand like a bundle of kindling. Pulling his glove off, he made a quick flick to ignite a two-inch flame that quickly caught the curtains on fire. A quick push forward, and the ball of flame was inside the bedroom. He stood a couple of minutes longer tracing the edges of the curtain with his lighter.

Rey stood back and regarded his handiwork. It could not have been any better. The wind was on his side, and within moments the interior of the room lit up with bright yellow-and-orange flames licking and then engulfing the room.

Rey quickly retraced his steps to his snow machine. No body, no toxicology, no autopsy. Nobody but Meara knew of the blood results, and Anchorage was not even aware of the death of Nora. His hand turned the ignition and his machine came on with a quiet purr of satisfaction that matched his grin. He was in the clear.

"The future is mine."

* * *

Meara's decision saved her on her way back to town. The buffer that the banks provided became her lifeline. As long as she kept moving, she was able to stay warm when she was out of the heat-sapping wind. Some places she was fully exposed to the penetrating gusts, but fortunately for her, sandy bluffs lined the river through most of its course.

The emergency blankets wrapped around her leg reflecting heat back to her was far from ideal, but the protection from windchill made a huge difference in saving her feet from certain frostbite. The heat created by her steady jog was keeping her going. Even the gauze dressing was playing a part in keeping her warm and alive. It was providing protection to her ears and retained heat that would have been lost out her head. The staples still announced themselves to her via the sensation of cold nails in her skull. She had taken full advantage of all the resources that she had found and had eaten the last of the rations to keep herself going.

Exhaustion wasn't strong enough of a word. She was using everything she had to mentally get herself back as well. She imagined each breath was filling her lungs with warm air that circulated through her body. When she wasn't focusing there, she was thinking of the ptarmigan soup she expected to be on Sophie's stove.

"If I control my mind, I control my survival. I do not quit."

Her jaw stayed firmly clenched as she drove herself forward. Her plan was to get to Sophie's or Verna's house. She had to admit that although she had always been used to plowing through her challenges by herself, the moose were right. There was safety in numbers.

Where should she make the turn to head to their homes? In the early morning hours, walking down the main street would make her too visible to anyone awake at this time. Unfortunately, there was one person that she could be sure was awake who would also be looking for her.

"I am not making this easy on him. I won't be a sitting duck in the middle of the road."

The choice had to be to continue to the end of the river and work back through the ice chunks where the river met the sea. Then she would work her way along the shore.

As Meara looked ahead, the silhouette of Sophie's house stood in front of her. She relaxed into the relief of knowing that the comfort of that loving home was just a short walk away after the long night's journey. She could see the inside of the house so clearly in her mind. The smell of soup on the stove and the warmth of the home and the hearts inside it gave her renewed energy to get there.

What she saw next stopped her in her tracks and pulled her immediately out of her reverie. Something was moving around outside the back of the house. She stopped to focus more.

That was no something. That was someone. She continued to move forward enough to recognize Rey's outline. She recognized that profile in snow gear from their date. What was he doing?

She gasped and flung her hand to her mouth to stifle the scream that came out. Her answer to the question about his intentions appeared as quickly as she had thought to ask. Yellow-and-orange flickers around the window took no time to turn into roaring flames.

"Sophie! Grace! Everyone! Fire! Get up!" Her pain and all thoughts of herself were irrelevant as she raced toward the house. She had to run to Sophie. If she stopped to hide from him, these people she had grown to love will all surely die. *I vowed that I would run toward and that is what I am doing. I would rather die trying to rescue them than to live with the knowledge that I hid in fear.*

Meara ran around the house to the front door expecting to hear the sound of the smoke detector going off. There was no sound other than the roar of the flames. Acrid smoke poured from the back-bedroom window as she ran by.

Meara burst into the exterior arctic entrance and pulled her glove off to put her hand on the interior door. It was not hot. Not yet. Pulling the gauze farther up around her mouth and nose, she pulled the door open.

"Fire! Everyone, wake up! Fire!" She grabbed and shook people awake as she moved through the living room. The room seemed deceptively safe, other than the beginning of smoke seeping in from under the bedroom door. There had been a towel rolled up across the base of it to hold the cold out of the rest of the house. That towel was now protecting them from the smoke.

She stood a teenage boy up by his shoulders and looked him in the eyes. "Listen to me, we need help. Now! Run to the VPSO for help." She noticed the CB radio by the front door. "No, get on the radio and call for help then run to the VPSO."

"Sophie! Grace!" She half yelled, choking back a sob as she ran down the hall to the other bedrooms. The smoke was making its way in quickly now. People were getting up and moving. She yelled to some men starting to stir. "Come with me and grab someone else. I need your help to get Grace out of here."

They bent low to stay under the smoke that was quickly filling the hallway. Working their way, they opened bedroom doors and pulled people out of them. The smoke seeped through the gauze and into her lungs. Her sobs became a choking cough.

Finally, they arrived at the last bedroom, where she found Sophie fast asleep. Her niece and the new baby shared the bed with her.

"Wake up! Fire!" She whipped the blankets off of the trio. Grasping the niece by the shoulders, she lifted her out of the bed and quickly put the baby in her arms and shoved her out the back door. Then, grabbing Sophie by her robe collar, she lifted the confused woman her out of the bed. She pushed them all toward the back door.

Now that they were safe, Meara glanced back toward the living room and saw that the flames had made their way in there.

"God, please make sure that everyone got out."

Sophie was now awake and struggled against Meara. "I need to get my Nora!" she screamed with hysteria, blindly sweeping her arms to get Meara out of her way.

"It isn't safe! You need to get out. Nora can't be saved."

Sophie had been a helper for her entire life, and right now she needed to help to stay sane. "Sophie, you have people that need you to stay alive. Gather everyone in front and make sure that we have everyone out."

It seemed to work. Sophie went from being rescued to the familiar role of rescuer. It seemed to bring her out of the panic and into a sense of purpose.

Meara noticed a fire extinguisher mounted to the side of the door. Quickly, she loosened it from its metal straps and pulled the pin from it. Then, holding the tank against her body as though it were a metal shield, she stepped back into the house in attempt to contain the fire. She crouched low to stay underneath the hot, smothering smoke and met the flames in the living room. She quickly swept the nozzle back and forth across the flames until its contents were spent.

By the other door, she could see two men approaching the flames with two other fire extinguishers. Meara ran and got behind them as they gave the flames all that they had. They were able to bring the flames back to the bedroom door, but just as they thought they had brought it back the flames burst again through the door with a renewed vengeance.

"Please God, have everyone out," called the older man.

The three of them ran out the front door into the awaiting storm.

* * *

Jim was working on the rescue team forming a grid, moving toward the sea after the dog took off in that direction with his nose to the ground. He had been called to join the rescue effort when Verna had pounded on the door to the airline bunkhouse and woke him up from his sleep. She must have decided that he could be helpful because she knew of his experience before he had arrived here in Alaska. While he worked on getting his hours in to become a commercial pilot, he had worked as a firefighter in Michigan. When he and Verna were dating, he had shared stories of working search and rescue. He had told Verna about searching for canoeists for days that had been lost in the thick, soupy fog that often engulfed the Au Sable River. Those rescued would be found cold, wet, and hypothermic. His stomach tightened and filled with dread about how they would find Meara.

Verna had given him her snow machine, and he had ridden along with Angus. They had been following the riverbed back to the sea. Every now and then, they would see the odd track that Meara had left behind at the VPSO station.

Suddenly, a loud synchronized squeal broke the roar of the wind as all the rescue radios went off at the same time. A panicked voice came through the static. "Fire at the Luckok house. Back part of the house in flames."

The team stopped spreading out and looked at each other, then back at Angus.

"Who said village life is quiet?" Jim broke the silence. "Search and rescue and a residential structure fire all at the same time?"

"We need to give up this mission to fight that fire. There were a lot of people staying there. We could have many people injured," said Angus.

Jim piped back up. "Who here is on the fire department?"

Seven people held their hands up.

"Angus, I was a professional firefighter in the lower forty-eight before I became a pilot. How about you stay here with the dogs and the dogsled for search and rescue? I will go back with the firefighting crew and help fight the fire. Then we don't have to give up on Meara."

Angus responded quickly. "Sounds good. Norman, Fred, and Frank, stay with me." He nodded to the dog handler.

Norman stood tall on his sled, shedding decades. "You couldn't get me to leave this mission. I am going to find that girl. I have only just started to teach her how to be useful around here. I am useless at a fire."

"Keep your radios on," Angus said to the departing crew.

Jim hopped back on the snow machine and raced off with the fire crew toward the fire station. When they arrived, two other volunteers were already there and had backed the truck out. One of the firefighters directed Jim to a cubby prepared with a full set of turnout gear. The volunteers suited up with the speed of a professional department. They all kicked their snow boots off and stepped into their bib pants set up over their insulated, fire-resistant boots. The coats hung above them, and the helmets were on shelves above the jackets. A quick, orchestrated dance, and they were dressed and ready to go. They hopped on the truck and rushed down the street to where the flames licked the darkness of the sky and marked Sophie's house.

Flames came out the kitchen window. The back roof was fully engulfed. Smoke filled the air, and Jim pulled his mask down immediately.

He scanned the front yard and street full of the people that had spilled out of Sophie's house. He could not see anyone seriously injured. A few men stood with their spent fire extinguishers that were helpless against the flames.

"Is everyone out?" Jim yelled.

"We think everyone is accounted for," called Verna's voice.

He hadn't even seen her in the chaos.

"I am bringing injured to the clinic and will set up shelter in the waiting room for now." She held the handles of a frail elderly woman's wheelchair. He thought he recognized her from flying. Verna was pushing her around as she gathered the few people that were injured but walking.

Sophie clearly held the greatest injury, and it wasn't physical. She stood in the road, supported on one side by her niece who also held her baby and on the other by a man. Her face was pale, her eyes were wide, and her body cried defeat. Her eyes were empty as she watched the flames eat her house, her history, and her daughter's body. She looked like a woman who had lost her soul.

The men planned their attack for the fire as they unrolled the hose from the truck. A volunteer yelled, "The sea is frozen over. We can't use the extra pump. All we have is this hose."

"Okay, let's contain this thing!" shouted another. Their efforts would be containment to prevent the fire from spreading to other homes instead of saving the burning house. The sparks traveled up in the air, getting caught in the wind blowing from the north.

This would be no small feat.

* * *

Rey remained hidden by the dark and snowbanks. He could not believe his eyes when he saw Meara running toward the house screaming. It was as if he were watching a ghost move across the yard. This woman could not be knocked down easily. For just a moment, she had turned and looked at him, making it clear that she knew what he had done. She seemed to dare him to follow her into the burning building.

She stumbled and limped, but she continued to run toward the building with all that she had.

He had highly underestimated her. He knew she was stubborn, but this was beyond reason. Why would anyone in their right mind run into a burning house? She was crazy.

He stood in the darkness watching the people pour out from inside as if she had flushed them out as she woke them. Maybe she was doing him a favor. The more people she got out, the less collateral damage from the fire. Nobody was going to get to the body. The flames had clearly taken care of that problem.

He held his hands together in prayer. "Please God, don't let her come out. She is the last piece of evidence that needs to go."

The village volunteers worked to rescue the house with fire extinguishers. Then she left the building with a spent fire extinguisher. She moved like a machine—a machine that he had to get rid of. She grabbed another fire extinguisher from the ground and ran to the back of the building.

The giant pumper truck pulled in front of the house, and all attention moved to the firefighters rolling out their defense.

He snapped to attention. "Thank you, God. You gave me an opportunity."

Turning the key of his snow machine, he sped forward with one thing in mind.

Her attention was entirely on the fire, and she did not see him approach. He pulled her across his lap with ease thanks to the distraction. And in a flash, she was upside down on his lap kicking and screaming in an attempt to escape. Her arms flailed wildly as she tried to grab his face.

He was sure he hadn't been detected. The crowd's attention was on the firefighters working on the other side of the house. Her screams and the roar of his engine were muted by the roar of the flames and the yelling of the rescuers.

Now, the only thing left to clear his way for his future was to get rid of his cargo.

* * *

Jim focused his attention on the fire. The local fire chief was directing the action. There was only one hose available to use from the big tanker truck. Other than a few more extinguishers stored on the truck, the main fighting tool was that single hose.

"A fire here in winter is a pretty definite disaster." All of the extinguishers were manned by locals. He busied himself with maintaining crowd safety of the last remaining people watching the building burn. The injured had already moved to the clinic. The remaining people who had been staying at Sophie's were safe outside. Some clearly were not dressed for the weather.

"Head to the clinic," he directed a couple. "You aren't dressed for the elements, and we don't need any more patients. You can stay warm there."

The other men worked together seamlessly. They had clearly taken their volunteer duty seriously. He was an extra cog in the wheel and wouldn't make it more efficient.

The house next door was close. The wind caught sparks and drove them in that direction. Fortunately, there was a layer of snow coating the roof.

Sophie stood there sagging into the arms of the people around her. Those dark eyes were distant and gone. It did not seem as if anything was registering with her now. Her face remained slack as she watched her house burn.

Suddenly, she stood tall. She pointed toward the back of her house and screamed, "Meara! Help her!" She struggled out of the arms of the people holding her up and ran to the back of the house.

A kicking figure lay across the snow machine speeding away.

"Meara!" Sophie's energy miraculously resurrected. "Someone radio for help!"

Jim snapped back to attention. The radio was in his hand still. He held the transmission button down. "Angus, come in. Angus."

There was only static for a second. Then, "This is Angus."

"Angus, we have a kidnapping. Meara was here fighting the fire, and some man on a snow machine just snagged her and took her away. He is heading toward the airport with her."

* * *

"Dr. Forester, Meara is missing. We have a house fire with an unknown number of injured coming in. I wanted to let you know that we may have many injured. We are staffed with two health aides that just finished session one. We have been working on our observation," Chelsey spoke urgently into the phone as she prepared the clinic for what Verna brought back.

It was one thing to treat Meara all by themselves today. But, now they were expected to handle multiple injured people by themselves. She had no confidence in her ability to do this. But, there was no choice. She and her sister were all that the incoming patients had.

"Use your ETT skills to triage and evaluate who you have. I will be waiting your call back. You will handle this fine. Just remember your ABCs," Dr. Forester reassured her.

Sure, just remember your ABCs. Fine to say when you were in the hospital with a bunch of people to help around you. And you had some big fancy degree after your name. Here, she was with just Verna. If more than two people needed help with the "A" for airway, they would not be available to deal with the rest. She could not imagine having to assign a person as unlikely to survive and give them no attention in trade for keeping the rest alive. *I don't think I can do that.*

Chelsey's fears were relieved when Verna came in the door pushing Grace, followed by four coughing people and one man with a burn on his arm.

"I think we have a miracle. This is it for patients. Losing a home is hard," Verna said, "but we can thank God we haven't lost any people in the fire. Grace appears to be fine, other than being shaken up." She turned to the burn victim. "Would you make sure she is alright while we take care of the patients with breathing issues? We will be back with you as soon as we see how these smoke inhalation patients are doing."

Chelsey observed the patients as they walked back to the exam room. One was short of breath when walking. The other three were coughing but appeared fine. The tension in her shoulders relaxed.

But they didn't relax completely. At least this part of the night's events might turn out alright. She was so grateful for Meara emphasizing that the evaluation happens as soon as the patient walks in the door. But, now what about Meara. She looked back at the door hoping that Meara would walk right through it and everything would be alright.

Chelsey needed to attend to what was here. She couldn't focus here and think of Meara. They could handle this here and would make her proud when they see her again. That was it, she needed to convince herself that Meara was fine and was going to walk in that door any moment. She snapped herself back to the situation at hand and decided she would take control.

"I will take this one. She is short of breath. Verna, you take the other three into the other room and make a brief assessment."

Verna gave her a "who died and made you boss" look but did what she said.

Chelsey led the elderly woman into the trauma room. "What is your name?" The woman appeared to be in her seventies.

"Julia Sitkof."

"How old are you?"

"Seventy-two."

"Besides the shortness of breath, do you have any other problems?"

"No. I do have diabetes and emphysema."

"Do you take any medications?" Chelsey wheeled the woman to the stretcher.

"Yes, I have inhalers in my purse. I also take metformin."

"What inhalers do you take?" She pulled out a stepstool

to help the rotund woman clamber onto the stretcher. Then she reached to sit the back of the stretcher upward to help the woman breathe better. She grabbed the oxygen saturation meter and put it on Julia's cool and wrinkled finger. The blood pressure cuff went around her arm while Chelsey waited for results from the pulse oximeter to find out her oxygen levels.

"Albuterol, Combivent."

"When was the last time you used them?"

"I used the Combivent at eight tonight." She opened her purse.

"Your O2 saturations are 89 percent." Chelsey listened to Julia's lungs. Inhalation sounded coarse, and the exhale had a prolonged squeal.

Julia was sitting taller. She tried swinging her legs back over the side of the stretcher as Chelsey tried to get her settled in. She pushed her hands into her legs, trying to straighten and prop her body up. Julie was trying to open her own lungs up to breathe by doing this. Her exhales seemed to be long pushes following a gasping in breath.

"I need to use my albuterol." Julia huffed the words in a staccato pace in between breaths. She rummaged through her bag and pulled the inhaler out. She stopped to rest before she shook it and plugged it into a long plastic tube. Then she put the tube to her mouth, compressed the canister, and breathed through the tube for a few breaths.

Chelsey was nervous watching the woman struggle to take care of herself. Chelsey reached behind the stretcher, pulled out a nasal cannula, and carefully put it into her patient's nose. Then she turned the big tank up to four liters of oxygen. Her own heart was beating quickly now, watching the woman quickly turn worse.

As Chelsey worked her way through the emergency CHAM, her patient gave short, quick answers. By the time she finished the evaluation, Julia was breathing with more ease, and her oxygen saturations went up to 94.

Chelsey was finally able to breathe a full breath herself when her patient breathed easier. After filling out the rest of the encounter form, Chelsey went to check the burn patient. By that time, other people had wandered into the warmth of the waiting room, and it was clear that Grace was anxious but alright. Family members were watching over her, and she had a cup of tea in her hand.

The burn patient was a young man in his late teens with a burn that went down his forearm. He had leaned into a metal doorframe as he escaped the building. She quickly assessed his SAMPLE history. She asked his symptoms, allergies, medications, past medical history, last meal, and the event from his perspective. The burn on his forearm was blistering with areas of white on it. She brought him back to the telemedicine cart and carefully took a picture of the burn with a ruler alongside of it to demonstrate the size. She created her patient encounter and sent it to Dr. Forester through the machine.

With everyone settled in, she walked back into the hallway and found her sister had just finished getting her patients set.

"My three patients all have clear lung sounds and good vital signs." Verna had her encounter forms set.

They called Dr. Forester together, giving her the rundown on what they had dealt with.

"Great job," she said. "Keep monitoring Julia for an hour. Let's see how she does. The three other smoke inhalation patients can be discharged. Now, the burn patient. You will wash the burn and dress it with Silvadene and gauze. We will have him return tomorrow, and Meara can debride it if necessary."

"What a relief," Chelsey drifted to the comment about Meara returning. Where was she?

"No kidding," replied Verna as if reading Chelsey's thoughts. "I hope they find Meara and find her alright."

"I don't know about you, but I am not ready to let her go. She trained us well and we survived this. But, I have to admit, I don't want to lose her as a teacher or as a friend."

The two girls spontaneously moved toward each other, held hands, and prayed for Meara's safety.

* * *

Meara was completely disoriented. One second she was running toward the fire, the next she found herself whipped across someone's lap on a snow machine. She tried to sit up but couldn't move. The speed of their movement had her glued against her captor. She was lying in an awkward position with her arm stuck under her body. An arm held her head down, and the way his fingers were digging into the staples in her head added to her immobility. She stopped wriggling. *I need to think. How am I getting out of here?*

"You had to mess with things," Rey's voice yelled over the roar of the wind and the engine. "Why couldn't you let things go? You know that I really cared about you, didn't you? But you didn't care, had to do things your way and pull more people in. It is all your fault that I now need to deal with you. I need to deal with you like I dealt with her."

"Let me go, Rey. You don't have to do this," she yelled back. He was irrational; she needed to stay calm. "If you let me go now, you can maybe work less of a sentence."

"There isn't going to be a sentence. They still don't know it was me with Nora. And nobody knows I am here, so once I get rid of you, I am in the clear. You are the only one that knows about the toxicology. And now that the body is gone, nobody will know as long as you are out of the way."

"Why did you kill her, Rey? What did she do to you?" She hoped that if she kept him talking, she could find a way to escape.

"She kept putting her nose into the importing. She was constantly trying to figure out where it was coming from. She couldn't mind her own business and was constantly asking Angus to dig in more. I had someone I was watching, and I was able to adjust my trips by knowing when she was coming in and out of town. Everyone suspected her, and it kept Angus busy looking at her and needing my help. Or, at least he thought I was helping. She kept him distracted, and I had a cover. But Nora had to keep pushing and pushing."

"You didn't have to kill her!" Meara yelled.

His arms relaxed a little as she talked, and she again twisted her body and tried to escape. His grip quickly tightened and stopped her fight.

She feigned defeat for a few minutes then quickly brought the knee closest to him up and into his ribs.

"That wasn't smart!" he continued unfettered.

This time, she stopped the struggle. *Think, Meara, think.* Then she remembered her running friend. She lay quietly. Slowly and cautiously, she moved her hand lower toward her left outer pocket. She was sure he would notice. She halfheartedly tried wriggling again to hide the sound of the Velcro letting loose as she moved her hand into the pocket.

She had to take advantage of the fact that he couldn't run the machine and grab his gun at the same time. If she didn't act now, she was dead for sure.

She wrapped her fingers firmly around the metal can in her pocket. She found the top with her finger. This was her only chance. Carefully calculating where she would need to twist to accomplish her goal, she planned the movement. It was a risk, but she had everything to lose if she didn't try. She wiggled her hand out of her right-hand glove to give herself a better chance and refine her grip.

Taking a deep breath, she pulled her left hand out of her pocket with her finger on the button. She twisted her right hand from under her side and reached to push up his helmet shield. The action met her target with ease, dispensing a full shot of bear spray directly into his helmet.

The snow machine came to a sudden stop as Rey's hand went from the accelerator to his eyes, throwing her off of his lap and onto the tundra snow. His screams pierced right through the wind.

Meara moved toward the snow machine one final time as she grabbed the keys to prevent his chase. He noticed her approach and blindly swept the space in front of him trying to grab her. He grabbed the hood of her parka just as she was ducking away. She instinctively used the self-defense she had been taught and had to use so often in working as a nurse in the past. Instead of pulling away, she moved toward him catching him off guard and off balance. He fell over the top of the bench seat and landed on the other side.

She turned and awkwardly ran down the trail praying that he would not pull out his gun.

Her prayers were not answered. Shots reverberated across the tundra.

She continued running into the night back toward the little village. A look back toward him made it clear this was the time for strategy. He was blindly pointing the gun in her direction. "Rey, I am not interested in dating anymore!" she yelled at her loudest. Then, she ran away from where she had left her last words. She even found the ability to smile as she watched him blindly direct his bullets in the direction that she had been.

She continued her run back toward the village where she hoped safety awaited.

* * *

The dog had his nose to the ground leading the search team forward. Angus and the men had followed Meara's trail along the river. A power bar wrapper lay on the snow next to the odd tracks they occasionally saw. They were going in the right direction.

Norman and his dog team ran the riverbed chasing directly behind the search dog. The dog teams' barking seemed to drive him to pick up his pace. Angus, Fred, and the dog handler rode alongside the river where they were able to scan the surrounding tundra. Their gazes methodically scanned the landscape looking for clues of the missing woman.

The radios went off, breaking the silence. The static made the men jump.

"Angus, come in. Angus, do you copy?" Jim's voice carried far with the wind.

"Copy that. This is Angus. What is happening?"

"Angus, we have a kidnapping. Meara made it back here. Sophie saw her being abducted while she was fighting the fire. The kidnapper took off toward the airport with her on a snow machine.

"Copy that. Search and rescue victim sighted and abducted. Suspect heading toward the airport from town." Angus shook his head as he put the radio back on his hip. This woman seemed to have nine lives. Her luck was going to run out soon if they didn't find her.

Norman pulled his sled team up and out of the riverbank and headed toward the back end of town and the airport. He turned on his sled to yell back, "What is taking you all so long to move? Are you waiting to give the guy an invitation to take care of her?"

The rescue dog handler hopped on the sled with Fred, and they followed behind the dog team. The search dog had reversed positions with the sled team and was chasing them, barking at their heels.

A gunshot pierced the night. Angus's stomach tightened as his hands gripped the handlebars. No, they couldn't be too late. His heart sank. He was not ready for this to become a recovery mission.

Ahead on the tundra, a disabled snow machine stopped across the trail. His heart quickened. A small figure was running toward town. Maybe they weren't too late!

Another shot went off as they neared the disabled machine.

"That was two." The worst fears Angus had calculated earlier in the evening turned out to be accurate. In front of him, his leader stood behind the snow machine with his 9mm Glock firing in Meara's direction.

Rey was normally a sharpshooter, but tonight that wasn't the case. Something wasn't right with him. His aim was all over the place.

The small figure stopped and turned around. She yelled then ducked and ran in a sharply different direction.

Rey shot more shots in the direction she had called from.

"Five, six, seven, eight, nine."

None of the shots were in the direction of the running target. The sharpshooter was clearly impaired.

The team rushed toward him. "Nine shots. He might have four shots left."

Rey faced the opposite direction.

More shots. So far Angus had heard ten. He had no idea how many Rey had fired off already. Angus could make a move when he saw Rey try to reload. He'd close the distance in the meantime. As a VPSO, he was not armed. He would need to sneak up and try to disarm Rey.

Fred took off ahead of the rest of the group screaming as he rode behind Rey. "Rey! I am back here. Rey, I am going to tell them everything." He climbed off his machine and waved his hands over his head and jumped up and down. "Rey, you need to get me to shut me up."

Rey turned and shot off two rounds toward Fred. Both whizzed over his head.

"I am moving forward." Angus yelled at the dog handler. "He could shoot at us. Do you want off?"

The dog handler on the machine with him reached for his side and slapped a cartridge into his gun. "I am with you."

Norman spoke up before he could be asked. "Follow me."

Another shot went off as Meara continued running away.

Fred grabbed his arm and stumbled.

Rey still did not seem notice the approaching team.

"Let's go!" Angus pulled back on the throttle and sped toward the lone figure and the snow machine. He passed the sled team on the way.

The acceleration caught Rey's attention, and he turned around, pointing the gun toward them. He squeezed the trigger.

Angus was looking straight at the nozzle. He held his breath, half expecting it to be his last.

Nothing happened.

There was no time to waste. He accelerated toward Rey as he lowered his arm and his hand reached into his pocket where he stored his spare cartridges.

Angus needed to get there now. He pulled up on one side of Rey.

"Hey, big guy. I did it. I turned you in. Your secret's out." Fred waved his arms revealing a darkened spot on the sleeve. "Looks like you missed, Rey."

Rey turned his blinded eyes toward the voice as he released the spent cartridge onto the snow.

"Hey, Rey. Make sure you know where I am. Maybe you need another murder in your books." Fred waved his injured arm above him.

The distraction allowed Angus to slip off of his sled. He was working his way to the other side of Rey, but his feet felt like concrete. He needed to get there before the gun was loaded, or there was no doubt that one of them would be the next victim.

Fred must have lost his mind. "Rey, you know because I was stupid enough to join you in your venture, my life is over. You already murdered me by getting me involved. Let us start down the list of buyers. I know all of them would love to see a trooper go down this way. You better shoot me before I start talking."

Rey finished lining up the fresh cartridge and slapped it into place with a loud click. He raised his hands in front of him, lining the gun up with Fred's waving body.

"Okay, you have—"

Angus sprang through the air, grabbing Rey from behind and pulling him backwards. A shot fired up and into the night sky.

He reached his arms to Rey's side, forcing his hands and gun into the air. He followed that with a knee in the back of his hamstring.

Rey dropped to the ground. His gun was still in his hand.

Angus's hands were around his wrists. Another shot rang off. Angus forced his elbow into Rey's throat as they fell to the ground. He lined up his knee to land in Rey's ribs. The gun loosened and fell to the ground as the two struggled.

Rey clawed for Angus's face as Angus continued to hold Rey's wrist, twisting it around his back.

Norman circled his team around them in a tight circle. The dogs' teeth were bared as they barked at the men rolling in front of them. Norman looked as agile as an Olympic hurdler as he jumped over the dogs' leads into the center of the throng. He had a lasso fashioned from his lead rope. He deftly slipped it around Rey's foot and swiftly pulled back. Rey dropped onto his stomach.

Fred grabbed one arm with his one functioning arm and forced it behind Rey's back.

Norman hog-tied the trooper in the snow with some extra webbing. From there, Fred and Angus got Rey into handcuffs locked tightly behind his back.

Norman pulled a pistol out of his pocket and held Rey at gunpoint. Fred picked up Rey's Glock from the snow.

"Here is how it is going to go for you, boss." Angus took a deep breath. "You are going for a walk back to the station. We have a gun on you. I don't advise making a run for it." He glanced toward town. "Hey, Norman, go rescue our damsel in distress."

The old man hopped on his sled, looking like a Roman gladiator racing across the tundra to rescue his young friend.

* * *

Meara stepped off the dogsled that had rescued her from her run on the tundra.

Norman tied the team up as he walked with her to the back door.

She searched her pockets and came up with some empty wrappers. Her legs felt like rubber, and her eyes were so heavy. Was that sound in the clinic? Who would be there at this time of night? She knocked on the door and waited for a response. Suddenly, all was black.

The moose were circling around in front of her. She peered closer. Were they holding something? She looked again. Were those dance fans? She opened her eyes. The vision of dancing moose disappeared and above her danced a white-tile ceiling with an operative lamp suspended from it. She heard muffled voices.

"Meara?" Verna's voice.

She turned toward it. Where was she?

"Meara, wake up."

The penetrating smell of ammonia under her nose quickly focused her vision. Verna's face was strained as she worked to get Meara's jacket off.

"Meara, what happened?" Chelsey's voice came from her other side.

She turned toward her face. Was that a tear forming in the corner of Chelsey's eye?

"*Aluk*, missy. You have work to do around here." A gruff voice with the slow Yupik canter. "I was just starting to make you useful. Don't you think you can get out of here."

She tried to smile weakly. She started to speak, but her lips were so dry. Running her tongue over her lips loosened the thickness. "Don't you worry, old timer." She raised her arm to her forehead and gave him the crispest salute she could muster.

"Blood pressure 90 over 60. Pulse 114. Respirations 14, O2 saturations 99 percent." We need to get you out of this coat." Verna worked with Chelsey to pull Meara's coat off.

"Ha, look at this. You never took the IV catheter out. Trying to make it easy on us?" piped in Chelsey. "You have no idea how worried we have been about you."

"To be honest, I was worried about me." A rustle to Meara's side let her know she was not the only patient in the room.

Next to her was an elderly woman with oxygen in her nose. She was watching over the action around Meara as if it was her own personalized version of *ER*.

"It looks like you handled everything without me. Good job. You make me proud. How many patients did you have?"

"Five. One with emphysema and smoke inhalation, three minor smoke inhalations, and one burn. Dr. Forester directed us. We were set because we had a great instructor who prepared us to be on our own a little sooner than we wanted to be." Verna winked at Meara. She stood taller, and her chin lifted as she gave their tally.

The girls must have loaded that intravenous fluid with an energy drink. The fluid coursed through her veins, and she felt her strength returning and her thoughts getting clearer. Then the memory of the disaster of last night returned, filling her with dread.

"Sophie! Where is Sophie? Is she alright?"

As if on cue, the treatment room door opened, and Jim stepped in with Sophie on his elbow. The smell of food followed them in the door, and Meara could hear the mumble of many conversations waft in from the waiting room.

"I am right here," whispered Sophie. When she got closer and took Meara's hand, her face crumpled, and she broke into sobs. "Thank God! I am so relieved to see you. I thought we lost you after you rescued all of us from the fire. I watched him grab you and take off."

"I am alright, Sophie. Tired, but alright. I am more worried about you."

"I will be alright. I have lost much, but I have much. I have family. I have community. I have God. I will be alright. I will never have my precious *panik* back, but I have her here." She placed her hand over her heart. The action seemed to give her strength, and the sobs settled down.

"Yes, I have lost my house and belongings. A house is not a home until people live in it. I have lost the pictures and the heirlooms, but the memories remain. The house can be rebuilt. This loss doesn't compare to losing Nora. But God doesn't give us anything that we can't handle."

She laughed, and Meara couldn't help but laugh, too. She had never heard Sophie talk so much. She was so exhausted she was struggling to understand the rambling of wisdom from Sophie.

"You, like me, can relax in the knowledge that he thinks our shoulders are broad. Trust that he will provide you all that you need. You know, sometimes I think we have losses to learn that we don't have to understand everything, but to reinforce our faith with an understanding that is much greater than ourselves."

"You are so strong, Sophie. You live what you believe. Even with faith, I don't know how you have held up so strong." She squeezed her friend's hand. "Speaking of Nora, I have news for you. Rey was the importer, and he murdered Nora. He drugged her when we were at the dance. He was such a thoughtful guy and brought us all tea. Only Nora's tea had a huge dose of benzodiazepines in it. Then he left. He then came back and picked her up when she was walking home and brought her way outside of town without her jacket.

"He admitted to drugging her then leaving her in the cold to die. I am sure he poured some alcohol in her mouth after she was unconscious because she had no alcohol in her blood work, then he planted her jacket with the bottle of alcohol in town. Last night when he arrived at the clinic, he said he was 'worried about me.' Everything came together for me when he offered me a cup of tea. I knew about benzodiazepines in Nora's labs and had been pushing him for an investigation autopsy, and he decided that I needed to go, too. So, I made a run for it. I was running for Agushak and their local police. I didn't know who was safe here. Then, I ran out of gas, and I had to run back to town. I came up behind your house just as he was setting it on fire."

"He set my house on fire? Why would he do that?" Sophie was visibly struggling to absorb all the information.

"To prevent an autopsy from happening."

Norman filled in the details that Meara wasn't aware of. "He is under arrest in his own station. Angus captured him with only one minor injury in the group. Fred has a scratch from where a bullet grazed him when he was distracting Rey from you."

Meara wiggled herself upright in the bed. "The good news from last night, if we were to find good news, is that we can bury Nora now with her dignity and respect intact. She served this village very well to the very end."

* * *

Angus was on the phone when Chelsey slipped into the VPSO building. "Yes, sir. I have him in the cell now, sir. Everything is in control. He confessed everything to the nurse practitioner when he was trying to kidnap her. He has shut up since I have had him in here though."

There was a pause as a voice spoke on the other line.

"Okay, sir, we will be expecting you in about three hours." He returned the phone to the receiver.

Chelsey's heart beat a little faster. It was a little more difficult to catch her breath, and her stomach was fluttering. "Knock, knock." She entered the room, trying to suppress the smile that was growing on her face.

"You are a sight for sore eyes. I bet you have heard the story from Meara." Angus fumbled with his hands, trying to find a place to put them.

"Yes, and I wanted to thank you. Meara has become quite special to us. You handled the whole ordeal well."

"I can't say that I am any more of a hero than you are tonight. You faced a large number of potentially injured people, and you stayed strong from what I have heard."

There was a knock on the door. Fred walked in.

"I should leave," said Chelsey.

"No, you don't have to," said Fred. "I screwed up, and I hurt people. My children need to live in this village and not be looked down at. I don't know if I am too late to save them from all the fallout of what I have done, but I need to own it publicly, and I need to make it up to the village. Angus, I am coming in now so that you can ship me out with Rey.

Chelsey, I was the distributor in town on his drug and alcohol runs. I was trying to find a way to get my boat payments so I could continue to fish for my family next summer. It was so wrong, and my judgement was fogged by my anxiety."

Angus stood quietly. He was actually smiling a bit as he shook his head. "Fred, you have turned yourself in twice at this point, and in between you have helped in search and rescue, and you put your life on the line to save others. Myself included. Yes, you made some terrible choices that harmed people. You can go out and tell people what you please, but you are free to go as far as I am concerned. I am going to recommend that you go in front of the tribal council for your trial. Go home to your girls."

Fred's hunched shoulders and downward gaze lifted some after hearing those words. "Thank you." He lifted his eyes to meet Angus's.

"I know you will continue to thank me and the village. And, thank you for your distraction. You made that arrest possible, and risked your own life doing it."

Chelsey had thought that she had liked this man on the surface. But the attraction had just increased exponentially with this private view of his depth shown by his compassion.

* * *

Meara went back to the break room and sat at the table as she called the CHAP director.

"Nancy, this is Meara."

"Oh my God, it is so good to hear your voice. We thought we had lost you when we heard you were kidnapped. That and your trip over the bluff. How are you doing? We can get you out of there today and in here for imaging."

"No, if I made it through last night, I don't think I have internal bleeding. I need an x-ray on my ankle, but the walking boot is working for now, and it can wait. My headache is calming down. I haven't lost consciousness again, and when I did this morning, it was from exhaustion. I want to stay. The funeral is today, and I really feel that we all need to go, and I want to finish getting Verna and Chelsey signed off for the session one observation. They handled all of this chaos without me beautifully. When can you get an experienced health aide out here to be with Verna?"

"Okay, you can stay if you insist, and you need to sign a waiver that you are delaying the imaging at your own risk. Post a note on the clinic that it is closed for the funeral, and you can remain on call during it. Most of the village will be at the funeral anyway. We are short traveling itinerant health aides right now. I have been working hard to do some moving around back here to get a certified health aide out there to be with Verna. That village is too busy for one beginning health aide."

"Alright. Sounds good. Thank you, Nancy."

"I think we need to be thanking you right now."

"I don't know about that. I can't say that I chose to do anything that happened here."

"Apparently from what I have heard from Chelsey and Verna, you chose not to give up on Nora."

"I guess so. I need to hurry and start getting cleaned up for the funeral." Meara went to her pack to find clothes that were close to appropriate for a funeral. She pulled out a pair of black pants and a blue long-sleeve Athleta top. Taking the clean clothes with her, she went to the bathroom.

The mirror caught her by surprise. Her red hair was a tangled mess around the blood-stained gauze that wrapped her wound. The left side of her face was bruised, working its way down to her eyes. The exposure and running in the night had reddened and chafed her face. Her arms were stiff from the combination of the pummeling off the cliff and the constant exertion of the night. Pulling her shirt over her head required effort. She sat on the toilet and loosened the walking boot. The freedom of the leg allowed the pain to flow back into the joint. She then slipped her pants down, revealing bruises down the side of her thigh. Her ankle was the size of a giant grapefruit, and it displayed colors ranging from red to purple. Her toes were still red from the cold last night.

She hobbled over to the shower and turned the heat all the way up. She felt so dirtied both superficially and deep inside. She had a stain that she felt she would never be able to wash out of her. She had fallen for a murderer. Not only that, but he had kissed her immediately after his murder. When she thought of that, she started to retch.

Stepping into the shower, she pumped on the wall pump and filled her washcloth with body wash. After gently working through her hair and around her ankle, she scrubbed. She scrubbed deeply around her face, her lips, her chest where he had wrapped his arms around her. She opened her mouth to the down-pouring water, hoping it would scrub any trace of his kiss away in the deepest core of her.

She was disgusted that she had felt safe in his arms. How foolish she had been.

She stepped out of the shower, her body red and scrubbed. How good it would have felt to have been in the maqii with other women instead of alone. They could have helped her to unwind her wrenched and twisted heart.

Getting dressed, she put her own feelings aside. Sophie and Nora's family needed support now. Her loss was frivolous compared to theirs.

* * *

In the ambulance, Verna and Joe approached what remained of Sophie's house. They had a grim task ahead of them. They could see the fire engine parked to the side. There was one lone figure sitting inside it. What remained of the house sent wisps of steam into the air.

They approached the truck as the door opened. They both stepped back a half step when they saw Jim climb out.

"Cama'i."

"Cama'i," they responded in unison.

"We came to see what can be saved of Nora's remains," said Joe. "It would be good for the family to have something symbolic for the funeral."

"That is a tough job but very kind. To tell you the truth, I think we have all avoided getting too close to that back room. I think it should be safe."

"Verna, you stay here. I will go back with your father and do that. Can you take over my job of watching for any coals rekindling?" Verna was grateful that Jim hadn't hesitated to separate her from the difficult job.

"Why are you still here?" she asked.

"I called the office, and they have allowed me to stay here and finish wrapping up the fire so that everyone else can attend the funeral. I used a personal day."

The two men walked around to the back of the remaining structure and tucked out of view. Verna leaned against the fire engine and waited. She was surprised to see Jim here and still working the fire. It was kind of him to stay. He was losing valuable work hours to do that. That was the kindness that had initially attracted her to him. She couldn't deny that it still did.

He had apologized. But she was still not sure about trusting him. A huge part of her felt that he deserved a chance. She gazed over the ruin, thinking about the times she had shared with him. The talks that had taken them deep into the night. The similarities in spite of their differences. It had made their getting to know each other interesting and fun. Her heart felt heavy with the thought of it being over.

After about twenty minutes, the men came around the house. Their faces expressed the grimness of the task. Nobody mentioned the topic.

Jim left her father at the back of the ambulance and approached her alone. He stood in front of her and took up one of her hands. He searched deep into her eyes. "Verna, I will be leaving as soon as the funeral is over. I am hoping with all of my heart that you may find yourself able to forgive me. I don't deserve your forgiveness, but I am hoping. And if that hope were to come true, I would like to start seeing you again."

Verna's heart lifted with hope but also guarded itself simultaneously. She felt more confused than ever. She moved her eyes away from him, looking toward the sky.

"He is a good man who made a mistake," her father said as he approached them.

She couldn't help but feel irritated that he didn't give them that moment alone.

"His mistake was nowhere near as bad as mine. As your father, I support you in choosing to give him another chance."

Was this what it was like to have a father? Protected and irritated all at the same time? She thought about her sister, and it was clear that Chelsey had moved on. Her eyes were clearly on Angus.

With a long exhale, she lowered her eyes to meet Jim's.

"How about we start as friends?"

* * *

The bell tower at the center of the village could be seen from all ends of the village and marked the Moravian church. Snow machines and four-wheelers lined the street in front of it, and families were unloading from them. The sky was a bright blue, and the sun was turning the snow into a scattering of twinkling crystals. The wind was not blowing for once.

Meara entered the church with the throng of people and wiggled her way in to wedge herself with the people lining the back wall. People lined the sides of the church as well, and soon the doorway was packed. Everyone old and young, with the exception of Meara, was dressed in qaspaqs. Some of the smaller children were wearing beaded mukluks and headdresses. They were running in and out as if a funeral were a normal day in church. Chelsey soon joined Meara.

Meara struggled with her anxiety of being in a church. She never understood why churches made her want to get out, and get out fast. However, she needed to be here for her friend's ceremony. She pushed the anxiety away by studying the room.

Sophie sat in the front row with Grace on one side and Nora's children on the other. They lined up between her and Frank. Sophie wore a red-and-black paisley qaspaq. Where did it come from? Was it Nora's?

The remains Jim and Joe had gathered were inside the casket. Its lid was closed, which was unusual out here, as she gathered from the surrounding conversation. In the middle of the podium sat a five-inch-wide beautiful handwoven basket of tundra grass decorated with a green-and-blue pattern and covered with its tight-fitting lid. Meara had been told that an elder basket weaver had donated this to the family when she had heard the body had burned.

On either side of the basket lay a pair of Nora's woven dance fans with fox fur edges. Pictures lined the sides of the altar. Chelsey told Meara that the rest of the village had gathered pictures of Nora they had in their own family photos to replace some of the ones Sophie lost in the fire.

The church was filled with quiet murmuring in Yupik. Joe Johnson and another man stepped up onto the altar with guitars and started a song. Soon, the church was filled with the tune of "The Old Rugged Cross" sung in Yupik. Meara joined in as one of the few singing it in English.

When the song was completed, a collared native man with short-cut graying hair and a round face stepped to the altar. He greeted the church and led them in an opening prayer. Although it was in Yupik, Meara thought the cadence was that of the Lord's Prayer.

After the traditional service, the priest brought up Pipnik. The strong little girl held a poem she had written about her mother. She stood strong and to her full height in her floral qaspaq. Meara was captivated by the strength that she had.

"The poem is about the lessons of her mother. About respect for community and culture and faith in a loving God. She is now calling up a group of children to do a dance for Nora that she had taught them before she died. Native dance is back in one of the churches that nearly killed it," Chelsey interpreted for Meara.

A group of six- and seven-year-olds went up in front of the podium. Nena was with them. Three young boys sat down at the back and started banging their drums in unison. The dancing boys sat cross-legged in front with their dance fans.

Chelsey continued to interpret. "They are dancing about the salmon that come in and fill the nets." The children danced the first round. "Now, they are dancing about the salmon that go past the nets for others to eat that live upstream." The children continued their dance. "Now, they dance for them to spawn so more can come to the nets." The children continued. "Now they are cutting the fish and giving thanks."

When the dance finished, the microphone was passed among people who wanted to share stories of Nora. Chelsey whispered interpretations into her ear. The service ended in a prayer, then the crowd was directed to empty aisle by aisle to proceed around the front pew to say regards to the family.

It was a long procedure as each person spent minutes sharing hugs and words with the family as they passed by. The line then proceeded to a community room at the side of the church where a potluck was set up.

Zach was the first to greet each person. Although he stood strong, he looked like a man that had lost himself. However, he showed his presence to his daughters with gentle squeezes and pats and looks as the crowds worked by.

"I am so sorry," Meara heard herself say. She knew the words were weak and inconsequential.

His head nodded in acceptance of the words that he had probably heard over and over again in a different tongue.

She struggled with the desire to explain herself, to give the full meaning of the words she had uttered. She was sorry for more than just the loss of Nora. She had been so judgmental and cold and most of all completely wrong in her interpretation of what she saw as red flags. Her intuition had certainly failed her there. She felt shame for the way she had treated a truly good and grieving man. But this was not the time, and she didn't know when there would be. "Thank you for catching me when I went down," she murmured awkwardly as she moved on.

She proceeded down the line, giving each of the girls a sympathetic smile and stopping to let Pipnik know how proud her mother would have been of her. Then she stopped at Sophie.

Sophie opened her arms first to take Meara into a deep and healing hug. Meara felt guilty that she was probably receiving more healing than Sophie.

"Thank you, Meara, for all that you did for Nora," she whispered into Meara's ear.

"I am the one that needs to thank you for all that you did for me," Meara whispered back. The two women pulled back from the hug, and their tear-filled eyes connected.

Meara followed the line into the community room and took a small serving of salmon. The smell of the smoke blended with the smell of the salmon wafted up and woke her. She had just stopped to smell the salmon.

It was in that moment that she felt the beauty of the salmon in this culture. The salmon symbolized love as did roses in her culture, but the fish had so much more power than the beautiful-but-fleeting petals. Here, the salmon was so much more than just a fish. Love was seen in the catching and the preparing of it as families gathered. It was the consistently shared food when people gathered in communion. It was the symbol of community and shared survival. It was the history of a people and their ancestors and would hopefully continue to be a shared part of their history with their descendants. The flash of its silver and red scales in the water showed the beauty of determination as it used its final strength to give birth to the next generation of both salmon and the people of the salmon.

She stopped, and this time she consciously inhaled all that came to her senses as she smelled the fish.

* * *

Meara checked in with the airline attendant. She had all her gear weighed in. She moved across to wait for her flight to King Salmon, where she would catch another small plane to Egulshik where she would be going to work with Chelsey for a few weeks. She was looking forward to seeing her again and how she was progressing in her skills after completing session two training. They would also have another new health aide training with them because this Aleutian village got busy with an influx of fishermen the first run of the season.

She pulled out her computer to work on some teaching documents she had been preparing. The new hat she had purchased sat next to her on the bench: sealskin. She still marveled that she actually had a sealskin hat, and she could not deny that it was worlds beyond the knit hat that she had arrived with. But it was practical, and it cut the wind. Although spring was here, there were still moments of cold, heavy wind, and she was told that the wind on the chain and peninsula could be strong.

Although it was spring, she was still dressed for winter travel. Her snow pants gave cushion to the unpadded seat she sat on.

"Meara!" a familiar voice called as the door to the tarmac opened up, letting in a group of arriving passengers from one of the villages. "I am so glad to see you! I was actually heading out to the hospital because I have something for you."

Meara embraced the warm welcome she had felt since the first time she had met Sophie at the steam. She stood and shared a hug that was as warm as the smile that had just greeted her.

Sophie stopped and placed her satchel on her chair and pulled out a Ziploc bag of green seaweed covered with little yellow eggs.

"Have you had *mulucuq* yet?" she asked. "Herring roe on kelp. It is an extra special treat in the spring. I pulled some from my freezer to make sure you had a chance to try it. Zach, the girls, and I gathered it. You can eat it plain or dip it in soy sauce."

Meara smiled. "I don't dip it in seal oil?"

She had confessed to Sophie about her strange reaction before she left Quyalaqaq, and they had laughed and laughed.

"You can if you want." Sophie chuckled as she opened her suitcase and pulled out a beautiful red qaspaq with a small paisley print in black. The trim was a simple black trim. It was not a skirted one, and it had a nice soft flowing feel to it as though it had been worn well.

Meara looked up at Sophie, who wore a somewhat pained look.

"Nora's?" she asked, although she already knew deep in her heart.

Sophie nodded. "I was going through her clothes, and this just stood out to me. I was pretty sure you didn't have one yet, and you should because you will always have a place with us. She would have agreed."

Meara held the qaspaq to her face and she breathed it all in.

AUTHORS NOTES

Agushak and Quyalaqaq are no longer villages but were once active communities. The names were chosen as fictional locations as an acknowledgement to their prior existence. The dialect and cultural representation of these villages were a blend of multiple Yupik villages. Each village in rural Alaska has its own very distinct community culture and dialect.

The main characters are fictional representatives of their careers. Any likeness to any individual person is purely coincidental. There are many dedicated health aides working out in remote Alaska and have been credited for saving the lives of not only their fellow villagers but also those who have been in trouble during fishing or touring in these remote areas. There are also many nurse practitioners, physicians, and physician assistants that travel to remote villages, teaching and sharing experiences with these health aides as well as providing health care alongside them.

The Alaska State Troopers do provide the supervision of the VPSO program that is on the ground in these villages. Rey and his choices were fictional choices of a character and not representative of troopers in general. In 2014, after some sad defenseless deaths of VPSOs, the troopers changed their rules allowing VPSOs to carry guns for self-defense. The death of VPSO Tom Madole stimulated this change when he was killed while running away from a suicidal patient he was trying to help. The memory of those lost and the service they provided is not lost to the communities they served.

Alaska's bush pilots as well as air rescue pilots and crews create a lifeline to those living and working in remote Alaska. They fly daily into some of the most extreme weather patterns on the planet and provide food, supplies, and transportation in both emergencies and non-emergencies.

I discovered the Alaska Territorial Guard while doing research for this book. I was surprised that we do not hear much about these men and women who patrolled and protected the coasts of the Alaskan territory. Their service was not only unpaid, but they also provided a lot of the supplies from their own reserves to keep their missions going. In 2000, Senator Ted Stevens sponsored a bill recognizing those that served with an honorable discharge and veterans' benefits. However, only a minority of them were able to be found and honored.

Last but not least, there are the heroes and heroines that preserved their culture in spite of adversity so that the history and stories of a distinct people could be passed on to their descendants. Saving dance may seem like an insignificant task to some, but dance shared the stories and the history of the Yupik culture. Agnes Aguchak and Maryann Sundown were heroines in their own right by being brave enough to continue and to then share their history in spite of laws preventing them from it. The American Indian Religious Freedom Act of 1978 changed that. Preserving history is vital to our survival, and lessons from the past from any culture can guide us in the present.

Finally, many people look to Alaska and think of Native Alaskans as Eskimos. This erroneous term which encompassed many of the circumpolar populations covered many of the Northern cultures. There are five different Native Alaskan cultural traditions within the state and over 170 tribes, each with their own individual culture. Join Meara in the next book as she finds herself teaching in and learning more about the history and different cultural traditions when she travels to villages on the Alaska Peninsula in Book 2 of the Alaska Hidden Heroes series. Sign up for the newsletter to receive updates at www.brendabowiewise.com.

BOOK CLUBS

Hello Readers,

I love the opportunity to connect and chat with my readers and enjoy the conversations that come out of book club discussions. These conversations add a whole new depth to a story.

I am interested in joining with you and your book club. I have some questions listed below, but please do not feel bound to them. The conversation is open to what your club desires.

Please contact me at www.BrendaBowieWise.com and we can set up a time for you and your group.

Questions:

1. Meara leaves her familiar surroundings to go to a very unfamiliar place to follow a dream of teaching.

Do you hold unfulfilled dreams like that? What would you be willing to give up to do this?

2. Meara arrives in a place where there seemed to be more differences than similarities at first. Is having different perspectives good? What do we gain by seeing life through other cultures' eyes? What similarities do you see in the two cultures? Do you think that the similarities are universal?
3. How did you feel about some of the foods and customs that Meara found as odd but participated in as a matter of respect for the local culture? Would you? What things are a part of your culture that other cultures may find as odd or hard to stomach? You may laugh at the old wives' tale in the book. What old wives' tales do you follow in your culture?
4. The salmon is the backbone of the Yupik culture. The year revolves around the patterns of this fish. Does your own ethnic culture have its own "salmon"? What is it?
5. In the typical health care system, there is a disconnect between the patients and those that provide health care because of the size of and mobility between our communities. Health aides take care of people they are connected to every day. How does this connection or disconnection affect coping? What

is it about the Yupik culture that helps promote resilience?

6. Death in the lower forty-eight is typically separated in this age. It all happens discreetly and there is a bit of taboo around it where we keep children separate from it. Do you like this disconnection? How do you think you would like a wake in your own home? What benefits are there to the "separated culture" over the at-home culture?
7. Deciding to have a "dry village" is one of the strategies that has been used to decrease the effects of alcohol. Do you think it works? What are other solutions?
8. We see racism happen in this book in both directions. Meara's experience made her think. This is a big question for a book club. How do we erase racism? Where does it start?
9. There is a lot of violence toward health care workers in this book. Meara discusses that it occurred both in the lower forty-eight and in remote Alaska. Does this surprise you? Would you return to a job where this was the norm? What are the solutions?

ACKNOWLEDGEMENTS

Where do I start? This book was affected by so many people and groups that it is difficult to begin.

I will start at home. I need to thank my husband, Tony, for supporting and believing in me as I ventured into a territory other than that of being a nurse practitioner. He cheered me on and gave me the space to get it done. I need to thank my youngest children, Matthew and Joseph, who, when they could handle it, gave me the space to write. I need to also thank my oldest children for believing I could do it and cheering me on. Then, there is my band of sisters, who pushed me forward. The day-to-day support we now share is priceless.

After family, I need to move to those that moved me to the book. Linda Curda, you inspire me like no other. Your story as a midwife, your role in the health aide program, and the work that you have done to preserve the beloved Yupik culture that you joined for so many years are amazing. The story you and Dale shared in Alaska is yet another unsung heroes' journey. Thank you for being you! I am truly blessed by your friendship.

To my friends and extended family that cheered me in the background. Thank you.

To all of the health aides and those that serve in AKCHAP, you are amazing! Your love, resilience, courage, and ingenuity in the face of crisis is appreciated by all those you help—even the ones who don't appreciate you in the moment. You often have to sacrifice yourselves and your family time to provide your service. Your sacrifice is noted. You make a difference.

To the VPSOs, your service in remote communities is also appreciated. I have seen you at work. You aren't just police; you make sure you are part of the community. The children admire you for your courage as well as your compassion, not to mention the humor I have seen.

To those bush pilots. Thank you. We couldn't get there without you.

To the storytellers that keep history alive, thank you for preserving the opportunity for us to learn from the past. It is a priceless gift.

Thank you to Agnes and Myron Naneng for sharing stories about Agnes and Maryann and preserving their culture.

To all of the patients who I have cared for during my thirty-two years in health care, thank you for allowing me the opportunity to see your lives and struggles and to have your stories integrate into my story. And, before you think I wrote about any one of you represented here, realize that I brew pieces of stories together to create unique characters.

Now, for this book. Thank you, Bev Rivard, for virtually walking next to me during a very difficult time and leading me back to writing. I have to thank Marisa Goudy and the Sovereign Writers group where I experienced the magic of just the right writing prompt. Marisa led me to Morgan Gist MacDonald and Paper Raven Books, who guided me through the process of writing this book. Last but certainly not least, to my writing coach, who took me from writing concise objective chart notes to writing a full novel. You passed on a reticule full of tricks, tips, and thoughts that made this happen, and I can only imagine the time it took for you to edit my fledgling skill of writing "deep point of view."

I am looking forward to getting the words on the paper for book two. I can tell you now that the research is fascinating. And for this story and those to come, I thank the muses of this world.

Sincerely,
Brenda Bowie Wise

www.ingramcontent.com/pod-product-compliance
Lightning Source LLC
Chambersburg PA
CBHW030333310726
48979CB00001B/4

* 9 7 8 1 7 3 5 4 9 7 0 1 3 *